REACH FOR THE DREAM

Connie Monk is the author of several previous novels published in Fontana Paperbacks, one of which, *Jessica*, was runner-up to the Romantic Novel of the Year Award.

She comes from a family of generations of musicians and her love of music, together with her knowledge of local history, combine to add authenticity and charm to *Reach for the Dream*, a story that will delight her many readers.

Connie Monk is married and lives in Devon.

CONNIE MONK

Reach for the Dream

‖‖ •PARRALLEL• ‖‖

This edition published 1995 for
Parallel Books
Units 13–17 Avonbridge Industrial Estate
Atlantic Road
Avonmouth, Bristol BS11 9QD
by Diamond Books
77–85 Fulham Palace Road
Hammersmith, London W6 8JB

Published by Diamond Books 1994
Published by Fontana 1991
First published by Judy Piatkus (Publishers) Ltd 1990

ISBN 0 261 66693 2

Printed in Great Britain

CHAPTER ONE

All day it had been hot. Not the clear dry heat they'd come to take for granted that summer, but sticky, the sky heavy. A yellow tinge in the light might have been a warning of what was ahead, but Penelope saw no further than being set free of the classroom.

'We're gonna go down to the beach, Penny. Wanna come?' Alf shouted. Only he and Tom were left in the playground by the time she came out.

Of course she wanted to come. 'Race you down the hill,' was answer enough. Already she'd put Herbert Peabody, the schoolmaster, out of her mind. She was free! The boys had waited for her!

Many of the children at Merchant Hill Board School came from poor homes; the elbows of their jumpers were darned, their aprons patched. Many of them, but not all. There were others like that hateful Rose McCormick who arrived on Monday mornings looking crisp and starched, aprons brilliant white, wearing hair ribbons to match their dresses. It was always Penelope who would be singled out for the master's cutting remarks. Passing out reading books that had to be shared, it would be: 'Penelope Drew, see you keep that head of yours away from your partner.' At other times: 'A nice bright Monday morning, a fresh start. At least for most of you,' with a smile that became a sneer as his eyes rested on her. A snigger from Rose McCormick and the starched brigade would be his reward.

Penelope was only ten but she knew very well why he did it: he wanted to make himself seem bigger and more important, and she was an easy target. Not for anything would she let them know she cared; she'd not give them the satisfaction of guessing how many tears she shed as she rubbed the lump of red soap on her washing, squeezed it with all her might in the small round bowl – washing that week by week seemed to look greyer as it hung on the line at the bottom of the area steps in Victoria Place for passers-by to see. When Herbert Peabody looked at her with that mocking sneer, she met his gaze squarely. Her day would come! Today she'd known when he'd spilt ink on the floor that it would be her job to stay at the end of lessons to scrub the wooden boards with cold water – and no hope of success.

But the sight of Alf and Tom put school and all that went with it behind her. Clutching at her battered straw hat she raced as hard as she could, her white teeth clenched with the effort. She and Alf were neck a' neck, but Tom stayed well in front. What matter who was the winner? They were free. The tide was out, the rocks waiting.

'Tell you what,' she called as she leapt deftly over a rockpool to land on the flat surface beyond, 'I'll run home and get Chummy. He's waiting, see.'

'All right. You'll find us along the beach by the boats.' Tom stopped speaking to listen. 'Hark! Was that thunder? Reckon we're in for a storm.'

'I'd best get a move on, then. Chummy's got to have his walk.' She stepped back towards the shore, taking a final spring to land on the wet sand. It must have been the rocks that had done it! That thin patch on the sole of her boot had gone through, she felt the water squelching between her toes.

'Last one to the pier's a sissy!' This time it was Tom who threw out the challenge. 'Ready, steady, go!'

Like a shot from a gun she was off, this time coming second to his first. The two lads ran straight on without a backward glance, to help old Shem Hardwick drag his rowing boat up the beach and see what he'd caught.

In her waterlogged boots Penelope squelched along the Promenade then up Kings Road towards Victoria Place. It would have taken more than a wet foot to dim the glow of the last half hour. Mostly she was excluded from the girls' games; it had been like that ever since she'd started school. Sometimes, though, the boys let her join in and to be honest she considered that much more fun. And always Tom and Alf were her friends.

The wind whipped up quite suddenly, coming from nowhere and tearing at the leafy branches of the trees in George Bradley Park at the far end of Victoria Place. She heard the distant rumble of thunder as she ran down the area steps to the basement where she could hear Chummy jumping against the closed door at the sound of her tread.

'Chummy! I'm home, Chummy!' Just inside the door she dropped to her knees, the scruffy black and white mongrel showing his delight by sneezing, jumping to lick her face, then rolling on his back, his tail beating a wild tattoo on the wooden floor. It was his routine welcome; whatever Penelope's life might lack it certainly was never a welcome home.

'Gonna be a storm, Chummy. Come on, boy, let's get your string, I must take you walks before the rain gets started.' It was clear they wouldn't be going back to the beach, the storm would soon break. 'Stand still. Yes, I know you're excited. I was too. D'you know where I been, Chummy? I went to the rocks with Alf and Tom. Did you think I was late? Come on boy, walks.'

But already huge splatters of rain were bouncing on the pavement. This was no shower, but the beginning of a deluge. They started off towards the George Bradley Park (given to the town of Challington by a local industrialist and named in his honour, his statue staring from its plinth in haughty disdain), but a clap of thunder stopped Chummy in his track, sent his ears down and his tail between his legs. The lamp-post at the end of Victoria Place would have to serve for today, then home; George Bradley's trees would keep for tomorrow. So they ran home, shutting the door against rain and thunder alike. Chummy shook himself, rolled on the worn mat, then with

7

a baleful glance at his friend as if to apologize for his cowardice, slunk shivering under the table.

'Pa'll soon be home.' Who was she reassuring, him or herself? The room was lit with a vivid flash. 'Soon be home, boy.' She went down on her knees and crawled to where he cringed. His too-long tail thumped the floor twice and he managed to put his fear behind him just long enough to lick her ear. The small, shaggy mongrel and the skinny child were two of a kind, they understood each other.

'You stay under here, I've got to mend my boot, Chummy.' A good thing it was hot weather. If she rubbed the inside of it with a towel it would soon dry off. And she knew what to do, she'd seen her father 'mending' his. She really needed something stronger but she had some brown paper; she'd fold it so that it was thick then cut it to the right size to slip inside. In her imagination the boots took on a new look, fine, strong inner soles keeping out the wet. A few minutes later she was so engrossed in what she was doing that she didn't hear Ethel Sharp, their landlady, clumping down the stairs from her rooms above.

'Anyone home?' and a loud knock on the door that divided them from the rest of the house.

'Yes, I'm here, Mrs Sharp.' Penelope opened the door that led to the stairway. 'Pa isn't home yet.'

'Not home, in all this weather! Can't think who he imagines wants him banging on the door asking for jobs in this storm, that I can't. Hiving up somewhere, I dare say. Well, it's 'im I want to talk with, been waiting to catch 'im. You tell him I've waited 'til I got tired of waiting. He'll understand what I mean.'

And so did Penelope. A shadow seemed to fall. It had happened before and somehow things always got right again, but she knew it meant that she and Pa owed Mrs Sharp the money for their rent. There would be threats. Pa's face would have that expression she dreaded: miserable, frightened, angry, trapped, not quite meeting her eyes properly.

Perhaps her own expression said something of this to Ethel Sharp: Poor mite, what a way to bring up a child! Be better cared for in a home, that she would! Dear, oh dear, as if I could throw them on the street. Yet, if I did, very likely she'd be put somewhere where at least she got a decent meal once in a way and was kept clean. Dear, oh dear . . .

But all she said was: 'What's that you're doing with your boot? You mustn't touch the scissors while this storm's on. And just look at that mirror. Haven't you got a towel or something to cover over it?' As she talked she put the scissors away in the drawer at the end of the kitchen table. Another crash of thunder, a whimper from Chummy – and in Penelope a new fear was born. She'd never liked to be alone during a storm, there was something in the atmosphere she hated, but she'd always told herself it was silly to be afraid. It seemed, though, she'd been wrong. Panting heavily Ethel stretched her solid body, reaching to drape the none too wholesome wiping-up cloth over the mirror.

'What you want in here is a good pair of curtains. It's not right having nothing across the window, the lightning coming straight in at you. Dear, oh dear, there it is again . . . now you count . . . two, three, four . . . ' Then the crash of thunder. 'Four seconds that time, that means the storm's coming towards us, getting close now. Four seconds – was six last time. Soon be right over our heads. Can't think what that father of yours is thinking of, leaving you on your own. Not fit for a dog to be out. 'tis to be hoped the lightning don't get 'im. And like I said, it's not right, no curtains at the window . . . ' She sniffed, her round face red with fright and exertion, the clump of grey whiskers that grew from a mole on her chin seeming to bristle.

'We are intending to get some very soon now, Mrs

Sharp, we were talking about it the other day, thinking what colour we'd choose.' There was a pathetic dignity about the child. Ethel might have been touched by it but for the vivid flash that put all else from her mind.

Then as the noise of the thunder died away: 'Humph! If wishes were horses beggars'd ride! You'd better come upstairs and wait along with me.'

'And Chummy? Can Chummy come?'

'You know very well I won't have dogs in my place, my Tiddles can't abide them.'

'Then, thank you just the same, Mrs Sharp, but I'll wait down here with Chummy. He's frightened, you see.'

'Enough to make anyone frightened! A storm like this turns my insides. Well, if you stay down here, no getting those scissors out, mind, not 'til the storm's gone by. Mending your boots, were you?'

Penelope nodded, trying to put herself between Mrs Sharp and the shabby footwear. She wished no one had seen. Uninvited, a memory returned — her father's expression as he'd looked at the worn soles the other evening. Fear? Resignation? Hopelessness? She heard the echo of his words: 'Look at you, not a decent rag to your back . . . boots all but through . . . I don't know . . . money, money, money . . . what can I do to make some money?' He'd been talking to himself and that had made it even worse. When she'd slipped her hand into his, he hadn't even seemed to notice.

Soon he'd be home. He'd be soaking wet; her boots had gone right through to a hole; Mrs Sharp was chasing him for the rent they owed . . . Then an even worse thought. Suppose the lightning had 'got' him like Mrs Sharp said!

'Well, any road, I gotta bit o' stout cardboard up in my kitchen. Just slip up with me and fetch that. That paper won't keep the wet out two minutes.'

Penelope's spirits rose and a minute or two later she was running back down the stairs with the cardboard in her hand, the moment of dread gone. Pa would be taking shelter from the rain; as soon as it stopped he'd come. Mrs Sharp had said she mustn't touch the metal scissors but while she was waiting she could lay her boots on the cardboard and draw out the shape, then as soon as she had a chance all she'd have to do would be to cut it out. She could do that later, even in bed.

'Pa needn't know.' She spoke to herself but Chummy obligingly poked his nose out of the shelter and twitched his ears. 'You know what, Chummy?' She sat down by his side, 'I don't really understand it but it's something to do with vanity – vanity's a sin, you see – and it's my punishment for that that made the hole come in my boot. 's morning at school when we knelt down for "Our Father", Rose McCormick was behind me. She's horrid – I hate her! That's a sin too, but I can't help hating her. Anyway she picks her nose even though she wears a big blue ribbon in her hair. She and Maisy Goodwin saw my boots. I heard them whispering and giggling. And I just knelt there, hating them.

'You see, Chummy, if I'd been thinking properly about "Our Father" I wouldn't have known about them – or if I had, it wouldn't have mattered to me. But I kept trying to push the hem of my skirt over my feet so they couldn't see.'

The little dog put his head in her lap as she sat close to him on the floor. He'd stopped shaking now; with the uncanny instinct of animals he knew the storm had passed. 'So it's my fault about the hole going right through. Be sure your sins will find you out, Chummy, that's what Mrs Sharp always says.'

Then she heard her father's tread on the area steps.

'Here I am, Tuppence,' Oliver Drew called as he threw open the door. 'What's all this, then? Hiding under the table? And what in the world is that cloth doing over the mirror?'

'I was keeping Chummy company, Pa. He got a bit

11

scared, you see. But I wasn't frightened. Mrs Sharp came down, she covered the looking glass.'

'After me, is she?' But he didn't seem put out by it.

Penelope looked at him curiously. There was something in his manner she didn't understand, something she wasn't familiar with. The package he carried gave out a smell so appetizing that Chummy's nose twitched and she was sure hers did too!

'Got a real feast for supper. Get the knives and forks on the table while I go up and see her.'

'You mean you're going up to find her?' For that was unheard of. It seemed to Penelope to be just looking for trouble.

'Tuppence, we're going to be rich! Just you wait 'til you hear what I have to tell you. I'll be down as soon as the table's ready.'

We're going to be rich . . . we're going to be rich . . . a hundred pictures chased each other around her mind. This room where they lived – they'd have a heavy chenille cloth on the table, one with a fringe all round like Mrs Sharp's green one, only theirs would be dark red to match the velvet curtains they'd hang at the window. (Hardly in keeping with the stone sink beneath it but to Penelope velvet represented luxury.) She imagined herself arriving at school wearing new clothes, really new, not clothes that other people had finished with. At the thought of the expression on hateful Rose McCormick's face she chuckled aloud. She knew just what she'd choose, she'd pictured it often enough: a blue and white gingham dress stiff with starch and her hair would be tied with a white ribbon. And just think of it! Pa would be able to have a new suit, perhaps even a gold watchchain across his stomach and a brown bowler hat on his head. As for Chummy, they'd give him real meat to eat and because they'd be such good customers at Mr Cload's butcher's shop, he'd never be short of a bone . . .

Oliver Drew came back from seeing their landlady, the smile still on his face.

'Wotcha gonna tell me, Pa?'

'What are you – going to,' he corrected. 'How often have I reminded you? Nothing lets you down more than a sloppy way of talking. It might be good enough for Merchant Hill Board School, but not for us, eh, Tuppence?' But his smile took any sting from his words. 'Who's to say where tomorrow will find us. We must be ready for it. "Wotcha gonna" indeed!'

'What are you going to tell me, Pa?' How much longer did she have to wait?

'We'll eat our supper first. Just you look at that! Meat, gravy, vegetables . . . the bowl's been well wrapped, it's still warm. Eat first, news after.'

She would much rather have had it the other way round. How could she savour each bite with full concentration when she didn't even begin to understand where it had come from?

The dish held plenty for all of them. Even Chummy ate his fill and finished off by licking their plates until they shone.

Only then did Oliver tell her. He had been given a job in the kitchen at the Grand Hotel.

'You'll see, Tuppence, there'll be plenty more where this lot came from. There's only one snag – it'll mean I shall be out every evening. You'll be in bed before I get home.'

The evenings were her favourite hours of the day. But nothing must cloud his success. So she beamed at him across the table as she answered. 'It's a good thing I'm growing up, Pa. Chummy and me'll be all right.'

'Chummy and I,' he corrected automatically.

She remembered times when he'd had other jobs. He hadn't always gone out each day knocking on doors, begging for odd jobs that would bring him a few coppers and sometimes a bowl of hot soup or a mug of tea. There had been the time he'd worked in the tobacconist's shop on

13

the corner of Bridge Street; he'd been there two or three months. Then, quite unexpectedly, he'd come home in the middle of a Thursday afternoon – the day before his weekly wage was due. 'If you're the boss,' he'd told Penelope, 'you can do as you please. Sacked me, said he could manage without an assistant.' She had felt offended on his account. And the following week, when she'd seen someone else in his place behind the counter, she'd thought it kinder not to tell him, so sure that he'd been unfairly used. The same sort of thing had happened at Mr Loveridge's, the ironmonger in Rupert Street. People treated Oliver badly. But now his luck had changed. From now on things would be good. Child though she was, she knew just what it would mean to his self-respect to earn a regular wage. So she gave not a hint of how lonely her evenings would be.

This evening there was an air of celebration in the basement room. The thunder had moved away, even Chummy was restored to his usual bouncing self, especially with a supper of meat and vegetables inside him.

Her father was looking at Penelope as if he were seeing her afresh. 'When we've a regular wage coming in we must get you some new clothes. You'll see, things are going to be different from now on. This hole isn't fit for a pig. Dirty hovel!'

But how could it be? She'd swept it, she'd even shaken the mat yesterday, and she always washed the plates after they'd eaten and pulled up the blankets in the morning.

'You're going to learn to dress properly, do your hair up pretty. You'll learn to be a lady. I know how things should be, you know, I wasn't brought up living like this. But I'll show them, I'll show the lot of them . . . '

Penelope was frightened by something unfamiliar in his voice she didn't understand. His mouth looked loose and wobbly, his eyes suddenly bloodshot with the sting of unshed tears. She went round the table and put her arm around his shoulders. Coming close, she found a smell about him she didn't recognize. Stale perfume . . . stale whisky on his breath.

'We're all right, Pa.' She tried to bring him back to her. 'Pa?' Perhaps he sensed her unease, he made an effort to pull himself together. ' . . . shall we, Pa?'

'Sorry, Tuppence, what was that?'

'I said, shall we make plans, about how it's all gonna be?'

'It's going to be different, Tuppence, that's how it's going to be. We'll find somewhere decent to live and – '

'You mean we aren't going to get the curtains for here? We'd planned to get them just as soon as we had the money, Pa.'

'Spend money on curtains for this hole! Not likely! We'll clear out of here.' He nudged her with his elbow. 'But that's a secret – not a word to anyone mind – not a word to that haybag upstairs.' His snigger made Penelope uncomfortable. 'Promise.' She nodded, a cold finger running down her spine. 'I've got a friend at the Grand. This is just between you and me, it was this friend who got me taken on.'

'What's his name, Pa? Have I ever seen him?'

'Her – not him.' He gave her a knowing wink as if the words had a special meaning and she'd know what it was. 'No, you don't know her. But I've been on "visiting terms", you might say, for a while.' Again that snigger. 'Ah, she'll see me right. It was Muriel – that's her name – who sent us our dish of supper. Like I said, she'll see me right, there's plenty more where that came from. She's got very fond of me, Tuppence. Look after Muriel and she'll see to it that my job's safe, never you fear.'

It wasn't a bit like him to use that tone. Penelope felt uncomfortable and out of her depth. To busy herself she picked up the plates; by now even Chummy had decided there was nothing more to be gained from polishing them with his tongue. She put an inch or two of water in the tin kettle and lit the gas ring. Making plans was her favourite

15

pastime; that they never came to fruition didn't detract from the pleasure she found in sharing the dreams with her father. And surely news like Pa had brought home this evening gave them plenty to plan for. He'd said they'd find a different place to live; perhaps it would be somewhere that was just their own. Into her mind sprang a picture of a house with steps to the front door, a garden bright with flowers.

The kettle sent out its first puff of steam and she poured the water into the small round bowl that served all their needs: Oliver used it to hold his shaving water; Penelope dipped their clothes in it and rubbed them with soap; she knelt on a chair and "washed" her hair in it too, rubbing that with the same lump of red soap that she used for everything else; sometimes it was stood on the floor, the nearest they ever came to having a bath; the potatoes were peeled in it; the dishes were washed in it. 'The Bowl' was an essential part of their lives.

Oliver took the towel from where it still hung over the mirror and dried the plates.

'Won't always be like this, Tuppence. I've let you down, I know I have. But no more.' If he'd spoken in a voice that sounded like his own she could have hugged him, reassured him. Something had upset him, she could tell it had, but she had no idea what. He never mentioned her mother, Penelope had no memory of her and knew nothing of her except that she was dead. Perhaps he was sad because she wasn't with them to share now that 'things were to be different'. With no idea of the way her mind was working, he viewed her, eyes half closed. 'Be a good-looking girl one of these days, Tuppence, feed you up and get a bit of flesh on your bones.'

Perhaps it was her mother he was thinking of as he stared at her with that strange expression. Perhaps if they talked about her it would make him happier.

'Who do I look like, Pa? Do I look like my mother?'

16

'Your mother? Who's been talking about her? That old haybag upstairs?'

'No one, honestly, no one. I just thought – '

'Well, don't. Not about her. She was no good to you – and no good to me neither. She's gone, you hear me, gone.'

'Yes, Pa. She died, I know.'

'Yes, she died. But she'd gone from me and from you too, long before that. Selfish bitch! You hear me? Selfish bitch, that's what your mother was.'

Penelope had never heard him shout like that before. She wished she'd not asked. Rather than cheer him up the mention of her mother had upset him even more. His face was working, his eyes red and bleary. She supposed he'd been treated very badly. It didn't occur to her that the way he'd spent his own afternoon, coupled with strong drink he was unused to, might have had anything to do with his lack of control. "Please don't let his face look like that. Please, don't let Pa start to cry." She lowered her gaze, unable to bring herself to look at him.

'I'm ever so glad about that lady helping you get taken on at the Grand.' Then, as if the words wouldn't be suppressed: 'But even if it hadn't happened, we were getting along very nicely.'

For a moment he rested his hand on her straight hair, hair that was lustreless for want of attention.

'We'll be all right, Tuppence.' And she knew by his voice it was safe to look at him again.

'Shall we have some games, Pa? Or shall we have a singsong?' For now they'd come to her special hour of the day. 'Then later I've got to finish mending my boot.' She'd not meant to let him know, but in the face of their sudden good fortune a hole in her sole was as nothing.

'I'll buy you new ones next week – well, soon anyway.'

New ones! Boots with smooth, shining soles that had never trodden the ground, boots that had held no feet but hers!

'It's gone through but it's all right, I've got a good stout piece of cardboard,' she beamed.

First they played dumb charades, each thinking of a word and acting it. Then 'Places', a game Oliver had made up, teaching her that the world didn't begin and end with Challington.

'I sailed across the Atlantic Ocean to – beginning with A?' he asked.

'America. I rowed along the coast until I came to – beginning with B?'

Just as she meant him to, he frowned in concentration before he suggested 'Brighton?'

Dirty hovel it might have been, but that basement of number seven Victoria Place held something that all the riches in the world couldn't buy.

Later, working together, they cut out the new inner soles. Under his breath Oliver hummed; Penelope joined in; Chummy's tail swished from side to side as he sat, head tilted, watching them.

Luckily for Penelope, the morning after the storm the roads were already dry and the good weather settled with them once more. For as 'next week' came and went, it was clear that boots for her were low on the list of priorities.

'I have to set myself up properly first, Tuppence. I can't remember when last I bought anything new to wear. Mixing with other people – well, I want to appear as good as the next.'

She dug her white teeth into the large slice of iced sponge cake he'd brought home for her, savouring each sweet crumb. Then she nodded.

'You gotta be smart as paint, Pa. And remember I finished school yesterday 'til next term so you don't need to worry. We'll go shopping for things for me in a week or two. We'll plan it out, think what we're going to get. I wouldn't be wearing new for play anyway.'

The tang of the lemon icing helped her to overcome her

18

disappointment. Something whispered to her that his friend Muriel might be behind his need to make an impression; but she wouldn't listen. Of course Pa must be smart as the next – and smarter! And even though everything he bought for himself put her shopping day that bit further away, Penelope's eyes shone with pride as she looked at him. Seeing the brilliant white of the new handkerchiefs he'd just taken from their wrapping, she realized how badly he needed new everything! If he went to the Grand looking untidy they'd tell him he couldn't stay. All too well she remembered how it had been when he'd lost his other jobs. She'd rather anything than that he should be given the sack again.

Over the first week or two of school holiday her boots were hardly important. Most of the time she was barefoot on the shore. Two boys, a girl and a small, shaggy black and white mongrel, each day they were there; if the tide was low they'd hunt in the rockpools, or, using a piece of wood for a bat, they'd play cricket on the sand. Sometimes there was a chance to earn a few pennies, helping mend a net or sort out a basket of fish.

In the days when Oliver had gone off each day looking for odd jobs, a hedge to trim, windows to be cleaned, a table to mend, even putting a fresh coat of distemper on a wall, he'd never rushed out in the mornings like people did who had regular work to go to. But now all that was changed. What free time he had during the day was in the afternoon. Sometimes he'd come home; more often he wouldn't. 'A lovely afternoon, I knew you'd be out to play,' he'd explain his absence during those weeks when Penelope wasn't at school.

So from first thing in the morning until after Penelope and Chummy were in bed and asleep, he'd be out. One wet evening in August she came home earlier than usual. The light was already fading. Down in the basement the only gas was for the cooking stove; light came from an oil lamp, its flame setting flickering shadows dancing across

19

the walls and ceiling. Outside the road was quiet; in this steady drizzle very few were tempted out.

'What shall we do, Chummy, boy?' He was agreeable to most things. If she'd had a book he would have curled up at her feet without a murmur; if she'd had a ball to spin across the stone floor he would have chased it and brought it back for more. But in answer to her question all he could do was put his head on one side and swish his tail. 'You sit there and watch. Right?' Her ever faithful audience showed no sign of boredom as she hummed and danced, swaying her small, thin body with a grace that neither of them appreciated. Tom had been to the concert on the pier. He told her that the dancers had kicked their legs high into the air, and there had been one who had ended up in what seemed to be called the splits. So she kicked hers, each time higher than the last, and then lowered herself gradually towards the floor. Practice, that's what she needed. And as her evenings grew longer, practice was what she had. Soon she could kick her leg straight towards the ceiling, and lower herself all the way down to the ground. She sang too, she knew lots of songs. How empty it sounded, though, one small voice all by itself.

Whether she would have had that promised pair of boots in time for school if Mrs Sharp hadn't brought down a parcel of her niece's girl's cast-offs, who can say? As it worked out, it seemed this autumn was to be the same as all the others.

'You wouldn't believe our Dulcie's not a year older than you, such a fine big girl she is.' Ethel dumped the brown paper package on their table, a table still without a cloth to cover the unscrubbed wood. 'Be on the big side for you I wouldn't wonder, but that's a good fault. Just stuff a bit of rag in the toes of the boots, there's plenty of wear left. Tell your Pa it'll save him a few bob.' Then nodding towards the window: 'Might drop him a hint that he can get those curtains you were talking about instead, make it cosier for you of an evening.'

'Thank you very much, Mrs Sharp. I'll write my letter and give it to you.'

Ethel turned to go back upstairs.

'That's it. You write your thank you, I'll see she gets it.'

Even after she'd gone Penelope bit hard on the corners of her mouth to hold it steady. She knew that if she loosened her grip she'd cry. And she wouldn't cry! She was lucky! Others years she'd always been so excited when 'the parcel' had been brought downstairs, she'd written her letter willingly. But this year was to have been different. Boots next week . . . get you new things to wear . . . next week . . . well, soon anyway . . . wait a while . . . She cut the string and took off the paper. There would be no new clothes, this would be her wardrobe. She heard a sob catch in the back of her throat – and felt the dab of a paw against her leg.

Brown paper was always useful, she knew she must fold it up and put it away safely in the cupboard next to the fireplace. What made her probe amongst the things in the cupboard she didn't know, she never had before. Soon clothes were forgotten, old and new alike.

That box on the shelf . . . Pa must know it was there, yet he never got it out . . . What was in it? Standing on a chair she reached for it, then climbed down and carried it to the table. A concertina, a squeezebox as Alf always called them, here in the cupboard and Pa had never said! Could he play it? Taking it from its case she slipped her hands through the leather straps, pulled it wide, pushed it closed, pressed each stop, listening to the different notes.

It was the first time she'd been glad to be alone – alone except for Chummy who listened with one ear cocked. She wouldn't tell Pa she'd found it, she'd learn all by herself to make tunes. She'd play the songs she knew, she'd sing and play.

Even the thought of another season in Dulcie's cast-offs had lost its sting.

There wasn't much that went on in the basement that

escaped Mrs Sharp's ear and she could hardly have failed to hear Penelope's first practice session.

'I heard you on that old concertina last night,' she said the next evening when Penelope carried the promised 'thank-you' letter up to her. 'Does your pa know you've got it?'

'No, not yet. I found it at the back of the shelf in the cupboard. I'm going to get better on it first, then surprise him. Fancy him not telling me we had it there. Used he to play it do you suppose, Mrs Sharp?'

'Not likely,' she guffawed, 'rather he'd never have set eyes on it, that'd be my guess. If I were you I'd keep quiet about it, not let him know you've been poking about in the cupboard. Nice for you to have a tune of an evening. Me and Mr Sharp won't blab.'

Penelope would have liked to ask more, but she didn't. She was never comfortable talking to Mrs Sharp about her father. No one had ever actually maligned him, but she felt the couple upstairs misjudged him. She supposed he must have tried to play it and not been very good.

In a way she was glad he wouldn't want to lay claim to it – she felt it was hers. Each evening she played, and soon she found that one voice alone didn't sound nearly so empty with the gusto she put into the accompaniment.

Oliver ate all his meals at the hotel, coming home each night with a parcel of food for her to eat the next day: cold meat, chicken joints, peaches, bananas, cakes . . . treats unheard of in the old days. If there wasn't much pleasure in her solitary meals, she wasn't going to admit it. Eagerly she accepted all he brought and never questioned his right to have helped the provisions find their way into his pocket.

There had been plenty of times when a large dish of potatoes had supplemented one small pie bought from Mr Pitt's shop in Kings Road and divided between them. She was remembering those shared suppers on this evening early in September.

'Never had real beef then, Chummy, eh boy?' Her faithful friend wasn't easily deceived; her bright voice didn't fool him. Oliver had put last night's 'spoils' between two plates to keep the flies off. Now Penelope lifted the top one and carried it to the table. She cut two slices of bread, one for her, the other broken up and mixed with his share of the meat for Chummy.

'There boy, isn't that good? Here, you have a bit more of my meat, I've got a banana for "afters". Never used to have "afters", did we?'

He sat at her feet, ears cocked, head on one side, his long tail swishing. She squatted down, sitting back on her heels. She knew how impatient he must be to get at his supper but she couldn't help it, she just *had* to touch him, to feel his never-failing lick on her face. She was ashamed. 'Being a proper baby, that's what I am. 's all right here, isn't it? Just you and me but we got each other . . .' Penelope sniffed. She wouldn't cry, she wouldn't! Chummy stood on his hind legs, his front paws on her shoulders so that he could reach to lick her ears. Her arms held him tight.

On the first day he'd started work at the Grand, Oliver had told her: 'I'll get home as early as I can – but I don't want you hanging around waiting outside the hotel. It wouldn't be right, it might make things difficult for me.'

'No, Pa, 'course I won't,' she'd promised. Not for the world would she have done anything to spoil his newfound happiness.

This evening she and Chummy were later than usual going for their last walk of the day. Already the street lamps had been lit. The large iron gates of George Bradley Park were still open, so just as she did every evening she untied Chummy's string and threw sticks for him to fetch back to her.

'Come along now, missie, lock-up time – and time you

23

were home off the streets too,' the park keeper called. He knew her well by sight and had his own opinion about parents who let a child wander on her own like she did.

'The evenings are drawing in. Come on, Chummy, the gentleman wants to shut the gate,' she answered in her best grown-up tone.

Pulling at his string, the dog led the way. She'd meant them to go straight home, but it seemed he had other ideas. And what was there to rush for? Pa wouldn't be back for ages yet. It would seem lighter on the beach away from the street lamps – and, as if Chummy had the same thoughts, it was in that direction that he pulled her. Here the game was much the same as in the park, except that now it was stones she threw for him and he splashed into the breaking waves in a vain search for them. Darkness fell; their eyes attuned to it, they hardly noticed.

Finally they turned away, his string again securing him.

Not far along the Promenade she could see the lights of the Grand. From here it looked like a magic wonderland, a bright beam piercing the darkness from every window. They'd stand at a distance and watch. She saw a carriage draw up to the steps, the doorman come to help a lady and gentleman down. She hadn't meant to move nearer, she'd promised not to hang about outside . . . just one peep.

It was so bright in the dining room that no one would see into the near darkness out here. The doorman had gone inside, there was no one to stop her as she climbed on to the low wall into which a rail was set then pulled herself up. She leant forward to get a better view. The bright lights of the chandeliers, the gleaming white table-cloths, the beautiful gowns, and the gentlemen all in evening dress . . . it was like some enchanting moving picture. At the far end of the room an orchestra was still playing. She strained her ears to try and hear. Chummy touched her leg with his front paw, silently asking her what she'd stopped for.

'Off those railings! Clear off, you and your tyke too.'

Penelope had been too engrossed in her thoughts to notice the doorman's return. His sudden shout made her jump and Chummy bark. She scrambled down, misjudged the distance from the low wall to the pavement; and that's how she caught her foot and tore the toe of the fragile sole from the upper part of her boot. Dulcie's over-large hand-me-downs had been stuffed with rag and put aside to come out fresh for next term.

'And don't let me have to tell you again.' The doorman meant to have the last word. But in fact it went to Chummy who, as she pulled him away, stood his ground on three legs and left a memento.

The doorman mustn't guess who she was. It wouldn't do to let her father find her here. She moved away, across the road, to stand in the shadows at the top of the beach. It couldn't be long before the kitchen staff finished and he'd come out – not down the front steps, but from the small door at the end of the building. She'd watch for him, let him start towards home, then chase after him as if she and Chummy had come up from the beach.

It was some time before a group of people came out through the staff door. But he wasn't one of them. At the top of the building a window was thrown open and, just at that same second, the gas in the room was lit. It was high up, yet in the surrounding darkness it was as if she looked at a picture. Pa throwing wide the window, top and bottom; a woman she'd never seen before coming to his side. Pa turning to her . . . putting his arm around her . . . moving his face against her neck in such a funny way, as if he were eating her.

Muriel – for Penelope was sure that's who it must be – reached to pull down the blind. The summer night was suddenly full of shadows. Chummy tugged at his string, leading the way home.

Evenings with the secret concertina were nothing new. She couldn't read a note of music but she had a natural gift, a good ear and a perfect sense of rhythm. Not that she realized any of that, to her the pleasure came from the fact that she had learnt to play some tunes and could accompany herself as she sang to Chummy. Tonight she found a new solace in playing. To be here with her concertina wasn't like being alone at all. Her spirits took an upward turn. What if Pa did have friends she didn't know, what was wrong with that? He didn't know that she'd learnt to play the squeezebox he'd kept hidden away, nor was he part of the fun she had with Tom and Alf on the beach. Anyway, he never forgot her. And as if to prove it, next morning she found a really huge slice of game pie, a lump of cheese, a wedge of fruit cake and three peaches.

Next morning, too, the glue pot did its job on the toe of her boot and life went on.

Oliver was a changed man. No longer was life a struggle, a losing battle. There came the day when he wore a gold chain across his stomach just like she'd imagined.

'I bought it from "Uncle",' he told her. 'Uncle' was the pawnbroker. If he'd gone to a jeweller's shop for his watch it wouldn't have spelled success as this did, for what better evidence could there be of their changed circumstances! Not taking their few treasures in to see what 'Uncle' would allow on them, but actually buying, possessing what someone on hard times had had to raise a loan on and then not been able to redeem.

It was an afternoon in November. All day the mist had rolled in off the sea.

'That tyke of yours has been whining to get out.' Mrs Sharp met Penelope hurrying home from school. 'Wouldn't be surprised you'll find a clearing up job waiting for you.'

'I'll take him straight to the park. He's never dirty, Mrs Sharp,' she defended her friend.

Nature was bothering him, but not in the way the landlady imagined. A faithful fellow was Chummy, faithful to Penelope and to a Jack Russell bitch who lived in Belmont

26

Street. It was pretty well a mile away from Victoria Place, but such was Chummy's loyalty – and his sense of direction – that on the rare occasions he went missing they knew he'd be found singing a baleful song at his canine lover's gate. The fact that he sometimes came home drenched from the bucket of water that had been thrown over him never deterred him.

On this winter teatime his greeting for Penelope was as warm as ever, his excitement as she tied his string knew no bounds. They ran all the way to the park where, in the murky dusk, she threw his first stick. Free of the string he was gone, tail up, ears back! Her shouting made no difference. By the time she set up chase he was already out of the gates and on his way towards his goal.

If it was nature that set the chain of events in motion, from here on fate took a hand.

'Here, Ollie,' Muriel called out to Oliver who was cleaning silver in the stillroom, 'wouldn't your Penelope just love one of these cakes while it's nice and hot? Why don't you take my grid and pop a couple of them round to her for her tea.' If the best way to a man's heart was through his stomach, then plump and generous Muriel must have been well along the road.

Not for years had he ridden a bicycle, but picturing Penelope's delight Oliver accepted the suggestion gratefully. With two hot cakes wrapped in a cloth and stowed in his pocket he pushed Muriel's cycle through the staff gate to the road. He'd heard people say that once you could ride, you never forgot. Gingerly he started on his wobbly way. By the time he turned into Kings Road his confidence was growing.

Penelope panted up Belmont Street, string at the ready to take Chummy captive. He heard her step even before she appeared in the yellow halo of light from the single gas lamp, light made eerie in the mist. His ears went down, his tail drooped between his legs. It was a fair cop! There was nothing for it but to let himself be dragged off,

27

although not without many a backward glance. From Belmont Street into Kings Road his hope faded but not his desire. At the corner of Victoria Place, with the end of his dreams in sight and just when Penelope was confident she'd won the battle, he made a sudden and unexpected dash. Her hold on the string was lost and so was he. She was after him, the chase was on!

And that's when Oliver saw them. Wobbling on his uncertain way, he recognized what was happening.

'*Chummy! Get home!*'

It was a roar not to be ignored! Chummy stopped dead, ears back, tail down. Then, as if all the fiends of hell were after him, he dashed blindly into the road.

It happened in seconds: the dog's panic; the jolt that threw Oliver over the handlebars as the front wheel of the bicycle was trapped in the tram-track; the juddering of the tram as it braked to a sudden halt; the shouts of the passengers; the crush of metal against metal as the mangled cycle was caught under the tram.

Only Chummy was silent.

In her front parlour Ethel Sharp cocked her head on one side and listened. Where was everyone running to? What was it they were shouting about? What was going on? She threw open the bottom window and leant out. Perhaps there was a fire somewhere. She couldn't smell smoke, but that could be because of the mist.

'What's the excitement?' she called to anyone who might answer.

'Round the corner in Kings Road,' a man stopped running just long enough to answer, 'accident – a bicycle and a tram. Just met a lad they'd sent running to get the ambulance.' Then on he ran as if to make up for wasted time.

Ethel slammed down the window and hurried to get her hat and coat off the peg in the passage. In her imagination she could see Kings Road spattered with blood – and worse! What chance would a bicycle have if it got in the way of a tram? It was a long time since she'd covered the ground as quickly, drawn towards the knot of people gathered near the stationary tramcar. And once she got there she wasn't the kind to stand at the back where she couldn't see. What were elbows for if not to forge a pathway?

'Is he hurt bad?' Again she spoke to no one in particular.

'He's still out cold. Some kid with a bloody dog running loose. Ran right across his path so they say.'

Ethel was no dog lover. The tone of her 'Poor soul' made that very plain.

'Won't be running loose no more. Made mincemeat o' the poor little bugger,' someone else said to anyone with ears to hear.

'Oh, dear Lord above us . . . Penelope!' By now Ethel had fought her way to the front.

Penelope didn't hear her. She knew there was a crowd . . . people . . . tramcar . . . mangled bicycle, she knew and yet couldn't take it in. Only Pa . . . Pa and Chummy. If Pa would move, just once, just something . . . His hat had been thrown halfway across the road and there was blood in his hair and trickling down his forehead on to the road, Pa's blood on the road. And Chummy . . . his fur red and matted, his back bent right over and his flesh hanging, torn. Chummy, his eyes staring at her and not seeing her, his mouth wide open. For the first time Penelope faced the finality of death, but even now her mind couldn't accept what her heart knew to be true. Chummy . . . Pa. 'No, please, please, no.' She didn't even realize she was crying as, kneeling by her father's side, she took his still hand between her own, pumping it up and down.

'Pa! Pa! Wake up, Pa. It's me, Penny. Pa, it's Tuppence. You'll be all right, Pa. You gotta be all right. *Please* wake up. Pa, Chummy's hurt bad. *Please hear what I say.*'

CHAPTER TWO

'I've given her a nice milky cup of cocoa,' Ethel said to Bert, her husband, 'she must be worn out the way she cried. Makes you want to cry too, that it does. Never could take to dogs, but where's the justice? About all she had was that tyke.'

'It's her father we should be worrying about. What's to be done if he can't get back to his job? Just when the rent was coming in regularly. Might've known it was too good to last. Perhaps he won't come home at all. A blow on the head could do anything to a man. Perhaps he'll wake up with his memory gone.'

'If ever a man was a wet blanket, Bert Sharp, it's you. The doctor said when they took him off to the Infirmary in the wagon that there were no bones broken as far as he could tell. Sound enough except for that crack on the head. Whatever's to be will be. I'll just creep down and take a peek at her, see whether she's dropped off.'

'Not very likely!'

Ethel thought he was probably right and that's why she went back down to the basement. Best let the child feel there was someone keeping an eye. And all because that tyke wanted to go sniffing after a bitch! She might have guessed that was what he'd got on his mind, howling and scratching the door like he'd been all afternoon.

Shock, fright and tears had all taken their toll. Penelope was fast asleep. Ethel picked up Chummy's bowl of water and emptied it, then wiped it round with the murky tea-towel and put it in the cupboard. Would only rub salt in the wound to see it on the floor when she woke in the morning.

When morning came, Penelope was roused by the sound

of loud hammering on the door. Half asleep, she stirred, expecting to feel Chummy jump from her bed, to hear his bark. Then she remembered. There was only her. Chummy wasn't here . . . Pa wasn't here. Someone must have come about Pa. Perhaps it could even be him home from the Infirmary. Throwing her coat over her outgrown night-dress (it was two years since Mrs Sharp's niece's parcel had brought it to her), she ran to pull back the bolt.

'Who is it?'

It was a woman's voice. 'I'm from the hotel. It was my grid your Pa was riding. I run all the way. Got to get back to see to breakfasts, but I had to know — what happened? Where is he? Did they send him home last night?'

Penelope opened the door to the woman she knew must be Muriel. It was just one more thing that tore the foundation of her old life from under her feet. She saw again that fourth floor window, her father nuzzling his face against this stranger's plump white neck.

For a second they sized each other up; that was all it took.

Muriel's first spontaneous thought: "Oh, you poor little mite!" It wasn't just that this was 'Ollie's Tuppence' that touched her generous heart.

"She's come chasing after Pa." Penelope's silent reaction was less friendly.

'Aren't you going to ask me in a moment? You'll get cold. You've got bare feet.'

'I'm quite warm, thank you. But please come inside.' Penelope stood to her full height and more! She pronounced each word carefully. Hadn't Pa always said that that was the way not to let yourself down?

'Tell me what happened. I only got hold of rumours, nothing from anyone who was there. I knew it must have been your Pa, what with him not being used to my old gridiron and then not getting back to his work. He was coming to bring you some cakes for your tea, all hot from the oven they were.'

31

Penelope tried hard to hold on to her dignity. But there was such kindness in Muriel's voice. It was as if she really cared about what had happened to Pa, and about her too.

'If I'd held tight to Chummy's string it wouldn't have happened.' She heard the croak threatening her voice. 'I thought I'd got him safe, but off he went. Pa saw him and shouted and Chummy didn't stop to think, he rushed straight into the road. Never stopped to look.' She gulped. 'Tram was right there. Pa must 'a seen and somehow got his wheel in the tramline. All so quick it was. They were all right then – ' she pushed her knuckles into her mouth, biting hard on her shaking hand.

'Poor little love.' Muriel wasn't clever with words. Instead Penelope found herself taken into a warm embrace. Oliver had never been a demonstrative man. Many children might take it as normal to sit on their father's knee, to be hugged, but not Penelope. That wasn't his way. She knew he loved her, they were partners, they looked after each other. But she must have needed that physical expression more than she'd ever realized. Now she hardly knew how it happened, but as she blurted out her tale and felt herself cradled against Muriel's plump breast she clung to her with all her might.

'If you get any news, you run and let me know. The minute I've done what I have to at the hotel, I'll go along to the Infirmary myself, find out how he is. Then, this afternoon, I'll come back here to you. Don't go to school, they'll understand why when you go back and explain. Get the place ready for your pa. I expect he'll need a bit of extra taking care of, don't you? Now, look, I don't need to run back for ten minutes, what about boiling up the kettle and we'll have a cup of tea together.'

Until this morning, although the subject had never been mentioned, Penelope had known in her heart she'd disliked her father's friend Muriel. Whatever she'd imagined her to be like, it certainly wasn't this. Plump, pretty in an untidy way, heavily scented; but mostly she was aware of the warmth. She knew that here was someone who really cared about what was happening at the Infirmary.

' "A trouble shared's a trouble halved", isn't that how the saying goes?' Muriel said as she took the mug of steaming tea Penelope poured for her. 'Hardly slept a wink for worrying – about Ollie and about you too. 'course I didn't know then about your Chummy. I'm ever so sorry, truly I am. But it must have been too quick for him to know. He wouldn't have had time to feel any pain.'

Penelope nodded. She dreaded talking about him, yet at the same time she wanted to.

'I can't remember him not being with us. He was nearly eight, you know. Pa told me how he found someone putting this puppy – that was Chummy – in a sack with a brick in it by the canal. He was only little, that's what Pa told me, hadn't had any life at all. So he brought him home to be ours.' She gulped her scalding tea, blinking hard. 'Would they let Chummy into heaven? Do you think dogs are allowed? Some people wouldn't like it. Mrs Sharp – she can't abide dogs.'

'Of course they let them in! It'll be all the lovely things he's ever dreamed of.'

'He used to dream sometimes. In his sleep he'd twitch, his tail would quiver and he'd make a sort of squeak as if he thought he was barking.'

'Dreaming he was playing with other dogs. Well, love, his troubles are all over now. He'll have fields to run in . . . never be hungry . . . '

Penelope nodded.

'I'm glad you came. You'll come back this afternoon, won't you?'

As soon as they'd drunk their tea Muriel had to hurry back to the Grand. Penelope was alone, uncertain of the hours ahead, looking up from the basement window as each pair of legs went by – just in case it was him coming home. No Chummy to take for a run . . . She wouldn't let her mind stray down that road, she'd keep telling herself that he was happy, there'd be other dogs to play with . . . wasn't that what Muriel had said? Now her thoughts were on her unexpected visitor. She sniffed, glad of the lingering smell of perfume.

Oliver had been concussed, but Bert Sharp's melancholy predictions were proved wrong. Not only was he to come home, but his memory was unimpaired.

Just for that one day Penelope stayed away from school. In the afternoon she was standing at the top of the area steps watching for the first glimpse of Muriel hurrying from the Infirmary with news. A hansom cab turned into Victoria Place. And there her Pa was, home! Muriel helped him down. His head was bandaged; his face pale. But he was home, he was going to be well again.

If he'd been anxious that time off might lose him his job, Muriel had soon put that idea out of his head.

'You're not to attempt to come back until you're quite fit. Next week you just stay at home and keep warm, the week after that too if need be. I'll see your job's safe,' she'd assured him on the drive home. And in the kitchens of the Grand Muriel wasn't without influence.

'Not at school, Tuppence?' But Penelope knew he was glad to see her.

'Of course she's not at school! She's where she should be, waiting to welcome you home.' And just as Muriel meant her to, Penelope felt herself to be important to his homecoming.

From that first afternoon, the atmosphere in the basement rooms became changed. Yet there were still no curtains at the windows, nor yet a cloth on the table. So where was the difference? What gave it the illusion of a comfort it hadn't had before? For the next week Penelope hurried to be first out of the classroom. ("Please don't let him say I've got to stay and clean up the room. Once Pa gets back to work again I won't mind, then I'll stay every day if You want me to, but please don't let him say I can't go quickly today.")

At home it wouldn't be just her father who'd be expecting her; Muriel would be looking out for her too. Yesterday's cold ashes had always been waiting in the grate – and would be again once he was well enough to work – but not now. Those children Penelope had felt such envy for, the girls with their crisply starched Monday morning dresses, could never have understood the wonder she found in hurrying down the area steps in the winter twilight, seeing through the uncurtained window into the room where the lamp was already lit, the fire burning, her father and Muriel waiting for her, the smell of cooking greeting her. All her life she would remember those tea-times.

Eight days after the accident Oliver was back at the hotel. Penelope returned each day to a home that held no welcome and no warmth. No Chummy waiting, his tail swinging, sneezing with excitement as she found his string. Now, in the empty room, his ghost was everywhere.

When the wind blew from the east, the fire would never draw, the smoke would blow back into the room, the sticks smoulder and die. Coming home today she'd met Mrs Sharp carrying a basket of shopping and they'd walked along together. Penelope liked that. It made her feel important that she and the landlady were both making for the same destination, each to her own front door.

'Be snow before morning, I wouldn't wonder. Have you got something warm for your supper, duckie?'

Ethel Sharp was kind, Penelope knew she was. Yet, behind the question, she detected a veiled criticism of her father.

'Yes, Mrs Sharp. Pa always sees I've plenty,' she answered defensively, 'and I've still some soup to re-heat.'

'Umph!' Which might have meant anything. Penelope gave her a sideways look. She wasn't going to have anyone

35

think Pa didn't see she was well looked after; but she hadn't meant to sound ungrateful.

'It's kind of you to ask me, Mrs Sharp.'

'Kind, nothing! It's not right, him being out every evening. I tell you what I think – I think you ought to be able to go and keep warm in the kitchen along with him.' As she spoke they rounded the corner into Victoria Place and the east wind hit them.

A quarter of an hour or so later the paper and driftwood that Penelope had used to try to light the fire would do no more than smoulder, and that same east wind was blowing the smoke back in clouds across the cold room. She heated her soup on the gas ring, then ate it, dipping her bread into it. The evening stretched ahead, empty and lonely. She rolled up more paper and poked it into the fire, then she held the towel in front of it like she'd seen her father do, hoping to make it draw. Soon it would be bright, she told herself hopefully. In the meantime she'd play some songs, have a dance – that would warm her up. With Chummy for her audience she'd spent so many evenings singing, playing the concertina, practising walking on her hands, bending, twisting, performing feats far more acrobatic than she realized. But that had been with Chummy. By herself, with a fire that did no more than blow clouds of dark smoke across the room, the fun had gone out of it.

Mrs Sharp's words came back to her. The kitchen of the hotel would be warm and bright, everyone would be busy, there would be chatter, laughter. If she were to walk along and ask, perhaps Pa would say she could come in. The coal slipped and gave up the ghost, sending a final swirl of smoke to hang around the mantelpiece. She saw it as a sign.

'Mrs Sharp,' she called up the stairs.

'Yes, duckie, something wrong?'

'No, but I thought I'd better tell you where I was in

36

case you wondered. I'm going along to the Grand – like you said.'

'Be a deal more comfortable for you. These dark evenings you'd be much better there, and no trouble to anyone.'

Her hands deep in her pockets, her coat collar turned up and her felt hat pulled over her ears, Penelope set off. Whether or not she'd actually go in when she reached the staff door of the Grand, she wasn't sure. 'I don't want you hanging about,' he'd said. But going right inside wouldn't be 'hanging about'; anyway, when he'd told her that, she hadn't known Muriel. In the hotel kitchen, Muriel reigned supreme. And imagine how warm it would be . . . just think of the lovely smells from the cooking . . . the bright light from the gas . . . the bustle of everyone working.

Suppose, though, she got there, looked into the kitchen and saw it just as she imagined – and then Pa was angry, sent her away? She wouldn't decide yet; she'd not look beyond having somewhere to walk to. She felt she had a purpose, just the same as everyone else, heads down against the icy blast of the wind. As she passed the Lifeboat Inn she could hear the sound of men's voices. At Mr Cload's shop half a dozen women waited, each holding an empty basin; they would be buying faggots to take home for supper. Penelope had seen it all so often, all a familiar part of her last walk of the day with Chummy. She pulled her hat down further, tried to believe that it was the wind that made her eyes smart so. If only she had Chummy . . . no, she mustn't start feeling sorry for herself. She must just picture him being happy now . . . picture his tail swishing, the way he used to pull at his string but keep turning round as if he wanted to make sure she could keep up with him.

Along Kings Road she had to pass the Prince of Wales Theatre. The lights were on in the foyer and already a dozen or so people were waiting at the foot of a wooden flight of stairs at the side of the building, the beginning of the queue for the 'gods'. The idea came to her quite suddenly! Of its own accord it sprang to mind, and she knew just what she was going to do as she turned to run back to Victoria Place.

There was no need to light the lamp, she could feel for the box at the far end of the cupboard shelf even in the dark. Before the queue was much longer she was back at the Prince of Wales.

At the sound of the first chords heads turned. Any distraction was welcome on a night like this.

'Bit of entertainment, by the looks o' things,' a man laughed, not unkindly, but his tone implying that he wasn't expecting much from her efforts.

Penelope wasn't deterred. It wouldn't seem nearly as cold and miserable out here if they'd tap their feet, join in a song or two.

> Once in the window of a pork and beef shop
> Two little sausages sat.
> One was a lady and one was a gentleman,
> Sausages are like that.

She felt the change in the mood of the lengthening queue. A ripple of interest, of pleasure. They'd stopped talking amongst themselves and all turned towards her. They were smiling and as the song got into full swing feet started stamping in time, hands clapping. Better by far than standing here freezing and, watching the little elf-like creature with her concertina, it was impossible not to smile. Penelope had natural rhythm. As she played it was as if her body wanted to dance to the beat of her music. The mood in the queue was changed. They'd been cold, watching impatiently for the door of the 'gods' to be opened. Now no one looked towards the top of the wooden stairs, all eyes were on her.

A new and heady excitement filled her.

Everyone was familiar with the song of the sausages. It was part of the whistling repertoire of many an errand boy.

'Come on, now you sing it with me,' she chuckled. This was fun! Her delight could be felt all along the line of people. If they didn't know the words 'la-la' had to do, but she sang loud and clear leading them on.

'Go on, gi' us another,' someone shouted to her as she squeezed her concertina into the last grand chord. And she didn't need any persuasion. She knew lots of songs.

She was the first to notice the theatre door open, so she whipped off her felt hat and held it out.

'Ought to be in the Halls,' was the opinion of the woman who dropped the first copper into it.

'Did ever you see such great eyes?' from her companion. 'Just you wait till that one grows up!'

'You'll be back one of these days, my girl,' one man voiced the opinion of many as he put in his penny, 'inside on that stage, not out here in the cold.'

Her heart was pounding with excitement. All these people, they'd all joined in the singing, they'd all enjoyed it! Pennies, ha'pennies, even farthings, every one of them given with a cheerful smile.

Then the queue moved away up the steps, stopping at the top to pass up their coppers to get in to the show, and Penelope was left. She scooped the money from her hat and put it in her pocket.

Hurrying back to Victoria Place she hardly noticed the biting wind. She'd get to bed quickly. Her mind was alive with dreams.

"You're a fool, Muriel Masters. Has he ever told you he loves you? No! You know he hasn't. Look at you. Thirty-five years old, not a spring chick any more, as lovestruck as a young girl with her first sweetheart! But then, who has there ever been for you to care about till now? Love isn't just for the youngsters though. Never had a twinge of wanting a man, not 'til I got to know Ollie. Must have been something special about him right from the kick-off. Reckon I felt it from the time he came to my kitchen door looking for the chance to earn a few pence. Never dreamt of encouraging a stranger in off the street 'til that day. 'Come back tomorrow, there's a chair needs seeing to up in my room . . . '

"Tomorrow and tomorrow – what a spring it was – afternoons walking on the cliff – then getting him taken on. Now look at me – give myself to him just like I hand over those slices of beef and chunks of pie for him to take to young Penny. And what about him, does he take me with no more thought than that? No, I don't believe it. Think of him just now, wild for me he was. Or are men always like that? Give 'em a willing woman . . . Am I a fool, then? Oh, but if I am, isn't even that better than not having him at all? If only I could put the clock back, be twenty-five instead of thirty-five."

She felt the contour of her naked body, wishing her waist were trimmer, her hips not so spreading. Despite his shabby clothes, Ollie had been enough to make a woman look at him twice. Now he was smart as mustard. Yet it was her he hung his hat up to. His hat? Her lips twitched. His hat and the rest, all of it, over the rail of *her* bed. "If only just once he would say it's me he wants, for my own sake."

'Ollie! No good going off to sleep. You gotta be out of that door before it gets locked for the night, else my head'll roll.' But even as she spoke, Muriel moved closer to him letting the warmth of her soft, naked body convey all she left unsaid.

Yes, she was a fool right enough. What man would think of marrying a woman who gave herself to him as eagerly as she did? She'd end up old and alone, cooking for people who didn't belong to her, nothing and no one of her own. A fool! There, she'd said it again. Her leg moved across his. Silently she begged him to chase her fears away. Half asleep still, Oliver pulled her closer, breathing the scent she always wore. He could hear the soft patter of sleet hitting the window pane, the east wind howled in the chimney. But in here the bed was warm and tempting; Muriel was warm – and did she know just how tempting? Her leg moved again on his. Yes, she knew. She reminded him that he had to be out of the door before it was locked for the night; yet even while she said it her hands were caressing, begging him not to go.

'Look after Muriel and she'll see to it my job's all right,' he'd told Penelope. He remembered it now, listening to the wild night. Willingly he let her pull him back from the sleep that had been overtaking him. He marvelled at himself, at his prowess that he could be aroused again so soon.

'Half an hour yet before they lock up,' he whispered, 'I'm not wasting it in sleep.'

Her reply was a gentle laugh, hardly a sound at all.

'Mustn't let you get the sack on my account.' No romance in his words, but he spoke them softly, tenderly, a hand fondling her bounteous breasts.

It would have been so easy to close her eyes, forget everything but the moment and his nearness. But she didn't. In the dim light of the low-burning gas she took in the whole scene, it imprinted itself on her consciousness: the barely furnished room with its sloping ceiling; the tiny grate set in the wall, a grate where no fire was ever lit; their clothes torn off and thrown over the iron rail at the foot of the bed. Just as earlier that same evening Penelope had known exactly what she was going to do, the idea coming to her of its own volition, so now with Muriel. Fool she may be but, despite his caresses, reason hadn't quite deserted her.

'You'd be for the sack too, Ollie, if they caught you up here with me. They think they own our souls in this place. We're not expected to have a life outside that kitchen.' For a second she paused, just long enough to add emphasis to her words. 'Me – I know what I'd do well enough if they told me to go. And I will do it too, one of these days. I was thinking about it back in the spring, then we got

41

friendly . . . since you've been here, well, it's all been different.'

'What would you do?' He asked it, but from his tone she knew his thoughts had moved on. With so few minutes left to them, this was no time for chatter.

'I've got a bit of money put by. Worked hard always and saved – and my aunt left me fifty pounds a year or so back. One of these days I shall open a boarding house. Rent somewhere with enough bedrooms. I could afford to furnish it with Aunt Jane's money. Cook in my own kitchen. I was going to look round for somewhere back in the spring, then I met you. Since you've been here,' she eased herself ever so slightly closer, the invitation he read in her movement speaking even more clearly than her words, 'since we've been like this together, well, I wouldn't want to go, not now.'

There, she'd said it! She couldn't have put it plainer if she'd asked him outright. For months she'd dreamed of it. A boarding house, their very own place. Ollie to be host to their guests. He was so good-looking and a real gentleman the way he talked. Now, always at the back of her mind, was the fear of getting pregnant. But once they were married . . . just think of it, she and Ollie with a family of their own. And it would be a proper home for Penny too.

Oliver didn't answer. Her breast filled his hand, her protruding nipple hardened under his touch . . . she turned on to her back, guiding his head. She felt his mouth, his teeth nibbling . . . then his weight as he moved on to her.

'Damn the door,' he muttered as he felt himself gripped between her strong thighs, 'can't leave you . . . should be together . . . can't leave you . . . not like this . . . '

Excitement at what she'd told him, fear that his hold on a second arousal in less than an hour would be short-lived, both gave him a feeling of urgency. Almost immediately it was over.

Before the night porter locked the back door he was on his way back to Victoria Place.

The charred wood was cold in the grate, evidence that tonight there had been no fire, but he didn't notice. It had usually burnt itself out by the time he got home. The concertina was back in its case; Penelope was asleep, her bundle of coppers tied in a handkerchief and pushed under her mattress.

That was in January. Oliver didn't rush into the proposal he knew Muriel wanted; he digested what she'd told him. He had no intention of letting her believe he was marrying her for the security she'd bring with her. A month later he'd not once referred to her dreams of a boarding house – nor yet her ability to finance it!

Leading the way up the last flight of stairs one night in February, Muriel took off her overall.

'You get the glasses out, Ollie. Help yourself to a good whisky. Nothing else I can give you tonight, I'm afraid.'

'You mean you're – '

'Went down on my knees and said thank God for it too! I'm never late as a rule.'

Oliver sensed this was his moment.

'If only things were different, Muriel. But how can I ask you to be my wife? Why, even while you're single and working, you must earn far more than I do. How can I expect you to accept the sort of life I could give you? I would have, though, I would have begged it of you, if only you'd not told me you'd got money of your own. It's a barrier I can't forget.' He picked up his glass with a hand that wasn't quite steady. 'But must it stand between us? I could look for something better than here at the Grand and bring home enough to keep us. Come and make a proper home of that poor hovel where I live. A man must be master in his own home, however humble.'

He knocked back his whisky and put the glass down, looking at her helplessly. 'I've no right to ask – to beg – you to say goodbye to your dreams just for my sake. You deserve your boarding house, you'd run a wonderful establishment. I'm no good to you, Muriel, no good to anyone.'

He gripped her shoulders. His face had that look that had frightened Penelope, his eyes suddenly bloodshot with unshed tears, his mouth trembling. 'I should go down on my knees too and beg forgiveness that because of me, because of the need I have of you, because you let me love you, you've been worried like that! I ought never to come here again, I know it. For your sake I ought to be strong. Yet, now, after all we've shared, I can't stop needing you.'

His hands moved. He touched her hair, untidy from a day at the ovens, then outlined her copious breasts, her thick waist, her sturdy buttocks. 'I'm no good to you. Your life was uncluttered before I came. Forget what I suggested – I know it can never be – I'll have to go away – I couldn't bear to be with you each day, not now, not when we've had so much – ' He took her hand and pressed it to his cheek.

She moved it, covering his lips. 'Hush, darling Ollie. Never leave me. Promise me you'll never leave me.'

'You mean you'll marry me? You'll forget the boarding house, come to live in Victoria Place?' It was a gamble he had to take. He could feel his heart pounding. No wonder his lips trembled. Supposing she said yes, she was prepared to do all that!

She sat on the bed, pulling him to her side, then as he leant towards her she took him in her arms, cradling his head against her.

'Ollie, try and see it my way. If we'd been man and wife when Aunt Jane died she would have left it to us both, now wouldn't she? So it's not mine, it's ours. We'll find a boarding house and run it together, Ollie. And you'll always be the master, of course you will, just like a husband should.'

He breathed in the strong scent she always wore, mixed with the lingering smells of cooking that clung to her

44

clothes. Not an erotic combination but one that, hearing her words, excited him.

'If I can't make love to you tonight, at least I can hold you,' he mumbled, his mouth against hers. Muriel's cup of happiness overflowed.

Often enough Muriel had been to the basement rooms, and knew Penelope's welcome was always genuine. But today Oliver was going to tell her about the engagement, today was different. Standing before the looking glass in her room, she pulled on her hat and practised her lines. 'I'm not trying to take your ma's place. If you can't think of me as a mother, then we'll go on being friends, same as we are already.' She steeled herself for Penelope's hostile expression; tried to put herself in the place of a child who had had no one to share her father's affection with. A basin containing an outsize portion of last night's sherry trifle was no more than she would have taken in any circumstances, yet today Muriel felt it would be seen as bribery.

But she needn't have worried. As she turned down the area steps she heard Penelope's excited shout: 'Pa! She's here! Muriel's come!' The girl flung open the door. 'Pa's been telling me all about it!'

'You're pleased? Penny, we'll have it that nice, you just see if we don't.'

From the doorway that led to his bedroom Oliver watched as the two of them hugged each other. It was as if a weight was lifted, a weight he'd carried so long it had barely been noticed – until it disappeared.

'I'm off along to Riley Street Market,' he said, 'I won't be more than ten minutes. I'll bring back some haddock and we'll have tea here with young Tuppence before we go back to work.'

'We'll make plans while he's gone, shall we?' Hearing Penelope's words, he was aware of a new sense of freedom. The responsibility for seeing those plans worked out would be someone else's now – Muriel's. Whistling under his breath, he marched off towards Riley Street. The plans they would be making spelt a new way of life . . . no wonder he whistled! As soon as they could find a suitable house, Muriel was ready with the rent. During the next few months they'd get the place ready in their free time, go to the salerooms and, using that money her aunt had left her, pick up the furniture they'd need to be fit for summer visitors. Seaside holidays were getting more popular with every year, people from the factories in the Midlands crowding down to the south coast.

He could picture himself welcoming the guests to his house. Muriel would ply the visitors with food as well presented as she knew how to from the Grand. A good class of clientèle was what Oliver had in mind. Young Tuppence could help wait at the tables and make herself generally useful. A few more weeks in the kitchen at the Grand and then he'd be his own master.

"Look after Muriel and she'll see we're right." He pictured her standing at the wooden bench at the hotel, rolling out her pastry, working with speed and precision; plump, rosy-cheeked, jolly, thirty-five years old and he was the first man to have got into bed with her; it would surprise them all if they knew how he 'looked after' her, ah, that it would, and how much she enjoyed being 'looked after' too! He bought his haddock and hurried home. Teatime in the basement today was a celebration.

When Mrs Sharp heard the basement door close in the evenings and Penelope's steps hurrying towards Kings Road, naturally enough she imagined her to be on her way to the Grand. 'A nice motherly soul,' was her opinion of Muriel, formed more from her shape than anything else for she'd hardly spoken to her. She hadn't given Oliver credit for having enough sense to look for a wife of her sort, not after what she'd heard of the first time round!

But it wasn't to the hotel Penelope went. Challington

46

had two theatres – the Prince of Wales, and off St James Street, the Theatre Royal. The small girl with the huge dark eyes soon became a familiar sight, sometimes at one, sometimes the other. Except for Penelope herself, the Sharps, Tom and Alf were the only people who knew about the concertina. Her busking was a secret she shared with no one. It wouldn't be right to tell other people before she told her father, and instinct warned her this was no time to take him into her confidence. He was intent on rising in the social scale; they were to have a proper house, furniture in all the rooms, guests. For Penelope to be playing her concertina in the street wouldn't fit into the new scene. So she said nothing. For her, status had nothing to do with it. Even the coppers she brought home to add to her pile weren't the driving force. Those people who waited for the 'gods' pay desk to open could be looking bored, miserable with the long wait. But she had it in her power to make them smile, to make them tap their feet with her. She'd heard their comments: 'Proper little natural, this one' . . . 'One day it'll be *her* name in the biggest letters'. The Pied Piper must have felt just as she did as the children of Hamelin followed him.

It was when she held her hat out as the queue started up the steps that someone asked: 'What's your name? We want to know who we've got to look out for in a few years time when you head the bill. Ain't that so?'

Foraging in pockets and purses for the coppers to put in her hat, they all agreed.

'Just Penny,' she told them. And what could have been more appropriate!

A house to rent was found in Alexandra Square, set back from the front. Certainly it wasn't at the smartest end of town; the promenade there gave way to the fishmarket and beyond that the dock. But it was large, it had gas lighting, it had a bathroom with a gas geyser and that in itself put it a cut above many of the boarding establishments – and with the sort of catering Muriel could provide, who was going to mind walking a mile to the pier? It was towards the centre of a terrace, each house with six stone steps to the front door. The grass in the middle of Alexandra Square was surrounded by a metal fence, a series of narrow iron arches, the smooth uprights just right for Penelope – and every other child – to run her hands along as she walked past. Even though this area of grass was public, the inhabitants of the Square looked on it as their garden. The back of the house wasn't as grand; a yard with two washing lines and a gate that led into Prospect Street, wrongly named if ever a street was, for it looked on to nothing except the tall brick buildings of a brewery. Clifford House, as number fourteen was called, had been used as a letting house previously, so Muriel not only took over most of the furniture but the bookings for the coming summer too.

Everything was arranged. Oliver and Muriel were to be married on the 7th May. It was a week before that, an evening with all the glory of summer, when half an hour before the curtain was due to rise at the Prince of Wales Penelope went into her first song. A little girl in her grey-white pinafore, still wearing Dulcie's large winter boots, her straight hair topped by the battered straw hat. Had she been one of the crisply starched brigade the queue mightn't have fallen under her spell so readily – although they probably would, for her happiness was infectious as she played, swaying her body, tapping her feet.

'Reckon we get as good a show out here as inside,' someone laughed as she finished her first song to the applause of the lengthening line of people.

Penelope beamed. The magic of it never failed.

'What in God's name do you think you're doing! Get off home this minute!'

'Pa!' But he never came out during the evening!

The queue fell silent. Penelope could feel their embarrassment.

'I was only – ' she started. These people had been her friends. Pa was making her look a fool in front of them.

'You heard me! Stop that racket and get home off the streets!'

'She plays a treat,' someone defended her, 'you got a real little natural there, Mister.'

Penelope's dark eyes sent him a smile of gratitude, but it was clear from Oliver's expression the remark had done nothing to placate him.

'Better get home,' she mumbled, fastening the concertina closed. 'Are you coming, Pa?'

'I am.'

Like a gaoler he marched her up Kings Road, neither of them speaking. She couldn't stand the silence any longer; she'd rather be shouted at than this.

'I was gonna tell you, Pa – about playing the concertina. But I wanted to get really good first.' Silence. 'Pa . . . ? Are you cross 'cos I took it without asking – or 'cos I went out in the street?'

'I hate deceit.'

'Didn't mean to, Pa, I'm sorry.' She'd never known him to be angry with her like this. It was as if she couldn't reach him. She slipped her hand into his.

'Can't think what came over you, going out like that!'

'I didn't think I was doing anything bad. They always liked it, everyone'd sing and – '

'You mean you've done this before?' They turned down the steps to their basement. She didn't need to answer.

'I won't go again, Pa, honest I won't. But can I just play you some of the things I . . . ' At the look on his face, her voice faltered.

'That concertina's going.'

'Oh, no. Please, no. Please let me keep it. I'll play it quietly, or when you're out. Please let me keep it.'

They were standing one either side of the table. He leant across toward her, his eyes screwed up. She couldn't look

49

away from him. He was peering hard at her as if she were a stranger, a stranger he hated.

'You heard me.'

She was crying now, quietly, rubbing the back of her hand across her nose. Mrs Sharp had said he must wish he'd never set eyes on it, but she hadn't expected him to mind as much as this. "Please, stop him looking at me like that. Please let me be able to keep the concertina." She watched as he put it in its box but tonight it didn't go back on the cupboard shelf.

'There's some pie in this dish. Muriel sent it. I've got to get back, I only meant to look in on my way past. I've got to sign something for the marriage records.'

'Not 'ungry,' she gulped. She dropped the 'h' to spite him while her brown eyes pleaded silently.

'I'll see you in the morning.' He picked up the box. It was going, he was taking it away.

The last of her control snapped.

'No, give it to me! You're not having it! You can't take it away!' She heard herself shouting, screaming, couldn't stop herself as she tried to pull it from him, fighting like a young animal. All she saw was the precious octagonal box. That it was her father she shouted at wasn't important, with all her might she fought to keep her treasure. Her booted foot struck his shin. Never in her life had she behaved like it, it was as if some madness had hold of her; and until now, Oliver had never hit her. He boxed her ears hard, the sting of his fingers leaving wheals. It had the desired effect: Penelope caught her breath, her screams stopped.

Tonight Mrs Sharp didn't stop to knock. Clumping down the stairs she walked straight in on them, taking in the scene with one look.

'Let that be a lesson!' Ignoring the landlady, Oliver told Penelope: 'Pull yourself together and start behaving. And eat your supper.'

Then he was gone, taking the concertina with him.

'Dear, oh dear, what a carry on. Never mind, duckie, don't you upset yourself like that. Not worth it, that he isn't. Ought to be ashamed of himself – and I'll tell him so next time I set eyes on him.'

'Was my fault,' Penelope gulped, even now defending him, 'said I was deceitful, but I didn't mean to be. Well, s'pose I did . . . didn't tell him purposely.'

Mrs Sharp seemed to be weighing up whether or not to say something. Then she pulled a chair to the table and sat down.

'Now just you listen. He's not going to tell you about things – and that Muriel won't know – so I'll have to be the one to do it. None of my business, that's what he'd say. Perhaps it isn't, but one day there'll be things you'll want to know and you won't be here with me then to ask. That squeezebox there was all that pother about – weren't never your Pa's, that belonged to your mother.'

'I shouldn't have taken it, I should have asked. Did you know her, Mrs Sharp?'

'Yes, I knew her right enough. They lived upstairs in those days, had my two best rooms. That's where you were born, up there in the front bedroom. Well, I was telling you . . . prettiest little creature I think I've ever clapped eyes on, great eyes as dark as dark. A dancer she was, used to play that squeezebox and dance on the pier. It was the theatre's first year, just been built there on the pier. Then when you were coming she had to give up.'

Wide-eyed, Penelope listened. Her mother, a dancer!

'Not the sort to content herself with a man and a baby – not the sort to content herself with no more than one man. The rows there used to be! Would have kicked them out but how could we with you only a little mite? A bad lot, no doubt about that – well, that's what people said. I'll tell you, though, I had a liking for that mother of yours, naughty girl or no. Made a mistake in tying herself up. She ought to have had a week or two's fun with him and let him go, just like she did all the others. Weak as

51

water, he always was. And that was no use to pretty little Anna, her shoulders weren't broad enough to bear all the burdens. Out of work as often as he was in. And all she wanted to do was get back on to the stage. Wonder she came to roost for as long as she did. You must have been coming up to three years old when she flit the nest, went off with the solo baritone from the Prince of Wales.'

'And left poor Pa.'

'Oh, don't you worry yourself about your pa. His heart wasn't too bruised. Glad to see the back of her, I reckon.'

'When did she die, Mrs Sharp?'

'Never heard that she did.'

'What I don't understand, if she didn't die – '

'I've told you more than I ought already. But with all that pother about the concertina, I thought you ought to hear it. That's why he wouldn't want you to be after playing it – he'd be frightened you were following after her, y'see.'

That night sleep was miles away as Penelope lay in bed. Until today she'd accepted herself as being her father's daughter; her unknown mother had had no shape in her imagination. Now, suddenly, she was real – the prettiest little creature Mrs Sharp had ever set eyes on, a dancer, a proper stage dancer. Anna . . . she even had a name. She must have known that wonderful bubbly feeling inside you when you led a crowd of people into a song, she'd have felt the power of that first chord on the concertina, when heads would turn and people stop to listen, wanting to hear more, wanting to join in the fun. Then her thoughts were back to the wooden box, each night put away so carefully on the cupboard shelf. It was not a bit of use crying, only babies cried . . .

But although she was miserable, all the anger and the spite she'd felt for her father had gone.

'What's up, Pen?' Tom came straight out with the question as the pupils poured into the sunshine at the end of lessons the next day. 'Are you upset because of your old man getting himself married again?'

'No. Muriel's nice.'

'Tell us, then. Go on, perhaps we can help.' This time it was Alf.

She'd not said a word, she'd even imagined no one would guess. But the scene had left its mark on her spirit as surely as her father had left the mark of his hand on her face.

'Pa's taken the concertina.' It had been at the front of her mind all day, it was a relief to talk about it. 'He's getting rid of it, he said. He never comes home in the evening as a rule, but he caught me busking at the Prince of Wales.'

'Go on! Honest?' Alf looked at her with new respect.

'Ever done it before?' Tom wanted to know. 'Why didn't you tell us? We could have come and led the clapping.'

'I couldn't tell you. As long as no one knew it didn't seem to matter not telling Pa. That's what I thought.'

'And he didn't?'

She shook her head.

'What a rotten shame.' Alf frowned.

As they'd talked they'd gradually drawn to a halt, here at the bottom of Merchant Hill. The boys were a year or so older than Penelope, three children all so different. She was thin, small; Alf short, rosy-cheeked with a mop of fair curls; Tom dark, well-built, a handsome child who would undoubtedly grow into a handsome man.

Tom was the most practical. 'If you've done it before, have you saved the money? How much have you got?'

'Lots. More than half a guinea. I've been doing it all the year. But money's no good. He'll have popped it at Uncle's.'

'Get hold of the ticket. I'll get it out for you, you needn't go to the pawnshop yourself. I'll see to it.' Tom took charge.

'Steal the ticket? Oh, but Tom I couldn't do that.'

53

'What's going to happen to it, then? Will your old man go and redeem it?'

'No.'

'Well then . . . ?'

'I couldn't. I couldn't go through his things, steal it from his pocket.'

'No, she's right, Tom.'

They walked on, all the worries of the world on their young shoulders. On their way to the beach they had to pass the pawnbroker's shop.

'Wait here,' Tom told them and disappeared inside. A minute later he was back. 'Yes, he popped it a couple of hours ago. Today's the 1st May. Now then, chaps, that means we have to have enough money to go in and pay whatever Uncle wants for it on the 8th May next year. Right? If your old man isn't going to reclaim it, that means it can't be sold for a year and seven days. And by then we'll have to have enough money ready to get it.'

He felt like the hero of the day, Alf was looking at him with respect — oh, wasn't that just like a girl! Poor old Penny, he supposed she couldn't help it, but wasn't that just like a stupid girl to start to blub!

'Come on, last one to the pier's a sissy. Get ready, get set, go!'

She gritted her teeth, ran as fast as either of them, and by the time they felt the scrunch of stones under their feet her tears were dry.

On 7th May in that year 1906 Oliver and Muriel were married. She moved out of her room on the top floor of the Grand; Oliver and Penelope shut the door for the last time on their basement home.

'Just you come and see me sometimes, duckie,' Mrs Sharp told Penelope. 'Don't get too grand for us in Victoria Place now that you're going up in the world.'

Today her too-large boots had been polished until they shone like glass; on her head was a hat that had been no one's except hers, a boater with a spray of pink flowers on it, Muriel had taken her to a proper hat shop to buy it especially for the wedding. Now she was actually wearing it, the day had come, Pa was already almost to the corner of Victoria Place on his way to the church and she'd have to run to catch up with him. She was so excited her tummy was full of flutters. So why was it she couldn't answer Mrs Sharp, why was it that if she spoke she would cry? She looked back down the area steps, seeming to hear Chummy scratching at the door as he jumped against it, recognizing her tread as she arrived home from school.

The best she could do by way of a reply was nod her head furiously. Then she was taken by surprise as she felt herself grabbed in a bear-like hug. It was the scratch of those bristles growing from the mole on Ethel Sharp's chin that helped her overcome her show of emotion.

"course I'll come and see you, Mrs Sharp.'

'Hurry up with your goodbyes,' she heard her father call to her, 'you'll see Mrs Sharp after the service.'

But that wouldn't be the same. That wouldn't be here, at the top of their own steps.

Penelope's bedroom was under the sloping eaves. Her window was in the roof, with a view straight up to the sky. If she climbed up to stand on the chest of drawers, then pushed the window open, she could just peer over the ledge. The joy of it! After a lifetime of looking at nothing but the legs of passersby, now she could see right across the rooftops, to the sea, the pier, the distant white cliffs further round the coast.

In that first week or two everything was new and different. At the back of her mind was a feeling of loss for the hours she'd spent making music, but only at the back of it, the front was full of activity; her long hours alone were a thing of the past.

'We're lucky,' Muriel talked as she worked, ironing curtains, 'lots of boarding houses won't be getting much doing until August. It's August when the factories have their week. The town will be full to overflowing then. A boarding house isn't like the Grand, folk who holiday there don't work in the mills and factories, they can choose their times to please themselves. Still, like I say, we're lucky with the bookings we took over.'

While she stood ironing at one end of the kitchen table, Penelope had her own job at the other. Each curtain had to be 'damped down', water sprinkled evenly over it and then the length of material rolled tightly.

'Wonder what they'll be like, Muriel. Proper stage people!'

Muriel laughed. 'You sound like your father. You'd think they'd got the plague 'cos they earn their livings on the stage. I'll tell you what they'll be like, love. Just like everyone else. They're all the same, rich or poor. Feed 'em up and they'll come back for more.'

But Penelope knew they weren't at all the same as everyone else. How could they be?

CHAPTER THREE

Penelope no longer attended Merchant Hill Board School. Instead she went to St James' next door to the church just behind Alexandra Square. Her pinafores had been boiled until they were as white as anyone else's, and Muriel knew that a dip in the bowl of starch would help to keep them clean; her hair had been washed and rinsed free of soap, there was a new sheen to it. She might not have a blue gingham dress, nor a matching ribbon, but no longer was Penelope shunned. The one regret Penelope had had about coming to live at this side of town was that she'd had to leave Merchant Hill Board School without hateful Rose McCormick ever seeing how things were with her now.

Her early days had taught her a lesson she wouldn't forget. Alf and Tom were her real friends, had been ever since she'd first gone to Merchant Hill, first because they'd been sorry for her and then because she was such good fun. 'Got a lot of sense, almost like a boy,' they'd agreed. Term time or holiday time they'd always known just where to look out for each other, and so they still did. After school, they would meet up on the beach.

And when Oliver said: 'Where's that girl? She ought to be helping, not leaving everything to you,' Muriel's answer was always the same: 'Leave her be, Ollie, children need time to play.'

On the second Sunday in June the first guests arrived, part of the troupe of players who were engaged for the season at the Theatre Royal. Rhoda Tidsley who sang ballads; Ted Kumley, a juggler; Terry and Christine Carstairs, a song and dance team; 'Happy' Harry Hastings, a comedian. With them came Gladys, Harry's wife, and Sylvia Carstairs, daughter of Terry and Christine. Seven of them, all travelling together from London to make their home here for nearly three months. Two cabs drew up outside number fourteen, bringing them from the railway station. From where she sat on the attic stairs, unseen but listening, Penelope guessed at the mountain of luggage that was being brought in. She heard each clump as a trunk was eased up to the first floor. Muriel had left her all-enveloping white apron in the kitchen while she greeted her guests. 'You'd think they'd got the plague,' she'd laughed at Oliver's reaction to stage people, but if that were his feeling he gave no sign of it today. He was host in his own establishment, his welcome as cordial as if his guests had come at his express invitation; today, wearing his best suit, a rose in his buttonhole, he was playing his own role.

The attic was on the third floor. Although voices travelled up to her that wasn't enough for Penelope. She wanted to see. So she crept down a few stairs and leant over the rail, deciding in her own mind who was who. One lady was really beautiful, her auburn hair piled up in curls, dressed entirely in a silvery grey. Penelope was just deciding she must be the singer when she saw a girl so like her there was no doubt it must be her daughter. So Mrs Lovely was Christine Carstairs and Miss Lovely her daughter Sylvia. Penelope had meant to stay in hiding, but step by step she'd drawn closer.

'This must be your daughter, Mrs Drew? Younger than you, Sylvie, but someone for you to go to school with.' Then, to Muriel: 'Poor Sylvie, she goes from one school to another. I wonder she learns anything at all. It's the only way though. Except for these summer weeks, we're on the move all the year, seldom more than a week in any town, certainly never more than a fortnight. But now Sylvie can go to school until the long summer holiday.'

Penelope had been given an opening. She felt important, the daughter of the house. Head up she came down the last stairs until she stood with Muriel.

'You'll like it at St James'. It's a nice school,' she told the auburn-haired girl.

'I've been there before. This is our third summer in Challington.'

The two girls took stock of each other while Muriel led the grown-ups to their rooms. Sylvie was half a head the taller, long legs, long arms, auburn curls tumbling on to her shoulders. She might have moved from place to place, never stayed anywhere long enough to make friends, but she looked as though her life had been a happy affair. Penelope thought her the most beautiful girl she'd ever seen. By comparison she felt herself to be tiny and colourless. It wasn't the whole truth. Certainly for eleven she was small; years with no more to eat than had been essential to sustain on would leave a legacy of slightness that would stay with her all her life. But there was an attractive elfin quality about her. High cheekbones, huge chocolate-brown eyes, honey-coloured straight hair; for Penelope life had been a serious business. In repose her expression was thoughtful. Yet when she did smile her face radiated happiness and was utterly transformed.

She smiled now, in friendship and in delight to see someone so pretty.

'When you've unpacked, you can come up to my room if you like.'

'All right. How old are you? Nine? Ten?'

'I'm eleven, eleven and a half. I'm just slow to grow.'

Sylvia laughed. 'You're that all right! I was twelve last week.' And when she said it she stood as tall as she could and held her shoulders well back. Just as she was meant to, Penelope saw the swelling of Sylvia's breasts. 'How old are you? Nine? Ten?' the question echoed. She looked down at herself and was ashamed. Lots of the girls in her class had a shape. She knew there were things they whispered about, but they always stopped if she, or any of the younger children, came within earshot. She wished Sylvia had been flat like her.

59

A few minutes later she forgot all about bosoms, or lack of them, as she drew the chair to the chest of drawers so that Sylvia could climb up and admire her view.

'Let's go on the beach. Can we?' Sylvia looked down from her high perch. 'Will your parents let you on a Sunday? I haven't seen the sea since last summer season. Can we?'

'I'll have to ask Mu – ' then she corrected herself ' – ask Mother.' Oh, just listen to the sound of it! Mother – just like Mrs Carstairs said to Muriel: 'You've got a daughter, Mrs Drew?' From now on Penelope would call her Mother. They were a proper family just like everyone else. 'I'll have to be back in time to set the tables and to carry the things through – that's my job, you see. But being Sunday won't make any difference. We've always done the same on Sunday as any other day.'

'We usually spend Sunday on the train, or unpacking in some rotten boarding house. Oh, I don't mean this! This is splendid, I love coming here, it's home all the way through the summer.'

Penelope's face broke into a smile.

There are some days in every life that, even at the time, are recognized as milestones; there are some that merge together, each one a single link in the chain that connects those milestones. Then there are others, days that try and masquerade as ordinary. Only later one sees them for what they were, realizes that like points on a railway track they changed the course of the future. Just such a day was that second Sunday in June 1906 for Penelope – and for Sylvia too. Yet as they dabbled in the cold rockpools and were joined by Alf and Tom they had no means of knowing it. None of them looked further than the hour.

Muriel took the tins from the oven, three of them, each holding a dozen small cakes. The main meal of the day at Clifford House was served at one o'clock, then the theatre folk liked a sit-down supper when they came home at

60

night. Now that they were halfway through July four other visitors had come, and for them there had to be a meal early in the evening. Muriel's day was long. Surely this couldn't have been what she'd dreamed of all those years! At the Grand someone else had prepared the vegetables, someone else had washed up, someone else had dealt with the grocer, the greengrocer, the fishmonger. Of course, Ollie was very good, he ran any errands she asked. She smiled indulgently, picturing him setting off with his list, like a child let out of school, glad to be free. And so he deserved! Precious little freedom he'd had in the past. What if he did like to pop into the Royal Standard for an ale or two before he came back? He deserved that too! Muriel sang tunelessly as she flipped the cakes deftly on to racks to cool.

'Smells good in here. Hot though, isn't it? Don't know how you can stand working with that fire on an evening like this. You're a good lass, Muriel.' Oliver knew just how to please her. He put his arm around her plump shoulder and, if an already red and shiny face can be said to flush with pleasure, hers did. 'I thought I'd wander down the Prom and listen to the band for half an hour. I'm no use to you here, am I?'

'You're always use to me, Ollie Drew.' She buffeted her head against his shoulder. 'You smell nice. Eau-de-Cologne?'

'Not so nice as those buns. One won't be missed, will it?' He winked at her as he dug his teeth into a hot cake. 'I'll go out the back way and remind young Penny to come in in time to see to the supper tables.'

Another minute and, his message delivered, the back gate closed behind him. Oliver was free. It was just about a year since he'd been given that job at the Grand. He'd come a long way since the days he'd gone from door to door begging for work. Nowadays he seldom so much as thought of the struggle it had been to make a home for young Tuppence. Even his nickname for her was forgotten along with the old life. On this summer evening as he walked along the Promenade, his step jaunty, no one would have recognized the good-looking, dapper man to be the same wretched creature who had lived in Victoria Place. One hand thrust in his pocket, Ollie jingled his loose change. He'd drop in at the Green Dragon presently, have an ale or two. Could do with it in this heat. He needn't hurry, it was always well after eleven before Muriel had the supper things out of the way. In the bandstand the Town Band was doing its best with the 'British Grenadiers'. Oliver sat down, leant back in his chair and tipped his panama hat to shade his eyes from the slanting rays from the sinking sun.

'I'll do the tables with you,' Sylvia offered. 'Your father doesn't do much, does he?'

Immediately Penelope was on the defensive. 'He doesn't do the tables, if that's what you mean. They're my job. He does his own things. We all have our own jobs.'

'Your mother's always working. I'd hate to keep a boarding house.'

'Well, your mother's always working too.' Penelope wasn't going to have that tone taken about Muriel, not even from her new friend.

'That's different. She never has to wear a beastly overall, she has lovely things for the show; her hands never get rough from horrid housework. Anyway, dancing with Terry can't be looked on as real work. Christine's beautiful, that's why the audience loves to watch them. You can't call it work, being clapped and told how good you are . . . '

'Why do you call them by their Christian names? Aren't they really your mother and father?' Just for a moment Penelope wanted to be spiteful, to knock Sylvia from her high perch where she seemed to think she could look down on Muriel.

'Yes, of course they are. But it's different with stage

62

people. Everybody always thinks of Christine and Terry as young. You should just see them behind the footlights! No one would guess that they have a daughter who's nearly grown up.'

'Don't you wish you could say Mother and Pa?'

'Goodness, no! Now it's my turn – you swing the rope and I'll jump.' The awkward moment was past, bonhomie restored.

One end of a rope was tied to the latch of the back gate, the other was swung, over and over, higher and higher, whilst they took turns skipping. Positions were changed; Sylvia started to jump as the rope came down, a little spring before each leap.

'When you – grow up – ' she spoke in rhythm as she skipped ' – do you – want a – board-ing – house of – your own?'

'No. If I tell you – it's a secret, mind – you've got to promise – '

''course I – prom-ise.'

Then, instinctively, she stopped jumping as Penelope let the rope hang limp.

'I'm going on the stage.'

'Oh, go on! That's because you've had *us* here. What would you do?'

'I'm not sure. Well, I'd like to sing and to dance. And it's nothing to do with having you here. I'd made my mind up ages ago, back last winter. If I tell you a secret, promise, cross your heart and hope to die, *promise* you won't tell a soul.'

Sylvia made the necessary sign of a cross over her heart. 'I promise. Hope to die.'

So Penelope shared her secret. They went up to her room so that Sylvia could see the hoard of coppers hidden in a box under a loose floorboard.

'He took the concertina away, you say?'

Penelope nodded.

'Well, I suppose he didn't like you busking. It's not like being properly on the stage.'

'*I* think it is.' Penelope stuck her chin up. Friend or no, she wasn't going to have Sylvia tell her the magic hadn't been there. Anyway, she added childishly to herself, *my* mother was a dancer too.

'It can't be. On the proper stage you have bright lights on you, you can't see into the auditorium properly – not to really see the audience. They're not the important ones – it's you – it's a grand feeling, everyone watching, everyone admiring you. I know, because last Christmas I danced in *Puss in Boots*. With all the lights shining on you you feel – special – important. You've never been on a proper stage. You have to walk the boards to be a real stage person.'

'Didn't say I was one, did I?' Penelope wished she'd kept her secret to herself. 'Just said that's what I'm going to be.' Even so, Sylvia represented experience, and she wanted to find out all she could. 'I'd be sorry not to see their faces, though. It was magic, Sylvie, they always looked cold and miserable when I got there; it was as if because I was happy they caught it off me, like smallpox or something. They tapped their feet, clapped their hands in time to the music, even joined in. I wanted to dance, but it's hard to when you're playing a concertina. All you can do is sway from side to side and move your feet – and you just have to do that, it's such a dancey sort of sound.'

'Christine teaches me to dance. Proper ballet steps. You need a barre to hold on to. If we had a barre, I'd show you.'

'Couldn't you show me holding on to the foot of the bedstead?'

'I could try. If you like, I'll teach you. But it's difficult – not like just tapping your feet in time to the music. Anybody can do that. You have to learn to do it right. It takes years to learn to be a real dancer.' Penelope was duly impressed.

Upstairs, she watched and copied. Then, on her own, she did as Sylvia instructed.

'Turn out First Position . . . good . . . well done . . . now Second Position . . . right . . . Third Position – that's harder – well done . . . now, harder again, Fourth. Pen, I wish we could share your secret. I wish we could tell Christine.'

'No. Don't tell. Just teach me all you can.'

'There's far more to it than you seem to think! Still, I can teach you a bit. This is a *jeté* – *jeté* to the right – *jeté* to the left. Now from that we'll try an *entrechât*. . . .'

If Penelope had felt the touch of magic on those cold winter evenings, she certainly felt it again now. There was no doubt in her mind that today was one of her milestones.

It was a sultry afternoon in August. The two girls had spent the afternoon dabbling in the rockpools with their shrimping nets.

'When's the baby coming?' Sylvia asked.

'Baby? It can't be this week, we're full up. Is there a baby with next week's people?'

'Silly! I mean yours, your mother's.'

'But she would have told me! How do you know? Did she tell Mrs Carstairs?'

'If she had I wouldn't be asking, stupid. I can tell by her shape, that's how I know.'

'It's you who's being stupid. You just don't know what shape she is. She's always been podgy.'

'Bet you a whole penny she's got a bun in the oven – that's what people call it. Did you know that?'

Penelope shook her head. She did wish Sylvia wouldn't try and make her look ignorant. 'Not people we know, they don't call it that. All right, a penny. I bet you're wrong.'

'We'll be gone anyway.' Then, seeing the boys, Sylvia forgot all about it. 'Look, they've been swimming. Tom's really splendid, isn't he? So handsome. But do look at Alf, what a titch he is.'

'Alf's jolly good fun.' One titch sprang to the defence of another. He must hate being small as much as she did.

Having Sylvia living here had opened her eyes to a lot she hadn't known about. She had learned from her what it was the girls whispered about. 'It' hadn't happened to her yet; Sylvia said it wouldn't until her shape started to come. Each night when she undressed, Penelope tipped the mirror that stood on her chest of drawers so that she could see her body. Even with her shoulders pushed right back she was as flat as a board, her nipples no more than two little dots. What chance had she of 'it' starting? She'd be the last one in her class! Perhaps she wouldn't be like other people. Each night she worried, she even asked in her prayers for some sign that she was changing.

Sylvia said that when you started to grow up you smelt different; she said you had to make sure you washed your armpits each morning. Another of Penelope's private rituals was hopefully to put her nose under her arm each morning and sniff. Nothing! Not a hint of growing up! But just to make sure, she washed like she'd been told, in cold water, standing naked at the marble topped washstand.

With these things in her mind she ran to catch up with the boys as they made their way gingerly up the shingle. Even if she wasn't prepared to admit it, Sylvia was right. Tom, a tough, well-built thirteen, might have been two or three years ahead of Alf – and to make matters worse, Alf's hand-knitted costume belonged to his elder brother and wouldn't stay on his narrow shoulders.

'It must be wonderful to swim.' Sylvia was wide-eyed with admiration. She looked at Tom as she said it and his silent answer acknowledged all she'd not said. The other two felt left behind.

But the moment passed, the rockpools called, and a minute or two later they were engrossed in lifting stones, hunting for shells, all the things that went to make up summer. Neither Tom's budding manhood nor Alf's drooping and waterlogged costume were of any importance. And by the time they got home Penelope had forgotten all about the silent message she'd been aware of yet not understood.

That evening she looked at Muriel with new interest. Yes, she was definitely fatter, but then people got fat if they were happy and she was always happy.

'You look worried, love. What's up?'

'I was just thinking, it would be nice if you could have a baby.' She opened the door for confidences.

'Who's been telling you my secrets then? Your pa?'

'You mean you are! You mean Pa knows and he never said!'

'It won't be yetawhile,' Muriel stood with her hands flat on her already rounded belly, 'but there's a babbee growing in there right enough.' The way she said it, babbee not baby, the way she rocked as she spoke, just as if the tiny thing were already in her arms, robbed Penelope of an answer. Muriel must have sensed her feeling of isolation for when did Muriel fail to understand? 'Here, come and put your hands just here. There, that's our babbee, can you feel?'

Penelope nodded. Still she couldn't find her voice. How silly to be crying, there was nothing to cry about. Wordlessly she flung her arms round Muriel's thick waist, burying her head against her.

The next day she took a penny from her hoard and gave it to Sylvia.

There had never been a summer like this one. Each day Penelope had her regular jobs to do, from serving breakfast, tidying the bedrooms, brushing down the stairs, dusting, right through to serving the supper. But often Sylvia helped her so that they could escape to freedom quicker. Sometimes it would be to the beach, sometimes to Penelope's attic bedroom where they'd share their secrets, and practise their dance steps.

In the middle of September the final curtain came down on the summer show in the Theatre Royal.

'I'll write to you often,' Penelope told her friend. 'Where will you be?'

'We're going back to London, Grandma's address in Clapham will always find me. But we shan't stay there long, only until Terry sees what the agent has for them. I expect it'll be in the Midlands or the North, it usually is. There's more doing there for Music Halls.'

How exciting it all sounded to Penelope who knew no further than Challington. Sylvia saw things differently.

'I wish I could stay here. You're the only real proper friend I've had. We don't stay anywhere long enough – and even if we did, you only make friends with special people. I never have before.'

'I haven't either – 'cept for the boys.' Just for a minute Penelope hesitated. Except for the incident of the concertina she'd never spoken of the past. Now, out it all poured . . . the basement . . . she and Pa taking care of each other . . . just Chummy and her . . . the concertina, how he used to listen with one ear up and one down . . . the accident . . . Muriel . . . even Mrs Sharp. Sylvia heard it all.

'I wish we were sisters. Just imagine, Pen, knowing we'd always have each other.'

'We can be chosen sisters, that would be almost as good. There's lots we haven't shared so far, but we can always be friends from now on. Let's promise.'

They shook hands and solemnly swore to be faithful always to their friendship. Materially Sylvia may have had more than Penelope, but both of them knew all about loneliness.

'Even when we're grown up, middle-aged, married and with families,' Sylvia held Penelope's right hand in hers, 'swear we'll still be chosen sisters, so that we share all the happy times.'

'And all the sad ones, too. Never have secrets.' Penelope's left hand came on top, then Sylvia's. 'I swear it. Cross my heart and hope to die.'

'We've been coming to Challington each season for ages – we'll just have to look forward to next year.'

But it could never be quite the same as these last months had been. By next summer the boys would have started work, there would be no long holiday for them.

'But that's ages away.' To Penelope a year seemed like eternity. 'And you'll have had your birthday. Probably you'll have been taken into the chorus and won't have any free time.'

'Stupid! Start work and give up the chance of our holiday. Not likely!' At the time, with her birthday still nine months away, she meant it.

Winter . . . gales that blew from the west bringing rain that lashed horizontally against the house . . . gales that blew from the east, made eyes run and ears sting. The smoke never billowed back into the haven of comfort that was Muriel's kitchen. As the weeks went by her added bulk made her clumsy but it never dented her good humour. Muriel was utterly content, she had all she'd ever dreamed of and more. With so much to be grateful for she certainly wasn't going to grumble about little things like swollen ankles or a bit of cramp. She'd given up hope of ever having babies of her own; now she was glad to suffer any physical discomfort pregnancy brought.

With no visitors in the house Oliver had his freedom. During the season he'd had to take the grocery order, or bring the fish from the market when the boats unloaded. Now they had the house to themselves there was no need; it wasn't a man's place. Life was extremely pleasant. He became a familiar figure taking his constitutional along the Prom, stopping off at the Green Dragon or the Royal

Standard. It was just before Christmas that Penelope saw him coming out of Tilly's Tea Rooms, holding the door for a lady wearing a pretty fur hat. When he got home his only comment about his afternoon was that it had been cold on the front but he'd had a good brisk walk.

'Here, love, pull your chair close to the fire. Come and get warm while I see to getting you a cup of tea. I expect you're ready for it.'

With all her heart Penelope wished he'd mention the lady, tell Muriel who he'd been out with, say he'd already had tea at the tea rooms. But he said nothing and inside her she had a hollow feeling of disappointment.

That was the first time. But there were plenty more. Once or twice he was with Mrs Furry Hat; then, when she was with Alf, Penelope saw him with a ginger-haired young woman on his arm; another time it was Madame Verte, the milliner, and Tom said he'd seen the two of them together plenty of times. And all the while Muriel blossomed into fruitfulness, singing tunelessly as she went about her daily round, sure that she was indeed blessed to be carrying his child.

Penelope kept her promise and made fairly regular visits to Victoria Place. She was surprised to find that going back there was like 'visiting'; even the basement window (draped with pink curtains now) and the area steps seemed remote. Only the washing line tied from a hook on the wall to the street railing touched a chord and awoke memories.

In January Merrick Oliver was born, a bouncing nine-pounder who, right from the start, showed himself to have inherited his mother's good temper. Good-tempered or bad, though, he took a lot of her attention, and Oliver could never be man enough to play second fiddle to a baby. Penelope knew exactly what was happening; occasionally she even followed her father, always with the secret hope that he'd take a solitary walk and come home. She knew that he had a life of his own outside Clifford House. A good-looking man with time on his hands, a pretty way with words and, although Penelope wasn't old enough yet to appreciate it, a need of flattery. That was a need she'd never experienced. Tom and Alf were as natural with her as she was with them, and they were as far as her knowledge of the opposite sex went.

The boys had both started work now. Alf ran errands and helped generally in Mr Sawyer's ironmongery shop; he was even learning how to mend holes in pots and kettles. Tom was in the boat builder's yard on the far side of the fishmarket. Wednesday was early closing day in Challington so that was when Alf was free, while Tom had Saturday afternoon off. They liked to think themselves grown up now that they'd left school, but change doesn't come overnight. As soon as the evenings lengthened they were on the beach, the boys and Penelope too.

None of them talked about the concertina but Penelope looked towards the 8th May with a mixture of longing and dread. She didn't have pocket money, but occasionally if she ran errands for Muriel she'd be given a penny for going, and at Christmas Mrs Sharp had given her a bag of toffees and a sixpenny piece. So by now her hoard was nearly twelve shillings. At last the longed for day came. How she could smuggle the concertina home, where she could hide it and when she'd have a chance to play it, she didn't even consider. Enough that it would be hers.

"Please don't let it be more money than I've got. Please let me be able to have it." With the money tied in a scarf and carried in her pinafore pocket, that was the thought that repeated itself over and over as the hours of lessons dragged by. A day had never been so long.

Then at last the bell was rung. She was free. Out along St James' Street, then a short cut through Foundry Lane took her to West Street. The three golden balls on the pawn shop had never gleamed as bright. For a whole year she'd dreamed of this moment. She knew just how the bell would jangle as she pushed the door wide and marched in, her bundle of coins in her hand.

71

'Well, missie, and what can I do for you. Brought me a ticket, have you?' For although he couldn't hand cash over to children, it wasn't unusual for them to be sent to redeem some treasure when funds allowed.

'No, thank you, sir. There's a concertina. It was brought in just a year and seven days ago and I know it's not been taken back. Please, sir, I've got eleven and tenpence, is that enough?'

'Must have been something special about that old squeezebox. I put it out in the window about twelve o'clock and by half-past it was gone.'

She couldn't believe it! All her money counted, tied up and waiting . . . she'd never even considered she wouldn't be in time.

'I'm right sorry, missie. Been saving up for it, have you? I got a nice flute in the window – cost a bit more than the squeezebox but I might consider putting it by – '

She shook her head. He meant to be kind but her throat ached so, it was hard to say thank you. Even the bell seemed to mock her as she closed the door behind her and left it swinging. Blindly she walked, making for the beach without even considering where she was going. The tide was high, the waves breaking almost to the top of the shingle. She ought to go home. What was the point in sitting here all by herself? She'd managed without it for a whole year, a year and seven days, so where was the sense in this dull misery? Someone else would be playing it, pulling it wide, hearing the first big chord; feeling the little buttons, each one so familiar. Determinedly Penelope pulled her hat down firmly on her head and started to walk towards Alexandra Square, the bundle of money knocking against her at each step like a living thing.

She knew they'd be there. The tide was going down and the sun too, but these evenings as soon as they were free the boys made for the shore. They hadn't remembered the actual day but they'd know how much she'd hoped that when the time was up she'd be able to buy it back . . . they'd understand . . .

'Here she is.' She saw Alf's head appear above the break-water then bob down again; they must be hiding. 'Ready?'

Then she heard it! No tune, not even a harmony, but a great sound as if every note was rushing out to meet her!

'Well, if you're not the limit!' Tom scrambled to his feet, the concertina held in both hands. 'Just like a girl!'

She couldn't stop herself. Tears ran down her cheeks, her face crumpled, and yet all the time she was smiling.

'Don't reckon she wants it, eh, Alf? What'll we do? Take it back to old Uncle?'

'Never thought it'd be you,' she choked. 'I went there straight after school with the money. He said it'd been sold. Thought it'd gone – '

'Cor, that's rotten, Pen.' Alf wished she wouldn't cry. Waiting for her to come, they'd pictured her being so excited. He pushed his hands deep in his pockets as if he'd find something there to cheer her up.

'Here, take it. It's yours.' Tom thrust the concertina at her. It was as if the year had never been. As the sun went down the three of them sat on the shingle, the boys watching with pride as she played.

'Suppose he takes it away again?' Tom was ever practical.

'How can he? It's hers now, he couldn't do that.' Alf was less realistic.

'Not 'til I give you my money, it isn't! If you wait here, I'll run home and get it.'

'No, we don't want you to. We've been saving up, a bit each week out of our pay.'

'We want to be the ones to give it to you, Pen.'

And on that they were unanimous. It took all Penelope's control not to disgrace herself again. Today tears were very near the surface.

'Now, listen to this.' Tom, the organizer, had the situation in control. 'I had a word with Mr Bayliss – he's foreman at the yard, you know – and he said just as long as I promise there'll be no mucking about with anything, we can go there, use the big shed. You can practise all you like there Pen, just so long as I'm with you, of course, 'cos I have to be in charge – it being my place.' He might be the bottom of the scale at the boatyard but Tom never lacked confidence.

The day had been one of highs and lows but it hadn't finished with Penelope yet. It was when she got home – without the concertina, for Tom had made himself responsible for that for safety's sake – that she was told there had been a change in the cast of the troupe coming to the Theatre Royal this year. The same producer, the same comedian, the same juggler, the same singer – the difference was in the names of the dancers. The letter on the kitchen table gave their names as Helen Banks and Jack Tuffnell.

That night, propped against her pillows and writing by the light of her bedside candle, Penelope wrote to her 'chosen sister', addressing her letter to Sylvia's grandmother in Clapham. She had to wait five weeks for a reply and when it came the postmark on the envelope was from Scarborough.

So much altered in the routine of Penelope's life over the next year. She, too, finished with school, but in her case it was to stay at home, run many of the errands that had been her father's job, help look after Merrick and, by the end of 1908, Amanda too. Like every young girl, she lived on dreams. But there was nothing of the Cinderella in Penelope. What she had to do in the house was done with speed and energy; at the first chance of freedom she was off.

Whatever magic it was that she'd worked on the queues for the 'gods', she now cast over the two boys – and anyone else who was still working into the evenings. She made music, they all joined in the singing. But singing was only half of it; Penelope loved to dance. And it was here that Tom, self-appointed 'producer' of these entertainments, came into his own. Out would come his harmonica. Penelope was as supple as a cat, and as graceful. Each night her feats grew more ambitious as she kicked her legs, stood on her hands, first on one and then the other, bent her body double; the evening came when her routine was brought to a climax with a mid-air somersault.

Her account of all this was written to Sylvia.

'Well done,' came the reply. 'Now, about me . . . I'm doing really well, last week I was given my first solo . . . '

The stage! The real stage!

It's so easy to fall into the pattern of working at one thing and dreaming of another. All too easily time can drift by. Penelope worked hard, she dreamed continually – but drift she never would. Always she practised and looked towards the future she meant to have. There was just one hurdle she wouldn't acknowledge – her father.

It was early in 1911, Penelope a skinny fifteen-year-old, when on the front page of the *Clarion* she read that Peter Somerville would be holding auditions in the Pier Theatre, looking for acts to be engaged in summer shows around the coast. 'Well-known talent scout', they called him, but she took that with a pinch of salt. She read everything she could lay eyes on about the stage and she'd never heard of him. She knew her time had come.

'You'll want me to be there,' Tom didn't mean to be left behind, 'it's the way we work. You play and sing, then I do your music for you while you dance. It's always been like that.'

Mr Bayliss overheard them. Worth anyone's money, was young Penelope in his opinion. Only a slip of a girl, though. It wouldn't do to have her walking about on her hands like she did, her skirts all over her shoulders.

'You'll have to get yourself something a bit more decent, m'dear, would never do for you to go out there showing off next week's washing. One thing here, just amongst ourselves. Quite another there with every Tom, Dick and Harry gawping.'

Costumes were something she hadn't considered. The three youngsters looked at each other for inspiration, none of them with much faith in finding any.

It was Alf who had the idea.

And the next week the curtains of the Pier Theatre parted and there was 'Tommy', a down and out, with his street urchin brother 'Young Perce'. Alf's old suit was too big round the waist but braces and a piece of strong twine held them up. His jacket had the elbow out. The scarf around her neck was all that was Penelope's own.

'Gotta wear this, it'll bring me luck,' she'd insisted. For it was the scarf that had carried her pile of coppers. "Please make us do well," she begged – but she made doubly sure by wearing the scarf to bring her luck. She wasn't taking chances.

They were allowed ten minutes, and into that ten minutes she packed all her dreams, all her energies, all her longing. Despite what Sylvia had said, for the auditions the lights were on in the auditorium. Peter Somerville sat in the front row, his bowler hat tipped to the back of his head, a cigar in his mouth. His expression gave nothing away as the act started, the banter between the 'brothers', Penny's clowning and acrobatics. Then, while Tom played his mouth organ, she danced. And it was then that she was first conscious of how hard the great man was concentrating, his cigar smouldering between his fingers. When, breathless from dancing, she took up her concertina, she wished they'd planned the act the other way round, let the singing come first. Still, nothing was going to deter her. "Please, please . . . " whether a reminder to her Deity or her muffler she hardly knew. He liked it! She could tell he did by the way he leant forward in his seat! The song over they took up the bantering, Tom chasing Perce off the stage. But how could she go without doing her *pièce de résistance*, her somersault in the air, just once more?

Her hair had been pinned up under Alf's cap, and the cap pinned too. The somersault was the final straw. As Penelope spun head over heels the last pin was dislodged, off came the cap and her long hair fell about her shoulders. Dumbfounded, she stood still. There wasn't a sound from the auditorium. Then the scout laughed, fairly shook with laughter.

"He liked us. Thank you, oh thank you . . . "

The truth was, though, that Peter Somerville recognized a spark of near genius in Penelope; Tom he hardly noticed.

'The material of your act is poor,' he told them when he called them down from the stage. Then, turning to Penelope: 'I could give you a slot. Your dancing's unusual.' She wasn't the first performer to impress him so forcefully, but not to any of them before had he given a hint of how impressed he'd been.

'We're a team, Mr Somerville.' It was Penelope who said it. Why, if it hadn't been for Tom where would she have practised all this time?

He frowned. 'Never thought of going your own ways?'

'No. We're partners.' This time it was Tom.

'Well, we'll have to do something with the act. Those jokes are as old as the hills.' He eyed them speculatively. The girl had the talent, and a gamin charm too; but the fellow had youth, looks . . . yes, a handsome young animal. With an appearance like that, he could ride along on her talent. It was too good a chance to miss; if he didn't get the girl someone else soon would. 'Tell you what, I'll give you a twenty-minute slot at Hastings. You'll go into rehearsal the week after next. Twenty-seven and six a week each, week after next 'til the middle of September.'

Tom could hardly wait to get outside where Alf was waiting. 'He's taking us on! We're to be given a slot in the show at Hastings. What do you think o' that!'

Alf said what they wanted to hear. And neither of them gave a thought to what his summer would be here at Challington without them.

For Tom it was easy. He was nearly seventeen, the middle son of five and earning only half a guinea a week in the boatyard. His family presented no problems. Not so for Penelope. She'd known there would be a struggle, but these days her father seemed happy to go his own carefree way; she'd let herself believe that he'd let her do the same.

At teatime she started to tell them – and came upon a streak in Oliver she'd never known existed. Oh, he'd been angry about the busking, then Mrs Sharp had helped her to understand the hurt that had made him behave the way he had on that spring evening so long ago. But that was just it: it *was* long ago. Here he was, married to Muriel, two babies of their own, a way of life that seemed to suit him down to the ground (with plenty of female admiration, she couldn't help adding silently), he'd accept now that she wanted something different for herself. Surely he'd even be proud to tell people: 'My eldest daughter, the one on the stage . . . ?'

'I don't believe what I'm hearing!' His voice cut into her like a knife. 'You and that conceited pup Tom Beasley, you say. I should have seen it! What have you ever done but hang around with boys? And you expect me to say I'll allow you to go off with him, leave Challington? Now you listen to me, my girl!' He leant across the table, his eyes narrowed. 'It's time you knew your place, time you realized what you owe. When that bitch went off and left me, all she wanted was to get back on the bloody stage – '

'Ollie, oh, Ollie! Don't say those things. Remember the babbees.'

'You keep out of this.'

Merrick, sensing trouble, let out his first howl and that triggered Amanda to make a duet of it.

'Gave up years for you, that's what I did! Coming home night after night to that filthy hovel, just you and that dog for company. Years when I could have been making a life for myself. Seems you're tarred with the same brush as she

78

was. Throwing her legs about – and opening them for anyone who fancied her. Whore, that's what your mother was!'

'Hush, Ollie. Please, love. Don't say things you'll be sorry for.' Muriel put her arm around his shoulder. 'Wasn't Pen's fault, she couldn't help the way things were for you.'

'Anyway, it wasn't a dirty hovel.' This time it was Penelope who shouted. 'It was home.'

'Don't cry, love.' She hadn't realized she was till Muriel said it. She felt sick, her heart was thumping into her throat.

'I told you, just keep out of it!' Oliver snapped again to Muriel. The children screamed even louder. 'Take those kids out of the way.'

'You can't stop me. My mother was a dancer – and so am I.'

'What do *you* know about your mother?'

'Just she was a dancer before you were married – '

'Men don't marry women like Anna Friedman, and just you bear that in mind. She came to live with me, she told me she was having my child. Then finally she cleared off, left you behind.'

'You mean you aren't really my pa?' Penelope's face was chalk white, her voice little more than a whisper.

He shrugged. Looking at her was like looking at Anna; she had the power to turn the knife in that old wound. To save himself he needed to hurt her.

'I might have been. Who could say?' His voice was full of contempt.

Even the children were silent. Penelope felt rather than saw every detail of the room that had held more comfort than she'd ever known. Muriel, jolly, hard-working, showing signs of burgeoning into pregnancy for the third time; her father – but was he her father? – his eyes screwed up and bloodshot, his mouth wobbly. Any second he would weep tears of self-pity, tears of anger.

79

When she spoke her voice was quiet: 'I want to go. And if you're not my father, I wonder you try to stop me.'

'No, lovey, don't say such things.' Poor Muriel was suffering for both of them. 'Ollie's just angry. Of course he's your pa. Come on now, Ollie, just you two make it up.' She cradled his head against her bounteous bosom.

'Just like her mother. Never a thought for anyone but herself . . . '

Penelope started to clear away the tea things.

An invisible barrier held Penelope and Ollie apart. Muriel was just the same as ever, trying to put the whole incident behind her. None of them referred to the audition.

Ten days later, at five o'clock in the morning, Penelope crept downstairs from her attic bedroom and out through the back door. She closed it quietly behind her. In a pillow-case she carried her clothes; in her 'good luck' muffler her money.

CHAPTER FOUR

The wonder, the magic . . . it was all just as she'd known it would be. Even during rehearsals Penelope could feel it. At this stage there was no orchestra, no roll of drums to bring emphasis to her acrobatic antics. Arnold Stubbs played the piano and for the first time in her life she had 'real' music to dance to. For Tom it wasn't quite so easy, he had to get used to an accompanist; but, that hurdle overcome, he felt a new pride in his performance. To him, it had taken on the hallmark of professionalism.

The bill at Hastings followed the same pattern as at any other seaside town: a comedian, a soprano to sing ballads, a juggler, a baritone, a conjurer, a song and dance act. Here, though, Hastings did vary slightly, for Penelope and Tom could hardly be described as that, not with good-looking 'Tommy' a sober feed man to 'Young Perce's' quips.

'You think you're so clever,' she'd bounce back when big brother had put her firmly in her place, 'just you tell me how many hairs there are in a dog's tail.'

'What a stupid question! How big a dog? How long is his tail?' Tommy would fall into the trap.

'There are no hairs *in* a dog's tail, the hairs are on the outside!'

The quality of the humour wasn't great, and in a strange way it was in the childishness of the jokes that their appeal lay, for what else would one expect from 'Young Perce' the ragamuffin? Big brother Tommy, trying to appear a man about town, was always pulled down to earth by mischievous, fun-loving Perce.

'Did you know that Adam was a good runner?'

'Where did you read that? How do you know?'

''course he was! He was the first in the human race.'

Of such were acts made in every music hall and pier theatre around the coast. If they'd had no more to offer than that, Peter Somerville would have left them behind at Challington. But they had. Tom Beasley turned many a young heart and there couldn't have been anyone who watched them and remained unmoved by the small 'lad' with the huge dark eyes so ready to twinkle with silent laughter. When Perce led them into song they all joined in, the merriment almost tangible. In the theatre queue all those years ago Penelope had believed she'd found what she'd been looking for; she knew now that it had been only the beginning of the road.

Often as the curtain started to close the audience would clap, stamp, even shout. That would be the cue for Tom's one and only joke.

'I say, Young Perce, why are we like a tight rope walker?'

The curtain would be still, half open and half closed.

'I don't know. Why are we like a tight rope walker?'

'Because we're en cored!' And while the audience added laughter to applause the curtain would re-open. The encore would be a song from Penny, then a dance always leading to her airborne somersault, from which she'd drop neatly into the splits; Tom, with his foot stamping in time, would play his mouth organ, the sound all but drowned by the orchestra once rehearsals were over and the season started.

About half the cast lodged with a Miss Brooks in a tall terraced house on Cartisbrook Crescent. She was probably no worse than the average stage boarding house landlady, but Penelope soon understood why it was that the players from Challington's Theatre Royal booked up so early to be sure of Muriel's care and cooking. Home, that was the one cloud on her horizon. Home and, most of all, Pa.

From her first pay packet she took ten shillings and sent it with a letter addressed to Mr and Mrs Oliver Drew. The hurt came from the rift between her and her father; perhaps if she sent ten shillings each week they could pay a girl to do the things she'd been responsible for and the bridge would be rebuilt. That he might write to her, 'forgive' her for doing what she'd known she had to, she wouldn't even let herself imagine. Her mind baulked away from thinking of those years when they'd had no one but each other and Chummy. Her memories had been built on shifting sand. The last time they'd really spoken to each other had been that dreadful teatime. It was as if the wound he'd inflicted had been bandaged, hidden from sight. To strip off that bandage, to let herself see the damage, took more courage than she could muster. So she sent her first ten-shilling offering with a note telling them her address, giving her love to Merrick and Amanda, and remaining 'always affectionately, Penny.' Each day she looked on the mantelpiece, where Miss Brooks put the letters, hoping for a reply. None came. The next week a second ten shillings went on its way. And still she watched.

Rehearsals were over and the show well into its stride by the time the evening came when she returned from the theatre to find no less than two envelopes waiting for her.

'Whatever must you be thinking of me!' She could almost hear Muriel's voice as she read. 'Your pa would have written to you himself, Penny love, but you know what men are when it comes to putting pen to paper. That you wanted to send me a bit of help with the money – well, you'll think me a proper softie, but I shed a tear, to think that you cared about the home here, when you're right at the start of your own proper life. Never was much good at putting down what I mean on a sheet of paper, Penny, but I don't want you to send me anymore ten shillingses. One of these days when you're rich and famous like that Marie Lloyd or one of those, then that'll be different. But what I want for you now, is for you to set yourself up smart in some nice new clothes and, if you've the shillings to spare, then take some dancing lessons like you've always wanted to. Running a boarding house isn't

for you, love, you and your dancing – many's the time
I've watched you out in the back yard, wished I'd had the
money to spare to have you taught to do it properly like
that young Sylvia friend of yours was learning.

'I thought your pa was writing you a letter when the
first ten shillings came, else I'd have done it sooner. Whatever must you have thought of us! Now, you're not to
worry about the work here, we're managing very nicely.
Ollie does any shopping I ask him, like he used to when
you were still at school. The other morning I popped the
babbees into their push cart and we ran out along to the
fishmarket. That's where I bumped into that Mrs Sharp
from where you used to live. Nice person. That pleased,
she was, when I told her about you, asked me to remember
her to you. Seems her niece's husband has just died, she
said you'd remember them, there were two girls, one about
your age. Well, this niece wants to do a bit of work, glad
of the money now that her man's been taken, and a real
nice person. She comes in of a morning and does the
bedrooms, then her youngest – not much older than you
but an ox of a girl to look at, poor child losing her Pa like
that – she takes the food through and serves up in the
evening. I think it'll all work out very well, and like I said,
you're not to send me any more money. When I look at
that poor woman, think of all she's lost, then I see how
well placed I am, I'm glad to pay out a bit that I can't
easily afford, seems like showing I'm grateful.

'I miss you being here, Penny love, having you to talk
to. Whoever it is that hands out what life gives us, has
been kind to me, given me all any woman could ask for.
I hope you get just as good. This babbee must be going
to be a big one, I didn't put on so much with Merrick or
Mandy as I am this time. Now, you just enjoy yourself,
don't you fret about any of that nonsense your pa talked.
People say hard things when they get upset. Mostly they
say them to the people they love best. Something we should
all of us remember, that is. Takes some of the sting out.

Years since I've written anyone a letter, never was much of a writer, but like I say I miss having you to chat to.

'When the summer season is over do you want to come back? If you could give me a hint of what you plan it would be easier to talk about it to your pa. Just that he was hurt, that's what it was that upset him so. I suppose when he was young he must have fallen real deep for your mother, but he'll never own up to it. Me, well, it was different with me. Bit like comparing silk with calico. Ha, ha! Calico's strong though, and he's safe with me, never you fear . . . '

The letter was long, the writing just as clear at the end as at the beginning. Unchanging, like everything about Muriel.

Penelope folded the three sheets of paper and put them carefully back in the envelope. Later she'd read them again, read each line and between each line. If the letter didn't actually heal the wound her father had made, at least it soothed it. On the practical side, that extra ten shillings a week was enough to lift her spirits. She told herself she'd buy something for each of the children, and for the coming baby too; that way her conscience needn't trouble her that she was so relieved to have the weekly burden lifted. 'Set yourself up with some smart new clothes,' Muriel had told her, and 'have dancing lessons'.

With a heart suddenly light, Penelope turned to letter number two. As soon as she'd found lodgings and had an address she'd written to Sylvia, as usual care of her grandmother in Clapham. Now, from Southsea, came her reply.

'I do hope you and Tom will manage. It's such a different life from what either of you have been used to, but at least if things don't work out the way you hope you've lost nothing, there's always plenty for you to do in Challington. That sounds quite unkind but, Penny, I don't mean it to. You've dreamt of dancing on the stage for so long but when things really happen they're not usually the same as

85

dreams. You may not even like the life. Digs are sometimes horrid – you remember I told you ages ago that not many landladies are like Mrs Drew.

'I wish we could have gone to Challington this summer. Even with you away I would prefer to have been there than here in Southsea. But Christine and Terry have been given top billing here and I've got a solo too. The show must come before personal feelings. That's the way with stage people. Perhaps that's why I can't see you taking to it. You really do have to be quite dedicated. Still, you've grown up since we had that time together, you may see things differently now. Fancy you being with Tom. Unless he's altered, I'd say that that would be enough to make any sort of life exciting. I thought him the handsomest boy I'd known – don't tell him I said that! But please remember me to him; remind him of that gorgeous summer we had together.

'When you write back to me, send to this address. We shall be here until September. Actually we just heard that my grandmother has had a fall and broken her leg. She's been taken to stay with Terry's brother and may not go back to Clapham. But I'll be here all the summer and shall be watching for your letters telling me everything that you and Tom do, whether your act goes well . . . '

The next page was full of a description of her costumes, her latest dance routine, the future as she planned to make it, the way the audience had applauded last night after her solo. ' . . . and when I got to the dressing room, do you know what I found? My first bouquet of roses! And on the card was written that they were from an admirer who wanted to take me to supper. Christine and Terry said I couldn't go, they said my admirer must have thought I was older. Parents can be so stuffy! I'm perfectly capable of taking care of myself. If ever anyone should ask you out to supper – although from what you tell me about your act, I shouldn't think it very likely that any dashing romantic would fall for young Perce's charms! – you'd have no one to please but yourself. Or is Tom your special beau? I shouldn't think so, he never seemed to have his eye on you. Isn't it thrilling, Pen? Here we are at the beginning of being grown up and the world full of such exciting possibilities.'

And, for Penelope too, that about summed it up. The future had no positive shape but over these last weeks she'd taken her first tottering steps in being herself, doing what she loved to do – and actually been paid good money for enjoying herself. She gave Miss Brooks ten shillings for her board and half a crown for doing her washing, something she had no choice about for there was nowhere for her to do it herself even if she'd wanted. Now that she'd been told not to send money home, she had seventeen and sixpence left, riches unknown. But the summer season wouldn't last for ever, and then what? So far she'd not seriously thought beyond September but that night, by the shadowy light of her bedside candle, she read both her letters again and realized that there could be no going back. Already she'd grown beyond the girl she'd been at home in Challington. A world full of exciting possibilities! Oh, yes, it was.

Penelope sat cross-legged on her single bed, her eyes like stars. Never mind about buying clothes – except something for Merrick and Mandy, she must do that – what she had to do was save so that when September came she had enough to live on until they got their next booking. They? Would Tom think it important enough to deprive himself of the luxury of money in his pocket? She hadn't looked beyond September; she certainly wouldn't let herself imagine a future without him. She knew he liked the feeling of money rattling in his pocket, he liked to 'blow it', as he called it. Who didn't? But she'd learnt her lessons young. All too well she remembered the sinking feeling in her stomach when she'd known Mrs Sharp had been watching out for her father, waiting for the rent that was owing. It was better to go without while you still had some money in your pocket than to 'blow it' and have nowhere to turn. Tomorrow she'd talk to Tom. She wanted to hear him say that the future so full of possibilities belonged to them both.

She climbed off the bed and started to undress. On one thing her mind was made up: she would never give in. She was a proper stage person now, she'd never be anything else. She crossed her fingers tight: "And Tom too."

In the weeks she'd slept in Miss Brooks' small back room she'd got used to the lumps in the horse hair mattress. Now, when she lay down, she knew just how to curl up so that she missed them. There had even been occasions when she'd imagined the feathered nest under the sloping roof of the attic in Clifford House with nostalgia. Tonight her mind wasn't on the bed. She wriggled deeper – to be stabbed in her hip by a particularly aggressive mound. It had no power to destroy her spirit nor dampen her resolve. She wasn't the first stage person who'd had to put up with Miss Brooks' lodgings . . . lumps in the mattress, lumps in the mashed potatoes . . . but what did any of that matter? The ladder she had to climb was long. This was but one rung that would carry her up to the next. She reached out to pinch the wick of her candle, sniffing its lingering smell.

"Thank you for making things not too bad at home for Mother. Luckiest of women, that's what she says she is. Yet look at the way she works. Popped out to the fishmarket, she said. Went herself, not Pa going for her. Wonder if he's really helping like she says or if she's pretending? Please," she pulled her runaway thoughts back into line, "I don't want to be unfair to him, say things about him that aren't loyal, You know what I mean, but please make him be as good to her as she deserves. I don't know much about men, and anyway it's not for me to be telling You what he should do and what he shouldn't, but it seems to me that it's not fair to expect her to do all the work, have the babies, be there when he wants her, look up to him as the head of the house – all that, and then he's off out, smiling and wearing his best clothes, likely as not with a rosebud in his buttonhole, full of charm for other women who've got time on their hands. If Mother were that sort of person, then it wouldn't matter. But she isn't.

"You do understand, don't You, it's not that I don't love Pa. I do love him. But I'm sure those happy times we had, the evenings when we were snug together, Pa, Chummy and me, I'm sure at the time he thought they were happy. Didn't he? Mother says he said all those things to me because he was hurt. But I'd never hurt Pa. She wouldn't either. Just imagine her, making excuses to get off out with other men! I just hope he's playing fair with her. Perhaps men are different. I remember how Chummy used to howl to get out. He loved me, I know he did; but if I called him he never came back when he had a mind to get off down Belmont Street. But he really was sort of married to that Jack Russell, he didn't sniff after just any dog. Pa seems always to like to have a pretty woman on his arm . . .

"Now, Tom, he's the handsomest young man I've ever seen, but he doesn't go chasing after the ladies." Again she tried to pull her thoughts into order. "Oh, I'm sorry, I was saying my prayers, wasn't I? I didn't mean to ramble on like that. I was saying thank you that I'd had my letters, both of them."

For good measure she shut her eyes tighter and lying in bed put the palms of her hands together, thinking as she did that she must look like one of those stone statues in St James' Church behind Alexandra Square. "Please make the baby – babbee, did You notice, she even writes it like that, babbee, just like she says it, thank You for making her be like she is – be born all right and keep things going well at home. And, please, if I do my bit, will You do Yours, help me to be famous like she says, as famous as Marie Lloyd? Me and Tom too. Sylvia says he never had his eye on me when we were children. But You see I'm not a child now. Please make Tom see that I'm grown up."

She didn't open her eyes. Already Penelope was drifting into sleep, happy in her new certainty of the way ahead. It was as if Muriel's letter had given her her freedom, and Sylvia's had confirmed to her the direction in which that freedom would take her.

In August Alf had his annual holiday. Never before had he spent it anywhere but Challington, but this year he had other plans.

'Here, listen to this, Pen!' Tom was chuckling to himself as he read. 'What a lark – old Alf wants to see if he can have a room here for his week off work. Poor old chap doesn't know what he's letting himself in for. I'll have a word with our Babbling Brook and see if she can fit him in.'

For Tom there was little that Barbara Brooks wouldn't have done. 'Such a beautiful young man', like the son she would have chosen had fate seen fit to give her a partner. 'Always got time for me to have a word or two.' That did much to commend him to her – and was how she came to be his Babbling Brook.

'Every inch is taken through August. Oh dear, I am sorry. Your friend from home, you say? I've even let my own room go and put my things up in the attic 'til the season's over. Attic, did I say! No bigger than a cupboard and I have to sleep with the door open to get a breath of air wafting in. It has to be like that in the good months, summer has to keep me going all through the bad days . . . ' Tom hardly listened to her. The smile on his face was sympathetic and that was enough to keep her babbling happily. 'Such a nice young man.'

'Tell you what, Miss Brooks, how would it be if Alf came in with me? He's only a pint-sized lad. We could sleep head to toe in my bed. He'd pay his whack, of course. He'd not try and do you down because he hadn't a proper bed.'

'As if I'd let him do that! A friend of yours, and you

90

giving up half your own bed to him. That's between you and him. Now, I tell you what, you write to him and say what you suggest and, seeing that he's a friend of yours, I'll give him his food and his hot water for morning ablutions the same as you get for seven shillings a week. Now, I can't say fairer than that, can I?' Her thin, pinched face creased into a smile, showing a broken front tooth. 'Fancy, him so concerned about his old friend from home. Not a bit turned by all the fuss he must get made of him there at the theatre.'

Alf arrived, wearing his best Sunday suit for the train journey, his straw-coloured curls topped by a new black cap and his everyday clothes carried in a small grip. Somehow, seeing him here, rather than bringing Challington closer made Tom and Penelope realize just how far they'd come in these weeks of summer. Yet, to be with him was all the fun it had ever been. Arms linked, with Penelope in the middle, they strode along the front from Hastings to Bexhill and back. Laughter came just as readily as it always had.

'Look at those three out there on the rocks,' Alf pointed, 'don't they take you back to when we were kids?'

'Last one to the pier's a sissy – remember?' Penelope laughed.

'Gonna be great when you two come back again.'

Alf's words echoed, unanswered. To say nothing was to let him believe they would be home in the autumn.

'We're not coming back to Challington, Alf. It may mean a bit of time looking for another booking, but we'll manage.'

'Never coming home . . . ?'

Penelope shook her head. 'You should never turn back. Whatever you do, you have to keep going forward.' It was the truth and she had to be honest with Alf, but she didn't want to look at him and see his disappointment.

'Mr Bayliss told me the other day they'd be glad to have you at the yard again, Tom.'

'The act needs the two of us. We're a team, Penny and me. And this summer's been great, hasn't it, Pen?'

His words were just what she'd wanted to hear, yet she slipped her hand into Alf's. The three children who'd been on the rocks chased up the shingle, two boys and a girl.

'Wherever we are, next time you have some days off work, Alf, promise you'll come and see us.'

'You bet I will.' He managed his normal cheeky grin. 'Maybe you'll be top of the bill. If you are, I shall expect a complimentary ticket.'

It was only the way his hand still held hers that told Penelope that the banter was a cover for his disappointment.

'Sylvia's still my best friend, you know,' she said, knowing that he'd follow her train of thought, 'she's written to me just the same wherever she's been.'

'The lovely Sylvia,' Tom chuckled. 'I'll bet she's a beauty by now, eh, Alf?'

'Bet she's not nearly as pretty as our Pen.' His brave words brought two bright spots of colour to his face, but today he didn't care; he was prepared to be bold in the face of what they'd just told him.

'That's my friend!' Penelope laughed his remark away. 'Seriously, I'm sure she's lovely, she always was. Already she gets roses sent to her dressing room.' She stopped in her tracks, one hand tugging each of the others back. 'Last one to the pier's a sissy. Ready, steady, go!' And she was off, her hair falling loose from one of its pins and her straw hat having to be held in place with the flat of her hand.

Tom came in first, Penny beating Alf by a short head.

'I don't see how you dance like you do when you have to be so sure your hair doesn't tumble,' Alf panted. Of them all, she was the only one not out of breath. Compared with the energy she put into each performance, a sprint to the pierhead was nothing.

'I wear an iron foundry of pins, that's how.' The seed

had already been sown in her mind; his words watered and nurtured it.

That afternoon she told them she had things to do, letters to write, some mending. To them it sounded dull. They left her willingly. But as soon as they'd disappeared in the direction of the Old Town, she had her hat and coat on. She'd promised herself she'd not waste money until she knew where the next was coming from. But this wasn't waste; indeed, it was all in the path of duty.

From downstairs Penelope could hear voices. Miss Brooks always gave her lodgers a pot of tea and either sandwiches or some toast before they set out for the theatre. Unlike Muriel she didn't have supper ready for them when they came home. Her mornings were taken up preparing such delights as watery stew, heavy dumplings and lumpy mashed potatoes; pretty well as soon as she'd cleared away the evidence of that it seemed to her it was time to start all over again making a great dish of sandwiches or a pile of toast. In all the years she'd been taking in lodgers that had been her rule: breakfast, a meal at one o'clock, something for tea and by then she'd finished. For ten shillings a week she considered they got a fair deal. Certainly they got all they were going to!

Just for a moment Penelope's courage failed her. The sight of herself in the speckled looking glass on her chest of drawers had completely taken away her last vestige of confidence. Count to ten, then head up, shoulders back, down she'd go.

'What in the world . . . ?'

'Your hair! Whatever have you done?'

It was clear what she'd done – she'd had it cut as short as a boy's. To be honest, when she'd first seen it she'd been rather taken with her new look, the straggly fringe combed forward. She didn't have a parting, her short straight hair fell just as it wanted from her natural crown. Not a pin – indeed not enough hair to put into one!

Until she'd got back to her room and seen it against the background of familiar things she'd been quite pleased with herself. Now the room was heavy with silence, every eye on her.

She lifted her chin, flicking her new fringe back.

'What sort of a sissy do you think Young Perce is,' Penelope forced a laugh, 'with hair like a girl's? Anyway, I'll be able to tumble about much more if I don't have to worry about the pins falling out.'

'A woman's hair is her crowning glory,' Edith Hacker, the soprano, pronounced, pulling herself to her fullest height and clasping her hands to support her overlarge bosom.

'All very well for Perce but, Pen, you're not always got up like a fellow. Now you've got to go about like that all the time!' Clearly Tom wasn't impressed by her new image.

They'd been robbed of words, but now their tongues were loosened, everyone spoke at once. And it was apparent they all thought her afternoon could have been better spent. The women tried to encourage her by saying 'it'll soon start to grow . . . ' and 'does it good to have it cut, so folk say, makes it thicker . . . ' The men gave no such cheer. Is there a man born who doesn't prefer to see a woman with plenty of hair? And up until then none of them had ever been confronted by a girl shorn to look like a boy. It was one thing to dress up as Perce on the stage, but this was carrying things too far, there was something not quite decent about it.

Only Alf spoke out in her favour. 'Well, I think Pen looks jolly nice. Not many girls could still look pretty with hair like that.' A back-handed compliment if ever there was one!

That was the evening when, as she wiped the grease paint off her face, a knock came at the door of the dressing room she shared with the other women.

Gladys Hopgood, who helped her husband in the box office, called to them that she'd 'got a real posh bunch o' flowers out 'ere. Young feller jus' 'anded them to Bert. Roses. Smell a treat.' Flowers for any of the concert party were unheard of, but Edith of the bosom opened the door expectantly. If there was an appreciative gentleman in the audience it had to be her he had his eye on.

'Oh, I say, what beauties.' She took the bunch of roses looking for the card.

Clearly Gladys had read it first. '"For Pen", that's what it says. Nothing else, not a sign of who sent 'em.'

But Penelope didn't need telling.

The gales of autumn came ahead of their time. Like a froth of ginger beer the sea was thrown over the iron railings of the pier. No one ventured along the promenade at high tide; the wind had force enough to blow any except the toughest off their feet. Each wave that broke sent the spray high and with it a hailstorm of pebbles. Only the beginning of September but the concert party could sniff the end of the season.

'What are you two young people planning to do when we move on?' Arnold Stubbs asked them as he closed the lid of the piano. It was Saturday night. They only had one more week of work left. 'I dare say Peter Somerville will have us all back – either here or somewhere else – next summer. Till then I suppose you'll go home for a bit of spoiling. Shan't be sorry to pack my bags from Barbara Brooks' place.'

'No, we shan't go back home. That would mean starting all over again next year. We intend to go to London, look for work there.' Such confidence in Penelope's voice.

Stubbs' kindly face took on a worried frown. Six months ago, if Penelope had conjured up a picture of a music hall pianist, he certainly wouldn't have been anything like Arnold. Of all the people who'd stayed at Clifford House none had been as 'ordinary'; Arnold was the sort of man who might knock on your door each week for your insurance pennies, or even serve on the haberdashery counter – except that he'd have to wear his Sunday suit for that. His thinning hair was fine, giving the impression of a baldness he'd not yet come to; his clothes were quite respectable yet somehow they hung on him as if they'd rather be somewhere else, his collar didn't sit well and his half moon glasses tended to slip down his nose. Even during the performance it was rare for him not to have a cigarette in the corner of his mouth, one eye half closed against the curl of smoke. Except for lighting these 'whiffs', as he called them – and that usually one from another – he seldom seemed to touch them. Even so his first finger was stained from nicotine.

A man you'd not spare a second glance. Yet, his fingers danced on the ivories, his playing seemed to have a life of its own. From the very first time she'd danced to his music Penelope had had a soft spot for him. At first it had been simply for his playing, but by now it was for Arnold himself. She supposed he had no family, for all he ever talked of it he might have had no past at all. Yet, like some kindly uncle, he was concerned for the two young members of the cast; if his concern was mostly for Penelope he gave no hint of it.

'London? I suppose one of you must have people there? It's a lonely city. You've got somewhere to stay?'

'No. But we shall go up on the first train of the day, we'll have hours to look around. Lodgings first, then the next day we'll start looking for work. You don't know any addresses, I suppose?'

Tom came over to join them. 'Yes, if you could recommend anywhere it might save us falling into another Brook.' He grinned hopefully. 'Some nice kind soul who enjoys cooking, that's what we're after.'

'It'll cost you a few bob more in London than it does down here. You sure you're ready? Why don't you give it another year? You're full young yet, either of you. Talk about dog eat dog – it's every man for himself, I tell you.'

'We'll be fine, Arnold.' Penelope wasn't to be deterred.

96

'Determined young lady, this one of yours, Tom.' His words put a new complexion on their partnership, one that Tom appeared to like. 'You take good care of her up there in London. I'll tell you what, I'll give you the name of someone I know. You tell him Arnold Stubbs sent you. He mostly finds places for straight singers – and for instrumentalists, that's how I first met him. He's found me my bookings for years. Don't know if he's quite the man for you, but it's wheels within wheels. If he can't help then there may be someone he'll send you to who can.'

'Wouldn't he count my concertina as an instrument?'

'You get a good tune out of that squeezebox. Trouble is you get it out of your head instead of off a sheet of music. Mac Masters is his name. I'll write it down for you and draw you a map so you'll know where to find him.'

'Where are you going next, Arnold? Have you got another booking?'

'Not 'til the pantomime season. A few weeks at home first.' Then, from his wallet, he took a much handled sepia photograph and passed it to them. A woman not only beautiful but elegant; and with her two children, a boy and a girl, both of them with dark curly hair, children as lovely as she was herself. 'That's my family. Lavinia, she's the wife, then Tess and Charlie. They're twins, be seven at the end of the month. I always reckon to get home for their birthday.' The drab little man spoke with pride, as well he might.

'And you have to be away from them all the summer? Oh, Arnold, you must hate that.'

'It's the first summer they've not come for a few weeks. Charlie got whooping cough, then when we thought she'd missed it, Tess went down with it. So, yes, it's been a long summer this year. Still, "men must work and women must weep", isn't that the saying? Not that Lavinia's one to weep, never has been. Can't have everything in this life and if I stayed at home in Slough giving piano lessons in the front parlour I'd never sniff the sort of money I pick up now. Got a nice home, bathroom, all the trimmings. Last time I was there I bought one of those tub things for the washing. All she has to do is put the hot water in and rub the soap on the clothes, then close down a lid and twiddle a handle on top. Does the lot for her in one go. It's clever the things they think of these days. Now, how could I earn enough for luxuries like that with teaching? No, I tell you, I owe a lot to Mac.'

He'd never talked so much. Perhaps it was the sight of the photograph, the thought that in a few days he'd be home with his family. And he'd seemed such a quiet, solitary little man.

Walking back to Cartisbrook Crescent with Tom, Penelope was still thinking about it. How well did any of them really know each other? She'd always looked on Arnold as being elderly. Well, so he must be, certainly he was older than her father. Whoever would have expected him to have that lovely wife and two pretty little children? So, what about the others? Living in the same lodgings, working in the same show, yet all of them alone here, each one an island. Somewhere had they families, sweethearts, parents, children, lovers?

'You hear what he called you, Pen?' Tom cut into her thoughts. 'My young lady! Sounds all right to me,' he chuckled, linking her arm through his, never doubting she'd be as taken with the idea as he was himself.

And so she was. They'd been friends as long as she could remember, all her secrets had been shared with Tom and Alf – well, nearly all of them. And far more than she realized it, she needed someone to lavish her affection on.

'We'll take London by storm, Tom! You just see if we don't.' Her ever buoyant confidence soared even higher.

That proved to be an exaggeration. But, thanks to a note Arnold wrote to Mac Masters, they were given an audition (not with Mac himself, but he knew a man who knew a man . . .) and from that followed bookings that kept them busy enough to pay their way even if Tom had precious little left over to 'blow'. Arnold's letter might have set the wheels in motion but the rest was up to them. Still the talent was Penelope's, the charisma too, but Tom was no fool. Those months at Hastings had taught him a good deal and nature was on his side. Tommy and Perce might not have taken London by storm in that coming winter, but before 1912 was very old they'd played in a good many suburban theatres and were beginning to feel old hands at the game.

Letters went regularly to Challington; those that came back were always from Muriel. 'If Ollie were in, he'd say to give you his love' or 'Your father and I both send you our love'. But her words didn't fool Penelope. Most of the time her mind was taken up with just living: tomorrow, next week, next year, the future beckoned her on. Young, healthy, full of energy, keen always to do better than her best and be rewarded by that unmistakable communication between herself and the audience, she was certain that what it held for her would be good. Usually that was enough, until from out of nowhere the shadow would fall and she'd remember how things used to be between herself and the Pa who had made up her childish world.

In 1912 they spent the summer season in Scarborough, staying north in the months that followed, working the halls in Bradford, Leeds, Manchester. Just as Sylvia had told her, there was more work in the north. But in all this time their paths never crossed; the nearest they came was in Birmingham where Penelope saw from an old notice being taken down in the theatre foyer that last week Terry and Christine Carstairs had been top of the bill, with Sylvia and the Dancing Dozen bottom.

By this time Tommy and Perce had climbed from last billing to about halfway. People saw them and remembered; the local newspapers gave them a special mention. Fame was a long way away, but the first pale light of recognition was dawning. Had it not been for Arnold

Stubbs and that letter to Mac Masters, they might have found themselves busking outside instead of walking the boards inside. But it wasn't until the following summer, 1913, that they heard of Arnold again.

Tommy and Perce were engaged for the season in Brighton, not half an hour's journey from Challington.

'What about surprising them at home on Sunday?' It was Tom's suggestion. His brothers had managed to see them when they'd been in London; his parents had even left the family to fend for themselves and made the journey, bristling with pride in their handsome son's success. Only Penelope heard nothing beyond the rambling missives from Muriel; but never any suggestion that 'surely you must have a week free soon? When are you coming home to see us?'

Now she chewed her bottom lip, picturing what it would be like to walk in unannounced.

'I don't know, Tom. I want to – I want to see Pa, to make everything all right . . . '

'And so it will be, Pen. When he sees you, still the same as you always were. Best thing you can do is just open the door and catch them when they don't know you're coming. Off guard he'll be pleased to see you.'

'What if he isn't?' Doubt wasn't usually a part of her nature. He put an arm lightly around her shoulder. 'What if it just stirs it all up again?'

'Look, Pen, your old man's been like a cloud hanging over you ever since we left Challington. Go home and make friends with him, let him see you haven't gone to the dogs just because you went your own way. I'll come with you if you like, if you think he'll be awkward.'

'No, don't do that. I'll go on my own. Do you know what I really wish? I'd like to meet him, just him, somewhere away from the house. Bump into him by chance. So that it could be just him and me like it used to be. I'm sure he can't have changed, not really, not Pa. When I was little he was so special. Funny isn't it, Tom? We didn't have anything in those days, yet — oh, I don't know, — there was just no one like Pa. There was nothing I couldn't tell him, I never had to have secrets from him. Well, not 'til I found the concertina,' she added, half smiling now at the memories, sad and happy, that the words evoked. 'Keep your fingers crossed for me, Tom, that Sunday gets rid of all the clouds. Anyway,' there was her old spirit in her voice now, 'it'll be lovely to see Mother and Merrick and Mandy. And Bruce too. Just think, he's walking already and I've never seen him.'

'And old Alf.'

'Oh, yes, can't you picture his face!' And the thought of Alf's pleasure chased away the shadow.

The sea broke on the shore with hardly a ripple as if nothing must disturb the stillness of Sunday morning. Two years had done nothing to change Challington. On the shingle one or two families had spread rugs where the ladies could sit with no fear of soiling their best dresses, for holiday or no, the Sabbath demanded no less. The tide was out as Tom and Penelope walked along the familiar Promenade.

'It feels as if we've never been away, Tom. Just look at those rocks. We could climb from one to the other right the way along — we know just where the difficult bits are.'

'Pen,' he took her hand, pulling her back, 'it's not the same, *we're* not the same. We were just kids then, but we're grown up now. And — well, Pen,' he grinned, his dark eyes laughing, 'it's hard to say these things in the morning sunshine . . . we ought to be under a romantic moon.'

'Just say them, Tom. Even in the rain I'd want to hear.'

'Honest? It's coming back here, remembering all of it . . . Pen, you're my girl . . . what I mean is . . . I suppose I must be in love with you. Can't imagine your not being part of my life. Wouldn't be much of a life without you.'

'Oh, Tom.' She saw him through a haze of stinging

101

tears. She couldn't help it. They spilled over, and try as she might her mouth wouldn't be steady. 'Go on, say it! "Just like a stupid girl",' she snorted. 'Always cried when I was happy.' The tears still flowed but now she was laughing, too. 'Reckon I'm a sissy –'

'Reckon you are. But I love you anyway. What about you? You didn't say.'

"course I love you. Wouldn't be making such a fool of myself if I didn't.'

Then, disregarding the Sunday morning strollers, churchgoers and holidaymakers alike, he wiped her face with the handkerchief he unfolded from his breast pocket (for Tom, like everyone else, was wearing his best suit and the crisp white handkerchief was all part of the ensemble) and for the first time in his life he kissed her. Not being experienced he wasn't sure whether his new trilby hat should be on or off, and between the two of them they managed to knock her boater over one ear. But none of that mattered. She was his girl, he loved her, they were partners now and always in everything they did.

Now she must go home, walk on her own to Clifford House. But suddenly she wasn't frightened of it anymore; it hadn't the same power to hurt her.

It was about half-past eleven and they promised to meet by the pierhead at four o'clock by which time Tom would have been the centre of his family's attention at Sunday dinner, then collected Alf. As they parted they turned back and waved at each other. Penelope walked on air; Tom did, too, but somehow it wouldn't have seemed manly to let anyone suspect it. A few days ago when first they'd decided to come to Challington she wouldn't have credited that she could have been so happy as she made her way to Alexandra Square. His words echoed in her mind, she felt glowing; surely it must show, everyone she passed must know. "My girl", "can't imagine a life without you", "in love with you". Tommy and Young Perce, Tom and Penelope . . . her feet wanted to dance as she hurried along the Promenade in the direction of the fishmarket and the less attractive end of town.

She'd thought Challington was unchanged, but she saw now there was one addition to the seafront: a new shelter with wrought iron ornamentation, the structure divided into four compartments, one facing in each direction so that no matter which way the wind blew it would always give protection. Muriel had mentioned it in one of her letters, but seaside shelters were all much the same and Penelope had seen plenty. So what made her turn and look back at it after she'd passed by she didn't know; it was almost as if something prompted her.

'Pa!' Hadn't she wanted their meeting to be spontaneous, hadn't she asked for him to be 'caught on the hop'?

'Your daughter?' His companion was first to break the silence that followed Penelope's surprised cry. She moved a little further from him on the bench, taking her hand from his. 'I didn't know you had an older daughter as well as Amanda.'

'Ah, well, I don't have to explain stage people to you. You know well enough how they can neglect their families.' Ollie was on top of the situation again; only for the first seconds had he floundered. Now he stood up and held out his hand. 'Penny,' he frowned, 'what have you done to yourself? Why, it's your hair! You've cut your hair off. You're changed.'

'No, Pa, I'm not.' And neither was she. In repose her face was still as solemn, the expression in her brown eyes still as honest. She came close and held her face up to kiss him. Even now, finding him wasting his Sunday morning with a pretty woman in tow, she had to find the Pa she was sure was still there if only she reached out to him. She felt his lips on her cheek and put her arms tight around him. 'I'm not changed, Pa.' Again tears threatened. They were always the outlet when emotions were too much to be contained. Tightly she clenched her teeth, putting all her strength into her grip on him.

'Tuppence,' she heard the name he'd not called her for years, 'little Tuppence.'

It was no use fighting. Her mouth twisted and she buried her face against his shoulder. All this time she'd shied away from remembering, from thinking about him! Now suddenly the cloud had lifted and he was her own dear Pa again. The very name 'Tuppence' – wasn't that his way of telling her how much all those years had meant to him?

'Lavinia,' he spoke to his companion over the top of Penelope's head, 'I've not seen Penny for two years. Penny, this is a friend, Lavinia Stubbs. I've been helping her with a little business problem that was troubling her.'

'And I'll be sitting here puzzling my poor brain with things I don't understand again tomorrow morning. But I expect with your daughter home you'll be busy.'

'Lavinia Stubbs, you say?' Nothing could have helped Penelope regain her composure quicker. 'Arnold's Lavinia? You don't mean – ?' Surely Arnold's beautiful Lavinia wasn't a widow battling with business problems, trying to bring up the twins alone! Her fears were soon proved unfounded.

'Arnold's at the Pier Theatre. We usually stay for a few weeks. But he's no businessman. I'm grateful to you, Oliver.'

'Any time, Lavinia. The pleasure's mine.'

And so it was, Penelope was sure of that from the expression on his still-handsome face as Lavinia straightened her stylish wide-brimmed straw hat and took up her parasol.

They watched her go, then turned away in the direction of Alexandra Square. Oliver held Penelope's elbow, propelling her along as he might one of his fair acquaintances.

'Fancy your having met Lavinia's husband. I suppose you've worked together?' He said it lightly, as if the whole thing were of no importance. 'Well, just between ourselves, if you meet him while you're here I wouldn't mention coming across Lavinia with me. He hasn't much of a head for figures, but he might not like to think she asked advice of another man. Some people are like that, you know, quick to start imagining things. And Muriel, too. No need to mention it to her, eh?'

Any wool they'd tried to pull over Penelope's eyes fell to the ground. As if she'd carry tales that would only hurt Muriel – or Arnold for that matter!

'Pa, what's between you and Lavinia? Truly?' She stopped walking and he had to stop too. 'She and the twins are all Arnold cares about – and don't you ever worry about hurting Mother? I can't understand – '

'Then let it rest. What you can't understand, don't meddle with. What's between the luscious Lavinia and me? No more than a bit of fun – is that such a sin? Muriel's happy enough at home. Some women are Marthas and some are Marys, there's room in the world for both. Two years knocking about like you have, I'd have thought you could understand.'

'Does Mother?' He thought he heard contempt in her tone.

'I deserve some sort of a life of my own. Do you expect me to fetch and carry in a boarding house all day? Is that what you want?'

'Let's go home. I want to see Mother and her babbees, I want to meet Bruce.'

He seemed glad to change the subject and half an hour later, when the first excitement had died down, there was no doubting his pride in his young family. He was like two people, and the Clifford House one was the Pa of her childhood. Perhaps Muriel knew no other.

Like old times, Penelope carried dishes to the dining room, collected empty plates. She had expected to meet the original owner of most of her childhood wardrobe, but it seemed that on Sundays Muriel was on her own. How easy it was to fall back into the old routine. Oliver sat on a wooden bench in the back yard reading the paper, Merrick and Mandy bowled a hoop on its wobbly way up and down the path while Bruce chased it on all fours, legs and arms straight.

'Everything going all right, Penny love?' Muriel turned from the sink, her reddened hands plunged into a bowl of hot water and soda. 'Nothing worrying you – it's not that that's brought you home?'

'The only thing that worried me was Pa, how it would be when he saw me.'

'Poor Ollie! Men aren't like us, they get hurt if things don't go the way they want. You know what I think? I think that you can waste good corn worrying about the tare. Does that make any sort of sense to you, I wonder? I'm trying to say we're all of us how the good Lord moulded us, and it's not a scrap of use trying to turn someone else into what we try to be ourselves. That's what I said to Ollie after you went. Like a bear with a sore head he was, oh, for weeks! And the babbees, poor mites, how did they know they mustn't mention your name?'

'Mother, I'm sorry. It's not fair that what I did – and what he said – should have spoiled things for everyone.'

'Never waste sympathy on a body who suffers for someone they love. Keep it for the person who hasn't got anyone to love. What's the use of all the comforts, all the money and smart clothes, if you've no one to really care about but yourself? And there are some like that, poor souls.' She stacked the last plate in the wooden rack. 'There, another meal eaten and forgotten. Now, we'll make ourselves a cup of tea and you tell me all about you and Tom Beasley. Went off no more than a slip of a child – not much bigger now, but you're two years on. So, what's life got in store for you, Penny love? Is Tom Beasley your Mister Right? Is that what you've come home to tell us?'

'It's not why I came but, yes, Tom and I are partners all the way now.' And in the newfound wonder of hearing him say he loved her, she couldn't help adding childishly:

'Tom would never be one of those men who chase after other women. He and I share everything.'

Muriel frowned. 'Well, love, before you get too free with the everything, make sure that you share his name! Falling in love is full of pitfalls. There, just take that cup of tea out to your pa, see he doesn't feel neglected out there while we've been chattering. And, Penny, what you said about Tom and other women – it takes all sorts, always remember that. The world'd be a dull place if it didn't. A pretty woman who knows how to flatter a man . . . well, who can blame him if he laps it up? Just think back to the Good Book, remember the Three Wise Men: did they all bring the same gift? No, 'course they didn't. What a man looks for outside his home isn't going to be the same as he finds inside it. Hark at me, will you? Who do I think I am with my sermonizing!'

So the visit passed, the old wounds were healed. Just as they'd known he would be, Alf was thrilled at the unexpected visit and the thought of a summer with them so nearby. And over the whole day hung the wonder of those moments on the promenade. Neither of them told their old friend how they felt about each other; somehow they knew it would have spoilt the few hours they had together. Plenty of time later.

As the weeks of summer passed, Tom would talk about 'one day' after they were married, but for the time being they took each one as it came, packed it with carefree fun whether they were on the stoney beach, in front of the footlights or striding along companionably in step as they thought of a new twist to their act.

Just before the concert party's season ended, Oliver surprised her by coming to Brighton to see the matinée. She knew as soon as she introduced him to Elspeth Dilloway, the blonde soprano, how he would be. At one time he would have kept his dalliances from her, but no longer. It didn't surprise her a bit to see him in the front row for the evening performance, but it wasn't until the next day that she discovered he'd taken Elspeth out to supper and finally found a room for the night, returning to Challington in the morning. She told herself it was for Muriel's sake she hated the way he behaved; but that wasn't the whole truth. No doubt he'd carry home the tale that he'd been with her. The 'little bit of fun' at Brighton would leave no lasting memory. But how removed it seemed from the Pa who'd helped her to make a cardboard inner sole for her boots, or who'd wiled away the winter evenings playing that favourite game 'Places'.

The carefree weeks and months were carrying them through another winter and spring. Every day brought its share of laughter. They hadn't much money to 'blow', nor yet had they made a name for themselves; with the confidence of youth they were certain that would all be part of their tomorrow, that and marriage too.

Then it was summer once more, the summer of 1914.

CHAPTER FIVE

'Read all about it,' the newsvendor shouted. 'Reallaboudit' was how the words wafted on the night air. 'Student murders Archduke.' That was clearer and, even though the title Archduke gave the story about as much reality as a newsflash from Ruritania, sale of the evening papers was brisk.

Tom passed up his penny.

'Who was he, Tom?' Penelope wanted to know, stopping under the gaslamp so that they could read. It was 28th June, only a week past the longest day, but the old man with his pile of papers was regularly to be found outside the railway station even at this hour of the evening. 'Archduke Ferdinand,' she scanned the front page, 'heir to the Austrian throne. Oh, how awful, not just him but his wife too, and killed on their wedding anniversary.'

'At some place called Sa-ra-jev-o.' Tom made hard work of the unfamiliar name. 'Yes, rotten. Still, Pen, it's a long way from here. I'm not even sure where the Balkans are.'

Penelope was better informed. The Places game had encouraged a natural curiosity; for her an atlas held the wonder of a magic carpet. But tonight even she was prepared to give no more than passing sympathy to the unhappy couple. She certainly had no clear understanding of the will of the Slav people of the Balkans to unite; of the propaganda spread by the society of the 'Black Hand' to which the student who'd shot the Archduke belonged. She knew enough to be aware of the tension between Serbia and Austria. To read what was going on in the world was important to her, if only because she hated to feel ignorant. Sometimes it was difficult to sort out the politics behind it all but, in her mind, ignorance went hand in hand with laziness. And that was something alien to her nature. Bad enough to be a shrimp, at least let it be seen that she had her head screwed on! And being a girl it was extra important for her to keep up with events; if women believed world affairs were beyond them then no wonder they still hadn't been given a vote. One day they would, though. They wouldn't be content until they did. And when that time came she was determined Penelope Drew's vote would come out of her own thinking, her own beliefs. Fancy Tom not knowing where the Balkans were after all they'd read over these months!

Tom was right, it was far away, remote from life this lovely summer in Tarnmouth. And there was something else at the top of her mind: when they got back to their lodgings this evening there ought to be a letter from Alf telling them which week he was having his holiday and visiting them.

'Come on.' Tom took her hand and they fell into step. At the corner of West Street they slowed down just as they did every night to admire the notice on the hoarding. 'An Evening of Fun, Song and Laughter at the Palace Theatre.' Then, at the top of the bill, 'Tommy and Young Perce', and underneath in small letters (so small that they actually had to stop to read them), 'You'll see them once – and you'll come back to see them again. Fun for all the family. *Evening Herald*.' Sarajevo might have been on another planet.

As the days went on it was easy enough to believe that the troubles were nothing to do with England. It must have been easy, for everyone managed to do it! They read that Austria had accused Serbia of being an accomplice in the murder and had refused to take part in conciliatory discussions. Still, the ongoing tale seemed far removed from their daily concerns. Penelope and Tom were young and as full of their own affairs as anyone else. Of much more consequence in their lives was the new dance routine she had introduced into their act, the extra curtain call

110

they'd been given after the Saturday night performance. On 28th July war was declared between Austria and Serbia. War! There was a sinister look to the placards. The word held drama, even a certain romance, especially when it referred to someone else's war. For, like everything that had led up to it, it had nothing to do with them. Especially today, the Monday of Alf's holiday! And this time they would have to tell him about their plans to marry.

It was on that same Monday evening that Tom was hailed by a stranger as they came out of the theatre.

'Excuse me, Mr Beasley. It is Tom Beasley, isn't it, sir?'

'Yes?' Instinctively he stood a little taller, his smile friendly yet aloof. The man with the black bowler hat and brown-checked waistcoat wasn't what he would have expected of an admirer, but who else would stop him in the street? And he was human enough to be pleased that Alf was there to appreciate it and take word home to Challington! 'I'm from the *Evening Herald*. On Wednesday there's to be a sports afternoon in Cricketfield Meadows, for the children, young boys. Now, it's been suggested that seeing you're accustomed to having a young brother (at which he nodded his head in Penelope's direction), one that's up to all the tricks as you might say, you'd be just the man to come and give the rosettes to the winners. Perhaps you could say a word or two, they'd like that I'm sure. We always try to get a celebrity and we'd be most obliged. The afternoon is sponsored by the *Herald*, sir. No fee, I'm afraid, but you'd be given good coverage by the paper.'

Celebrity! The word rang in Tom's ears.

'I'd be only too happy. Just me or were you wanting Miss Drew?'

'With due respect, miss,' again he nodded his head in her direction, 'just you, sir. Best they don't see a pretty young lady; not much like that scallywag Perce.'

'You'll take care of her for me, won't you, Alf?' And

111

Tom put a possessive arm around her. This sudden rise to the ranks of the famous had given him a feeling of superiority.

'Two-thirty in the Meadow then. And I'm obliged, sir.'

As he walked away the three of them turned and looked at each other. Tom's broad grin said far more than any words.

Alf was the first to speak. 'You wait 'til I tell 'em at home! Come on, I'll buy you a supper. Not every day I can treat a celebrity!'

Tom was much too pleased with himself to detect the over-cheerful tone. Penelope noticed it, but she tried to believe her imagination was running away with her, and all because of a bunch of red roses. She linked her arms through theirs.

'That sounds like a good idea, Alf.' She steered them in the direction of the quay. 'Let's go to the Harbour Café – they'll still be open and their fish is lovely. I'm starving, it must be excitement.'

At the top of the slope leading down to the harbour the gaslight cast its glow on the newsvendor's board that he had left standing there. 'War Declared.'

'Aren't we lucky? Being us, I mean.' Penelope, walking between them, her arms linked through theirs, hugged them to her. '"For I might have been a Prussian . . . "' she sung, altering Gilbert's words to fit the occasion, to be joined first by Tom then Alf too '" . . . For I myself have said it, and it's greatly to my credit, that I am an Englishman, yes, I am an Englishman."' Gilbert's words (almost), Sullivan's tune, seemed to cast a blanket of safety over them and a peace they took for granted. War was for other countries, hotheads, fanatics. England was strong, it had no reason to pick quarrels with anyone.

It was on the Wednesday afternoon that Alf referred to the worsening situation.

'I wonder what'll happen to us all if war comes, Pen.'

'But their squabbles are nothing to do with us, Alf. The

112

newspapers talk about countries honouring treaties, but war can't come that way, coldly, dispassionately.'

'You're wrong. That's just the way! Germany's been arming for years, I was reading about it the other day. It said the situation was dangerous. Russia's on the brink of mobilizing, France too. If it happens it'll be different from the old sort of wars. Weapons are modern, deadly. The world is mechanized.'

She thought he was exaggerating, but for all that she looked at Alf with new respect. He obviously tried to keep abreast with what was going on.

'Sir Edward Grey won't let it happen, not to England.'

Alf frowned, sitting forward on the shingle. Like her, he was still a shrimp! How thin his wrists were as he sat with his hands clasped around his drawn up knees.

'Pen,' he blurted out her name and she sensed that whatever it was he wanted to say, he had to get it out before his courage failed. 'You and old Tom, are you just work mates – or are you his sweetheart? None of my business – except that the three of us have been pals so long and –'

'Of course it's your business. Sweetheart seems a funny thing to say about Tom and me. It never sounds,' she had to be sure she found the right word, 'permanent, somehow. I'd say we're partners – that's much bigger than being sweethearts.'

'Yes, but are you going to marry him? Are you promised to him? You don't wear a ring.'

'We've never talked about a ring but we shall be married one day.' She saw the way his Adam's apple wobbled in his thin neck. Dear Alf. She mustn't let him think she noticed. 'And what about you, Alf? Is there anyone?'

'Me marry? I'll tell you what I'm going to do. If this war comes – oh, I know you say it won't, but I'm not so sure – I shall join the Army. I'm thinking of joining anyway. Travel, see the world. A soldier might be sent any where in the Empire. Just think of the opportunities, Pen.'

113

'War! Army! What talk is this for a sunny day at the seaside? Let's go and put our bathing suits on and swim, shall we?' She emerged from the wooden changing hut a few minutes later to find him waiting for her. 'Race you down the beach. Last one in the water's a sissy!' With Alf she didn't want to grow up, she didn't want anything to change between them; dear Alf, he'd always understood her, he'd never needed to have things explained, neither tears nor laughter.

Along the sands at the water's edge children dug, ladies paddled; one or two, clad in bathing dresses and with scarves tied around their heads, ventured to bob up and down in the waves. But that wasn't for Penelope. Long ago the boys had taught her to swim. Now she raced over the stones and straight into the water, wading out until she was waist deep then hurling herself forward without a care for her cropped hair. She was just ahead of Alf. He'd let her be the first to take the plunge. She saw it clearly today, even if she never had before.

The cold water took their breath away and drew a veil over their talk of war, of sweethearts.

'Stand with your legs wide open, Alf. I'm going to swim between them.' Then their howls of laughter as he lost his balance, both of them going under. Their pleasure knew no bounds, both of them completely at home in the water. Penelope stood on her hands, her feet sticking up over the waves. If some of the ladies who dipped their toes envied them their carefree youth, there were others who raised their eyebrows and couldn't think what young people were coming to!

This Wednesday afternoon was another of those special times. In their memories the blue of the sky would be deeper, the water not quite so cold; these few golden hours were to stay with both of them, the joy highlighted by what was so soon to follow.

*

'Here, Pen, look at this! Your luscious Sylvia in a national paper.'

'Sylvia! Let's see! Where is she playing?' For the 'chosen sisters' had drifted apart. After Hastings there had been a couple of brief notes, one from Manchester and one from Berwick-on-Tweed. Then nothing. For a while Penelope had kept on writing, saying that letters to Alexandra Square would always reach her, but the nearest she got to a reply was her own letters returned with 'Gone Away' or 'Present address not known' on the envelopes.

'I should think she's finished with the dancing girls,' Tom chuckled, 'just listen to this. "Captain Kenneth Greenaway, eldest son of the late Mr Henry Greenaway, was married today to the beautiful Miss Sylvia Carstairs. On his father's death Captain Greenaway, together with his brother, inherited the family business, Henry Greenaway and Sons, well-known as manufacturers of highclass cutlery. The couple met in the spring when Miss Carstairs, a dancer, was performing in Sheffield where the bride groom was visiting relatives whilst on leave from his regiment, having returned to England after serving in India." No,' he looked up from the paper, 'my guess would be your friend Sylvia has trodden the boards for the last time, from now on her performances will be for the captain's private viewing. There's a bit more – "He is now attached to the British Expeditionary Force in France, where he will return after a brief honeymoon."'

'Oh, Tom, don't you just hate the war? There's Alf a soldier; Sylvia having to say goodbye almost as soon as she's married; the call-boy at the Empire told me tonight that he enlisted this morning. Just ordinary people . . . Well, Sylvia's captain is a proper soldier, I suppose. Everyone said it would be over before this. Six months, and all we hear is that more and more people are going.'

It was nearly midnight. They'd bought the paper as they'd come out of the tube station at Finchley Road on the way home from the theatre. London had been home

115

to them all the winter. A week at one theatre, sometimes a fortnight at another, they'd moved round the circuit of the music halls. Sometimes they felt they spent half their working lives on tube trains, but they were prepared for that simply to have their names on programmes in the capital – albeit sometimes as the first act of the evening, with a second appearance following the interval, while people were still settling down. Usually they finished their day together; either she went with him to his room or he to hers.

'We'll have things clear from the start,' Mrs Fellows, their portly landlady, had told them when she'd shown them their rooms last September, 'I run a respectable house. Got my living to earn and a reputation to look to. I tell all my ladies and gentlemen the same thing. No hanky-panky, if you please, not under my roof!' With a feeling of guilt they'd close the door after them, sometimes in his room, sometimes in hers. If Mrs Fellows suspected she gave no sign of it. She'd come to know them well over the weeks. 'As likely playing tiddly-winks as getting up to what they didn't ought!'

Like most theatre people Penelope and Tom were night birds and were never in a hurry to get to bed. Although it was the bed they sat on now, side by side, the paper dropped to the floor. He held his arm around her shoulder, drawing her towards him. What she'd just said, what they'd just read, none of it could be pushed aside. His mind was leaping from one thing to the next and back again. He was no hero, and he had no burning passion to rush off into the mêlée. But neither did he want to be seen as skulking at home, letting someone else do the dirty work – and get the glory. Old Alf – seeing him the other day weighed down with those great boots, wearing a khaki tunic that looked big enough for him and another one his size too – somehow that had brought the war right home. Now reading this about Sylvia . . . Pen was quite upset for her, and worried about old Alf too. Silly to resent her

116

worrying about other people, speaking about them with respect like she did. The truth was he was jealous. She was *his* girl, she always had been. If she had to be worried then it should be about him . . .

His mind still in turmoil Tom put his hand under her chin and turned her face towards him. How pretty she was, her huge dark eyes so solemn. Trouble was, he was so used to what she looked like that he hardly noticed. He ran his fingers through her short honey-brown hair. Her lips parted, she leant closer, so close that he felt the warmth of her breath.

'I've got to go too,' he heard himself say, somehow his mind suddenly clear, his decision made. 'Pen, it's you I'll be fighting for, you and the life we'll have together when it's all over. You know I've got to go, don't you?'

She nodded. ''course I know. You were always the bravest of us all, even when we were little. Oh, Tom, dunno what I'll do without you.'

'We'll be married first, Pen. The same as Sylvia and her soldier. Soon as we can get the licence, we'll be married.' He'd kissed her plenty of times before, but never like this.

As children they'd been like brother and sister; for nearly four years they'd shared each day; neither of them had had any sweetheart except each other; and each loved the other dearly. That one day they would be married was accepted, and looked forward to. But even Mrs Fellows had soon recognized that she'd had no need to worry about them breaking the house rules.

Penelope heard the wheezy chime of the clock on the dining room mantelpiece. Midnight. Sylvia's wedding day was over, already it was tomorrow. A day nearer to Tom's going away. A day nearer to her being his wife, left behind the same as all the other wives, watching for letters, living on a knife edge of fear. There'd be no Tom to come home with each night. No Tommy to keep Perce in order.

'Sorry.' She rubbed her palm across her wet cheeks. 'Just . . . can't think of me being without you.' Then, with

117

an attempt at a laugh: 'Young Perce'll get right on top of himself, no Tommy to keep him in his place.'

They clung to each other, both frightened of a future that had no shape. First they'd be married. But even that was making a game of what marriage should be. A few days, a few nights – then what? Tonight was full of new emotions, emotions that heightened their need to hold on to the moment, to each other and their need of each other.

There was nothing unusual in their sitting on the edge of the bed together, nothing unusual in his drawing her near to him, her head nuzzling against his neck, in their kissing. But tonight these new emotions were carrying them to strange ground. They both knew where they were heading, carried on an avalanche of passion that once set in motion there was no stopping. Their pulses raced with excitement. Memory nudged at Penelope: 'Before you share everything else, just you make sure you share his name.' Muriel might have spoken the words aloud.

That Tom was as aroused as she herself was thrillingly obvious. As if in answer to Muriel's reminder Penelope's hand caressed his throat, his chest, down . . . down . . . her eyes entreating him; her hand came to rest, almost his undoing.

'Soon be husband and wife . . . can it matter . . . ?' He spoke for both of them. And reading the answer in her face he tore at the restraining buttons to feel her hand, warm, tender, eager. 'Pen, I love you. Never done it before, but Pen, please . . . can't be wrong . . . '

It was she who pulled them both back on to the bed, guiding his hand, those silly tears telling him more than anything she could have spoken.

Words tumbled out in whispers, barely audible.

'Your hand, Pen . . . guide me . . . not sure . . . '

'Here . . . here . . . ah . . . '

'Tell me if I hurt you?'

'Hurts . . . I want it to hurt . . . closer . . . '

And upstairs in the attic Mrs Fellows slept, happy in

her ignorance of what was going on under the roof of her nice respectable house.

In February the world stirred before first light. It was the sound of hurrying footsteps that woke them, a cart rattling along Finchley High Street, a motor car horn.

Soon they would be man and wife, but in the meantime Tom had to get back along the corridor! With all the stealth of a cat burglar he felt for his hastily torn off clothes. Wearing his shirt, carrying everything else, he silently opened the bedroom door then, the passage dark and empty, he crept back to where he belonged. From downstairs came the sounds of morning: yesterday's dead ashes raked from the kitchen range; a sudden gush of water into the pans to be heated ready for Mrs Fellows to bring round presently. Safely behind his own closed door, Tom climbed into bed.

Penelope listened to the start-of-day symphony too, smiling that it could sound the same as usual, as if this were an ordinary morning. But it wasn't. She lay very straight, stretched her full five foot one inch, holding her arms towards the ceiling as she lay there. No, it wasn't the same, she wasn't the same. She'd never be the same girl as she had been this time yesterday. She was a woman. And Tom, not the boy she climbed the rocks with, not the lad she'd left home with. He was a man – her man. She felt it must be written all over her, plain for all the world to see. Her mind turned to Sylvia. Chosen sisters; kindred spirits.

That day Tom did two things: he applied for a marriage licence and enrolled in the Army.

Since Penelope and Tom were both under age, parental consent was needed. To obtain a licence wasn't as straightforward as they'd expected, nor as quick. He was fit, he was strong and, as hoardings proclaimed at the turn of every street corner, his country needed him.

The very next Sunday they went to Challington for the day. There was no time to be lost or he'd find himself in the Army and still a bachelor! With only a few hours at home they parted by the pierhead, he going his way and she hers. A bad move on his part. Oliver hadn't forgiven him yet for 'enticing' Penelope away; it did nothing for Tom's cause that he didn't present himself humbly to ask her hand in marriage.

'And what sort of a young man is it who hasn't the courage to speak for himself? Before I consent I want to know how he intends to provide for you.'

'Pa, I love him. Anyway, of course he can provide. We're a team, Tom and me, you know we are.'

'You say he's enlisted. Suppose he comes home crippled. They've taken Prospect House as a hospital, I've seen some of the men sent back from France. You're hardly more than a child yet – '

'I'm not! And I've seen some of the wounded soldiers too. That's why I want us to be married before he goes. Please . . . '

'Wait until he comes on leave. Have a few months without each other. He's the only sweetheart you've had, you can't know your own mind.'

Penelope's lips set in a firm line.

'I can't marry without your consent. But I shall live as if I'm his wife.' She held her chin high.

Across the table brown eyes glared into blue. Watching them Muriel recognized Oliver's jealousy of young Tom Beasley; Penelope's hurt at what she saw as his lack of understanding.

'Just stop and take breath, the pair of you.' She put a soothing hand on Oliver's arm. 'This war pushes everyone along so fast, Ollie, makes them frightened to wait for tomorrow.'

'Are you saying you agree with her wanting to tie her life to Tom Beasley's? You think that conceited young pup is good enough for her?' Even Muriel seemed to have deserted him.

'Ollie, there's no man living you'll ever see as good enough for her, nor shall I come to that. But we only get one chance at this life and if they love each other we've no business stopping them snatching what happiness they can.'

He didn't answer, but she had his whole attention now. Penelope stood watching them, waiting.

'Very well,' he said at last. 'But before you go back to London I want young Beasley to have the courtesy to come and speak to me – to us – ' he corrected himself.

And, that evening, 'young Beasley' arrived. Penelope left him alone with her father. She knew the battle was won, there was no one could stand out against Tom's charm.

Finally the licence was obtained. They were to be married at Challington on Monday 21st March. They even planned a week's honeymoon. But the Army's need of Tom was apparently too urgent for that; papers arrived instructing him to report on the 23rd. The honeymoon was to be no more than one night in his childhood room, his younger brother Cliff's side of the bed given over to Penelope. Then back to London on the 22nd.

'I Penelope take thee Thomas Edward to be my lawfully wedded husband . . . ' Her voice was clear and sure, her eyes full of happiness.

Muriel did her best to provide a good wedding breakfast even though shortages were making catering difficult. A girl only gets married once and nothing was too good for Penny, that was her opinion. Pity Alf couldn't have been there to be the best man, but Cliff was managing very well. And good-looking as Tom Beasley might be, there wasn't a man in the church to compare with her Ollie, bless him.

The 'breakfast' over, all the Beasleys went home, Penelope with them. Today there was no room in her heart for anything but joy; she wouldn't let herself admit the cold glint in Oliver's eyes as he'd bid Tom goodbye and good luck. He was just a bit jealous, that's what Mother would say. To make him feel better she gave him a tighter than usual hug and promised to come back to Challington very soon. Then the Beasley brigade were off, walking the half mile or so home.

Younger than Tom, his three brothers and one sister were filled with giggling curiosity.

'I think you'll be comfortable. I've filled the jug in your room with water – and I'll bring you up some hot in the morning, don't you bother to get up for it.' His mother seemed to take the occasion in her stride; so, too, did Tom.

Penelope wished they could have gone somewhere else, even back to London. Yet, once upstairs in Tom's old bedroom, alone with him, all her misgivings melted. She was his wife. She had a new silk nightgown, the prettiest she'd ever bought.

'Turn your back while I undress, Tom.'

He frowned. 'Funny way for a wife to talk,' he joked.

'Silly! It's just I want you to see me at my best, not undressing and getting ready. I'll keep my back to you too. Then we'll turn round.' She spoke in a whisper.

Stealthily they took off their clothes, she slipped the cool silk gown over her head, he stepped into the trousers of his modern pyjamas, leaving the jacket unbuttoned.

'Ready when you are.' Her words were barely audible. They both turned. She'd imagined his look of appreciation as he looked at her. Only for a second was she disappointed that the new nightgown went unnoticed; his arms were strong, his mouth on hers masterful. Tears of joy too great to contain blurred her vision, she felt choked with it.

Suddenly he released her, almost pushed her away, flinging open the door. Two young boys scuttled back a couple of steps, the smiles wiped from their faces.

'Go on, push off. Hey, before you go – what have you done with the key of this door?'

'Nothing, honest.' Bill, aged nine, was the first to find his tongue. 'Wasn't one there.'

'Which means you looked. Well, go on, clear off to bed before you get Dad after you.' Then, the door shut behind them he pulled a chair in front of it, the top spar wedged under the handle.

Just as if nothing had interrupted him he came back to Penelope, carrying on where he'd left off. In less time than it had taken them to undress, he found his goal.

'They're back, Tom. Listen. Can't you hear?' she whispered against his ear.

'They can't get in, the chair's against the door. Forget about them.'

But she couldn't. She tried not to listen as Mrs Beasley marched them away down the corridor and closed their door firmly on them. This was her wedding night, she was his wife, Tom's wife. He was heavy, it was hard to breathe, but she kept her mind on the beauty of what was happening. They were one, she and Tom, they'd joined their lives together just as they were joining their bodies. As he'd turned out the light she'd pulled back the curtains and now, moving her head to one side in an attempt to find air, she caught sight of the night sky, the clouds pale in the moonlight. Even her giggling young brothers-in-law were forgotten as she gripped Tom tightly, her legs twined round him. They were one. Everything they did would always be for each other. "Thank you, thank you," she cried silently.

There was nothing gentle in Tom's lovemaking, his thrusting movements tore at her small frame. But as he quickened to a climax she was proud that she was his woman. This was marriage. Tom was strong, vigorous; love was part of the life they would share.

The next day Mrs Fellows welcomed them back as if they were family. She'd told the tale of her young lodgers

123

to her friends and between them they'd overcome the shortages and on the dining table was an iced cake, its cochineal lettering bidding her favourite boarder to 'Come Back Soon Tom'. For tomorrow he was to report at the depot. He'd be marched up the road following the band, just like they'd seen so many young men go these past few months.

It was late before the cake was cut. Their fellow guests had to have time to get back from the theatre before the party could start. Already the wedding was overshadowed by something so much bigger. This was Tom's party, he was the centre of attention, he was the hero of the hour.

'Don't rush into anything, Pen,' he said presently, lying in the darkness of what used to be just her room. 'You can see they'd be pleased to have you back at Challington, glad of you I expect through the summer. Why don't you do like I say, wait until I get home again and we'll pick up the threads. The act needs us both.'

''course it does, Tom. By the autumn perhaps it'll have us both again too. But I can't go back. Could you? Or Alf? Could Alf mend pots and kettles again? Could you take your old job in the boat yard, forget all we've done?'

'That's different. I shall be fighting, like Alf is. Out there in France before I know it. But it's not the same for a woman. You'll have enough on your mind with me to worry about, I should have thought. Not jigging about as if you hadn't a care in the world.'

'You know as well as I do, jigging about as you call it hasn't got anything to do with worrying or not worrying. What are you saying? Close the theatres? Don't have anywhere where people can try and forget their troubles?'

He didn't answer. This was their last night, their only night truly on their own, without the prying eyes and ears of his giggling brothers and sister. If only they had more time! Time to adjust to being torn apart before they learnt to accept being together.

'Tom, forget tomorrow. Just for an hour, forget it all. Please. Don't let's wrangle, not tonight.'

He felt her little body nestling against his. How thin she was. As his hand moved on her naked flesh he could feel each rib; her stomach wasn't just flat, it disappeared into a hollow; her legs were supple as a snake, he felt her wrap them around him. Tomorrow was still there, a shadow that fell across them. But they pretended not to see it. Into tonight they must crowd memories to carry them until they met again.

Next morning she watched him march away. She could hear the band getting nearer, the sound of it bringing people out into the street, fetching them from everywhere within earshot. Friends and neighbours . . . always a chance there was a lad they knew who deserved a wave and a cheer. At only five foot one, Penelope's view was blocked. Elbows had to come into play. Ethel Sharp herself couldn't have done better than she did as she carved a way through to the kerbside.

'Tom!' She yelled his name, waving her handkerchief. 'See you soon, Tom.' "Please, please, I'll see him soon, won't I?"

'Left – left – left, right, left . . . ' At the back of the line of civilians was a man in khaki, a sergeant. 'Left – left – left, right, left . . . '

'God speed, lads,' shouted an old man from the saddle of his knife-sharpening machine parked in the gutter. It looked as if it took all his force to turn the pedals that propelled the grindstone. He never took his eyes off the line of youths, but all the time he watched so he worked. After a lifetime of sharpening it was second nature to him.

"God speed," Penelope echoed silently.

'Soon be back, Tom!' He was near enough to hear her now but none of them could turn. Already they felt themselves to be soldiers, shoulders back, heads straight.

Within feet of where she stood frantically waving that silly wisp of a hanky he rolled his eyes in her direction,

125

then shut one in a broad wink. If he'd just marched by without a sign she could have stood it, but now it was a physical effort to hold herself back, not to run down the road by his side. She could see the bulge in the left hand pocket of his jacket and knew just what it was. She'd put it there herself as he was leaving. His mouth organ.

'Ah, good girl,' he'd said, 'I might have gone without it! We'll have a bit of fun with that.'

Fun? What fun would there be where he'd soon be going? The newspapers told them little enough, lists of casualties, reports of glorious victories, even retreats had a mention; but nothing of the men, how they felt, how they lived. The doorman at the Palace had a son who'd been sent home wounded. Penelope had heard stories of the life they had in the trenches. Tom must have heard them too. Yet he could still smile, still leave her with a cheerful wink. Her chin went up an inch. If he could do it, so could she.

That night when the curtains opened on the act shown in the programme as 'Tommy and Young Perce' there was a solitary ragamuffin sitting on a box on the centre of the stage.

'Gotta behave myself, that's what he said when he went. Learn to stand on your own two feet, Young Perce, behave yourself — and take care you don't get up t' no mischief. Me? Now, would I? So I'm man o' the house now, for the duration. 'cos Tommy's gone off to help knock old Fritz into shape.'

'Good luck to 'im, laddie,' someone shouted from the gallery.

'Good luck . . . ' Gallery, circle, stalls, the message came from every quarter. Not just for Tommy, she knew that, but for all the sons, husbands, lovers, brothers, all the Tommys. She could feel the greasepaint smudging as she tried to brush away her 'silly tears', tears for Tom, tears for all the others too. And something more than that. Her heart was banging, her arms and legs felt weak with an emotion she couldn't name . . . this tug between her and the people in the audience, this magic that never failed her.

'Soon be over . . . ' Another voice.

From the wings she could sense a feeling of unrest. All very well to bring an audience into a show, it was done every night, but not like this!

"course it will. And 'til it is, we won't let old Kaiser Bill get us down, will we?' And that cheeky grin, as they roared their response. 'Life may not be all we want, but it's all we're gonna 'ave. So let's 'ave it. Stick a geranium in our 'ats and be 'appy.' The volume of their applause was for her spirit, she knew that. She took up her concertina and went into her first song.

That night saw the beginning of a changed act. With no big brother to keep him in order Perce had lost his feed man. More songs, more dancing, more acrobatics; but it wasn't just that. Tommy wasn't there, but he was still part of the act, his absence and his scallywag little brother's loneliness without him giving a new pathos to Perce, alone for the duration. 'Young Perce All Alone' the billing read, and Penelope had no shortage of bookings.

Alf had been almost the first young man in Challington to join the queue at the recruitment centre. He'd had no special skills to offer, nothing except determination to show the Kaiser who was who! The same as thousands like him, Alf had been put into the Infantry, the footsloggers; dressed in his ill-fitting khaki, a rifle and a pair of boots were the tools of his trade.

Now it was Tom's turn. Penelope sat crosslegged on the bed, reading his first letter. He'd been gone just a week and tonight she'd come home to find this.

'We get lots of drill. Looking at some of the lads, I can see I'm fitter than most. I suppose, Pen, the act has kept me in good shape, holding you up, lifting you. I can't see how you're going to manage. So many of your balancing tricks need me – standing on your hands on the floor's not nearly as clever-looking as when I lie flat and your hands are on mine. Pen, you won't get some other chap in to take my place, will you? Some skulking blighter frightened to go and fight. No, I know you won't. The act is ours, yours and mine. I still think you'd be best to pack up and go back to Challington 'til this lot's over. It won't take long now I'm here to get it sorted!

'Anyway, I was telling you about what it's like. The lads are all right. No one else from the stage. Chaps from shops, offices, ordinary sort of jobs, they all think it grand to have a performer among them. I play the mouth organ in our hut, and we have a sing-song. A couple of them have seen Tommy and Perce. Couldn't believe it when I said Perce was my wife. My wife! Can hardly believe it myself. Me, a married man. Some of the men have photographs of their wives. They pass them round for us all to see. Not one of them could hold a candle to you. I want you to go to the photographer's studio and have a picture taken for me. Don't send a big one, I may not have room to carry it, just something for my pocket. When I come on leave we could sit for one together – send a print to old Alf, he'd like that.

'It's nearly "lights out" time, Sgt Crisp will be round. We have to have everything folded and in our kitbags, corners of the blankets squared. Reckon they expect us to go to sleep lying to attention! But it's all right. Most of them are kicking against the pricks, but I'm not. To be honest, I think it's all a bit of a lark. Not the fighting bit later on, nothing funny about that. But all this bull, the spit and polish; and the drilling's great. Tell you who'd take to it easy as wink – Young Perce. Wish I could have brought him with me . . . '

Of course she was glad that despite everything he was enjoying himself. She uncrossed her legs and climbed off the bed, going to the wardrobe where his clothes hung. Touching his jacket, she ran her fingers round the cuff, let

128

her hand feel the lining; she held the material to her cheek, sniffing it, trying to bring him close. Clothes, empty clothes. Even his hats might have belonged to anyone; just hats.

Hurriedly she got ready for bed. She'd read the letter again, she'd read it last thing before she went to sleep.

She read it – but sleep eluded her.

"Is it because he's having a good time? Am I as selfish as that? Oh, I can't be. I want Tom to be happy. Why, if he'd written a miserable letter, hating it all, I'd have been in a dreadful state." And as was her way her prayers were one with her self-analysis. "Please help me not to be selfish, make me glad that he isn't desperately sad at leaving me and at not being in the act. 'cos, that's the truth of it, isn't it? You know that without me having to tell you. I wanted him to say his life was empty without me. Mind You, I ought to have realized it wasn't, it's taken him a week to write! 'course he might have had lots to do, drilling and spit and polish – what do You think they spit at? What's it got to do with battle training, I wonder? I'll ask him when I write. And now that I have an address I can send my letters. One every night I'd done – and all he's written is a single one after pretty well a week! Still, he's not miserable, and honestly, truly, I do say thank You for seeing that he isn't sad. Please keep him safe and bring him back to me and the act soon so we can get on with being a proper couple."

By the beginning of May his initial 'square-bashing', as he called it, was over. He was ready to be sent to the war. In the newspapers she read the casualty lists, names of men killed at a place called Ypres; it was rumoured that soldiers were returning to be cared for in military hospitals suffering from gas poisoning. And Tom was ready to be sent into that!

'I was determined to get a chance of something better than footslogging. You'll never guess, Pen. I'm being transferred to the Army Service Corps, I'm going to be taught

129

to drive a vehicle. Just think of it! If I can drive a lorry I'll be able to drive a motor car when I get out of the army again. How do you fancy that? We won't spend our Sundays on bleak railway stations any more. We'll travel in style on four wheels. There are one or two chaps going to the Engineers, me and a couple more to be drivers. The rest of them will be shipped out to France, I suppose. Bit of luck, eh, Pen!

'I've always said you've got to play your cards right, take every opportunity that comes. Some of them have moaned and grumbled here, but not me. What's the use? Better to keep your eyes skinned, grab at every chance. Like I did. Put my name forward for the Engineers same as the others, but then I got called to the Captain and told I'm being sent tomorrow for driver's training. Better than being an engineer. After all, what use would that be to me? I'll not be coming home to build bridges.

'I'm glad you've managed to change the act so that you can do it on your own. The title you give it isn't bad – but it's a pity the name Tommy couldn't have been kept in: "Perce – But Where's Tommy?" something of that sort. Can't be as entertaining with only one, but in a way it's better than you just packing it up 'til I get back. By yourself, yet talking about Tommy, that way I won't be forgotten. Like keeping my side of the bed warm for me. And do that too, Pen, because as soon as I've done this driving course I'm sure to get some leave. Just about ready for a bit of wifely attention.' Halfway through writing the next sentence he must have changed his mind, for he crossed it out so that she could only manage to read it by holding it first at one angle, then another: 'Living in a hut with a crowd of blokes – ' Whatever he'd been going to say, she was left to guess.

That summer she didn't go to the seaside. These days there was no 'out of season' period for theatres, or for anything else in London. Edwardian England had flocked to the Music Hall; now it was the Palace of Variety.

Already the evening dress of the stalls was giving way to uniform. But let an audience dress as it pleased, Penelope never failed to feel the pulse of its heartbeat.

On the 15th July Tommy was coming on leave; on the calendar in the girls' dressing room Penelope had put a ring round the date. He wasn't expected until evening, so he'd written that he'd come straight to the theatre, try to get there before she went on. When the curtain opened on that solitary urchin sitting on his wooden box, she was still waiting. Any second he'd be here; he was probably walking up the road this very minute. Tonight it tested her skill as an actress to bring out the pathos in the ragged little figure of Perce; she wanted just to sing for joy. She put all her pent-up excitement into her dancing. Had she ever kicked her legs so high, or leaped into her airborne somersaults with such abandon? As the curtain started to close the audience went wild. They loved her.

'Want to ask you something!' She held a hand up to quieten them.

They may not have heard what she said amid the clamour but they saw her speak, saw the movement of the curtains halted. Silence. The curtains re-opened.

'Got a question for you. Tommy asked me this once – and I'm asking you. Why am I like a tight rope walker?' The childish pun of their very first performance . . . Someone halfway back in the stalls, too far away for her to see properly, made a movement. He was here! He'd come!

'Because I'm en cored,' a familiar voice called, and immediately she pulled her concertina into its introductory phrase to lead them all in a final chorus.

Two curtain calls and she was free, rushing towards the stage door. Tom would be sure to come backstage now that her act was finished.

'Got his leave all right then,' Bert Wilkie, the stage door attendant, greeted her. 'Left his kit bag in here for me to keep an eye on. They said they'd see you after the show, but I bet he'll not sit through the rest now.'

'They? Has he brought someone on leave with him?'

'Not a soldier, not this one. A young lady. Felt I ought to know her – can't place her though. Good-looking . . . ' He got no further.

'Pen, look who I've found!'

Good-looking. Oh, yes, she was certainly that, but then she always had been. Sylvia! Breaking away from Tom's side, she ran forward and hugged Penelope.

'What a day of excitement. I only arrived in London this afternoon. Penny, you haven't changed a scrap, haven't even grown an inch.'

'Wasn't it like fate, Pen? I came out of the station at Euston Square lugging that great kitbag and there she was, just being helped up the step of the one and only cab.'

It wasn't a bit the way she'd imagined her first minutes with Tom would be. A friendly peck on her cheek was a far cry from the romantic embrace she'd dreamed of. But to have them both here was so wonderful she had no room for disappointment. He was home, they had a whole week just for each other. To have Sylvia appear so unexpectedly gave the evening a touch of magic.

'I'll talk to Bert while you go and change, Pen,' Tom told her. Then, to Sylvia: 'You go with her, they won't mind you in the dressing room.'

'So I should hope. I've used it times enough.'

'Now I've got it!' Bert snapped his fingers in triumph. 'Sylvia Carstairs. Now I know who you are. Been bothering me all evening.'

'It's the posh clothes put you off, Bert,' she laughed, taking Penelope's hand and pulling her towards the once familiar dressing room. While Penelope took off her make-up, Sylvia sat and watched, something wistful in her expression. From her evening bag she took a cigarette holder, fitted a cigarette and lit it. There was a new elegance in Sylvia. No, Penelope decided, watching her, the elegance was 'on' her, not 'in' her. Fundamentally, she hadn't changed.

132

'Well?' Her friend was aware of the scrutiny.

'There's so much I want to know. Sylvia, what happened? You never answered my letters.'

'I didn't have any letters. Grandma died, you know, she never went back to Clapham at all. It was really up to me. I ought to have made more effort, but I couldn't remember the address in Challington and – oh, time went on, we were all of us caught up in struggling to become rich and famous.'

'Well, from the look of you, you succeeded!' Penelope laughed. 'Tell me about your husband – Kenneth Greenaway. I remember his name. We read about the wedding in the London paper.'

'I've a photograph at the hotel. He's really quite handsome, very striking. An excellent horseman – well, he would be, he's in a cavalry regiment.'

It was hard to pinpoint exactly why Penelope felt that something was wrong. The first clue came as she took off her tatty suit and shirt and the 'good luck' muffler she still wore.

'I'll just hang "Perce" away and pop a dress on, then I'll be ready.'

'Penny, you don't know how lucky you are.'

'With Tom home, you mean? Oh yes I do! And lucky that he won't be fighting in the trenches, too.'

'Lucky that you have a career, that you're yourself, making your own way. They don't like me, you know, my in-laws. I think they consider me only one stage better than a tart because I'm a dancer. *Am* a dancer? Was one, more like. I'm expected to be nothing now, just Mrs Greenaway, setting a good example in the district like my strait-laced sisters-in-law, rolling bandages at the centre. In the village I'm supposed to remember whose sons are in France, to be sure to enquire if they've had letters. "And the Captain? Good news from the Captain I hope, ma'am?" There isn't one of them I really know, any more

133

than they know me. And why should they? Just because Ken saw fit to land me in their midst.'

'I suppose it's like war work, Sylvia. Would it make it easier if you looked on it like that?'

She stubbed out her half smoked cigarette, grinding it into the lid of an empty tin that stood on the bench.

'You, you of all people, know me, Penny.' Her blue eyes were troubled. 'What am I going to do? Nearly five months I've been there, and honestly I've tried. It's not the life for me, not there on my own. If Ken were home . . . But then, when the war's over and things are normal, I'll be able to travel abroad with him. I'll see the world. By then he'll be far more than a Captain, I'll have a proper role to play. I know I'm making a rotten fist of it now, I'm failing him and I hadn't meant to. But I'm so bored. Bored, bored, bored!'

Outside Tom was waiting. This was the evening Penelope had planned for so long. Yet now she knelt in front of Sylvia, holding tight to her hands.

'You were on the stage when Ken fell in love with you. Do what you do best, Sylvia. That's war work, too, you know. When the lads come on leave they need to be entertained. I don't mean be disloyal to Ken.' Her dark eyes twinkled. 'Be like me, home on the tube to my solitary little bedroom. No kicking up my heels on the town.'

'I hate my own company. But, Penny, I must do something or I'll end up resenting Ken as much as I do the rest of his narrow-minded family. It's not fair on him, and it's not fair on me.'

A hammering on the door put an end to her tale of woe. 'Come on, you two. Haven't you put Perce to bed yet, Pen?'

'Coming! I'm just ready.'

Later they'd go back to Sylvia's problems, but the next two hours were given over to enjoying themselves. When Tom suggested he take them both to supper, she insisted they should be her guests. It was Tom's second visit to her

West End hotel, for instead of him sharing her cab as far as Baker Street tube station as he'd expected, when she'd heard that he planned to see Penny's performance that evening she'd had a much better idea. Tea at her hotel, the luxury of bone china, cucumber sandwiches, even cream cake; the hut he'd shared with thirty-one other new recruits was like a fading dream. A leisurely tea, they'd sat over it for more than an hour, yet the time had flown. For months they'd both been starved of the joy of talking 'theatre', of common interests, shared experiences, reminiscences of backstages good and bad; in the unexpectedness of the meeting laughter had come easily. No wonder time had flown. Then she'd left him ensconced behind *The Times*, a glass of whisky in his hand, while she'd gone to dress for the theatre.

Some of the gaiety was with them still, but underlying it now was what Sylvia had told of her life in the Yorkshire village where she felt she had no place.

'I've been telling Sylvia she ought not to be wasting herself,' Penelope told Tom, sure of his support as she picked up the threads of her earlier conversation with her friend. 'If you'd made a place for yourself in the village before Ken went away, if you'd ever shared a life with him there, then I can see you'd feel you ought to stay there. But it's like digging up a flower and re-planting it in a vegetable patch, not even watering it, then wondering why it wilts.'

'Wilts? Do I look as if I'm wilting?'

'You look lovely, you know you do.' There was no jealousy in Penelope. 'What do your parents say?'

'Terry and Christine went to America last year. They were there when the war started so they didn't come back. I don't think they ever will. They're not on the stage any more, they're running a dancing school. What do you think, Tom? You're a man, and a soldier too, you must see it from Ken's point of view. I'm just so useless there,

I'll never fit in. It all seems such a waste of time, and no one up there likes me or wants me.'

'Have you told him, asked him what he thinks about you dancing again? Some men might not like other chaps to be drooling at their wives . . . you know what I mean. It's different for Pen, a scraggy underfed young brother. She won't get the British Army lusting after Perce!'

They all laughed at the idea of it, but Penelope wouldn't have been human if she'd not felt a pang of hurt at his words.

'I know! I've hit on an idea!' They both listened to him. It was like that golden summer all over again. The sudden ideas had usually been his; it had been Tom who'd made the rules and led the way. 'You and Pen find a place to live. A couple of rooms, enough space so that when I get leave I can fit in too. If Captain Ken comes home, then I take it you'd go to Yorkshire. You'll soon pick up some work. Sylvia Carstairs was doing well enough, and married to the boss of Henry Greenaway's they'll all jump at engaging you.'

'I'd still be Carstairs. Ken's people wouldn't like their name dragged into show business. Even Ken wouldn't, I don't think, although he was proud enough that I was doing well.'

'Right. That's settled then.' Tom had taken it in hand and there was no turning back. 'I'm home for a week. Leave it to me, I'll find you a place. I'd like to know before I go back where you're going to be living.'

They clinked their glasses together, drank to their reunion, to their future. The evening's aura of happiness cast a reassuringly rosy glow on all they planned.

CHAPTER SIX

Their door was at the back of the building, opening onto a narrow alleyway. Tonight there was no moon but hurrying from the underground station Penelope's eyes had become accustomed to the darkness. And even if they hadn't, she would have known when she reached home by the stench of rotting vegetables. The shortages of war meant that nothing must be wasted. Each morning she and Sylvia heard the metal bin being dragged to the end of the alley for collection.

It was as good as an alarm clock to the girls.

'The pig man cometh,' one of them would shout to the other, knowing neither who he was nor yet where he and his pigs came from. Indeed, pigs seemed a far cry from Hampstead, but who could say in these days of emergency? It was an unspoken rule that whoever heard him and shouted first was privileged to stay in bed while the other got up to light the gas under the kettle.

Avoiding the bin of vegetation, Penelope ran her fingers down the door to find the keyhole.

Someone was coming! Groping along the alley from the street, someone not familiar with pitfalls – the gully that ran down the middle of the passageway, the position of the drains. It was obvious from the shuffling step that whoever was coming was a stranger. It took a lot to frighten Penelope but to be followed down a dark passageway leading to nowhere is enough to frighten the stoutest heart, and as she fumbled to get the key in the lock hers was hammering a wild tattoo.

'Can you help me? I want to find the person who lives over the top of the vegetable shop. Do you know which is the right door?'

Alf! Here in London! It was six weeks since she'd heard from Muriel that he'd been sent home to a military hospital in Kent. 'Not much hurt, his mother tells me . . .' Three times Penelope had written to him in Challington with 'Please forward' on the envelopes, but there'd been no word in reply.

'Alf! I've been so worried about you! Why didn't you answer my letters. I wanted to come to the hospital.'

'Pen! It was you all the time!'

Leaving the key in the lock she turned back to steer him safely past the ingredients for tomorrow's pig swill. Her hug was as natural as if he'd been a brother. He held her tight, so tight that he crushed the breath out of her, not kissing her, but rubbing his cheek against her, almost knocking her velvet beret from her short straight hair.

'They've given me a twenty-four hour pass. I came straight here, Pen, I had to see you . . .'

Something was wrong, she sensed it. What use is a twenty-four hour pass to a man, and why had he rushed here to her? Did he know something about Tom? Did he want to be the one to break the news to her? But how could he? Tom was in a transport camp in Yorkshire. News of him would hardly filter through to a military hospital in the south east.

'Come inside. Sylvia will be home soon, but I'm always first back.'

'Sylvia Carstairs. I'd forgotten she'd be there. Pen – let's just walk.'

Yes, something was very wrong with Alf.

'All right. Wait for me just inside the door. I'll run upstairs and leave a note for her, tell her you'll be coming back for the night. Then we'll go for a walk by ourselves.' She wished she could see his face. Perhaps she was imagining things, perhaps if it weren't for this wretched darkness everywhere she'd see the familiar lop-sided smile.

Upstairs she drew the thick curtains, lit the gas and on the back of an envelope wrote: 'Can I share your bed

138

tonight? Alf is here, he has a twenty-four hour pass. We may be late home.'

Back up the alley, she holding his hand and leading the way, round the corner and up towards the High Street. Neither of them spoke. His grip on her fingers was like a vice.

'Can you walk as far as the Heath?' she asked him after a few minutes. 'I don't know where you were hurt, why you were in hospital. Tell me if you'd rather we found somewhere to sit.'

'I can walk anywhere. I wasn't wounded. Reckon I'm going barmy.'

They stopped and turned to look at each other, although it was memory rather than sight that gave their faces any familiarity.

'Wouldn't be the first,' he went on. 'Barmy, loopy.'

'Let's walk. You're not barmy, Alf. Bright as a button, you always were.'

He was silent. Somewhere in the distance she heard a clock strike midnight. She linked her arm through his, but still he gripped her fingers. Then he walked on, hurrying now; it was as if they had to get to the Heath. Only then would the dam burst and he'd be able to talk. That there was any truth in what he'd said didn't seriously enter her head.

At last habitation was behind them.

'Stop now.' He pulled her down so that they both sat on the ground. 'Listen . . . just quiet . . . still.'

'Umph. You can almost hear the silence, Alf.' Then after a while: 'Tell me. Tell me all the dreadful things.' He sat in his favourite position, his hands clasped round his drawn-up knees. She could see his outline clearly now, no bigger than he had been as a boy. No bigger, but so much older in what life had done to him. Her hand reached towards him, touching his thin wrist.

He made no answer and it was a minute before she heard the small, stifled sound. Alf was crying. Not loud,

139

harsh sobs of hysteria; tears of utter misery. She cradled him in her arms, ran her fingers through his straw-coloured curly hair as if he were a child.

'Sometimes it can help to talk, Alf. I'd never repeat anything – not even to Tom.'

' . . . rather I'd been killed . . . all over . . . finished.'

'No, Alf, no. One day it'll be behind us. You'll come home. You've done your share out there. Perhaps they won't send you back to France.'

'I can't go back . . . Pen, I can't . . . can't eat, can't sleep . . . ' He gulped, wiping his sleeve across his eyes. 'And when I do, where am I? Climbing through barbed wire, Jerry hurling shells, men yelling . . . then I wake up and find all the row was just me. Tied me down at the hospital, they did, Pen. They had to tie me down. Look at me.' Even his voice wasn't his own. It was higher, frightened, breaking on a squeak that took her back to when they'd all been children. Tom's voice had broken and settled into manhood; Alf's had wavered unable to make up its mind, dropping to his boots and squeaking by turn. No wonder now her own face was wet with tears. 'Look at me! Pride of the Army, aren't I? Snivelling, blubbing – '

'You, Alf, and lots of men older and tougher than we are. I'm crying too, crying for all the misery, all the lost hopes. Crying 'cos I can't bear to see you miserable.'

He pulled away from her.

'I don't care what I tell you now, I can say anything.' He'd obviously reached rock bottom. 'I want to tell you. Since we were at Merchant Hill, Pen, I've always loved you. There'll never be another girl for me. If I'd had you to come back to then I could have stood it all. I'd have been brave, strong . . . '

In these minutes they'd not looked beyond themselves. It wasn't so unusual to see the beam of a searchlight scanning the dark night sky. Now though there was an added sound. Gunfire!

140

'Jerry!' came Alf's strangled cry.

'Up there. See, they've got the Zeppelin in the beam! It won't drop bombs here, we're too far out. Who'd want to bomb the Heath?'

The gunfire was louder. Alf turned to her, buried his head against her. The Zeppelin had passed overhead. Perhaps it had already unloaded its bombs and was making for home. Somebody's husband, somebody's son . . . Would he get away over the coast? And if he'd dropped his bombs, how many lives had he shattered? It was as if in Alf's broken spirit Penelope held every mother's son. She felt his hands moving on her, and still she cradled him; in her he found something to cling to, he needed to reassure himself. How he trembled still.

Giving of herself so generously, she wasn't prepared. Alf was a shrimp, he always had been, but he was stronger than she for all that. She found herself pushed backward to the ground, the weight of him on top of her. Her first instinct was to fight, to cast him off. But she didn't. She lay quite still, the only sound now the choking sobs that he didn't try to stem. His hands moved on her, outlining her breasts, the top of her legs. Whether he would have had the strength to rape her she couldn't guess, for suddenly she knew she had nothing to fight. Alf was a dreamer, for years she had been his dream. But his tears were for so many things: he was like a child, a lost, impotent child. And that she recognized it must have stripped him of his last vestige of manhood.

For a long time they stayed on the Heath. Gradually his crying stopped and only then did he tell her something of what life had been like in the trenches. There was a new stillness about him. Perhaps talking about it would lay the ghosts that haunted him, help him find the courage to look for a ray of hope in the future.

"Poor Alf. He's not going barmy. Just wishes he could, rather than face it all. Please look after him." She gazed at the infinite darkness of the starless sky, the same sky

141

here as over the men in those rat-infested trenches; the same sky as over Tom; over Sylvia's Ken; over whoever was in that Zeppelin. So vast, so unchanging, part of an omnipotence that was beyond her understanding.

Sylvia was already in bed when they got home. And the next morning Alf left early to catch the 9.35 train out of Waterloo. They kept him in hospital another six weeks, then gave him seven days' embarkation leave. This time he went home to Challington.

Sylvia's return to the stage had done nothing to endear her to her in-laws. One of a glittering cast in the revue 'Rings on Her Fingers', her foot was firmly back on the ladder of success. And despite reading between the lines of his family's letters, Ken was proud of his showgirl wife, proud to see the admiring – and envious, he was sure – glances his brother officers gave the photograph beside his camp bed.

It was a week before Christmas when his letter came telling her that he expected to be home on leave during the first week in the New Year. Fourteen days! He'd come to London to collect her and then they'd go north together. Most of the letter Sylvia kept to herself, but the plans for leave she read aloud to Penelope.

'A nice New Year present for your understudy. Is she good?'

'Not bad.' Then with an exaggerated swagger in her voice and a twinkle in her eyes: 'Can't be compared with the real thing, of course. Fancy, Penny, a whole fortnight's holiday together! It's funny, but I don't even mind going up to face that miserable lot now. Once Ken's there it'll be fine – and I've made my stand, they know I'm not staying.'

Tom hadn't been home since the summer when he'd found them these rooms over the greengrocer's shop in Hampstead. He was due for seven days in February. There would be no understudy for Penelope though. For them leave wasn't a time for holidaying; it was a reassurance that their future was waiting for them, a chance for him to get backstage again.

Christmas had never been a high point in Penelope's life. As a child she'd dreaded it for it had always put that worried look on Pa's face. Instead of being a period of plenty for them it had been a time when no one wanted odd jobs done. She'd sensed his mood, felt his frustration as the two of them had played games or walked on the beach with Chummy. For his sake she'd always pretended Christmas was splendid, everything she wanted.

After Muriel came on the scene it had been different. At Alexandra Square she'd felt the warmth of the festival. Even that was a long time ago now. Since she'd left home, she and Tom had enjoyed it together. In the boarding house would be a special dinner of prime beef and mince pies; childish games, laughter, community singing, a bottle or two of port to lubricate their throats. 'A day off with knobs on,' that had been Tom's idea of Christmas Day.

And this year? No house full of lodgers to share the fun. But then how could this year be the same? What sort of a Christmas would Tom be having? Would it be a day off with knobs on or just another day? And what about Ken – and Alf, back again now in France?

'Ken was out there last Christmas.' Sylvia was sitting in front of the mirror, pinning up her lovely auburn hair, trying to find a new style that would make Ken take one look at her and fall in love all over again. 'What do you think, Penny? Pulled off my face? I'm not sure.'

'It suits you well enough. But men like something softer, I know Tom does. It seems more feminine. Not like mine!'

'Umph, perhaps you're right.' And out came the pins so that she could start again. 'Yes, I was saying – Ken told me about it. He wasn't right up at the front, but he'd spoken to people who were, people who said that our soldiers and theirs crawled out of the trenches, actually

143

met on No Man's Land between them. All the fighting stopped. Like a game at half time.'

'I know. Alf told me. But that was last year. Will it be the same this time? After all that's happened in this dreadful year, can they just cry "Pax" for a few hours – then go and throw shells at each other the next day? Human beings can't behave like that, surely. Alf said that last year on Christmas night when it was quiet if they came outside the trenches and listened they could hear the Germans singing carols – some of them the same tunes as our Tommies recognized. Then a few hours later they were blowing each other to bits.'

'Poor little Alf. He wasn't cut out for soldiering. Anyway a lot goes on that doesn't seem human these days. To call a halt even for a day must be better than nothing.' She finished tweaking her hair, satisfied with the result. 'What shall I wear when he comes to collect me?' she mused, not expecting an answer. 'Oh, Penny, don't you just long for the lovely coloured silks there used to be? I often think of the beautiful shimmering gowns Christine wore. Probably still does. And there she is, middle-aged. Colours can't look as good on her as they would on me.' Then, as an afterthought: 'Or on you. It's all very well for people who had lots of clothes before things were in short supply, but that's no use to us. When had we the chance to build a good wardrobe? I bet Ken's sisters have clothes for every occasion,' then she giggled, 'and look frights in all of them. Honestly, Ethel's the eldest, she must be about forty – and I should think she said goodbye to her shape too long ago to remember. She's like Humpty Dumpty without his smile. Next is Désirée. How she came by a name like that I can't think, for anyone less desirable I can't imagine . . .'

Penelope only half listened to her. The first time Ken's family had been described to her she'd tried to find excuses for them, even to persuade Sylvia the trouble came because none of them understood each other. If they did, then they'd learn to get on. These months that she and Sylvia had lived together had shown her just how hurt her friend had been by her in-laws' treatment. So now she was prepared to listen, to build in Sylvia the confidence to withstand their cutting comments.

As they came to Christmas the festival was pushed into insignificance by Ken's leave, coming so soon after. It would be more than ten months since he had returned to France at the end of their brief honeymoon. Now Sylvia was as excited as any bride.

'You know, Pen, what's so thrilling is that all the time I'm with him, I'm getting to know him.'

Penelope laughed. 'A bit late for that!'

'No, it's what's so wonderful. I know I love him, I fell in love with him the first time I set eyes on him. He said it was like that for him too. But there's so much that's a closed book. And it's exciting.'

'There are so many different ways of loving.' Into Penelope's mind came a picture of Muriel, her hands plunged deep into a bowl of washing up. 'The gifts the Wise Men brought were all different.'

'What?'

'It's not a bit like that with Tom and me. We must be able to read each other's thoughts after all these years. I love Tom like I love sunshine and rain and songs and laughing. As if he's knitted into my ordinary everydays.'

'I suppose I ought to envy you that. But I don't. What was it you meant just now about the Wise Men?'

That had been on the morning of Christmas Eve. The next day there was no pig man to rouse them. It must have been the spirit of this special day, a holiday with knobs on, that woke Penelope. Under her pillow she had a present for Sylvia, a silver picture frame, wrapped in tissue paper and tied with a red ribbon.

"Happy Christmas, Tom – and Alf, oh please make it be a happy one for Alf! Please don't let him be frightened of all the dreadful things. It's not a bit of good saying

145

please don't let there be dreadful things, 'cos I know there will be. Happy Christmas, Pa. Please make him stay at home today with Mother and the others. They'll play games, I expect, the kitchen will be full of lovely smells . . . "

She got out of bed and pulled on her wrap, then went through to the sitting room. This was in the front of the building, looking out on to the High Street. The window drew her, as if she expected to see something different about the scene on this special day. The postman was coming. This morning as he put the letters through each door he gave a loud rat-a-tat on the knocker. 'Happy Christmas,' it seemed to say. On up the High Street then round the corner. She listened. If there was post for them he'd bring it down the alley to their door. A minute went by, a long minute as she waited. Rat-a-tat came his greeting.

She ran down the stairs to see four or five letters on the mat, but before she picked them up she opened the door and shouted after his retreating figure.

'Thank you. Happy Christmas!'

Tom's writing was on the top envelope; one for Sylvia with a Field Post Office postmark; one from Challington in a childish hand, it must be from Merrick; another Field Post Office, this time for her, Alf's hand unmistakably.

Back upstairs she collected the present from under her pillow and took the mail into Sylvia's room.

'Happy Christmas!'

'Umph, and you, Happy Christmas!' Sylvia rubbed her fists against her eyes, then opened them wide and sat up foraging under her bed for a parcel. 'Letters too. Lovely! But first let's have presents. I'm dying to give you this. Go on, open it.'

The parcel was heavy, it had to be dragged out from under the bed. Silence in the room except for the rustle of tissue that wrapped the picture frame and the tearing of

146

the large sheet of brown paper on the mysterious outsize gift.

A canteen of silver cutlery, enough for twelve people.

'For me? But Sylvia . . . oh, they're beautiful. But they must have – '

'Cost more money than I've got?' Sylvia giggled. 'They're for you and Tom. So that when you're rich and famous and have dinner parties your table looks fit for a prince. I wrote and told Ken what I wanted to give you. He arranged it. See, on the handles, H. Greenaway & Son – the old firm! My picture frame's lovely. I'm going to keep it until after our leave, we'll go and get a new photograph taken. Now that Ken's a Major he'll have a crown on his uniform. I'll wait for that, not put the wedding one in.'

The letters were on the bed. They didn't rush to look at them. Knives, forks, spoons, ladles – these things were too lovely to be hurried. Never had Penelope dreamed of owning anything so elegant. A little ghost from long ago was peeping over her shoulder . . . Tuppence, dreaming of curtains at the kitchen window . . . Never had her plans encompassed such beauty as this.

'Penny, what's the matter? You don't like them?'

Those 'silly tears' blurred her vision and trickled down her cheeks. 'It's 'cos I like them so much – 'cos you gave them to me – just happy – ' She gulped, digging into the pocket of her wrap for a handkerchief.

'Come on, let's read our letters. Oh – ' Sylvia's tone changed – 'I thought it was from Ken. Whoever else do I know in France?' She knew no one else. They looked at each other helplessly, frightened of the next step. 'Open it for me, Pen, use one of your knives to tear the envelope.' Sylvia swallowed, her mouth dry. 'See who it's from . . . '

She watched as Penelope scanned the single sheet. She didn't need to ask.

'It's from his Colonel. He says . . . oh, Sylvie . . . ' What he said could come later. Sylvia didn't need to be told.

Silently, the girls clung to each other. Tragedy wasn't something that just happened to other people; on that Christmas morning the war was brought right home to them.

'The show must come first.' It was the maxim Sylvia had been reared on. Her grief was real enough. In losing Ken she'd lost all the dreams that had been weaving their coloured pictures in her mind. She'd been so certain of the way things would go. By the time the war was over he would hold an even higher rank; the name of Sylvia Carstairs would be well-known; her retirement from the theatre would be noted in the newspapers; she would go with him wherever his regiment went, acclaimed, respected. And in her dreams she saw herself and Ken, each constantly discovering some new facet in the other to enrich their relationship, keep their romance young and new.

There seemed no stemming her tears until by evening she was drained, her face white, eyelids so swollen that it must have hurt her to open them at all.

'Penny, I don't want to lie there all on my own. Can't we make room for us both in my bed?' Then with an effort at normality: 'You're only a shrimp.'

'Plenty of room. If you really want me with you.'

She felt helpless. What was there to say? How could she, even with her special affection for her 'chosen sister', get near to sharing the journey Sylvia must make on her own? Once in the single bed they lay very straight, Penelope right on the edge. Here in the darkness at least she could give a physical comfort. She could hold her friend's hand, make her know she'd never be alone; she could listen, stay awake and listen.

Whatever she expected, it wasn't what Sylvia said.

'Do you think my face will look all right by tomorrow? Never had eyes so sore, they really hurt. I'll look such a fright tomorrow night.'

'But, Sylvie, you're not dancing tomorrow! They

148

wouldn't expect you to be there. Let your understudy go on.'

'She'll not get her chance now, will she?' Her voice croaked, but staring hard at the dark ceiling she made herself say it: 'Now that Ken won't be coming, I shan't go on leave.'

How could Penelope stay perched on the edge of the bed? Instinctively she turned, her thin arms pulling Sylvia close.

'Give yourself time, Sylvie.'

'To sit here thinking, picturing what might have been? Or out of respect for the dead?' Her voice was hard. 'What about the last week? Every night I've danced, I've laughed, I've been happy. And all that time Ken was dead.'

There was no answer to that. They neither of them knew how to deal with the stark reality of the news.

'Time, you say. But time for what? Pen, I don't know how I can go on as I was, not now. "Rings on Her Fingers" was such fun, and always like a backdrop was the thought of it leading on to all the exciting things Ken and I would have ahead of us. Take away the backdrop and the show loses all its colour. I can't just go on.'

'Let your understudy have her chance, give yourself a week or two. And you can't talk of just going on, as if you were still the Sylvia Carstairs you used to be. You were Ken's wife. Perhaps you'll have to go north. Solicitors, all that sort of thing.'

Sylvia had always been the worldly one, but from the long silence it seemed she hadn't thought of Ken's vow: '. . . with my worldly goods I thee endow.'

After a minute she said: 'In the morning I'll have to write to Ethel and Désirée. They're not next of kin, they won't have heard. What a slap in the eye for them.'

Penelope's hold on her tightened. Tonight at least Sylvia was entitled to lash out. Who could blame her?

The next night she was back on the stage, her grease-paint a little thicker, her smile set a fraction too brightly.

'The show must come first.' And making herself live up to the code she'd never questioned helped her through those first hours. Just one concession she allowed: she let Penelope go to the theatre in the afternoon and take the news. Sylvia was realist enough to admit to herself that there was disappointment mingled with her grief. It was thoughts of the future she had lost, as much as of Ken himself, that still had the power to bring tears to her eyes. She'd spent the morning rinsing her eyes in cold water every quarter of an hour or so. The first sting of tears and all the good she'd done would be gone. Concentration on her dance routine, the sound of the audience's applause, the rush to change from one costume to the next – these things were her salvation.

A week later a long parchment envelope was dropped through the letter box. Even before she opened it she could tell by the quality of the paper that the letter conveyed something important. It was from Messrs Hamworthy and Dryson, Solicitors to the late Major Kenneth Greenaway. On the 4th January Penelope went with Sylvia to Euston, waving her on her way, wishing desperately that she could have gone to Yorkshire with her. What a cruel twist of fate! Today, the 4th January, the very day that Ken had been expected in London, and Sylvia must travel alone to face his inhospitable family.

But of such is life in the theatre made. Penelope had commitments, it didn't enter either her head or Sylvia's that these might be broken. For Sylvia it was different; she had an understudy waiting eagerly each night to step out of the chorus line. Her tragedy was Tilly Tidmarsh's chance. The show must go on, the audience mustn't be disappointed.

It was the following weekend. Resolutely Sylvia was going through papers in the bureau, ruthlessly burning anything that seemed to her to have no relevance.

'There's nothing here that needs you. Run off back to

150

London and the bright lights,' Ethel had told her. That had been on her first evening here, when her sister-in-law had come calling. Word had quickly spread that that red-headed tart Ken had been bewitched by had been seen going into Mr Hamworthy's office. The two sisters had no need to put into words what they felt – but they were wise enough to keep their opinions to themselves in front of Ethel's husband, Frederick Hurd.

Just like Ken's younger brother, Robert, Frederick was involved with the family business. That Ken had chosen a career in the Army had been headstrong and selfish, or so thought both his sisters. Ethel was the eldest in the family, now a badly preserved forty-three, shapeless and unsmiling; Désirée was two years younger, a thin woman whose swarthy skin and poor teeth gave the impression that she and soapy water weren't too well acquainted. Ken would have been thirty-five had he lived until March, and far behind was Robert, twenty years younger than Ethel, an afterthought when their mother had believed her childbearing days were over. And perhaps they had been, for she'd lost her life in the effort, leaving the baby to be cared for by his two grown-up sisters. Away at boarding school Ken had been too old to come in for their attentions, too young to be independent. But right from the start he'd been determined that a soldier's life was for him. Had his father lived long enough to take him seriously and appreciate that he had no intention of coming into the family business, he might have left things differently. As it was Ken had been his main beneficiary, the chief shareholder in the family business; Ken had inherited the family house; Ken had inherited two-thirds of his father's substantial capital, the remaining third to go to Robert.

All that was years ago. When Ethel had married Frederick Hurd, manager of the company, they had taken a large house on the edge of the village, Désirée carrying on the running of the family home in Ken's absence – and bringing up young Robert. Three years ago Robert, always the

151

apple of his sisters' eyes, had fallen in love with the daughter of the minister from the chapel, a plump little blonde called Charity. Charity had loved him too, not wisely but too well. A hurried wedding had been enough to alert the local gossips, and they hadn't been disappointed. Seven months later Charlotte had been born. Robert brought Charity to live in the old family home, an arrangement that suited Ken well enough until the day came – if ever it did – when he wanted it himself. Désirée moved to live with Ethel and Frederick. Their daily life turned once again on oiled wheels.

There hadn't been a cloud on the horizon until Ken had been hooked and landed by that red-headed tart. Nothing but a disgrace, and when there was no one to hear them, Ethel and Désirée voiced their opinions forcefully. To think of a Greenaway parading her body, any Tom, Dick and Harry paying his money to feast his eyes while she kicked her legs about! What dear Mother would have said they dreaded to think. Least of all to Ken did they give vent to their feelings, but there are things women don't need to say to each other. From day one Sylvia had understood the silent message they passed to her. With Ken there it hadn't mattered. After he'd gone, leaving her to face the village on her own, her unhappiness had come far more from her longing to get back to the life she knew than from anything his sisters could say. Plump Charity, good-natured Robert and a rather whining Charlotte hadn't moved out, and why should they? The two girls hadn't much in common, but from Sylvia's point of view in those miserable months before she'd decided to visit London, met up with Penny and Tom and been persuaded to work again, any company had been better than none.

But what should she do now? The house was hers. Everything that had been Ken's was hers. If she were wise she'd sell it. Have her dividends from the company sent to her, invest her not inconsiderable fortune . . . 'Go back to the bright lights, leave us to sort it all out' . . . Oh yes,

152

they'd like to get their hands on everything that had been Ken's.

For a minute she sat idly gazing into the flickering flames of the fire, lost in thoughts that gave her no pleasure. If his sisters had really cared for him, if they'd loved him like they obviously did Robert . . . but they hadn't. They'd not even pretended to. It wasn't Robert's fault, and it certainly wasn't Charity's, she was as soft as butter and hadn't the guile to outwit anyone, not even young Charlotte. So, oughtn't she to let them go on living in the house?

'You've got a visitor, Sylvia.' Charity opened the door of the sitting room. 'No one we know round here. Said to tell you it was Tom.' Neither had she the guile to hide her curiosity.

'Tom!' Sylvia rammed the pile of papers back in the bureau and closed it. 'I'm in here, Tom. Oh, you don't know how good it is to see you!' A familiar face, someone belonging to her own life, and even more important, someone belonging to Penny. It was as if she'd been floundering out of her depth and suddenly been thrown a lifeline.

'I was just going to take Charlotte for a walk. I expect you'd rather I stayed here now, wouldn't you, Sylvia? I don't mind, truly.'

'Whatever for?'

'I just thought – well, you know how people love to gossip. But I suppose it's all right. Babs is in the kitchen. Shall I tell her to bring you some tea?'

'No, you just forget all about me and have your walk. Tom, I'd forgotten you were in Yorkshire.' And Charity was out in the hall, the door closed on her.

'I had a letter from Pen yesterday saying you'd had to come up. I came as soon as I could get a few hours off. I've never been in business, but sometimes two heads are wiser than one. Anyway it evens things out a bit to have someone from your own camp. Bet you're swamped, aren't you? Who was the chubby blonde? Pretty face.'

153

'She's a sister-in-law. Ken's brother's wife. Charlotte's her little girl. They live here, you see. Ken was always happy for them to, he only came home on leave.'

'He's in the Army, this brother?'

She shook her head.

'I imagine they feel the family was represented by Ken. *If* they thought about it. The village and the business is about as far as their horizon stretches.'

'Umph, well, I suppose this brother is head of the business, Ken always being in the Army.'

She stooped down to shovel more coal on the fire.

'Robert's always worked there. Then there's Ethel's husband, he's managed it for years. But,' she stood up to face him, a mischievous twinkle suddenly dancing in her blue eyes, reminding him of the child he'd first met on the beach all those years before, 'I suppose in fact *I* am head of the company now. Can't you just picture their faces if I presented myself to preside over their next meeting!'

'Nothing stopping you. Why don't you?'

'Because I'm a dancing girl, that's why.'

Tom had spoken the truth; he knew nothing about business, no more than she did herself. Somehow that didn't matter. As he'd said earlier, he was someone from her own camp. He'd dealt with the landlord and a place for Penny and her to live, he'd not wasted any time about that. So she repeated to him all she'd learned from Mr Hamworthy. Some of the burden of responsibility seemed to be lifted even though he'd done no more than listen. And much of the warmth in having him here came from the fact that Penny had asked him to come. Sylvia wasn't alone.

Ten days later she came back to London. On the surface she appeared to have closed the door on that brief spell of happiness she'd found with Ken, and on the unfriendliness of his sisters too. Only Penelope, who knew her so much better than most, understood that she could never pick up the threads and pretend the pattern hadn't changed. Tilly Tidmarsh was making a success of her part in the revue, the show would go on equally well with or without Sylvia. She seemed restless, yet in no hurry to rush back to work. Such is the freedom money brings!

Already January was three-quarters gone. She'd been back nearly a week on the night Penelope came home to find her engrossed in a new copy of *Stage*, kneeling on a chair with the paper spread open on the table in front of her.

'I've got it, Penny! I thought you'd never get here, I've been bursting to tell you. I'm not going back to "Rings on Her Fingers". Listen – or have you read it? They want more entertainers to travel to service bases, giving shows for the troops. Now, that's proper war work.'

These months had been so good, living together, coming home sometimes to sit talking into the early hours. Penelope tried to hide her disappointment.

'But this would be your base? You'd still get back here often, Sylvia . . . ?' She needed reassurance.

'Yes, I'd travel from here as often as I could. Silly I suppose when I've got the best chance in the West End I've ever had. But somehow, Pen, I feel I ought to do this. I'm so afraid – I'd only ever say this to you – if I just go on as if the war hasn't touched me, it'll be as if I'd never been married to Ken at all. To entertain the soldiers is – is – well, he was a soldier.'

'I do understand, truly I do. I think if Tom were abroad I'd do the same. But while he can sometimes get home I want him to be able to come to the theatre, feel he belongs still.'

Another turning point in the road they travelled. Poring over the paper together they both felt it: this decision was the right one.

Sylvia wasn't one to let the grass grow under her feet. By the time Tom came home for his week's leave she was already gone, a card from her on the mantelpiece saying she was somewhere in Lancashire. For the first time

Penelope and Tom found themselves on their own, not sharing a room in a lodging house but in what they liked to think of as their own home. It was when Penny dragged the large canteen of cutlery out of the built-in cupboard to show him that he first mentioned Sylvia and his visit.

'She's quite an heiress, you know, Pen. I had a meal there with her. The table was full of silver, not just cutlery but the lot!' He picked up a knife and read the inscription on the blade. 'Yes, Sylvia's never going to be short of a bob. But what's the good of it? Won't buy happiness.'

And as if to demonstrate the happiness that can't be bought he pulled her towards him and covered her mouth with his. A few months in the Army had taught him more than how to present arms! Tom had listened to the earthy talk amongst the men, listened, learnt and remembered. He was no longer the uncertain fumbling boy he had been when instinct had been their only guide.

Has time any true meaning? That single week in February was so soon just a memory. For months Penelope had made his leave the peak she'd striven for. She'd bought a new blouse, not in the drab unbleached white, nor grey or black as so many of the clothes were now that dyes were hard to come by, but a rich red silk. But had she worn it? No. 'I'm keeping it for February,' she'd said as she'd hung it in her cupboard, somehow having it there bringing the magic seven days nearer. And so with everything that hinted at being a treat, all of it 'for February'.

Then it was over, Tom gone. But still he was to be in England, living under canvas at a transit camp on Salisbury Plain.

Sylvia had taken the hardest knock. From it she was determined to build up an immunity, make sure nothing could hurt her again. She was away far more than she was at home; Perce moved around the circuit, first in one variety theatre, then another; Tom was safe from danger. Over those next few months if life held no highspots at least it spared them the troughs. It was so easy to fall into the trap of feeling untouchable.

It was Sylvia who brought the news. She'd been away for a week or more, to Plymouth, to Tidworth and, as it now transpired, to that camp where Tom was based.

'You saw Tom?'

'Yes.' Clearly something was wrong.

'Is anything the matter with him? I had a letter yesterday, he sounded fine. What is it? There's something, isn't there?' Penelope was suddenly frightened, her brown eyes could never mask her feelings. But what could there be to be frightened of?

'Tom's all right. No, that's not true. He's dreadfully upset. Penny, he'd had a letter from his mother yesterday morning – it was yesterday I saw him – she'd seen Alf's mother, it seems.'

'No . . . oh, no!' And she had believed herself to be so snug and safe.

'He's not killed if that's what you think. He's been injured – burnt – his mother had been to see him and apparently she was in a dreadful state when she talked to Mrs Beasley.'

'But he's alive.' And wasn't that everything? In her relief Penelope could think no further than that. For a second she'd thought he'd been killed, but he hadn't. Wounded. Perhaps he'd be sent home, back to Challington where he'd be safe, away from everything he'd hated so much . . .

'They'll try and patch him up – but, Penny, it's his face. He'll look dreadful, he must do. As Tom says, poor Alf, still alive but wouldn't it have been kinder if a shell had finished it for him? I've seen one or two of them about, these men who've had the flesh burnt off their faces. You must have, too. Would you want to face every day looking like an ogre?'

'Stop it! An ogre is something evil. Alf is good, the best person I've ever known, he wouldn't hurt a soul . . . ' This time they weren't 'silly' tears, they were tears of com-

157

passion, of love. Just as Alf had understood the little girl she'd once been, so now her heart reached out to understand what he must be suffering. Poor, frightened Alf.

'Tom knew you'd be upset. Well, we all are. He is, dreadfully. They've been pals all their lives. It hits home when it's someone you care about.'

Those last few words wiped out what she'd said before, about being better if Alf had been killed. ' . . . someone you care about.' And who should know better than her?

'Wouldn't be better if they'd killed him,' Penelope sobbed, 'he's still here, doesn't matter if he looks different.'

Sylvia held her close.

All Penelope's letters went unanswered. Was it that he couldn't write? But if that were so, a nurse would have done it for him. Couldn't? There's more to writing a letter than penning the words. His silence told her as much as any outpouring could have.

After three months in hospital Alf was sent home. It was Muriel who wrote to tell Penelope. Not that she'd seen him, but she'd met his mother on another of her regular trips to the fishmarket.

'Poor woman, she's at her wit's end with him. He won't go outside the door, hides himself in his room most of the time. There's just him and his mother but I suppose he's feared of visitors calling, feels safer out of the way. Just won't see anyone. And from the years it's put on to her, my guess would be his scars aren't pretty. Poor boy. Nice little chap, always was. Where's it all going to end? Makes you frightened to think. Or even, will it ever end at all? Seems no sign of it. You must take comfort from knowing Tom is safe in England – but be proud that he volunteered himself. Still, from now on the lads will get sent for, whether they want to or not. Conscription, isn't that what they call it?

'The only other bit of news from here is that Hawkins & Blacker, you remember the metal box factory up the

158

top end of Prospect Street, it's been turned over to making some sort of weapons – or parts for a weapon. I can't see they'll be turning out anything very mighty, the place isn't that vast. Your father said it's all come about because of this new Ministry of Munitions that's been set up. Anyway, don't they always say there's a silver lining to every cloud? He went along there and straight away got taken on. It's mostly women who do the actual work, but of course each shift has a man in charge, an overseer they call him. Naturally enough the man who interviewed could see that Ollie was the sort he wanted.

'He's in charge of about twenty – "my girls" he calls them, pleased as Punch with himself, and so he should be! The bottom's fallen right out of the holiday trade, but this is better, Ollie is earning regular money, and I've taken four of his "girls" as permanent boarders. But no one will be sleeping in your attic, Penny love, and if you can get down your bed is always waiting. I was just thinking of young Alf. You and he were always good pals. Perhaps he might not hide himself away from you like he does everyone else. Pity Tom's been sent so far north again, if they'd left him on Salisbury Plain he might have managed to get down. It's what poor young Alf must need, someone he can talk to.'

That was at the end of September. The following Sunday saw Penelope on the train heading towards the south coast. 'The show must come first', Sylvia's often repeated creed echoed in her mind. Settling into the corner seat, Penelope considered what she'd done. Never before had she cancelled a booking; previously it would have been unthinkable. Perhaps all those years ago Sylvia had been right, perhaps she wasn't a proper stage person, perhaps she never could be. She loved to dance and sing, she loved the relationship between herself and her audience. How often had she heard it said that great artistes were always petrified before a performance; didn't that prove she wasn't a real artiste? Her only emotion as she waited in the wings was excitement, eagerness to get out there, to make contact with a new set of people. Each performance was just that bit different, not because of her but because of the audience. She couldn't imagine doing anything else. But none of it was important compared with comforting someone she loved. She wished Tom could have come too. However badly burnt Alf had been, she had to make him realize that the three of them needed each other. They were like a triangle; each side propped the other two up.

She meant to stay a whole week, there was no need to rush. But until she'd talked to Alf she wasn't ready to go to Alexandra Square. He was at the front of her mind all the time.

'Penelope Drew!' In her surprise the old name slipped out as his mother answered the knock on her front door.

'I've come specially to see Alf, Mrs Johnson.'

'He won't . . . it's no use calling him.' Her voice was just a whisper. 'Hour after hour he just sits there in his room, hardly eats enough to keep alive.' Her already bloodshot eyes filled with ready tears. 'Such a happy little boy he used to be – bloody war, damned bloody war!' She was as small and gentle as one would have expected Alf's mother to be. Words so out of character were evidence that she, too, was one of the casualties of war.

Penelope nodded. 'Don't tell him I'm here,' she whispered in reply. 'Just let me creep up and open his door.'

'You don't know what you're saying. You won't know him.'

'He's the same underneath. The last time we talked it was in the dark. He's the same, whatever he looks like.'

'I don't know – if he sees the shock on your face – not a bit like him, his mouth pulled right down on one side, his eye too – ' She was wringing her hands, chewing her lip, her words rushing out in a whisper that was barely audible. 'Makes him look evil – my little Alf – '

'Now you've warned me, I'm not going to be shocked. Just let me try. Which room?'

160

'Up the stairs, then along to the right. End room. Looks out on to next-door's wall. No view. He won't move. Just sits.'

Penelope was already creeping up the stairs.

She didn't knock, just quietly opened the door. On the far wall was a table. Alf sat at it, his back towards the door.

'I'm not hungry, Mum.'

'Good. I've not brought you anything to eat.'

He started as if at an electric current but didn't look round. 'What do you want? Don't come in, Pen. She'd no right to let you in. Damn it, why doesn't she listen! Just go. Please, Pen. Clear off.'

She tried to answer him but was afraid to speak. "I mustn't cry. Please, I mustn't cry. Let me sound strong and firm. I don't even know what to say to help him – but I must. Please if You exist at all, please help me. But if You exist, why did You let it happen? Alf never did a mean thing in his life."

Thoughts rushed so quickly one after another that they were hardly coherent. Penelope crossed the room to stand just behind Alf's chair. Even backview he was changed. From one side of his head the fair curls were gone; his scalp looked like withered parchment.

'Remember that night on the Heath, Alf? Remember the Zeppelin? Suppose one night coming home from the theatre I got hurt in an air-raid, badly hurt.' Then, taking all her courage, 'So that I looked different – '

'Just clear off, Pen.'

She put her hands on his shoulders. 'No, Alf, listen to me. If I did, would you feel changed towards me? Or if Tom comes home maimed' – "Please, I'm not tempting fate, I'm only trying to help Alf, don't let anything happen to Tom" – 'would it make any difference to what we feel for him? You know it wouldn't.'

She mustn't flinch, she mustn't fail him. It was Alf, she must hang on to that. Whatever he looked like, he was

161

Alf. She moved to stand in front of him. He couldn't meet her eyes and in that first instant she was thankful. She'd told herself she was ready for anything – but there was no way of preparing herself for what she now saw.

Downstairs his mother could wait no longer. She crept halfway up and listened. Voices, Penelope's, Alf's too . . . up two more stairs . . . not that she could hear what was being said, but the tone was reassuring. Nearly twenty minutes young Penelope Drew had been in there with him. Hark! Couldn't be sure whether he was crying or laughing. Either was better than sitting as if he were made of stone. Ah, movements . . . she was just going. Alf's mother hadn't moved down those stairs so fast for a long time!

'Half-past nine then. Outside the boatyard.'

'Pen – oh, just – thanks. Sorry I made a scene.'

She went back to him and dropped a kiss on the parchment-like scalp. 'You'd earned the right to a scene, Alf Johnson! Don't be late this evening – promise?'

She felt as though she were made of feathers. For a moment she stood still, staring blindly at the waves breaking on the shingle. It wasn't like an illness . . . from an illness there was hope of recovery . . . but not for Alf. She thought of his tears there in the darkness on Hampstead Heath. Had some inner sense warned him? She strained towards the normality of home, yet dreaded it too; the familiar comfort seemed a betrayal, as if she wanted to forget that Alf sat in his bedroom like a prisoner in a cell. Her thoughts were with him still as she walked on, going to the back gate in Prospect Street.

Before she reached the kitchen door she could hear voices, laughter. Of course, there were women lodging there who worked at the munitions factory. The sound alienated them from her. It was as if they neither knew nor cared that Alf's life had been shattered. Mid-sentence they all stopped talking as she walked in, the sudden silence unnatural.

'Penny love,' Muriel dumped the saucepan back on the range, 'we've been looking out for you this half hour or more. Was your train late?'

' . . . went to see Alf . . . '

Muriel's bearlike embrace was an answer in itself.

'Go and tell your father, Merrick, say Penny's come. We'll have our dinenr and you can all get to know each other as you eat.' Nothing like good food to make folk feel right with the world, that had always been Muriel's philosophy.

In most households carving was the man's job. Not here. It probably had something to do with experience, for while Muriel had learnt how to slice the beef thinly in the hotel kitchen, the sort of fare Oliver and 'Tuppence' had shared hadn't given him much practice. At Clifford House it had been a job he'd gladly passed up, especially in the summers when the dining room was full. Now the four boarders lived as if they were part of the family, all eating at the large wooden kitchen table.

'What do you think of my war effort, Penny, eh?' As Muriel had said in her letter, Oliver was pleased as Punch with himself. 'Your mother's told you all about it, I suppose.'

Before Penelope had a chance to answer, one of the girls chimed in with: 'War effort! Keeping us lot under the whip, and he calls it a war effort! You love every moment of it, you know you do.' It was the one they called Mavis who spoke, a woman probably in her late twenties, not a beauty by any means if beauty is judged by face alone; her rounded bosom, trim waist and neat ankles hinted that the best of her could only be guessed at.

Of the four there was one who was quite lovely, her skin clear and soft as a child's, her eyes a blue that was almost violet, her dark curly hair pinned up to expose a delicate neck. Yes, she was exquisite. But when Muriel

163

passed her her plate, Penelope could only guess at her 'Thank you'. 'Han hu' was how it sounded to her ears. No one else seemed to notice. Bruce helped himself to a spoonful of potato and passed the dish to her, taking the 'Han hu' in his stride. Other than that she said nothing.

The other two were sisters. They told Penelope about themselves during dinner. Just as Muriel had known it would, good food set them all at their ease. Peggy and Cath Carling, middle-aged, unmarried, sufficient unto themselves — and each other. Until this last year they'd had parents to care for but: 'When Father died and Mother and her sister decided to share a roof, we thought — we thought — freedom at last! Isn't that right, Peggy?'

'Right indeed. A life of our own. One thing this war has done is given women a chance to stand on their feet. Without the war, where would we have been given work together, earned enough to be able to go on living together?'

'Quite a Pankhurst, this one,' Oliver teased, egging Peggy on.

'And so I am! So we both are! If women are good enough to help win the war, then they're good enough to help sort things out once peacetime comes.' Peggy swallowed the bait and the good-tempered teasing went on, Oliver enjoying himself with 'his girls'. Not that he took their nonsense seriously. Could anyone imagine consideration being given to allowing housewives to have a say in who sat on the local council — let alone who was sent up to Parliament! It was a bit of fun, though, seeing the way they got so hot around the collar about it all.

'Alf let you in did he, love?' Muriel asked in an undertone from her seat beside Penelope. 'Very bad, is he?'

'He'll always be just Alf.' Her voice was unnaturally harsh, as if defying anyone to tell her different. 'If only he'd face going out, so that people could get used to what's happened to him. Lose a leg or an arm, it's hard, but no one is embarrassed. So why should they be because it's his face?'

'It's early days yet,' was all Muriel said, but Penelope knew she understood and cared.

Across the table the lovely dark-haired girl wasn't saying anything.

'Have some more veg, Emma love?'

'No, han hu, I'h hlen-y.'

'Elbows off the table, Mandy. What about you. More?'

'Thanks Mum.'

Knives and forks clattered, conversation hummed. No, nothing had changed, nothing ever could where Muriel reigned supreme. Penelope stayed there until the following Saturday. Not once did she get Alf out in daylight, but every evening they met and walked on the sand if the tide was low enough, on the promenade if it wasn't.

It was Friday afternoon. Ollie and the girls were at the factory, the older children about due home from school and young Bruce busy folding paper to try and make a boat.

'Mother, I've always hated matchmakers, I'm not trying to start a romance – but – '

'You been thinking along the same lines as I have.'

'Even after just a few days, I find I understand almost all the time. Has she always . . . ?' With Bruce there they talked in innuendoes.

Muriel touched the roof of her own mouth. 'Not got . . . Now fold it over this way, look, Bruce, like this . . . ' His curiosity gave way to more important things.

'You going out as usual this evening?' Which Penelope took to mean, 'Where will you be?'

'Yes. The tide's up so we shall walk on the promenade. Thank goodness for the blackout or we might not be out at all.'

'Umph. Well, I'll put my thinking cap on. That's lovely, Bruce duckie. Now, be a good chap and run up to my bedroom, will you? I've come down without a hanky.'

'They may not even like each other,' Penelope said as the little boy clumped up the stairs. She wasn't sure they had the right to play at God. 'But they won't know if they don't have the chance to find out. So, we'll see what we can do for them.'

'Poor little souls, the pair of them. Oh, but we're lucky, Penny love, that we are.'

Emma had heard something of the talk about Alf; Penny had told him about the four boarders: the self-sufficient sisters, the would-be flirt Mavis, and beautiful Emma who had no hard roof to her mouth. That night fate played into the matchmakers' hands. As she and Alf strode along the dark Promenade, the wind gusting in their faces from the south west, she heard footsteps hurrying towards them.

Too dark to see but Emma had been sent on an urgent mission; she had to overcome her dread of speaking to strangers. 'Hhenn – Hhenny – ish hu?'

'Yes, it's me. Emma, what are you doing all on your own in the dark?'

'M-rel seg M-hish Schar- shee hu.'

It's unlikely that Alf understood the message, but Penelope followed Muriel's mind. Mrs Sharp wanted to see her before she went back to London. And they were almost on the corner of the Promenade and Kings Road. She could be there in two or three minutes if she hurried.

'Alf, this is Emma. She lives at Clifford House. You remember I told you there are four girls there from the weapons place? Emma, this is Alf. Alf, don't go away, I'll only be ten minutes or so, it's no distance to her house from here.' She took the bull by the horns. "I don't mean to interfere, but they're both so lonely, they're both dears . . . " 'Wait in the shelter for me, both of you. *Please*.' And before Emma could form a word of protest or Alf could collect his wits enough to think of a means of escape, she was gone. In fact she'd already called on Ethel Sharp earlier in the week, but having got them together she was determined to leave them long enough to

166

overcome the first hurdles. So a 'quick goodbye 'cos I'm off in the morning' stretched into twenty minutes and a cup of tea.

'Well?' Muriel asked her later, at their first opportunity to speak privately.

'I don't know. I think they were talking – but they didn't give me any hint. He brought us right to the door, like he always walks home with me. Well, I couldn't ask . . . '

Muriel chuckled. 'That'll teach us to mind our own affairs. Pity if it didn't come off, though. You'll see him to say goodbye. Perhaps he'll say something then.'

All he said was: 'Emma's one of a family of five, did you know? Like the birds do, they threw the weak one out of the nest. Poor kid.'

'Emma's no weakling. She's had too much to overcome to be that.'

No doubt he'd think about it after she'd gone.

Down the dark alley, grope for the keyhole, unlock the door . . . there was something depressing about going home to her empty rooms. But halfway up the stairs she noticed a ridge of light showing at the bottom of the sitting room door.

'Sylvia. Is that you? I wasn't expecting you for a fort-night yet.'

The door opened. Tom!

'There's a welcome for a chap! Home to an empty house.' He hugged her.

'When did you come? Why didn't you let me know? I'd have come back sooner. How long have you got?' Questions rushed out one after another, not giving him time to answer. She buffeted her head against him, raised her arms and twined them around his neck. At Challington she'd been so aware of a cloud of sadness. Not now. This moment was enough to convince her all heaven had drop-ped at her feet.

'I've got 'til tomorrow evening. I arrived last night, but

it was no use thinking of coming on down to Challington. I knew you were leaving sometime today and might have passed you in the train. I had seventy-two hours. I'll have to leave tomorrow evening.'

'All that way for seventy-two hours!'

'It's embarkation leave, Pen.'

The clouds were back, clouds so black the future was lost in them. It couldn't be happening, not to her and Tom! Those dreadful stories she'd heard about the mud, the rats, the stench of death. Frightened to speak, she buried her face against his chest.

'It's not France. I've been issued with what they call tropical kit – shorts, lightweight shirts.' He tipped her face up towards his, winking at her. 'I cut quite a dash in them. Wait 'til those eastern lovelies feast their eyes on my manly beauty.'

The only war zone she'd heard anything of at first hand had been Europe. Tropical kit meant sunshine, sunshine meant happiness. The 'silly tears' were her safety valve. As he kissed her, he tasted the salt of them.

So much had to be crowded in to this brief time. Perhaps they were closest when they talked of Alf.

'I ought to have got down to see him.'

'In seventy-two hours, how could you? It's not fair, Tom, such a little time. Whoever heard of only three days for embarkation! And goodness knows when you'll get leave, long enough leave to come home again, I mean.'

'No, Pen. Probably not 'til it's over. I can't see them sending me all that way for seven days. Have to indulge in the flesh pots of Cairo.' But she knew as well as he did that he was boosting his own confidence. 'And talking of flesh pots . . . '

She needed no encouraging. Tonight was all they had. Tomorrow was uncertain, neither wanted to think of it.

When Ken had been killed Sylvia had found her strength in the show, the applause, the smell of the greasepaint.

168

Now that Tom had gone, Penelope sought to find hers in the same way. It had never failed her before. But for the first time that empathy between herself and her audience eluded her. She understood why it was that Sylvia had wanted to entertain the troops. Easy for her, though. She could afford to offer her services free. Earning a living was no longer a necessity for her.

It was while swaying homeward in the tube train that Penny made her decision. She'd book herself half the time in the theatres, earn enough to keep her going but leave weeks free when she could visit the camps, introducing Perce to the soldiers. Her mind made up, she felt happier and wished she'd had someone to tell. Another week and Sylvia would be home. They'd make plans then, perhaps even travel together.

Down the alley, avoiding the pig bin; indoors, groping on the doormat for post that wasn't there; then upstairs, humming under her breath at the prospect of a war effort of her own. In the dark she drew the curtains, felt for the matches . . . the same routine every night. It was only when the gas was lit that she turned, pulling off her tammy.

'Sylvia! Sylvia, wake up! What's wrong? Are you ill?' Such silly questions, for one look at the figure stretched out on the chesterfield gave her all the answers. Sylvia, her face the colour of parchment, her bright hair fallen loose from its pins, her skirt undone at the waist. On the table by her side was a half full glass of water and two paper sachets, both empty.

CHAPTER SEVEN

Penelope felt, besides fright, a feeling of failure that Sylvia could have believed herself to be so alone that she was driven to this.

'No . . . no!' For a moment horror drained Penelope of all ability to think clearly. 'No.' She bit her knuckles, her teeth leaving marks, yet didn't even realize she did it. "Why's she done it? My fault? She hadn't anyone but me – I must have failed her – I ought to have stayed with her – didn't know – "

Instinct rather than reason brought her to her knees by Sylvia's side.

'Sylvia! What've you done? What've I gotta do?' She might have been a child again, helpless. The pale face, the colourless lips, told her that Sylvia must have been lying like this for hours. She would be cold, her skin would feel different. Penelope reached out a small hand, put it tenderly on her friend's forehead. But it wasn't cold! It was warm, sticky to the touch. 'Sylvia, listen to me! Oh, hear me, please hear me!'

This time she took the lifeless shoulders. Whatever she expected it wasn't this: though still not awake the inert body was suddenly convulsed, the movement and the choking sound bringing all Penelope's reason back to her. Whatever it was those sachets had contained, it wasn't too late. She pulled Sylvia towards her, bending her forward, thumping her back. The only thing to hand was the aspidistra that had come to them with the furnished rooms. The way Penelope yanked it, pot and all, and dropped it on to the floor could have done it no good but its china container had never been put to better use. The shaking had dislodged the powders Sylvia's body rebelled against;

the thumping did the rest. By now her bloodshot eyes were open. She was beyond caring; she vomited, she cried, she moaned.

Then at last, weak and breathless, she rested her head against Penelope.

'You'll soon feel better.'

'Penny . . . so ashamed . . . ' she wept. 'Dear, good Pen. Don't know what to do . . . so ashamed.'

'It's me should be ashamed. I should have understood better how much you missed him.'

Silence. The seconds ticked by.

'I took that stuff – a backstreet chemist gave it to me – '

'Thank God you've got rid of it.'

'Might have worked . . . he told me it might . . . I mixed it together, ergot and quinine.' She forced herself to sit up straight, and to meet Penelope's eyes. 'I've got pregnant, that's why I took it. Trying to get right again. Don't know what else to do.' She must have seen the bewilderment in Penelope's earnest expression.

'But, Sylvia, I didn't know there was anyone. Why didn't you tell me? Did you expect I'd think you were being disloyal to Ken or what? Are you going to marr–'

'No. He's married already. Anyway it's all finished, all over. Shouldn't have happened. So ashamed – was lonely and – '

'Well, you're not to be lonely now, and not about this. Look, Sylvia, what's done is done. We have to look forward. We'll work it out, we'll make plans together. You're not on your own.'

'You don't know what you're suggesting.' Another burst of determination. 'I won't have it. I'll find a way. There are things a girl can do. Someone once told me how they'd poked about with a knitting needle. I've even tried that. Oh, Pen, you've no idea. It's so degrading, so humiliating.' She did up her skirt and pushed her tousled hair off her face. 'Do you believe in God?'

171

'Suppose so. I don't know about a gentleman with a beard, flowing robes, all that – but, yes, I believe in something. Well, you have to, Sylvia, or how can you tell right from wrong?'

'Perhaps that's the trouble. I didn't, did I? Perhaps the devil got me into his camp.'

'What rubbish you talk! Anyway, as if the devil has anything to do with a tiny, innocent baby.'

'Don't, I'm not having it! I swear I won't!'

That night, as she had when they'd heard about Ken, Penelope offered to share Sylvia's bed. This time though the offer was refused. It was almost as if Sylvia was frightened of the confidences night might tempt from her.

Nothing made so much as a dent in her determination. Somehow she would get rid of the baby. It was about a fortnight later that Penelope came home on the Saturday night to find her in a state of excitement.

'I'm going to be all right! I told you I would!'

'After all these weeks. Did it just start?'

'No, silly. I'm nearly three months, how could it just start like that? No, I've been told about someone. I went to a chemist – oh, don't look worried, not the one down the road, he wouldn't have helped. This was a sleazy little place. I thought it looked promisingly mucky, just right for what I was after and no one would have known me there. The man said he had a friend. I'm to go tomorrow evening. Penny, you will come with me, won't you? I purposely made it Sunday so that you could come. He said I may feel a bit rough after, I ought not to travel by myself.'

Penelope chewed her lip, her dark eyes saying so much more than her simple: 'Are you really sure? It's dangerous, Sylvia.'

'He won't get caught. He says not to have a cabby wait outside or anything like that – '

'I mean dangerous for you. What if something goes

172

wrong, or if you find after this you can never have any babies?'

'Please, Penny. You can't make me change my mind. I will *not* have this child. I've made a big enough mess already. If you don't want to come, then I'll go on my own. I've got the money in my purse all ready.' And when Penelope heard how much, it did nothing to quieten her fears.

Of course Penelope went with her. They walked from the underground station, finding their way in the dark to the back door of the chemist's shop. It was opened to their knock and they were ushered into a passageway. Only then was a candle lit, by an elderly man, round-shouldered and with a shuffling step.

'Your friend can't go up with you,' he told Sylvia. 'She can wait down here with me, he'll want you on your own. You brought the cash, did you? Likes his payment before he starts work.'

'Do I give it to him, or to you?'

'It's not for me to take money from his clients. Got my reputation to guard.' He handed Sylvia the candle. 'Top of the stairs then on the left. You'll find him ready. We'll wait below, in the shop. Have to manage without a lamp, wouldn't do to pull the blinds down on a Sunday evening. All the busybodies would wonder what was going on.'

Even his voice made Penelope's flesh creep. She could picture the pair of them sharing their illegal bounty after closing the door on their departing 'client'. And what sort of a state would Sylvia be in to walk to the main road and find a cab? She remembered when Merrick and Mandy had been born, she'd seen the midwife clearing up. So much blood. But three months couldn't be the same – or could it? Birth was natural, there was nothing natural about what was happening to Sylvia. Supposing she fainted out there in the street, haemorrhaged and a doctor had to be sent for. What tale would they tell?

"Please, please don't let anything dreadful happen to

Sylvia. The man was far more wicked. He had a wife. How would his wife feel now if she knew what was going on upstairs? Whatever happens, it's always the woman who has to be the one to forgive. So many different ways of loving, or so Mother says. What a dreadful mess it all is — because of the war, because of Ken being killed, husbands and wives parted. But I'm a wife too, and so lucky. Mother said that too. Please keep Tom safe, bring him back so that things can be like they used to be. Is that selfish, to ask for what I want for us when Sylvia ought to be having all my thoughts?"

The silence was rent by a scream from the room above, followed by a 'Tut — tut — tut' from the chemist. Then again all was quiet. The seconds ticked to minutes. Movements overhead, another stifled yell that made Penelope jump to her feet.

'Just you be patient. These things don't shift that easy.' Then, with a mirthless chuckle, 'It's not like having your corns cut, y'know. Your friend wants to be sure. He's come 'specially to see to her. No good asking him back for a second bite at the cherry.'

Penelope shivered.

Another minute and they heard the upstairs door open, then footsteps on the stairs.

'Best go out the back way, same as you came in. And now, mind what I told you, miss. No mentioning my name to your friends. I don't make a habit of this sort of thing. Like I said, I've got a reputation to consider.'

Penelope had become used to the dark. She could clearly see Sylvia in outline, standing gripping the doorway to the passage. She wanted them just to be gone.

Once out in the street they walked with arms linked, Sylvia bent forward with pain so that anyone might have thought her no taller than Penelope.

'Try not to think about it. It's done now. A good night's sleep and you'll wake up feeling like a new person.' Penelope hoped what she said was sensible, but how could they know what to expect?

'Not over. He says,' Sylvia caught her breath, 'says – what he's done will make it start. Says – this is normal. By tonight or – or by tomorrow – it'll come away.'

'But the pains?'

'Like – going into – labour – he says.' She didn't seem to have the breath to speak. 'Oh, Pen, can we stop – minute.' She held on to the post on an unlit streetlight.

Even taking a cab all the way the journey seemed endless. In fact they would have been much quicker on the underground, neither horse nor cabman were in any hurry to get to Hampstead. But at least in the carriage they were alone, there was no one to hear the occasional whimper. The journey was long – but nothing compared to the seemingly endless night that followed.

'If having a baby's like this, then I'll never have one, never, never,' Sylvia moaned.

'Try and bear it. I remember when Mother was having the babies, the pains beforehand were awful.'

'But it's getting worse.'

'Hers did too, the pains came nearer and nearer together – then the babies got born. Try doing what she had to, Sylvia, try pushing hard.'

She pushed, she strained, she wept – until finally, in the same single bed with Penelope holding her close, they both slept.

Morning brought no sign of the promised miscarriage. Even the pains had eased, leaving Sylvia feeling bruised and sore. But perhaps that was what they must expect, perhaps that was the way it happened. They looked at each other helplessly, not knowing. And there was no one to ask.

Days went by. There was no suggestion that Sylvia should find work. In fact, because she so obviously avoided mentioning plans for the future, Penelope didn't press her. But they couldn't bury their heads in the sand for ever.

Before long she would show signs of pregnancy. No more did she say: 'I will not have a baby,' but she didn't even mention it at all, any more than she mentioned the rogue who had brought her hope and humiliation, and taken her money for nothing. Penelope hated leaving her so much alone. Each night she knew a surge of thankfulness to get home and find her still there. But she wasn't blind.

Knitting needles but no wool. Sylvia was no knitter – and she'd mentioned those needles before. What went on during her lonely evenings? Penelope saw the half empty bottle of liquid paraffin. Then there was the night that she came home to find Sylvia with her head on the table, sound asleep, the room smelling of gin. The undiluted spirit wasn't without its effect, it made her ill all night; but it did nothing to dislodge the baby. How much more could she take? And then what? Penelope longed to tell someone, she must tell someone. Never before had she kept a secret from Tom, but loyalty to Sylvia still prevented her mentioning it in her letters. That's when she made her decision. It was as if a great weight had been lifted. The next night, alone in her dressing room between her first and second appearance, she took a pencil and a sheet of paper. That was on a Friday.

Monday teatime, after Penelope had left for the theatre, a letter dropped on to the mat addressed to Mrs Greenaway.

'I remember when you and Penny were thick as thieves all those years ago, and what a happy summer it was. I'm no good at putting things down on paper. If you were here I could talk to you, make you know that there's a place for you. I dare say you think I'm too old to be able to understand – but give me a try, why don't you? An extra is always welcome here, and as for a babbee, nothing I love more. This war's got a lot to answer for. You losing your man. Nothing knocks one off course more than troubles. But, Sylvia love, this babbee won't be a trouble, it'll bring you love. They all do, given half a chance.

176

'Now what I suggest is that you come down to Challington just as soon as you like. What you tell folk is up to you. I don't think even Ollie took that much notice of dates, he might remember your husband was lost – that sounds a hard thing to say, that he might remember, but his life is full and busy, it wouldn't mean that he wouldn't be sorry – but he wouldn't remember when. You're a widow, expecting a babbee. If you want to let it go at that, then it's up to you. Far as I'm concerned, you're the little dancing girl used to kick her legs about with Penny in the yard here, and if you want to come home to us, then that's where you should be.'

Penelope had had no doubts of Muriel's reaction to her cry for help, but she had grave doubts of Sylvia's acceptance that someone else be let in on her secret. To share it was to accept. And did she accept? Even now her very silence was evidence that she didn't.

That Monday, just as every other night, Penelope stepped carefully round the pig bucket and let herself in.

'I'm home, Sylvia. Are you still up?' "Please let her answer, don't let her have done anything . . . "

'Pen, I've had a letter from Challington.'

'I had to tell her, there wasn't anyone else I could tell. And we can't just go on keeping it to ourselves.' Two at a time she ran up the stairs. 'I felt so helpless. Trust her, Sylvia, she's kind – she understands things without being told.'

Her brown eyes pleaded; she was so afraid Sylvia would think that handing the problem over to someone else meant that she didn't care.

But there was no anger, no hurt, only a suppressed excitement in Sylvia's tone. 'Here, read what she says. Home, she calls it. Come home to us, she says.' She tried to smile but her eyes were brimming. She'd steeled herself to accept criticism. Heaven knows, she hated herself; each day she hated herself more. Kindness such as Muriel had shown caught her unprepared, found a chink in her armour.

'And you'll go to her?'

Sylvia nodded.

'I'll come down with you on Sunday.'

'No, there's no need. I've already written to her and found out the train times and everything. My bags are almost ready. I'm going straight away, 10.40 from Charing Cross tomorrow morning. You'll come and see me off, won't you?'

This was a new Sylvia – or perhaps it was the old one now the weight of worry was lifted. Almost as if these last weeks had never been, they sat up late talking, not about babies but about themselves, the theatre, the concert parties that went to entertain the troops.

'The pigman will be round before we get our beauty sleep.' Sylvia laughed, standing up and stretching her arms high. Night hawks though they were, it was long past time for bed. Then, as Penelope turned the gas tap and threw the room into darkness, she went on: 'I can't believe it, you know, Pen. One extra makes no difference . . . nothing better than a baby in the house . . . '

'You couldn't be scared with Muriel there. And when it's all over we'll work out the next step.'

The room was in darkness now, somehow emphasizing the long pause before Sylvia answered: 'If this baby lives at all – and if the God you say you believe in really exists then it won't – it'll be a monster, it won't be normal. How could it, after all I've tried? Not just the man we went to.' Penelope felt the shiver in her voice as she remembered. 'You don't know what it's been like, night after night here on my own. I've tried all ways, drunk the filthiest concoctions 'til I wonder I've any inside left. It can't be normal, by now it must be a freak – '

'Your baby will be perfect, of course it will.'

'My baby! Don't call it that. It's just something I have to endure 'til it's over. Like a tumour that's growing there.

178

I hate it, Pen. I can't help it.' With the thick curtains pulled the room was pitch black. 'I want just to get it over, to get back to work.'

'Sylvia, tell me one thing – honestly, tell me. Were you in love with this married man? And him – was he in love with you?' She'd no right to ask. Yet it was the one thing she'd never understood, she who believed she knew Sylvia almost as well as she knew herself.

Again a pause. She wished she'd not probed.

'Yes. I didn't know love could be like it. But it's over, finished. For him and for me too. I told you – he's married, not to some dragon who doesn't care. If she were, then it would be easy. What we had was wonderful, as if we compressed a lifetime's loving into those few months.'

In the dark only Penelope knew how the 'silly tears' flooded her dark eyes, tears of compassion for the girl she loved so dearly. 'But the baby, his baby, how can you not want it?'

'How can I make you understand? My love was just for him, his for me. The baby was sent to spite us, to punish me for taking what wasn't mine. It was what we dreaded, always we tried to be careful.'

'Does he know?'

'I told you – it's over. Having to get fat and ugly, not being able to dance, all that is my punishment. But another five months and it'll be finished. Come on, let's go to bed. We've had such a lovely evening' (Evening? It must have been nearly midnight when it started), 'don't let's spoil it.'

The night was short, they had to be at Charing Cross in time for Sylvia to catch the 10.40 to Challington. That guilt she'd talked about had apparently been pushed comfortably to the back of her mind. It was Penelope who was more troubled as she made her way home. Ought she to have let Muriel be dragged in? Was it fair? She had her own life, a husband, three children, four lodgers; willingly she'd give shelter and care to 'the little dancing girl' she remembered from that happy summer, help her through

179

her confinement. But what then? Penelope could already see the writing on the wall.

In normal circumstances it wouldn't have taken Sylvia long to become bored with life in the household at Clifford House. But there was nothing normal about seeing her lovely figure change. She'd been given Penelope's attic bedroom, the room that had heard so many of their confidences, had witnessed their vows of faithfulness to each other. 'We'll share all the good times and all the bad ones too.'

Just as she did so often in the afternoon, today she retreated up to its privacy. To rest, she said. To rest her body perhaps, but not her mind. Lying flat on the bed staring at the sloping ceiling with its window carrying her vision upwards to the grey scudding clouds, the already fading daylight, her thoughts carried her back to those months of such happiness she hadn't known existed. If it hadn't been for the mess it had led her to, would she still have had this sense of shame and guilt? No. The answer was clear. He'd vowed to be faithful to the girl he'd married – but had she been robbed of anything that had been hers? No. Again the answer was clear. And Ken? Had it changed her towards Ken's memory? No. Loving him had been the path that had led to – oh, to so much more. She hadn't known . . . Perhaps if Ken had lived she never would have known. They would have had good years together, travelled, probably had a family . . . always getting to know each other a little better. Ah, but that was the difference. Memory carried her back to the March evening when she'd danced at an army camp, the temporary stage at one end of a huge tent. That had been the beginning. Or had it? Had it begun long ago, been lying dormant in her subconscious? In his too?

A tender smile played around the corners of her mouth, her eyes closed. Timed perfectly to bring her feet firmly back to the ground came the first flutter of movement within her; as if some satanic power prodded her, reminded her that it had the final victory. Her eyes shot open. Penny's room. A room where the spirit of those two children still lived. It was here she'd taught Penny her first few ballet steps, using the iron rail at the foot of the bed for support. Taught her? More likely snatched the opportunity to show off to her how much she knew herself. If was here they'd come on that very first afternoon, both of them recognizing from the start that they'd found a friend. And here too that she'd heard about the concertina; over by the chest of drawers was the loose floorboard, she could see Penny now, easing it up and bringing out her precious hoard of coppers wrapped in the muffler. Poor little Penny, so determined that one day she'd buy the concertina back. But the boys had got it for her, the boys had always cared. Penny, Tom and Alf . . . Penny, Alf, Tom and her. When you're young everything is so simple.

She must have been more tired than she'd realized. A few minutes later Muriel plodded up with a cup of tea, saw she was asleep and crept back down again.

Sylvia gone, Tom too far away to get to England for his leaves, the rooms in Hampstead had lost their appeal. Penelope could never be a homemaker simply for the sake of it. To her, 'home' came from the people who lived there, not from the furnishings, the curtains, vases of flowers, plants (and certainly not from the dust-harbouring aspidistra that had been re-housed in its china container and stuffed on top of the what-not out of the way).

In the girls' dressing room she was busy grease-painting her face. She'd give up the rooms, find a place in a lodging house again. At least she wouldn't have to bother about housekeeping; there would be warmth and light to welcome her back at the end of the day.

' . . . what you said you wanted. Come with us, Pen.'

'Sorry?' She hadn't heard a word.

'Peter Somerville – you were with him once, weren't

you? He's getting up concert parties to send to France. Don't expect there'll be much money in it – after all it's war effort, they don't pay the poor Tommies a fortune, do they? What do you say? He's auditioning on Wednesday and Thursday mornings at the Fortune Theatre.'

'You bet!'

'Pity your Tom's not in France, you might have seen him. Not that we shall be near the fighting lines. You may be sure we shall only see the lads who are kicking up their heels on leave.'

'Suits me,' one of the chorus chortled, and from the remarks that followed it suited all of them. What better than a chance to help the boys on leave to have a good time? They'd have a bit of spare money in their pocket, coming from the fighting, and they'd need all the cheerful company they could find. The chorus consisted of anything from aspiring beginners to some who looked better with the help of greasepaint and footlights, the first bloom of youth having faded. One thing they had in common was that they were fancy free and ready for anything. They'd kick their legs and waggle their behinds with that bit of extra panache. If anyone deserved it it was 'Tommy Atkins'.

'Peter Somerville might not want your sort of act, Penny. Trench-weary soldiers aren't going to be uplifted to see Young Perce at home waiting for Tommy. Rubbing salt in the wound.'

Penelope was afraid there might be truth in the warning. That night she sat up late even by the standards set when Sylvia had been with her. The act must be changed. Still, she was Perce. After all, as Tom had said, she had to 'keep his side of the bed warm' 'til he came back. But the spirit of Perce had to have a remould. As she sat and scribbled a new script to work on (not that it was ever more than a guide, each performance being different), Perce was transformed. No longer the young lad, alone and lonely without Tommy; it was time he felt himself ready to join in the fray. Too young, they said, but his spirit was strong. A fresh dance routine, based on army drilling while a Union Jack was raised. The audience would love that! She was a natural comedienne; how she'd mock as she goose-stepped, her legs kicking high. Alone over the greengrocery shop, the furniture pushed back to the walls, she worked out what she would do, laughing to herself. Yes, they'd love that too! Then into her Cossack dancing she'd bring all the acrobatic tricks she'd learnt and practised. No longer the pranks of a mischievous urchin, but managing to convey the strength and courage of Perce and the thousands of other young lads at home, anxious to take up cudgels. She wouldn't sing about keeping the 'home fires burning', she'd tell them she was ready to 'pack up her troubles in her old kit bag'. Then there was a ballad people were beginning to sing, 'When the Bells of Peace Ring Out'. She'd buy the music in the morning, learn the words ready for Wednesday when she saw Peter Somerville.

Ready for bed at last, she undrew the curtains. Wearing only a nightgown, her bare feet on the cold lino, she looked out over the rooftops. The full moon, hidden by thick cloud, cast an eerie light over the scene below.

"He liked me before – Peter Somerville, I mean – please let him like me again." Perhaps it was her silent communication with the night sky that sent her thoughts tumbling back just about a year, to the night she'd sat on Hampstead Heath with Alf. "I want to go to France – I don't see there's any sense in feeling I'm doing it for Alf, but in a way it's true. Poor Alf! I do wish he and Emma could fall in love. Surely it would be wonderful for both of them – wouldn't it? He'd understand her clearly – the children can – he would if he could learn to love her. And she'd see him, the real him. Isn't that so? Isn't that what love is all about?" She turned away from the window, then back again to add: "And Tom – please keep Tom safe. And make Sylvia's baby normal."

The next morning she went out to buy her song sheet.

'When the Bells of Peace Ring Out', words and music by Laurence McLeod.

Five years on from that first audition, but Peter Somerville had recognized her as a winner then and so he did now. She was to leave on her first tour at the end of February.

'You mustn't worry about Perce and me,' she wrote to Tom that Wednesday afternoon, 'I think from what I can gather we'll be visiting leave centres, hospitals. But I don't know where and of course I won't be able to give you an address. So, Tom, can you write to me at Alexandra Square? I shall make that my base – at least I shall leave the things there that I can't carry. Pa will send letters on to me if I'm able to tell them where. We are giving up the rooms in Hampstead, it's silly to keep them empty.

'I've not mentioned this before, it's something only Sylvia and I knew about until recently. Tom, she is expecting a baby. You're not to jump to conclusions and think badly of her. She must have been lonely and sad after Ken died – anyway this wasn't some light affair she had. He was a married man, fond of his wife – but they fell in love. It's so dreadfully sad. Poor Sylvia, she would have made a good wife to Ken, but she lost him; then she found her real love, and she lost him too. She's very 'closed up' about it all, but from the few times she has talked I know how deep down unhappy she is. We're so lucky, you and me. Once the war's over and you come back we know just how it's going to be. We fit together like a hand and glove. Do you know what one of my favourite 'getting to sleep' games is? I imagine the first night the curtain goes up on Tommy and Perce. I plan the act, think how we'll play it. Somehow doing that makes it feel closer, as if I'm expecting you back soon. And going to sleep with happy thoughts in my mind sometimes makes me dream such real dreams that you're home.

'I was telling you about Sylvia. She's gone to stay with Mother until after the baby is born. It's due in April, so I expect she'll be there until later in the summer, before she feels ready to go back to her dancing. When that time comes – oh, so many things might have happened. Perhaps peace will have come, perhaps you'll be coming home. Anyway, as I said to Sylvia, we'll take the next step when we get to it. Between us we'll manage . . . '

The rest of the letter was personal, much the same as wives everywhere were writing, full of dreams, hopes, plans for that 'one day' they all waited for.

Before she joined Peter Somerville's concert party she had a few days in Challington. A canvas camp bed was put up for her in the old room that this time she and Sylvia would be sharing.

Just as she'd known it would, the house had absorbed Sylvia, slotted her into the pattern.

'It's working out all right, is it, Mother? She looks ever so fit.' A few moments alone with Muriel was a rarity. Penelope had to come straight to the point.

'It's the right age to have babies. But, Penny love, she's not softening towards it, not one bit. Almost like it's got nothing to do with her. An illness he's got to go through, won't be better 'til it's over.' Then, her face lighting into a look of pleasure: 'Tell you what, though – every night, wet or dry, out goes Emma.'

There Muriel stood, beaming at the thought of happiness coming to someone else, caring for them all, worrying over their worries. Above everything Penelope was aware of how dear she was. The sudden haze of 'silly tears' robbed her of her voice, but Muriel went on: 'Brought him in the other evening. It was the day we'd had your letter about going off to France. Raining cats and dogs it was. Emma knew the girls were doing overtime and Ollie was playing in a darts match at the Royal Standard. Sylvia never stays up late. I heard their voices and her key in the lock, so I thought: "Now's your chance, Muriel my girl, you just bring the poor boy in, let him see he's still the same Alf as he always was."

'Opened the door on them – bother the light, I thought, let it show just for once, catch him on the hop. "Come in out of this weather. And you, Alf, I'm just making a drink." Stand them by the fire and they'd fill the kitchen with steam, that wet they were. Just for a second he hesitated; reckon he'd kept himself hidden from her as much as he could. Poor little devil! Seemed to square his shoulders. Then in he came, took his trilby off. That was a test of her feelings. Well, she came through with flying colours. Hangs on his every word, she does.'

'And him?'

'If he'd kept them hidden in the dark all these weeks, he'd not had a chance to look at her either. Here in the kitchen he couldn't take his eyes off her – and no wonder.'

'Just what we hoped.'

'Don't rush them. He's got a big hurdle ahead of him before he asks her to share his life.'

'Because of how he looks? But that's silly. It might have mattered before she knew him, but you say she loves him. Surely she'll just see him as Alf.'

'Don't rush them. They'll get there when they're ready – and in the meantime, they're enjoying the journey. Pop the cloth on, there's a love. The children will be home starving in a minute.'

Because Muriel was as she was, the house had a feeling of content. Time and again over the next few days Penelope saw it. They all brought their troubles to her, not because she was clever but because she had time to listen and she always cared: Peggy and Cath, who'd been upset by a letter from their mother saying that if they'd not been so selfish she would still have had her own home; Emma who couldn't even start to voice her fears but knew Muriel understood without being told; Mavis and her latest 'bit of fun' as she called each new admirer; Sylvia whose hopes were pinned on those words 'nothing I like better than a babbee in the house'; the children who took her for granted in a way that Penelope couldn't, for even after all these years she remembered so well the days without her; and Oliver who went his own way (and Penelope believed he avoided the house particularly when she was there) knowing Muriel would always be there when he came back.

Sylvia ate as little as possible, she walked each day whatever the weather, she exercised with no regard for the discomfort of the unwanted 'thing' that daily made her more cumbersome. She was determined not to get stiff and out of condition. With tunnel vision she saw the time when she would be slim again, these months vanished like waking from a nightmare.

'I'm so glad to be able to think of you here while I'm away, Sylvia. By the time I get back from this tour you'll – '

'I'll almost be a human being again.'

Penelope didn't dig deeper. The baby would be normal. Surely Sylvia's baby would be more than normal, it would be beautiful. She would feel different when she held it. It was easier not to question.

Each day she was in Challington she went to see Alf. About Emma he was wary, Penelope could only guess at his feelings. "Don't rush them." She heeded Muriel's warning and didn't question. Mostly they talked about France, and that in itself was a step in the right direction. If he wasn't ready for a future at least he wasn't hiding from the past.

'More!' 'Encore!' 'More!' Following the troupe of dancers, she hadn't expected Perce to be so well received. Usually she had an early spot in the show; the daring chorus kicking their legs and showing their temptingly frilly underwear were kept 'til last.

'Must be because it's a hospital,' one of them had laughed when their stage manager had told them Perce

187

was to go on last, 'they're frightened we won't be good for their blood pressure.' It was said good-naturedly enough; after all an audience of men in wheelchairs didn't promise to be much in the way of after-show fun. Now, hearing the applause, it was evident the choice of finale had been right. Perce's message had come as a tonic; it would leave the men feeling they'd had a glimpse of home.

To those men who'd been wounded, in fact to most of the forces in France, it seemed there were two different worlds, the one they inhabited forgotten by so many in England who clung on to the old life. How much did the people at home know? How much did the people at home care? England, almost untouched by the hell they'd lived through out here; England, where it was a matter of national pride to carry on and not let Kaiser Bill have the satisfaction of believing he could make a dent in their equilibrium. Some of 'the boys' had been home on leave, had felt themselves to be strangers, aliens; not from their own families but from the snug life that even now, after nearly three years of war, prevailed. Certainly there were shortages – but there were those who found their way round them, resented them for the inconvenience they caused in the even tenor of their lives. The dancing girls, the juggler, the comic, the soprano who'd sung her love songs dressed as she might have to dine in high society, these belonged to that other world. Young Perce came like a breath of fresh air. There was no doubt 'he' was really a girl, but that made her act even more fun.

They hooted with derision and shouted for more as she mocked Jerry; they applauded her unashamed patriotism as the Union Jack was hoisted; somehow this slip of a girl made them feel proud that their injuries were in the cause of freedom. Young Perce, sitting on his box with his con-certina, led them into choruses of songs they all knew, talked about home and the folk in 'his' street. She ended on a sentimental note, singing Laurence McLeod's 'When the Bells of Peace Ring Out', and as a man they felt nearer

188

to that peace, closer to home, even better understood by the people there.

'Excuse me, Miss.' A young VAD nurse came to her with a note in her hand. 'I was asked to pass this to you.'

'You deserve the biggest bouquet in town. But there is no town – and no bouquet. Will this do instead? I wish you'd let me hear you sing it. L.M.'

The short note was attached to a piece of manuscript paper on which a song was written, words and music. 'Hold Fast to Tomorrow', Penelope read, she even tried silently to hum the tune.

'Who sent it?' she asked.

'Gentleman at the back of the room, Captain McLeod. That's him, see, in the wheelchair stood next to the trolley.' There being so many wheelchairs it had to be pinpointed. Penelope's gaze sought out the man next to the trolley; she glanced again at the note and the handwritten score, then back again to him. Even from this distance she was sure there was a twinkle in his eyes as he watched her.

'Thank you, nurse. I'll go and have a word with him.' Often enough members of the audience sent messages to the performers. Of course they did; so far from home there was no other chance of a visitor.

But this man who signed himself L.M. didn't look to her to be pining. Both his legs were in plaster but if his legs were broken it was clear that his spirit was intact.

'Penelope Drew,' he greeted her, 'that was a quite remarkable performance.' His accent was unfamiliar and his manner different from the usual admirer's. Some of the young soldiers she'd talked to became tongue-tied, out of their depth because she was on the stage; others tried to flirt, showing varying degrees of experience in the game. This man did neither. He spoke with confidence, with authority, while his very blue eyes laughed, whether with her or at her she couldn't be sure.

How often she'd longed for a savoir-faire she could never find. His praise was genuine, there was no doubt of that. She felt her cheeks and neck grow hot with pleasure. "Like some gauche sixteen year old," she told herself in disgust, embarrassment robbing her of the quick and witty response she felt the situation needed. Rather than meet his gaze she lowered her own. And that was her salvation. "If he can be cheerful with two legs in plaster, Penelope Drew, just stop thinking about yourself and make him glad to have a visitor."

'The song – "Hold Fast to Tomorrow" – you want me to sing it. I would if I could, but I can't.'

'Can't?'

'I can work it out – slowly, sort of measuring my way – but I really only read music when I know it by heart.'

This time he laughed aloud.

'Then wheel me up to the piano and I'll teach you the tune.'

He was a Captain in the Royal Flying Corps – what could be more English than that? – yet his voice had no familiar ring of home. McLeod, the nurse had called him. Irish?

'Since I've been in here we've had two or three shows. Not an act to touch yours. You sure touched the right note.'

'Thank you.' Walking behind the chair, pushing him to the other end of the hut where the piano stood, it was easier to sound composed. 'I've done Perce for so long we're almost one person now.'

'Aren't you ever yourself? Are you always this hobo kid?'

'Hobo? Is that the same as urchin? I've never heard it.'

'You say tramp, ragamuffin – back home we talk about hobos.'

'Where is back home?' She had to ask.

'You can't tell? Back home in the USA.'

'Of course! Now you've told me I can recognize the accent.'

Again he laughed, holding his head back to her as she pushed him.

'Like the music.'

And this time she laughed too.

'You didn't answer. Are you always Perce?'

'Yes. You see, I'm only half the act. The other half is Tommy, but he's in the army. When he comes home it'll be Tommy and Perce again.' Then, moving the chair that stood in front of the piano and pushing him as close as the plastered legs would allow: 'There, can you reach from there? I can't get you any closer.' She stood the sheet of handwritten music on the stand.

He ran his hands over the keyboard; it was as if he caressed it. The brake pushed hard against the wheel of his chair to hold it steady, Penelope waited. There are those who learn the notes and play them; there are those others whose touch is like that of a lover, drawing the rhythm and melody to them. In the first few notes, Penelope was caught and held under the pianist's spell. He didn't play the music she'd put on the stand but something she'd never heard before, a rhythm that was strange and exciting, pulsating . . . The piano was in front of the raised dais that had served as a stage. Now, not making a sound, she hoisted herself to sit cross-legged on the wooden platform, lost in the wonder of that thrilling beat. Apart from anything else, she'd never heard anyone play with such skill, as if he and the piano were one. Most of the audience had either been pushed or made their own way back to the wards but those who hadn't already gone came to gather by the piano.

As he played, she watched him. Compared with so many of the troops they'd entertained this Captain McLeod wasn't a boy. She didn't consciously consider his age, but saw him as mature, his craggy face looked 'used', although she suspected the crow's feet around his eyes came from laughing more than from time; his hair was prematurely greying, wiry and cut short. If he was imprinting himself

191

on her mind she was hardly aware of it; for a moment nothing mattered except the music. After a few moments the rhythm changed, throbbed like a heart bursting with grief, the melody a plaintive cry. How she'd love to dance to that! Not her usual acrobatic, comic dancing, but letting her body express the longing, the loneliness . . . Later she'd come to call it 'the blues', but that afternoon she knew only that it tugged at her heart, made her yearn for something though she didn't know what. The man who played wasn't important, except as the medium that led her first through the wild abandon, the crazed pounding of the jazz, and now to this soulful, lonely cry. To her it was the heartbeat of the war-torn world; but more than that, it was a rhythm and beat that was new to her. Tomorrow's sound.

She gave no thought to her own appearance, nor Perce's either, for she was still wearing the tatty suit, cap and muffler. Her dark eyes were huge in her pale face, her short hair falling in an untidy fringe and her cap pushed back on her head. As he played the wounded captain glanced at her, her lips parted, her thin body leaning forward as if she couldn't hold back from the music. By now some of the dancers had come in to gather by the piano. They were aware that they radiated a glamour, they clicked their fingers, tapped their feet, drawing attention to themselves as the visiting artistes. Penelope was aware only of a strange, unfamiliar emotion. There was a quivering hollow feeling in her chest, she wanted to dance, she wanted to cry. The sound of 'the blues' was another milestone.

Then, just as suddenly as he'd turned from jazz to 'blues', so he struck up the opening chords of the song in front of him. His voice was pleasantly on key, an easy voice.

'Well,' he turned to her at the end, 'do you think you know it well enough to read it now?'

'If you play – or we could sing it together.' She uncrossed

her legs and stood up in one light, supple movement. 'Where did you get it from? It's a lovely lilting tune.'

'Good. I thought it would suit your act. You could alternate it with the "Bells of Peace" thing.'

'Well . . . ' It was a risk. People were beginning to know 'When the Bells of Peace Ring Out'. 'But "The Bells" is a Laurence McLeod – ' Her mouth dropped open. L.M. he'd signed his note. He was from the United States. 'You're not . . . no, you can't be . . . '

'We'll go over it a few more times. Get your concertina.'

She might not read music but once she knew the tune she was as sure on the buttons of her concertina as he was on the keyboard of the piano. Disregarding everyone else they started work in earnest, and sensing that the fun was over the impromptu audience drifted away.

When the nurse came to push him back to the ward he gave Penelope the sheet of manuscript.

'That's for you. You'll come again, won't you? Please. We've been so taken up with holding fast to tomorrow we've not had time to talk.'

Laurence McLeod – suggesting she should come and talk! Laurence McLeod! One of the foremost names on Broadway, whose songs were whistled by every errand boy and sung in every variety theatre! Tonight she'd write to Tom, there was such a lot she wanted to tell him.

But she hadn't forgotten that stupid blush when he'd praised her; this time she wasn't going to let her excitement show. 'We're travelling out each day from our local base here.'

'Please.'

'Yes, I will, I promise. We're being taken somewhere to a transit camp in the afternoon tomorrow. Would the morning be any use?'

'I've nothing in my engagement book,' he answered as the nurse started to push him away. 'Make sure you bring your concertina. We'll run through your song again.'

*

Her appearance must have been a surprise. Until now he'd only seen Perce. Hand-me-down clothes, boots that let in the water, these things would always be at the back of Penelope's memory, and from them had developed the care she took now in how she dressed. Never as smart as Sylvia, never as flamboyant as so many of the concert party, but always wearing the clothes she felt were right for her.

'So!' And in that one word he managed to convey not only surprise but appreciation of what he saw. The brown skirt was the new, shorter cut, a fashion brought about to save material, and came to about six inches above her neat ankles. With it she wore a coffee-coloured silk blouse, with a brown silk tie knotted at her throat and a tammy of the same shade pulled jauntily to one side of her head. Yesterday she'd been an impish lad, today she was transformed.

Laurence thought she looked charming – young, fresh, eager – yet wasn't fooled into looking on her as a child.

'I brought my concertina,' she said unnecessarily, 'and I've been through the song lots of times.'

'Good. Then get a chair and come and talk to me, Penelope Drew. Tell me how it is you hide yourself behind Young Perce, why you don't let the audience see you for yourself.'

His voice fascinated her. She'd heard Irish, Welsh, Scottish accents, dialects from every part of England. In her travels she'd even met foreigners who were difficult to understand at all. But never had she talked to anyone from the United States, the country that led the silent picture world. If those films could only speak, is this what they'd sound like?

She realized she was staring at him. He was still waiting for her answer.

'Well? You find me curious?' He raised his eyebrows.

'Sorry, I wasn't being rude. It's your voice, I've never heard anyone from the United States talk. I like it. I listened to it so hard I didn't hear what you said.'

'If ever a girl talked in riddles! And I'm not a true

194

American. My mother was English. In fact, I still have a grandmother living in Penzance. I've visited your country – partly my country too – before the war brought me over. You know, Penelope, we're a funny lot, we Yankees, we all dig to find our roots in the old world. Well, mine are in Cornwall. Whether or not America will ever come into this war who can say? I couldn't wait at home to find out. I guess if you want to keep your roots healthy you have to take care of them. That's why I came over and joined the Flying Corps.'

She nodded. It made sense. It fitted the sort of man he looked to be.

'Now I've told you how I came to be flying an aeroplane, you tell me how it is you present a character so unlike the real Penelope.'

'But he isn't! He's me, through and through. You can't judge a sausage by its skin, nor a gentleman by his overcoat. You see, in the act I'm Perce. Tom – he's my husband – plays Tommy, my big, protective and bossy brother. We started like that long ago, when we first left home. It just grew from there.'

Her mind jumped back to those days in the boatbuilders' yard where she used to practise. She remembered Mr Bailey telling her that she was too big to stand on her hands showing her drawers to the world. Perched on the edge of the platform she told Laurence McLeod: 'There was this audition in Challington where we lived. I made up my mind this was the opportunity I'd been waiting for. But I never considered that I'd need a costume. Alf, he was a friend, a shrimp for his age like me, gave me his old suit. So Perce was born.'

'But you're doing a solo now – and if acquiring a costume presented a problem then, I'm sure it wouldn't now.' There was no laughter in his eyes now, this was Laurence McLeod with ten years' Broadway experience behind him. 'Perce is great, I recognized it yesterday – he's great

195

because you create him. But he stunts you. You move too well to waste yourself as a comic dancer, Penelope Drew.'

'You don't understand, though. Perce and Tommy are a partnership. Why, I even base the way I talk on Tommy.'

Laurence shook his head. 'No, I don't understand. That concertina you play – and play well, too, as long as you know the tunes first,' he teased, 'imagine you were suddenly without it. What would you do? Tell the audience about how it used to be, how it would be again when you got it back? No. You'd fill the gap. Take the act forward to the next stage. And the next stage could be tremendous.'

'You don't understand . . . '

His answer was to start to play, that soulful melancholy sound. His voice was soft. She moved closer.

> Since you went away,
> The sun don't shine,
> Through each empty day
> My heart do pine –
> Hear me cryin' the blues.

From the top of the piano he passed her a piece of scorepaper. Even if she couldn't 'measure her way through the tune', with him playing the piano she wouldn't get lost. The words were written clearly. It was as natural for her to sing and dance as it was to walk and talk. Usually her songs were jolly, suited to Perce. Now her voice was low, tender and husky. It held a world of loneliness and heartbreak.

When the last chords died away he sat looking at her.

'Don't understand, you say. But I do. I understand that you've been given a gift and you're only half using it. Penelope Drew, you could hold every man in your audience in the palm of your small hand. God knows why, but it's surely the truth.'

'Can we try "Hold Fast to Tomorrow" once more?' She was taking avoiding action and they both knew it.

196

'OK, in a minute we will. Tom, this husband of yours, will you get to see him while you're in France?'

'No. He's in the Middle East. I had a letter from him sent from Cairo when he was on leave.' ("I wonder if he found the fleshpots." Mentally she smiled, so sure that he wouldn't have looked for them.) 'Captain McLeod – '

'Laurence . . . '

'Laurence, then . . . please don't try and persuade me to abandon Perce. It'd be courting trouble. Don't you see, I'm keeping the act together for when Tom comes back.'

And how could he argue with that? He didn't even try.

'He's a lucky man.'

'It takes two to be lucky. And we are, that's why I can't tempt fate to notice and spoil things. Is it wicked to be superstitious, do you suppose? When we were children there were three of us, Tom, me and Alf – he was the small one I told you about. Poor Alf had a beastly war, and now he's home . . . ' Her words trailed off, somehow stopping him asking questions. Then, looking at him earnestly: 'So many people have had their lives spoilt, spoilt for ever I mean, not just for the time they have to be apart. Sometimes I get frightened that fate hasn't noticed Tom and me, we've got away with it all so lightly. So I'm not going to attract attention. I'll just go on keeping the act going until Tom comes back.

'Now tell me about you. I suppose it's a cheek to ask, I mean, you're important and all that. But you told me a bit, about having a Grandma in Penzance. Is there anyone else?'

'Oh yes, there's Helen, my wife. And my son, Laurence Jnr whom we call Sonny. I've been away nearly two years. I guess that's the hardest part, knowing how he must be growing and changing and I'm not part of it. He was eight when I last saw him. Ten now – and God knows how old by the time I get back.' She noticed the nervous way he drummed his fingers on the sides of the wheelchair, saw the tightening of his lips.

197

'Come on, let's "Hold Fast to Tomorrow", that's what we have to do. Today'll be yesterday before we know it.'

She suspected that work would always be his surest pick-me-up. Now his smile told her she was right. She was beginning to recognize his mannerisms: the way he threw his head back when he laughed; the flourish as he played his introductory chords and arpeggios.

Before they finally moved on the concert party came again to the military hospital. Even in those few days there had been a change round in patients, some who'd not been fit to see the show before were brought in, others had only just arrived – and some had been sent back to England to convalesce. Laurence was still there. Penelope noticed him talking to a man in civilian dress, presumably a visitor. It was after the show when she went to say goodbye that she learned who it was.

'Under her disguise this is Penelope Drew. Maxim Pilbright, war correspondent for the *Morning Herald*. I've asked him to take a photograph of Perce for me. You'll pose, won't you, Penelope? His camera is set up ready in the office across the corridor.' She felt flattered – no, that wasn't the whole truth. She felt more than flattered – excited, gratified. Laurence McLeod wanted a photograph to remember her by.

It was April when she got back to England. She told herself it was because she was a bad sailor and the sea had been unfriendly that she had this feeling that something was wrong with Sylvia. But 'herself' didn't listen. She went straight to Challington. It was the middle of the day. The children would be at school, Pa and his girls at the factory. She'd let herself in the back way, walk in on Sylvia and Mother.

'Penny love!' Muriel's greeting never failed. 'She's upstairs getting on with the job now. I sent a note to fetch Mrs Crisp about eleven o'clock.' The kitchen was full of steam, saucepans of hot water at the ready.

'I knew it, I knew something was wrong!'

'Nothing's wrong. Sylvia's as healthy as a girl could be. With a first one, the babbee can't be here just yet, a first always takes its time. Why don't you pop up and have a word while I make a cup of tea? Ask her – and Mrs Crisp – if they could drink a cup.'

'But she can't stop to drink tea!' Penelope remembered that dreadful night after the visit to the chemist and his friend.

'Be glad of a cup in between whiles.' Muriel smiled confidently. 'Your turn'll come, you'll find out. Oh, yes, and that reminds me, the post girl brought post from Tom. One for you and one for her. Good boy he is, often drops her a line. And a blessing he does – she gets no other letters except for one or two from the solicitor who looks after things for her. She needs friends at a time like this.'

Penelope found Sylvia propped up in bed, her hair rumpled, her face pale.

'Oh, Pen! Oh, it's awful. Worse than – you know. Worse than I thought . . . '

Penelope took her hand.

'Soon be over. All these months, now in a few hours it'll be done.'

Sylvia caught her breath as the contraction gripped her. Her nails dug into Penelope's hand. 'Damn it, damn it!' She could hardly breathe let alone speak but there was venom in her tone.

'No good taking that attitude.' Mrs Crisp never had been the most sympathetic of nurses. She believed it did some of these girls more good to speak sharply, make them help themselves and get on with the job. No use kicking up a fuss. What went in had to come out and there was no other way to do it. Bit of a madam this one, she'd thought when she'd come to meet her beforehand. "You'll be one to make hard work for yourself, I can see that, my pretty madam," she'd decided.

The pain had taken the whole of Sylvia's attention while

it lasted but now, as it faded, she saw the envelope in Penelope's hand.

'For me?' she panted, still breathless.

'Yes, from Tom. One for you and one downstairs waiting for me. Can you manage or shall I open it for you?'

'No, leave it. I'll read it presently. No hurry.' She pushed the envelope under her pillows. 'You go and read yours – oh, the pain – oh – oh – ' Then a sudden and piercing scream.

'Now perhaps she means business.' Mrs Crisp pulled the blankets off the bed. 'Lie flat now.' And so saying she whipped the pillows from behind Sylvia, dropping her on to her back and Tom's letter to the floor. 'That's it, good job we've got the draw sheets in. Can you tell Mrs Drew I'll be glad if she'll bring a pail of hot water?' Then, turning back to Sylvia, 'Not a happorth o' good you kicking up that shindig. Just you start pushing. Remember, the Lord helps those who help themselves.'

Sylvia was crying. 'Lord's got nothing to do with this. The devil – ooohh – '

"For two pins I'd smack her bottom. Doesn't so much as try to help things along!"

But Muriel arrived with the water so the nurse overcame the desire. And once there Muriel stayed. She was still there when first the children arrived back from school, then Emma home from the factory. Oliver and his girls had been on the early shift today, the others had just stopped off at the Standard on the way home but 'hey'll hoon ge heeer' told Penelope that they'd soon be here. Peggy and Cath arrived, then presently Mavis.

Still no sign of Oliver. Halfway up the stairs Penelope hovered, listening to every sound. She knew that down in the kitchen the girls were seeing to the meal; she ought to go and help but she couldn't go out of earshot. And the thought of food made her feel quite sick.

She didn't hear her father come in, but turned at the

200

sound of a movement on the stairs behind her and there he was.

'Pa! Mother's upstairs with Sylvia — '

'Bloody dancing girls. Like the rest of them — thinks I can't add up. Who's bastard is she dropping? Eh?' He pushed his face close to Penelope's, his breath heavy with whisky fumes. She hated the smell and instinctively turned her head away. Something had upset him, this wasn't brought on just by what was going on upstairs. The whisky was unleashing a fury that under normal circumstances he would have controlled. With a hand that was unsteady he tilted her chin, forcing her to face him. 'Look at me when I speak to you.'

Always her undoing, those 'silly tears' stung her eyes; she could only see him through a haze.

'You're all the same, the lot of you. Her upstairs scream-ing — ha!' He spat the word. She felt his saliva on her face. 'Doesn't like taking her medicine, does she? And you, pretending you don't know whose brat it is — all one big happy family, the lot of you — and what about this, eh?'

He held up a piece of sheet music, pushed it towards her so that it was only inches from her face, so close she couldn't focus on it. He'd seen it in the window of Hawk-ins and Daintree, the music shop, on his way home from the Standard.

Holding her head back she read: '"Hold Fast to To-morrow", words and music written by Laurence McLeod for Penelope Drew', and there, complete with concertina, was a picture of Young Perce.

'Eh? What about that then? "I met Laurence McLeod",' his voice took on a false sugary tone as he repeated what she'd written to them. 'Think I was born yesterday? Eh? Think I don't know how chits like you get favours from his sort.' His leer was worse than his anger. 'Opened your legs, just like she used to, gave him what he wanted.'

She was standing a tread higher than he on the stairs. As he talked, his eyes screwed up, his face only inches from hers, she moved a step at a time towards the landing, he following close.

From the attic came a new sound – the cry of a baby.

'Hear it?' Ollie's mouth wobbled. His eyes were suddenly bloodshot as he rocked on his feet. 'I remember the night you were born . . . '

'Pa . . . ' Just for a second she seemed to have glimpsed the Pa who'd been the centre of her young life. If he hadn't stayed so long in the Royal Standard she might have been able to reach him – but then if he hadn't stayed so long in the Royal Standard, none of this would have happened. Now, even as she said his name, the moment was lost.

'Go off together again now the brat's arrived, I suppose. Share it, is that what you'll do? One big happy family.' He screwed up the sheet of music and threw it on the ground then staggered into his bedroom and slammed the door.

Sinking to the top stair, Penelope listened to the cry of the newborn baby while smoothing out the sheet of music . . . written by Laurence McLeod for Penelope Drew.

CHAPTER EIGHT

'Just hold her, Sylvia love. You'll feel different if you feel her. Innocent little pet. It's none of it her fault, she didn't choose how it was she came to be here. See her feet – what is there about a babbee's tiny feet? Who could think that one of these days perhaps she'll be a dancer like you.'

Nothing for it but to dump the tiny bundle on its mother and let nature do the rest.

But Sylvia seemed devoid of all the normal feelings. She stared at the baby as if it belonged to another planet, then shut her eyes and leant back on the pillows.

'No,' she answered wearily, 'it's not her fault. But I can't pretend. Mrs Drew, help me to get it taken into a home. There's a place in Cumley Street – I've often walked past and looked at it.'

'The orphanage? But, bless her, she isn't an orphan. You're tired, of course you are after all you've just been through. By morning you'll see things clearer. You won't have any milk yet, but just let her nuzzle.'

Sylvia's eyes shot open.

'I'm not feeding her! I won't!' Tightly she folded her arms across her breasts. 'Can't you understand? For nine months my life's been ruined. Take her away, why can't you just take her away . . . ' Her face crumpled and she cried. The tiny bundle was laid carefully in its crib (a legacy from Merrick, Mandy and Bruce) and Sylvia felt herself taken into Muriel's embrace. Kindness was her undoing. She sobbed helplessly, choking on the words she'd bottled up for so long: ' . . . shouldn't have been like this . . . truly I loved him . . . wasn't like you think.'

'Then love his little daughter.'

'No, I just want it all to be over. He's gone. I won't

even look at her. All I did to get rid of her – and there she is – I've been punished – all these months, I've been punished. Send her away, help me to finish it, please, please . . . '

'Never mind worrying tonight. You let me take her down to my room. In the morning things'll look brighter.'

With a husband made maudlin by drink and a newborn baby thrown out of the nest by its mother, Muriel's own night showed little promise of rest.

The only difference a good night's sleep made to Sylvia was to strengthen her determination. Mrs Crisp had been there for the delivery but, that over, her job was done. When Muriel opened the front door in answer to the peremptory knock she was surprised to find the midwife on the step again.

'Thought I'd just see everything's going all right,' she announced. Her manner was businesslike, giving no hint that she'd ridden here on her bicycle out of concern for Muriel. She didn't trust that madam upstairs. She'd have poor Mrs Drew waiting on her hand, foot and finger! She'd met her sort before. Nothing told you more about a woman than how she behaved when nature had her cornered and the only way was to grit her teeth and help herself. Cora Crisp had brought most of the local babies into the world, learning from experience – and it was that experience that had prompted her to pedal from the other side of George Bradley Park on this wet and blustery April morning.

'She's had a comfortable night.' Muriel was never good at pretence, her bright answer didn't fool Cora for one second.

'Now, don't you bother coming up with me. I'll go and check everything's in order.' "And give her a piece of my mind if she's not behaving herself."

Downstairs Penelope and Muriel waited.

'It's no use,' Muriel was certain, 'nothing's going to

204

make her love that baby. So are we right to try and foist her responsibilities on to her?'

'I've told her we could take a place together. I've said it right from when we first knew about the baby. Sylvia needs to be back in the theatre, Mother, it's the only life she's ever known. It's not like any ordinary job of work, I can't explain . . . She needs the tension of waiting for the curtains to open, she needs to know she's part of it all again. She's not poor, and with both of us bringing money in, we could easily have a housekeeper.'

This talk of theatre was outside Muriel's imaginings.

'And what about when Tom comes home?' Family life, that she could understand.

'Tom's her friend; he's never resented that Sylvia and I have been so special to each other. He wouldn't mind.'

'And what about this poor innocent?' Muriel bent over the baby. Just as she had when each of her own had been very young, she'd brought a drawer from her wardrobe down to the kitchen, lined with a blanket and with a large pillow to make a nest. The bundled newcomer stared at nothing in the unfocused way of those fresh to the world. 'A housekeeper, paid to see she's fed and kept clean! 'tisn't money that makes a home for a child and well you know it. She needs love. Don't you my little angel?'

'I'll off to see Alf. If Sylvia asks for me, tell her I'll keep her company when I get home. Is there any shopping you want?'

'Good girl. I don't want to have to leave our little pet with her, not just yet.'

So, with basket and shopping list, Penelope set off. Nothing changed at Challington. A few hours here and she slipped back into her old groove – where even Perce had no place. For a week or so it was wonderful, knowing that that's all it was – a week or two but not for ever. No wonder Sylvia fought for her freedom! And yet, if she really had loved the baby's father as she said, how could she not want his child? All the way to Alf's she pondered the problem.

A smiling Mrs Johnson answered her knock, telling her: 'He's through in the kitchen.'

Penelope's brown eyes asked the silent question, Alf's mother nodded in reply. Yes, things were improving. He might not have got back into the swim of things yet but at least he'd put his toe in to test the water. No longer was he sitting, silent and morose, in his room all day.

'Visitor for you, Alf. It's your friend back from her travels,' she said as she ushered Penelope down the passage and into the kitchen. 'I know Alf will want to hear all about it so I'll leave you and go to the shops. Mr Geary told me he'd be making sausages today. There may be a queue, but I'll be back as soon as I can.' As she talked she rammed her hat on and spiked it with a long pin to hold it down in the wind. 'Better take a gamp, although it's blustery enough to turn it inside out. See you look after Penelope, Alf lad, there's cake in the tin.'

Then she was gone.

'Your Mum's looking better,' Penelope said, which was the nearest she could come to putting into words what she really meant.

'No use fretting, is it, Pen? What was it you used to say about life not being all you want?'

' "It may not be all you want," ' she quoted in a voice Perce would have recognized, ' "but it's all you're gonna 'ave. So 'ave it. Put a geranium in yer 'at and be 'appy." '

He giggled, one side of his face turning up into a smile, the other remaining the same ghoulish mask. It was the nearest she'd seen yet to the Alf he used to be. She wanted to reach out, take his hand and hold it to her cheek. But she was stopped by the memory of that night on the Heath.

'Well, that's about it, isn't it?' he said. 'If you've only got a shrimping net, you're not going to catch a bass. But what's wrong with shrimps, anyway?'

'I think, Alf, it depends who you eat them with. Doesn't

206

matter whether it's shrimps, bass or the finest caviare so long as you're happy in their company.'

'Yes, well, I'm not likely to be eating them with anyone. Honest, I am trying to get on top of things – but that's something I'm not on top of yet, Pen. Eating by myself, I mean, for always.' He took up the poker and proceeded to stab at the coals burning in the range.

Now she did reach out, her small hand covering his.

'You're fond of her?' As she said it the thought struck her that not with anyone else could she have talked as she did with Alf. Not a single direct question and answer, yet both of them always understood what was left unsaid.

He nodded. 'We used to meet every night in the winter. The evenings are drawing out now, I can't expect her to want to be seen – well, can I? She comes here.'

'Can you talk to her, Alf, properly talk to her?'

'I haven't told her I care about her, if that's what you mean.'

'Actually it wasn't. What I meant was, can you have a conversation with her? Understand what she says?'

''course I can!' he sounded quite offended. 'Wouldn't have thought you'd say a mean thing like that, Pen. It's rotten for her but you can't think a thing like that's important. Not like being seen walking out with – '

Now it was her turn to giggle.

'Oh, Alfred Johnson! Dear kind little Alf who I've loved since we were at Merchant Hill Board School – I never believed he could be so – so – ' lost for the right word she floundered ' – self-important.'

Alf frowned – at least, one side of his face did.

'Self-important? Precious little reason for that!'

'Listen, Alf,' her eyes were full of tears, 'I wish I was cleverer at saying things. It's never any use trying to hide from the truth. Your face is changed, scarred; but what we look like only matters with strangers. And how you feel about your scars is just the way Emma must feel about the way she can't speak like you and me. We know her, we hear her half-formed words, but it's what she says that matters to us, not how it sounds.

'I said you were self-important 'cos you're just worried about you and think her troubles are nothing. You say it's not important, but imagine what it must have done to her. All her life – children at school taunting her, probably mimicking her.' She looked at him earnestly. 'You're you, same now as you always were. And if Emma didn't want to be with you she wouldn't have wasted every evening for months out of pity.'

He gazed into the flickering flames, digesting her words. Finally he turned to her, half his face lighting in a grin that tore at her heart.

'Reckon I ought to get myself a shrimping net.'

'Reckon you had. And see if you can't catch enough for two.'

She stayed a few minutes more, told him about the baby. They talked about where she'd been to in France, about Tom and the latest letters from him. But she could tell that Alf's thoughts were on the shrimping expedition he was planning. She took the shopping basket and went on her way, leaving him to his dreams.

'We're going on the rocks, Penny, the tide's low,' Merrick told her at breakfast on the Sunday. 'Do you want to come with us?'

'Outgrown clambering over the rocks, I expect. Haven't you, love?' Muriel laughed.

'It's one of the things I dream about when I'm away. Of course I'll come with you. What about you others? Emma? Mavis?' At the look on Peggy and Cath's faces she knew *their* answer; in any case they were both in their chapel-going costumes and had brought their hats and gloves downstairs with them ready.

'Not me, ta.' Mavis was hardly the type to clamber on the rocks. 'I met this chap at the Albany last night, he's taking me out for the day. He's on a seven days.'

'Ang Gime heeig Algh,' which, now that they were so used to her, they all heard as: 'And I'm seeing Alf.'

April is early in the year for dabbling on the water's edge, but they were all adept at jumping from one rock to the next and keeping dry.

'Last one to the pier's a sissy!' A shout so familiar yet so unexpected that Penelope missed her footing and slithered into two inches of water. Alf! Out of doors on a Sunday morning! She turned to see him coming down the beach towards them, hand in hand with Emma. She saw them and at the same moment registered the expression of the children's faces. It was another of life's milestone moments, she realized in an instant. If one of the children had had a wetting everyone would have laughed. Instead they looked at her anxiously and waited. She belonged to the world of grown-ups! 'Last one to the pier . . . ' But Merrick, Amanda and Bruce knew nothing about that, they couldn't see the ghosts of those other children, always Tom coming first, Alf hanging back so that Penelope – one hand holding down her hat – could come second. Now here was Alf . . . She pulled herself together, made a face at the children and shook a wet shoe in their direction. They laughed. In their relief the incident became suddenly hilariously funny. Alf and Emma . . . 'Last one to the pier . . . '

'I'd beat you, Alf Johnson, 'cept my shoes are full of water.'

'Excuses, excuses,' he laughed. 'I saw you down here, wanted to say – Pen, you didn't bring a shrimping net, did you?'

She looked from one to the other. What was he telling her?

'Whe cu hu hell ou.' They'd come to tell her. Still she looked from one to the other.

'To tell me? You mean . . . ?'

Alf nodded. Two Sunday morning strollers walking along the Promenade whispered one to another, each turning to look back, pretending it was something else that took their attention. Such curiosity he would have to live with, get used to. Today, mercifully, he didn't even notice. Penelope knew that Emma did, though. She knew it by the possessive way the girl took his arm.

But what did strangers matter? Not at all in that moment of hugs and happiness, congratulation and confidence. A minute ago yesterday had merged with today; now today looked forward to tomorrow. Alf had a future again.

'Wish old Tom was here.' He looked at his lovely Emma with such pride. 'Just you wait till he meets Emma.' In anyone's eyes she was exquisite; in Alf's she was perfect.

The children had thought of Penelope as 'a grown-up'. Now, as she looked at Alf and Emma, she knew that growing up depended on experience, and for all her travels, her life in London, her marriage, even the beginning of making a name for herself, her photograph on a sheet of music, she knew nothing of the mystery these two had solved. 'Love is in the eye of the beholder'; they'd found their way beyond any physical shortcomings. For a moment, she almost envied them. Overhead, in typical April fashion, the white clouds rushed across a blue sky. Looking up she felt she could see for ever. "Thank You for making him happy. Please let it always be just as good for him as it is today. You've given him more than his share of bad times, and now You can see he deserves things to start to get better. Thank You, thank You . . . " She sent her silent message into that infinity of time and space that held all her secrets.

Her wet feet were like blocks of ice.

'Come on you three, you heard what he said. Line up here, that's it. Last one to the pier's a sissy. On your marks, get set, go!' They were off. Alf, Emma and Penelope watched as Amanda came first, then as soon as she was home Merrick rushed the last few yards and Bruce, so much younger, brought up the rear. Could it be that Challington was rearing another of nature's gentlemen?

*

210

'Merrick! Is that you, Merrick?' Sylvia called when she heard the boy come out of the other attic bedroom.

'Yes. Do you want me to get you something?'

'It's just these letters. Look, I haven't any stamps. Pass me my purse, can you?'

'I expect Mum's got some stamps.'

'I thought we wouldn't bother your mother. I thought you might like to earn yourself some pocket money.' She used all the guile at her command – which wasn't much, restricted as she was to sitting up in bed. 'If I give you sixpence, will you go to the post office and get the stamps for these two letters? You could put them in the box on your way to school couldn't you? That'll give you four-pence change – for yourself.'

Fourpence was wealth indeed. Planning what he'd do with it he hurried downstairs, then put the envelopes inside his cap on the hall table so that he wouldn't forget. Not very likely, with fourpence at the top of his mind as he ate his breakfast porridge and kipper.

Ten minutes later, ready to set out for school, he threw his cap on his head and went to put the two envelopes in his pocket. Penelope had considered he had the makings of one of nature's gentlemen, but he would have been more than human if he hadn't looked to see who Sylvia had written to. One letter was addressed to a theatrical agent. It was the other that took all the pleasure out of his highly paid errand. He turned it over in his hand, held it to the window as if he expected the light to shine through it, letting him read. But did he need to read it? No one had talked to him but he wasn't stupid.

"Thought we wouldn't bother your mother . . ." What ought he to do? Sylvia was trusting him. But she was grown-up, able to take care of herself. What about the baby? Poor little scrap, hadn't so much as a name yet and it was ten days old. "Cumley Street Orphanage" . . . what could Sylvia want with them? His kipper seemed to have stuck in his chest.

211

'Buck up, Merrick, the others are halfway up Prospect Street by now. You haven't lost that cap again, have you?'

'Coming, Mum.'

And as if that had been the cue she'd waited for, Penelope came running down the stairs. Thankfully he turned to her, the burden suddenly lifted. Never mind the fourpence, they had to do what was right.

'Penny, Sylvia asked me to post her letters.'

'Have you got time? Do you want to leave them for me to take?'

'I got the feeling they were private, she didn't actually say so. But – look . . . ' He held them out for her to take. 'I got time, 's not that. Don't know if I should.'

He waited as she read the addresses but he couldn't tell what was going through her mind. She kept her eyes lowered and gave no hint. 'You hop off and catch the others up, I'll see to them.'

'She said I could keep the change. But – I'd rather you sorted it out – never mind about the money.'

'You're a good chap, Merrick.'

That fourpence would have held all the guilt of thirty pieces of silver.

He'd got rid of the problem, but that didn't mean the problem had gone. Penelope sat on the bottom of the stairs deciding her best approach. Sylvia had heard her plan that they should live together, find someone to keep house and look after the baby. (Ten days and no name . . . how much longer were they supposed to call her just that, 'the baby'?) She'd never argued against the suggestion; probably she'd never seriously considered the possibility of it. Penelope looked at the envelope: "Cumley Street Orphanage". Into her mind crowded so many memories of long ago, the life she'd shared with Pa. When her mother had left them, he could so easily have shrugged off his responsibilities; Penelope could have found herself at Cumley Street Orphanage. Sylvia had money – Pa had had none; Sylvia was the baby's mother – Pa hadn't even been sure whether

212

or not he was the father. The 'dirty hovel' . . . oh, but it had held something that no institution could give. Here on the stairs Penelope let it fill her mind. She knew exactly the feeling of the wooden handle on 'The Bowl', the way the shadows fell across the room from the legs of people who walked by, the drawer at the end of the kitchen table where they'd kept everything from bits of string to a pack of dog-eared playing cards . . . Chummy, the sound of his tail thumping on the ground. Memories that would stay with her as long as she lived. And Sylvia was prepared to deprive that tiny mite of a home of her own!

Tearing the letter into small pieces she climbed to the attic.

'Penny, I'm glad it's you. They say I've got to lie here until the end of the week. Well, I'm not going to. Now you're here, you can help me make myself presentable.' Sylvia was ready for life again: the tilt of her chin, the sparkle in her eyes, told their own tale.

'If you feel ready, yes, I'll help you.' She put the little pile of torn-up paper on the bed in front of Sylvia. 'I found it in Merrick's cap – he put your letters where he wouldn't forget them. I told him I'd take them.'

'You tore up my letter! How dare you interfere!'

'And how dare you try and take that child's freedom away from her before she knows what life is? Sylvia, she's a little girl, like you were, like I was. What if Christine had said you were an inconvenience?

'Don't be frightened, you're not on your own. We'll make a home for her together, and when Tom comes back – '

'You'd no right to touch my letters. I tell you I don't want her. She'd be better off in the orphanage – and I can give them money.'

Penelope felt helpless, but she tried again.

'But I can help you get back on your feet. Look, Sylvia, I'll tell you what we'll do. When I go back to London on Sunday, you and the baby come too. We'll find somewhere,

213

get a housekeeper. It'll be weeks before you're trim and back in practice to work. By that time we'll have the establishment running on oiled wheels.'

'I'm coming back with you, I'd already decided. But I am *not* being lumbered with a baby. I want a new start, Penny, can't you try and understand?'

Neither of them had heard Muriel coming up the stairs, drawn by the sound of raised voices.

'Now then you two, 'tis not a bit of use wasting all your energies going over the same stony ground. I've heard some of what you say – now it's my turn.'

'Another one come to badger me!' The pendulum of Sylvia's mood had swung the other way. She brushed ready tears from her eyes.

'I'm with you not against you on this one.' Sylvia's eyes shot open, Penelope started to speak but was talked down. 'Do you think I'd see that little mite bundled into a railway train and taken off to goodness knows where? Take her to London on Sunday? Why, Penny love, you must have taken leave of your senses! It's no life for a baby, being packed up and carted around as if she's luggage – nor yet being left at home with some stranger paid to look after her.'

'So, I'm right. I told Penny she had no business to tear up my letter. It'd be better off in Cumley Street. You could visit there sometimes, Mrs Drew, if you wanted to make sure everything was all right, and I could pay for – '

'That child is a little girl, not an "it". First things first. It's time she had a name. Even in an orphanage she'd have to be called something.'

'Oh, I don't care. If she'd waited another week or so she could have been called May.'

'That's it then, born in April, we'll call her April.' Muriel was satisfied that at least one thing was settled.

'Not April, Mother. I was in France at the beginning of April – Avril they call it there,' Penelope remembered. 'Why not Avril? That's a lovely name.' But what was the good of a lovely name if you had to live in that gaunt, grey house in Cumley Street? 'Sylvie, just let's give it a try –'

'I've not done yet,' Muriel cut in. 'I've no rights, it's not for me to say. But, Sylvia, she's not been a ha'porth of trouble. Nothing I like better than a babbee about the place, I've said so before. Before we know it she'll be smiling, getting to know us, learning a bit more every day. I've no rights, I can only try and make you see the wisdom of it. Last night I had a talk to Ollie. He's master of the house, I told him, if he was against the scheme then I'd have to let it go. But Ollie could never see a child thrown out . . . as if I didn't know it! None of us is perfect, but Penny knows as well as I do, Ollie's a good pa.'

Penelope nodded. Her throat was dry and tight. 'The best Pa,' she managed. And there spoke the little girl who'd shared her dreams with him, who'd learnt about the world with the Places game. Then, sure of her voice again: 'Say yes, Sylvia, let her stay with Mother and Pa and the others; she's one of us.'

Sylvia didn't answer. One look at her face and Muriel took her in her arms. Poor child, what a year she'd had. Ollie saw things differently, of course he did, he was a man. But, like she'd said, Ollie would never see a child badly used. And wait a year or two, little Avril would have him twisted round her little finger just the same as the others did.

The following Sunday the two girls were taken off in a hansom to catch the train to London. It was May. April – April and Avril too – were gone. Sylvia watched out of the window eagerly. Life was waiting.

Penelope had arranged to take a room with Mrs Fellows in Finchley High Street, and a letter sent ahead saying that Sylvia was coming with her led to their being given the double room she used to share with Tom. The girls had both had their share of stage landladies, good and bad;

Mrs Fellows was one of the better ones and they intended to make a base there even if the room was often empty.

In France Penelope had sensed the feeling amongst the troops: they believed the war was no more than a minor inconvenience to the people at home. Here in London she sometimes believed they were right. She took bookings in the music halls, her audiences still warmed to her in the same way; any change was in her, not in them. It was years ago that she'd felt the first touch of magic when the queue for the Prince of Wales had joined in the chorus of the song of the two little sausages. Since then she'd learnt the lesson that any successful showman must know: once you walk on to the stage you become what the audience expects. In short, she'd learnt her craft. Perce was still the same combination of fun and pathos. She took him to the Army camps, she took him to Portsmouth and to Plymouth. This was her 'war work'; in playing to the troops she felt she was keeping faith with those who felt themselves to be forgotten.

The summer months of 1917 took their toll, the lists of casualties grew longer. The wounded were sent home: men never to recover from poison gas, men who'd lost limbs, men who'd lost sight. Each one of them someone's husband, someone's son or brother, each one of them coming home just like Alf had to fight another and more personal battle. And in France, around a village called Passchendaele, the British Army was mounting an offensive. But could they be winning it? It would have been easier to keep her head buried in the sand like so many more did, but Penelope had seen too much for that. Each day she looked at a new casualty list in the newspaper, and each day it took just that bit more skill to breathe life into Young Perce.

It was October, six months after Avril had made her appearance. Sylvia was somewhere in the north, Penelope playing a week's music hall in Holborn. She'd come up in the world over the last couple of years. She had a dressing room to herself these days and her name was at the top of the bill.

A last look in the mirror, a dab more colour on her cheeks, an adjustment to her muffler, then picking up her concertina she was ready. When a knock came on her door she thought it was her call.

'Thanks, I'm coming.'

'These just been brought for you, Miss Drew. Made some of 'em sit up and take notice. Did ever you see such beauties?' Gertie Russell had spent more years than she cared to admit backstage helping the girls dress. 'Old Gertie' they called her. 'One for the books, Young Perce getting the flowers.'

The bouquet was magnificent – and flowers for Penelope something unusual. Perce sang and Perce danced, indeed no one danced like 'him', but any flowers that came backstage were for the more glamorous members of the cast. A basin of jellied eels would have seemed more to the taste of the urchin they all loved!

'For me?' Dumping the concertina on the make-up table she took them, feeling amongst the blooms to pull out the card. Tom! He must have been sent home! For one wild moment she expected to see his writing on the card.

'This time there is a town and there is a flower shop. You deserved the biggest bouquet then and so you still do. L.'

'Is he still here?'

'Yes, 'e's out front. Said to tell you he'd be round after you finish. Never told me 'is name, said you'd know.' She waited, hoping to be told, then craned her neck to read the card. 'L' told Gertie nothing. 'Wasn't a person I recognized . . . ' Then, putting first things first: 'Hark, there's the end of Nick Bollom's tricks, 'e'll be off in two shakes. You'd better get yerself out there. Here! What about this squeezebox, ain't you taking it? Blimey! Some o' you girls! Forget yer 'ed if you didn't have it screwed.'

Week after week Penelope had gone through her act,

had given to it everything that was in her. She'd believed it was because of what she'd seen in France that she'd lost some of the empathy she used to have with her audiences. Now, waiting in the wings for her entry, her heart was pounding with excitement. She didn't try to analyse why that was, simply accepted that it had to do with Laurence McLeod and the chord in her his music had touched. The band started to play her introductory bars. Perce and his antics were a far cry from emotions she'd hardly understood when he'd played the blues, but none of that mattered now. He was here, he'd sent her flowers, flowers for Perce . . . The few bars led to her entry chords – and she was off! Tonight all the old magic was there, tonight harmony flowed from her to the audience and back again. She brought the act to a close with 'Hold Fast to Tomorrow'. They loved it. This was the song they'd come to hear, this one was especially her own, her photograph blazoned on the front cover in every music shop window.

When she took her curtain call she saw someone stand up to applaud her; immediately others followed suit, some stamping their feet. It was that first one she noticed though, sitting two rows from the front of the stalls. Perce touched his cap to him.

They went by underground to the West End, then to his hotel. Top of the bill she might be, but supper at a grand hotel wasn't part of her routine. The last time had been with Sylvia and Tom. Over two years ago.

'Well? You're a long way away, Penelope Drew. Where have you travelled?'

'In my thoughts? Not far actually. Only just across the Square. I was thinking, it's over two years since I came to a smart hotel after the show, when Tom was home on his first leave.' She smiled across the table. 'A treat's even better when it comes as a surprise. That's all I was thinking. Nothing very deep. You're far more interesting. You

218

don't so much as limp, I watched you 'specially. So you're quite better?'

'Not only better, I'm flying again. And stationed in England for the time being — in Oxfordshire.'

Strangely, she had a sense of disappointment. They were talking like polite acquaintances. It must be something to do with his having two good legs again. While he'd been dependent on his wheelchair she had felt more useful, more of an equal. Now she was conscious of being young, nothing interesting to her.

She was aware that he was watching her closely, almost as if he were looking for something in her . . . subconsciously she sat straighter, ready to eat her food carefully as if she were a child again and Oliver drilling into her how important these things were.

'I told you I had a grandmother, do you remember?'

'Yes, of course I do. She lives in Penzance.'

'She did. Actually she lived a few miles out of Penzance, but that was the nearest place you would have heard of.'

'Lived?'

'She died. While I was still in hospital in France. I was sorry, I would like to have seen her.'

'I'm sorry too. She represented your English roots, didn't she?'

'Guess she must have been nearing ninety, she'd probably had enough of life. I shall go down there when I get some leave — it seems she left me her house. She had no other direct descendants. Reason tells me I ought to sell it. I'm an American — what use could I have for a house in Cornwall? Yet, I don't want to sever that last fragile tie. Then there's Sonny. I'd be depriving him.'

'I don't believe you can force people to see things the way you do. What I mean is, you can't say to Sonny, you had a great-grandmother in Cornwall, we have a house in Cornwall, therefore something of you belongs to Cornwall. You can't do that any more than you can sever your own ties. Don't you see? If someone told you that your grandmother hadn't really been your grandmother at all, it wouldn't make any difference now. You've grown accustomed to believing that you have a link to Cornwall, and nothing can take that away.'

She looked at him so earnestly; he wondered about her, what her own background was.

'A girl blessed with big brown eyes, a natural talent — and a husband called Tom. Do you realize that's all I know about you? But there's more to you than that, Penelope Drew. Tell me.'

It was so easy to talk to him. Once she started she found the years rolled away. He refilled her wine glass, asked just enough to keep the flow coming. In the background the small orchestra played, but background was all any of the room about them was. Laurence could seem to hear Chummy's tail thumping on the floor in his never failing welcome, or Mrs Sharp's heavy tread on the stair, something in the purposeful approach warning the child that she was 'coming after Pa 'cos of the rent'. Penelope's huge eyes were bright with affection (made brighter probably by the third glass of red wine) as she told him about the winter evenings she and her father had shared.

'Making plans, that was my favourite. It was almost as good as really having the rich red curtains and a cloth on the table. Just talking about it, knowing we both wanted the same thing. Pa taught me much more than I ever learnt in Merchant Hill Board School — he made me want to know about things. The Places Game — I don't think it was a proper game, I think Pa made it up.'

It was only much later, thinking back to that evening, that she realized that even to Tom or Alf or Sylvia she'd not taken the lid off her early years as she had to Laurence. He heard about the concertina, about Tom and Alf, even how the 'last one to the pier's a sissy'. He listened, topped up her wine glass to encourage her to talk.

The musicians who entertained during the evening were packing up. It was nearly midnight. And like Cinderella she was suddenly brought back to earth, realizing in alarm how much she'd been talking and not even too certain what she'd said.

'I've gotta go.' Her cheeks were pink with embarrassment. 'Dunno what you must think. I've been going on – and all about myself. Never done it before.'

'Good. I'm flattered. And tomorrow it'll be my turn. There are things I want to talk to you about. But not tonight. I must get you home.'

'I can get home on my own. I do every evening.'

'This is no ordinary evening. Please, I have a forty-eight-hour leave. I don't intend to spend it having early nights.'

"But he can't want to spend it with me for company. He's successful and important – and I've talked too much – think I've drunk too much too, the table keeps bobbing up and down and there's a funny humming noise in my head."

But she wasn't going to let anyone know how odd she felt, least of all an important person like Laurence McLeod. People he mixed with would all be used to having lots of wine with their food. If only the tablecloth weren't such a dazzling white it might not jitter about like this! She stood up very straight, one hand on the back of her chair, her chin high and a look of concentration on her unsmiling face. She hoped she gave an impression of sophistication. Her embarrassment would have been absolute had she been able to read his thoughts as he steered her arms into her coat.

Outside he guided her through the dark streets.

'We'll take a tube, that'll be quicker than a cab.' For most of the cabs were horse-drawn again now, petrol being in short supply. She was quiet, it took all her concentration to get on and off the escalator. When the tube came in he armed her on to it, trying not to let her see his concern at her white face. What a fool he was. Why hadn't he realized that she wasn't used to drinking? Hadn't she told him it was two years since she'd been to a 'smart hotel'?

'Jus – jus – shall we jus – jus walk – little bit?' she mumbled through dry lips. They must have been about halfway to Finchley; all she wanted was to escape this swaying prison.

'Sure, nothing I'd like better than to be out in the fresh air,' he agreed.

Another escalator and this time he bodily lifted her off her feet when they came to the top. Then they were out of the station, the night refreshingly chill.

The world had been transformed in those minutes they'd been rushing through the bowels of the earth. The search-lights were making a criss-cross pattern overhead, and then a noise that she'd never heard before, a noise that made her blood run cold. It sobered her as nothing else could. Or was it being thrown to the ground that did that, feeling his body on hers? It all happened in seconds, a distant rumble of falling bricks, someone screaming, footsteps, shouting. She lay quite still, above all else conscious of the banging of her heart and the echoing throb right through her.

'It's OK. Did you see the Zeppelin? It's gone, there won't be another bomb. Sure you're all right?' He was on his feet, bending to help her up.

'I'm sober as a judge, truly.' Which answered his unspoken question.

There was something unreal about the next hours. The bomb had fallen on a derelict building, known round about to be where the local down and outs slept. Houses nearby had broken windows, fallen ceilings, but nothing worse.

'Give a hand mate, can you?' someone called.

'Sure I can.'

Penelope heard and expected to help too. But apparently shifting fallen bricks was man's work.

'I'd like to get my hands on the bastard who did this,' a woman said, coming out of the house opposite the tramps' lodging. Then, to Penelope: 'You not hurt, my duck?'

222

'No. Can I sweep up the glass for you or something?'

'Not 'arf you can't! Should just see the mess inside. Daren't let the light shine out o' doors. Here comes Mill and Babs to see what the bugger's done.'

There was a camaraderie about the neighbourhood, and rather than shutting her out it included her. Friends or passers-by like herself and Laurence, all were united. Penelope found herself with a bass broom sweeping away glass from shattered windows, picking up pieces of broken household china, shaking plaster from bedding. Two o'clock and somebody – who, she had no idea – came from a less damaged house nearby with mugs of tea. At quarter-past two the lifeless body of an elderly man was brought out from the bombed building. At half-past, Penelope and Laurence were on their way to Finchley. Chance had brought them off the underground at that particular place and that particular time; for a few hours they'd felt close to those people, yet after tonight they'd probably never see any of them again – nor yet recognize them if they did. But that wasn't important. They'd all been part of the same human experience.

Laurence had intended to see Penelope safely indoors, then hoped to find a cab to take him to his hotel, but at this time of night and so far out of the city centre he thought it far more likely he'd have to go to the underground station and wait for the first train of morning. However, Mrs Fellows was careful of her house's good name, she'd made that quite clear to Penelope and Tom when first they'd taken two separate rooms with her. Lying in bed she cat-napped and listened. Staying out all hours, what was the girl thinking of? Hark, there was her key in the door – oh, and voices too. Mrs Fellows was out of bed like a shot. She'd known Penelope Drew for years, never any trouble, but she'd stamp on this caper before it started, that she would!

'What's all this then? Coming home here at four o'clock in the morning – and who's this with you? I'm not having – '

223

One look at them, covered with dust and grime, and she stopped, holding her candle high so that it cast its light on them. In her concern she forgot her own appearance, her teeth in a cup on her dressing table and her hair in rags. 'Whatever's happened to you? What a state you're in.'

Laurence explained why they'd been held up.

'I knew there was trouble somewhere. Heard the Zeppelin – and the guns. Well, what are we going to do with you? You won't get a cab this time of night and the tubes are all closed down. Not my custom to take any but stage people, but at times like these we have to make exceptions. If you want to use number six it's empty. I dare say someone will lend you a razor in the morning.'

'That's mighty kind of you, Mrs . . . ?'

'Oh, sorry. This is Mrs Fellows. Mrs Fellows, this is Laurence McLeod.'

'Well, I'm jiggered! Got the music of plenty of your songs in the parlour in the piano stool. Well, I'm jiggered.' She flashed her gums at him in approval.

'I'm grateful to you for saving me from a night on the underground platform, Mrs Fellows.' If he'd been introduced to Queen Mary herself he couldn't have shown more courtesy as he shook the landlady's hand. She blinked and sucked in her lips. Indeed she was jiggered. Music hall artistes were one thing, a songwriter known both sides of the Atlantic . . . As Old Gertie would say, she'd 'come over all unnecessary'.

Next morning Mrs Fellows threw out hints; she'd found the sheet music she'd told them about. If they cared to go over any of it, have a tune perhaps, it was on the piano. After the hospitality she'd shown him, Laurence could do no less.

The piano left a lot to be desired, Mr Hodges who used to tune it had gone into munitions back at the beginning of last year. But Mrs Fellows listened spellbound. Who would have thought this time yesterday that here she'd be listening to Laurence McLeod playing his own songs in her front room? Not only playing them, but singing them too! She could hardly wait for him to finish so that she could rush down the road to her friend Mrs Cload and tell her. Mrs Cload's lodgers were a very dull lot, one worked in the bank, two at one of the Ministry offices. Wait 'til she heard about this!

Almost as he closed the piano lid she was gone.

'Is that all?' Penelope was disappointed. 'In France, do you remember – the blues?'

So he opened the lid, and this time he played just for her.

> Don't you hear me cry
> To the heavens above
> What use am I
> Since I lost my love
> My tears are fallin'
> Oh, hear me callin'
> Callin' the blues

He sang, first the verse then the chorus, then nodded to her. Could she remember the words? Falteringly she started; he joined in. The second time around she was confident on her own. Her voice was low, husky, the cry of a broken heart.

'What are we going to do about you, Penelope Drew?' He swivelled round on the piano stool to look at her. He wasn't joking.

'Sorry. Wasn't I any good? It's not the sort of thing Perce sings, you see.'

'Penny,' he took both her hands in his, 'forget Perce. Weren't you any good you say! You wouldn't have a dry eye in the house. Your voice – ' he groped for the right word ' – your voice melts.'

'I'm not a real singer, I mean I can't get high pure notes like the soloists. Singing has always been, well, just a happy thing to do. But the blues is different. Makes you feel – oh, I don't know, I'm not clever at saying things. The words aren't the important part of the song are they? They're simple, just a sort of cry. It's the feeling.' She heard herself sounding gauche and tongue-tied; she was ashamed. 'Not just singing, though. Imagine dancing to that, expressing all it's trying to say in your movements . . . '

'You would be sensational, I've no doubts at all. Penny, I've seen artistes enough to judge. The gift that you have is something no one can learn. Pack Perce away. I've contacts here in London, I could get you an audition. No one's going to be interested in hearing you if all they connect you with is Perce. I'll make an appointment for you with Douglas Mountford.' Surely the first name in musical comedy in London. 'I'll tell him what I think of you and he'll hear you. That's all it'll take. He'll know just as surely as I do. You're supple as a snake, too. Your body is wasted on comic dancing no matter how clever.'

'No, I can't.'

'I recognized it in France. I'm doubly sure now. Do you want to spend all your days in music hall? And, Tom, if he were here he'd want you to climb to the top, now wouldn't he?'

'Yes, of course he would. If he were here and said so it would be different. But I told you before, I can't do it – I don't want to do it! I just want Tom to come home safe and things be fun like they used to be. Being famous, having everyone recognize you – like Mary Pickford or someone – that's not what I'm after.'

'So you're trying to tell me you prefer to romp about with comic songs than music like this. Is that what I'm to believe?'

He was playing again. Behind him she started to dance, standing almost on one spot, moving only her body and arms, her silent posturing saying as much as and more than the plaintive music.

'Well?' he asked her again as the last notes died away.

226

'I thought you'd understand.' Her eyes were luminous with tears. 'Don't you believe in trust, in keeping promises? Anyway,' she swallowed and blinked hard, then went on in a voice that brooked no argument, 'most important thing is to get Tom home. I'm keeping the act going, I've told you so before. Call it my war work if you like. I'd be courting trouble for us, throwing his future away by going solo under a different name. Anyway, I don't want to. It's tempting fate even to think about it. We've always been Tommy and Young Perce; I'm even planning the new act for when he's in it again.'

'When you write to this Tom of yours, tell him from me he's a lucky guy.'

She shook her head. 'I'll not tell him anything about this at all – just that Perce is waiting.'

He closed the lid of the piano. It was time he left, he said, he had one or two people to see while he was in town. That night he didn't come to Holborn. Gertie had put the flowers in a jug of water and there they stayed, until ten days or so later they were finally thrown out.

The months and years of the war followed the same repetitive pattern, at least for Penelope. Others were less fortunate. There was nothing to make any of them believe the end was in sight the following spring as the German Army reached the Marne and Paris was shelled. But, like a fresh wind of hope blowing over the Continent, Yankee Doodle came to town. Three-quarters of a million Americans were landed in France, men far from battle weary, worn down by years of struggle and food shortages. This new army was fit, well fed, eager to let it be seen what the New World could do. By September the tide had turned, the British had recaptured Cambrai, the Americans were fighting in the Argonne Forest and at Verdun. Even those at home who had been ostriches for the last four years pulled their heads out of the sand and took note of the good news.

The Middle East seemed so much further away, Penelope regularly hunted for every bit of news she could find. Even the Places Game hadn't prepared her for names like Beersheba and Askalon; but it had made her keen to learn and in the bedroom she and Sylvia either shared or used according to which of them was in London she kept an atlas where the progress of General Allenby's army was charted. In October she put a large red ring around Damascus to show that it had surrendered, then not many days later around Aleppo. Every red circle was a stage on the way towards bringing Tom home. By the end of that October in 1918 the Turks were utterly defeated. It couldn't be long!

In November the great day came. The Kaiser had fled, the Armistice had been signed. All over the country the bells rang out, bells of joy for some, bells surely with a hollow ring for so many more. But for everyone they were a hymn of thankfulness. It was over.

It was the end of that same month, November 1918, that the bells rang out for another reason. The bells of St James' Church, Challington; the occasion the wedding of Alf and his lovely Emma.

It was spring again before Tom came home, brown and somehow larger, older, even more handsome than they'd remembered him. He'd hung up his boots and his tropical kit too. Tom was ready for the footlights. But he wasn't ready to make his home under the ever watchful eye of Mrs Fellows.

'Time I was home sorting things out for you girls!' He beamed at both of them across the table of the small Italian restaurant in Vine Street where they were having supper. 'And that's exactly what I've been doing. Got to make the most of my freedom. Another couple of weeks and Perce'll have me back in harness.' A wink in Penelope's direction. He'd been home two days and intended to be foot-loose

in his old London haunts this week, go down to Challington next, and come back into the act the week after.

'What have you been doing?' Penelope prompted him.

'What about this? Bijou, the agent called it. Cramped is
nearer the mark. But it's got two bedrooms, mod cons –
well fairly mod, the bath is in the kitchen with a lid on
top of it – but what do you say? We don't want to spend
our lives with Flora Fellows laying down the law worse
than some sergeant major, do we, Pen? And you, Sylvia,
wouldn't you prefer a bath in the kitchen with us to a
hotel without us?' For now that he was home she'd moved
to a hotel nearer the West End, vacating her half of the
bed.

'It wouldn't be cramped for just the two of you,' Sylvia
said. 'I know what you've always said, both of you. But
– truly it's better not. Let's just leave things as they are.'

'You know what I always hoped, Sylvie. She's two now,
and she's gorgeous. If only you'd – '

'No!' Sylvia's face flooded with colour. 'You don't know
what you're talking about! I've said no. And to the house
too. I'm comfortable enough where I am, at any rate for
a bit. After Mrs Fellows, I can tell you the freedom is
wonderful.'

'Sylvia, forget what I just said. We're a good team, we'd
have a lot of fun together.'

Sylvia looked down at her plate, undecided; then
towards Tom.

'We can handle it, Sylvia,' he said.

Penelope laughed. 'Handle it, indeed. It'll be great fun.'

'Give it a try, why don't you?' Tom added his persuasion.

She almost let herself be swayed. But not quite.

'You two move in – I'll come and see you so often you'll
get fed up with me. And, if you don't then I'll think about
moving in. But seriously I do like the hotel. I'm my own
mistress there, I've nothing to worry about, no responsi-

229

bilities. And it's not like Mrs Fellows', I can have who I like to my room.'

Penelope was disappointed. But perhaps later on Sylvia would change her mind, and in the meantime she and Tom would enjoy a new freedom too. She giggled.

'What's up?'

'I was just picturing what fun it could be – supper in the bath.'

'Welcome Home, Tommy'. The choice of name was Tom's. 'You've done jolly well to keep the thing ticking along without me, but we want to make an impact now, a title to let people know that it's not just you any longer.'

Certainly it was a name that struck a note with demobilized soldiers wherever they played. But still it was Perce who stole the show. To Penelope that wasn't important. They were together. Surely her life now held everything she wanted. She certainly believed so in those weeks of spring and early summer. Like a child with a dolls' house she enjoyed housekeeping; each evening – with a Saturday matinée – she'd throw herself heart and soul into 'Welcome Home, Tommy'; at night they'd go back to their bijou house near Swiss Cottage where the day would end with their making love.

It was all just as she'd imagined it would be. One day she might look back on those weeks and think: "I ought to have realized." But for now she didn't. She saw only as far as her own narrow path of happiness.

CHAPTER NINE

'Come on, Tom! Buck up! You've not even cleaned your face!' Penelope stood with her back to him so that he could fasten the buttons of her dress.

'You go on without me. Think I'll get some air before I go home. Damned hot under those lights tonight.'

She heard it with a sinking heart. It wasn't what he said, it was the flat tone; lately she'd noticed it more and more. Tom had lost his sparkle.

'Tom,' it was easier to ask it with her back towards him, 'why won't you tell me what's the matter? Lots of soldiers are finding it hard to settle at home again, I was reading about it in a magazine.'

'Don't talk rot! You can't imagine I want to be back out there.'

'Is it the act? Do you want to change something? I know it was me who made it up, but it doesn't have to be like it is. Cut some of Perce's numbers — why don't you do that? Give one of the songs to Tommy?'

'Oh, don't keep on, Pen. The act's fine. It's just me. I'm sorry. Honestly, I don't mean to be such a bear with a sore head.'

Now she turned to face him. His monotonous voice told her nothing, she had to look at him.

'Let me come close, Tom, don't shut me out. I could help if you'd only talk to me.' She wound her thin arms around his neck. 'When you look around you, then at us — we're so lucky.'

'Oh, for heaven's sake, I can do without a sermon.'

Her mouth was raised to his, her finger caressed the back of his neck then moved down his spine. For a second or two he stood quite still, then gave her a light kiss on the forehead.

'You go home, Pen. I just want to walk.'

'Couldn't we walk together?'

'Drop it, can't you! I'll come when I'm ready. You get home and go on to bed.' She had never been able to keep any hurt she felt from her eyes. He saw it now. 'Pen – I'm sorry. It'll all work out.'

She nodded. ''course it will. And, Tom, I do understand, honest. You've got used to having a lot of men for company. It's not much fun for you having only me, living with me, working with me . . . You go for a pint of beer, have a chat at the pub. I'll see you later.' She kissed his chin, then turned and pulled her straw toque on to her head.

These new fashions might have been designed for her: slim and straight, the low waist hinting at neither bust nor hips. The shorter skirts exposed her slender calves and the buttoned shoes accentuated her neat ankles. At last materials in pastel shades where appearing again. Tonight Penelope was wearing a soft apple green frock with a cream lace collar.

For the first time that evening the old affection showed in Tom's smile. That was all it took. Penelope's eyes shone with happiness.

'How many years is it you've trodden the boards?' Then, answering his own question, 'Eight. You're like Peter Pan – still a child.'

'I'm a woman. A married woman. Hurry home, Tom, so that I can prove it to you! Don't walk about on your own for hours, promise? Go and find some company.'

'I promise.'

As she closed the dressing room door behind her she looked back, confident that he'd be watching her, the look in his eyes reassuring her. But he'd sat down at the make-up table, already plastering his face with cream.

Still, that one small smile had banished all her anxiety.

She'd do as he said, leave him to walk or have a drink or do what he wanted. Soon he'd come home. She'd wait up for him. Not checking how long he'd been, but making him glad to find her there. A smile played at the corners of her mouth as her mind leapt ahead.

The other day she'd bought a sheer silk nightie with matching negligée. Then the moment hadn't seemed right to give it a first airing. Tonight she took it from its tissue wrapping then lit the geyser in the kitchen. Scent in the water, her new nightie waiting on the back of a wooden chair. She wouldn't hurry. Let him find her in the bath. The thought excited her — so it would excite him. Luxuriously she soaped each leg, holding it high, pointing her toes; sensuously she rubbed her soapy hands all over her body, dipping and wriggling in the warm water.

Midnight. The water was getting cold, the soap leaving a scummy rim on the tub. It took a lot to discourage Penelope, it always had. Best to get out quickly, clean the bath and put her nightie and negligee on. She smelt nice from the scented water. She'd lie on the sofa and wait for him. None of this boring pyjamas and bed. The night was warm. She'd planned her seduction scene to get them no further than the sitting room rug. Oh, she wished he'd come! Perhaps he hadn't understood the hint she'd dropped . . .

One o'clock. Supposing something had happened to him? Wherever could he be walking to be out as long as this? Then she supposed something so much worse that she couldn't even let the idea take shape. He couldn't be as miserable as that — no, no, of course he wasn't! He must have met someone, perhaps someone he'd known in the Army. He'd think she was in bed asleep. He wasn't to know that she'd be standing here at the window trying to will him to come. The street lamps stayed on all night, each casting its own pool of yellow light.

Two o'clock. Even at this hour the silence never held for long; there was the occasional rattle of a horse-drawn cart, the roar of an automobile. The warm night was breaking with a storm. She could tell it was coming by the way the wind suddenly rattled the window panes. Then, some way away, thunder. She shivered. Her arms were covered in goose pimples.

"Silly to get cold." Which was a silent acknowledgement that when he did come home it wouldn't be the moment for him to appreciate her scent and sheer silk. She went up the narrow stairs, a flash of lightning timed to illuminate their bedroom as she opened the door, followed by a roll of thunder. Senseless fear of storms had been born in her long ago, the first seeds sown by Mrs Sharp and nurtured by Chummy. With her back to the window she changed into her everyday dressing gown, then went back downstairs. She'd planned to let him find her lying on the sofa, she'd even practised the most alluring position. That's where he did find her, sound asleep, her face buried against one cushion, a second on top to block out the noise and sight of the storm.

'Why in the – ?'

She woke at the sound of his voice.

'Oh, thank goodness.' She knelt up. 'I was so worried. I was frightened – ' but now that he was home she saw the stupidity of her fears. 'Did you meet someone? Where were you? You're not even wet?'

'What's this, the Spanish Inquisition?' His lips looked tight.

''course not. Just I was worried. I thought you'd walked too far and got caught in the wet. But you're dry? You went home with someone.'

'That's right.' He ran a hand through his dark hair. 'Pen, don't keep badgering me, for Christ's sake! Just give me space.'

She drew back as if he'd inflicted a physical blow.

'I'm sorry, Tom. Honest, I don't mean to badger. Well, now you're home, we'd better get some sleep.' With what she hoped passed for dignity, she led the way up the stairs,

234

lighting the gas in the bedroom, while he turned it off in the sitting room and followed her.

As if he hadn't felt wretched enough without getting home to this! It wasn't fair. Why couldn't she build a life of her own, why did she have to make it so obvious her happiness only came from being with him? Poor old Pen. She'd always doted on him. Good kid, she always had been. Wasn't as if she was one of these 'hole in her nightie' sorts like lots of chaps' wives. No, it wasn't her fault.

She took off her dressing gown and he noticed the sheer silk.

'New nightgown? Umph, very nice too.' ("Poor kid, must have worn it specially, been waiting for me . . . ") 'Pity it's so late, eh? Or should I say early. The milk cart'll be coming along soon.'

'Put it on because it was so hot,' she lied. 'It's thin.' Only her eyes told the story of her night.

Women! Let's hope she wasn't going to start blubbing. He pulled off his trousers, and tipping back the mattress put them under it to keep the creases. 'In you hop,' he said as he laid it carefully flat again. But she was staring at something, her eyes wide. He followed her gaze to the red mark on his thigh. Lipstick. Now she'd seen one mark the others, less bright, were clear.

Oh those 'silly tears'! She blinked, gritted her teeth.

'Pen, try and understand.'

'Not tonight. Not now.' It was hard to talk through clenched teeth. To hang on to her composure became the most important thing; concentrating on that she didn't have to think of anything else.

Back to back they lay there, neither speaking. She believed all the anguish was hers. Had he known when she left him that he was going to another woman, or had he fallen for the temptation of some streetwalker. But why? Why? After the show when he'd seemed cut off from her, she'd been so sure of the way to get closer to him. But it hadn't been her he'd gone to. Again she saw herself getting ready for him to come home, she'd been so sure . . . but it hadn't been her body he'd wanted. Purposely she breathed deeply, feigning sleep; by her side, Tom did the same.

Perhaps she had been immature to have expected anything else. Plenty of men behaved like it. 'He's a lad for the ladies.' She'd heard it said often enough, said with a ring of admiration – but not about Tom. Pa, now, he was one for the ladies; he liked nothing better than a pretty woman on his arm. There are all sorts of ways of loving, hadn't Mother said so? But a lady on his arm wasn't the same as lipstick on his body. She bit her pillow to stop herself from crying out in jealousy and pain.

The next day by unspoken agreement they avoided each other, hardly coming face to face until they were in the flood of the footlights. That performance was the hardest she'd ever played. Yet Tom, who'd not spoken a word in the dressing room, and who showed even more signs of strain than she did herself, struggled to keep up a semblance of normality between them.

'I saw Sylvia this afternoon.' The show over, he was creaming the make-up off his face as he spoke. 'She invited us for supper – I said we would.' Anything was better than going home obviously.

She'd always thought there was nothing too private to share with Sylvia but saw now that she'd been wrong. Lots of men had women outside marriage, she'd told herself so a hundred times during the day. "But not Tom." She was haunted by memories of a day – it seemed a lifetime ago – when Sylvia had been talking about Ken, saying she was always getting to know something new about him. Penelope had listened and been so confident, so smug in her confidence. There was nothing she and Tom hadn't known about each other, she'd thought, believing they were two sides of the same coin. But this was something she couldn't talk about to anyone, least of all Sylvia. "We'll share our good times – and our sad times too." Automati-

236

cally she cleaned her face, pulled her dress over her head, ghosts and echoes all around her.

'Miss Carstairs is expecting you,' they were told. 'She said would you go straight to her room when you arrived?'

'This is the way to live,' Tom made a forced attempt to be bright. 'No going home to bread and cheese for Sylvia.'

'I thought we would have met her in the dining room.'

"When you stop and listen to what you say, there's none of it worth saying. I wish we'd waited downstairs where there are lots of people. Tom looks quite ill." Penelope gave him the hint of a smile. She couldn't help it; he must be feeling wretched about it all to look so drawn and pale.

Sylvia answered the knock and ushered them in to her room. It was large and at one end held a gate-leg table which was opened up and set for supper.

'No mixing with the rabble tonight, I see.' Tom's teasing couldn't have sounded natural to any of them.

Penelope expected Sylvia to make some comment, but his remark passed her by.

'Pour some drinks, Tom. Or better, mix us a cocktail, surprise us.'

He would have preferred straight whisky, but mixing the cocktails kept him occupied hunting out a dash of this, a splash of that. He knew nothing about cocktails, but what he put in the shaker ought to be enough to give them all the Dutch courage they needed.

They sipped, blinked, sipped again.

'What in the world have you put in this?' Sylvia laughed.

'I don't remember.'

'And by the time we've drunk it, I shouldn't think any of us will be in a state to guess!'

The atmosphere was contrived, there was a forced gaiety, but it helped the minutes along until the waiter had brought their meal and left them alone. Then, as if she could play games no longer, Sylvia dived straight in.

237

'Penny, I've written to your mother. I expect she'll be quite upset – but I've decided to have Avril back.'

'Are you sure? Sylvie, you've never even been down to see her. Why now, after all this time?'

'I've seen her.' It was Tom who spoke, a remark that had no bearing on anything.

'You always said I should have her with me, get a housekeeper.'

'What I said was, let's make a home for her together. On your own – well, you'll be tied. I know a housekeeper would look after her but . . . Sylvia, think of her as well as yourself, that's the only home she's ever known. They're her family – her roots.' What an evening for ghosts this was turning out to be! She remembered having a similar conversation with Laurence McLeod. She'd read about his latest musical opening on Broadway . . .

' . . . never meant it to happen. I thought we could handle it.'

Penelope held her musing in check.

'Sorry, I missed what you were saying. I was just remembering something.'

'Penny, I've even rehearsed how to say it. Over and over I've pictured how it would be to tell you – I've never seen her – but you have. And you didn't guess, you didn't even suspect that – '

Tom came to Sylvia's rescue.

'Pen, what Sylvia's saying is – Avril. I'm her father.'

She felt nothing. It was as if she stood outside herself, watching, listening. She'd heard of people feeling numb; so it wasn't just an expression, it really happened. She couldn't take in what they were telling her, yet neither did she reject it. It was words, just words.

'Was he here last night?' she listened to herself asking, as if that would give her the answer to everything.

'Pen, not just last night. I'm sorry, honestly I'm sorry for doing this to you. We've been pals since we were kids. If you know what a heel I feel about all this.'

238

'Do you?' No spite in her voice. Rather she was curious. This was Tom, the boy she'd known so well, the man she'd believed she knew as well as she did herself.

'It was after Ken was killed,' Sylvia took up the story. 'I don't know what I would have done without Tom. I turned to him for everything.'

Penelope nodded. 'So it seems.'

'We didn't mean it to be like that. Well, we'd always been a bit keen, even when we were children. Remember, Penny, how I used to say he was the handsomest boy I'd ever seen?'

'And you were his – what was it, Tom? – "luscious Sylvia". Wasn't that what you used to call her?' The numbness was going. Yet still she was on the outside listening to the sarcasm in her voice that had nothing to do with the ache in her arms, the hollow emptiness in her chest. They were her secret, she'd not let anyone know. Easier to sneer, easier to hate . . .

'Then after I lost Ken, and his family were so beastly to me, I had to have someone. Tom was there. We thought that's all it was, a bit of fun. He was lonely, I was miserable, we helped each other.'

'And why not?' Those brown eyes scorned the pair of them. 'Hadn't we sworn to share – all the good times, all the sad ones. Which was Tom? A good one?'

'I don't blame you for feeling spiteful, Pen.' Tom took a too large swig of his fiery cocktail. It made his eyes water. 'But Sylvia's right, we were both upset about it, about hurting you. She didn't write to me when I went overseas, and I didn't try and contact her. We thought it was over. We were pretty sick about it, but we knew it had to be like that. Then you wrote and told me she was having a baby. Of course, I knew it was mine – '

'What sublime confidence!'

'Oh, shut up!' Sylvia, the least emotional, was crying openly. 'Of course it was his. I know what I did was wrong – taking my friend's husband – but, Penny, it had to

239

happen. I truly loved him. I told you that right from the start. I told you it wasn't a casual affair – '

'Oh, I misunderstood. I thought you just called it a bit of fun?' If only she could think of something cutting, something clever, but her mind was still reeling from shock.

Now Tom joined the fray. 'That's all we meant it to be. Oh, damn it all, Pen, sometimes things get out of hand. I don't mean because we slept together.' He reached across the table and took Sylvia's hand. Now the numbness had gone. In that one simple action he brought Penelope alive with pain as he turned to her and said: 'Pen, we didn't want to have to hurt you, we've tried, we've fought against it. Then, when you and I went down to Challington, when I saw Avril – I can't understand how everyone doesn't guess. Why, she even looks just like me!' There was pride in his voice.

'That was weeks ago.'

'I know. I wanted to spill the beans then, get it settled, but Sylvia – '

'I said no,' Sylvia chimed in. 'It's no use, though, we can't go on like this. None of us is really happy. Penny, you can't want it to go on now, knowing how Tom feels. Can you?'

Penelope ignored her and turned to Tom.

'You're leaving me, is that what you're saying?' She knew it was exactly what he was saying, but she asked it, gave him one last chance to remember all the good times they'd shared. Could he really imagine he could wipe it all out so easily – that she could? 'We've been pals since we were kids.' He'd said it so often.

'I'm sorry, Pen.'

'Does Alf know – about you and Sylvia, about the baby?'

''struth, no! That's a rotten thing to suggest. As if I'd talk about it, tell anyone what our marriage has come to

240

and that I want my freedom. Not to anyone, Pen, least of all old Alf.'

Sylvia had recovered from her tears, her bright future beckoning.

'No need to tell anyone more than you want to,' she said. 'Penny will have to cite me, but the past needn't be dragged in to it. She needn't even tell the solicitor. Anyway, you've lived together since then, I don't expect it would count.' She looked uneasily from one to the other. 'It's the future that matters – and, more immediately, the present. Will you go back to Swiss Cottage tonight, Tom, or . . . ?'

From numbness to hurt and now finally to anger. Penelope had never believed there was such anger inside her.

'He can go where he likes – but not home with me!'

"Not home with me – I can't be saying it. Tom . . . not coming home," her heart was screaming, but they couldn't guess at it from the sneer as she repeated their words.

'Poor little Pen, mustn't hurt Pen. I should be crying alleluya that at last I'm not being cheated.'

There was a dangerous note in her voice, hysteria not far beneath the surface. A silent message passed between the other two. Best to be gentle with her.

'There's no point in my staying any longer.' She pushed back her chair.

Tom stood up too. It was over, the thing he'd dreaded for months. It was done. He'd told her.

'Best not to talk about it any more now. I'll come and see you later. There's not much chance in the theatre – '

'Theatre? We shan't be at the theatre.'

'This needn't make any difference to our professional lives. We've always worked well together. Tommy and Perce are doing fine. It's a great team, Pen. You didn't imagine I was suggesting throwing you out of a job too! We've got bookings for weeks. The act needs both of us. I know you kept the show going on your own before, but that was different. Wartime, people understood. They accepted that things had to be at half cock.'

241

Every pulse in her body was hammering. Everything was against her, even her height, as she looked from one to the other, both of them so much taller than her. What could she say that would knock him off his perch?

'Now it's full cock, I suppose you think? Well, you can keep it – cock and all! And I hope she enjoys it!'

'Don't be like that, Pen. Not after we've been pals so long. It isn't as if I've picked up with some tart. You're hurt now but don't say things you'll regret. Just let's keep on with the act.'

But her one brief outburst had released the safety valve. There was no going back. Like a cloak she wrapped a new dignity around her.

'People have made bookings for this week, I shan't let them down.' She was pleased with her quiet, even tone. 'After that, the act is your affair.'

'But, Pen . . . '

She raised her chin, meeting his gaze squarely. And for once those tell-tale eyes kept her secret; she might have been looking at a stranger for all the interest there was in them.

'You will see a solicitor, Penny?' Sylvia took the new-found calm as an opportunity to press her point.

Penelope shrugged her shoulders.

'I don't know what I intend to do yet. Tom, I shall be out in the morning. Perhaps you'll collect your things.'

'No rush, Pen.' Did he honestly think he'd hurt her less by not seeming anxious to cut the final cord?

'I'd be glad if you'd clear them.'

'If that's the way you want it,' he mumbled, not looking at her. 'You will do something about a divorce? I would but – '

'Oh, I'm sorry.' Her smile was brittle, her voice as cold as ice. 'I've not given you grounds, have I? What must you think of me! Such a nice, cosy family you'll be, the three of you, and I'm letting your name be soiled with talk of unfaithfulness, adultery.' She picked up her purse, ready to go.

'Penny!' It was Sylvia, rather than Tom, who nearly broke through her defences, grabbing her hand and holding her back as she made for the door. 'Don't go like that, not with bad feeling. We're more than ordinary friends, we always have been.'

Tearing her hand free Penelope escaped. The lift was standing there empty, but she didn't take it. She ran down the stairs, not stopping until she was outside in the night air. Looking neither to right nor left she hurried away.

A young woman alone at this time of night. 'What's the rush?' . . . 'All on your own then?' . . . 'Hey there, missie, what about a bit o' comp'ny?' was the gist of the comments. She hardly heard and certainly didn't care. Like a wounded animal making for its nest, she crossed Leicester Square, heading for Piccadilly Circus. Then the swaying underground train and a short walk home. At last she was inside, wrapped in darkness and solitude. As if all the devils of hell had been on her heels she locked the door. Leaning against it, the fight drained from her.

'Hello, I'm home.' Stupid to call out, she knew it was; she had to turn the knife in the wound. Stupid to speak aloud too. ' . . . nobody . . . nobody here . . . just me . . . never coming home . . . never wanted to be here . . . but why? Tom, why . . . ?' Tonight there was nothing 'silly' in her tears, nor in the great gulping sobs that rose from deep inside her. Only a few minutes ago, dry-eyed and determined, she'd hurried through the London night. Now her legs hadn't the strength to support her. She went down on her knees, her head bowed to the ground in front of her. Just as she cried unrestrainedly, so she talked, wailed aloud her grief and betrayal, over and over again, until there was darkness in the room, darkness in her heart, no glimmer of light or hope anywhere.

'I knew you'd come. I told Ollie – ' But what she'd told

Ollie Muriel didn't say as she enfolded Penelope in her never-failing, warm embrace.

'Mother, I tried to talk her out of it. What will you do without her?' With Avril taking in every word, Penelope didn't mention her by name. 'She's like your own.'

'If she's all right then I shall be too. Keep telling myself it's for the best. She's not short of a bob or two, be able to give her a better chance than we could. That's what I keep telling myself. Anyway, nothing else for it, I've no rights. Oh, look, Avril! There's Tibby jumped on your dolls' pram again. You run and shoo him off before he sits on Rosie.'

Off went Avril to attend to more important things than grown-ups talking.

'A woman out every evening, someone paid to keep an eye . . . It's no way to rear a child. It's time the little soul needs, time and love. Do you think Sylvia is really ready for her?'

Penelope turned to watch the little girl with her pram. A glorious-looking child with dark curly hair which in the July sunshine held a glow of red, and vivid blue eyes. It was easier to speak with her back to Muriel.

'It won't be like that. Well, not quite like that. Avril took to Tom, didn't she, Mother?'

'That she did! Followed him everywhere. That pleased with himself he was, too.'

'You're as green as I was. We neither of us guessed.' Come on, now, say it. You can't put it off any longer. Say it while Avril's outside. But she didn't have to say it.

'Green as you . . . so your Pa's right? Is that what you're telling me? "They'll be one big family, I've always known it," that's what Ollie said. But I wouldn't listen. Penny love, how can you want to live like it?'

'Me?' She started to laugh, but there was no mirth in the sound. 'Me? Oh, I haven't been invited! Pa's wrong there. He talked to me about one big happy family, the

244

night she was born. I didn't know what he was getting at. You mean, he knew, even then?'

'Never mind then, Penny love. What do you mean, you're not invited? You mean Tom wants to set up home with Sylvia? Avril's really his? You're sure of that?'

'Yes, I'm sure. It seems they've been playing a "being kind to Penny" game all these years. Green, like I said. Heaven knows I was green! Well,' she turned round, her chin up and her lips forced into a bright smile, 'I'm not green any longer. And I can live very nicely without pity from either of them.'

'Better without them! What a way to behave. That husband of hers could hardly have been under the ground when she and Tom started all their nonsense.'

'Anyway, that's years ago now and they want to make a fresh start, have Avril with them.'

'She's not got as much maternal instinct as our Tibby! At least Tibs cares for her kits when they're tiny even if she can't abide them a bit later on.'

'It'll be different now. Tom dotes on Avril.'

'Looks like him, that's about why. Conceited young fop! Ollie said so right from the start, but I wouldn't listen 'cos after all he was your choice. You're naught but a child though, Penny. Plenty of time ahead for you to find proper happiness with a good man. Look at me! I was thirty-five when I met Ollie, and a virgin at that.'

There was silence for a while. Penny was lost for the right thing to say; Muriel lost in memories. She sensed it was easier for Penelope to listen than to talk, so she went on eventually: 'Never thought Tom wanted a family. Or was it you, perhaps, who didn't? None of my business, I shouldn't pry. But life's a funny old business, Penny love. If a woman's beautiful, good figure and all that, everyone expects she'll want a man in her bed. I remember thinking that before I met Ollie. But I learnt. Somewhere along the way you see the turning you've been looking for. Thirty-five and a virgin, never been in love and never had a man want me, not even just on a borrowing basis let alone for keeps. Then – all that was changed. First Ollie – and you to love – and before the year was out a babbee of our own.' She put her arm around Penelope. 'Your road'll have the right turning too, never you doubt it. And if that's the way he could behave, then you send up a little thank you that you got shot.'

'It's nice to come home.'

''course it is. That's what homes are for, to be nice to come to. None of your rushing off again. You let me have a chance to put a bit of fat on you. Why, child, you're no more than six pennorth of scrag.'

Again Penelope tried to laugh. It tore at Muriel's kind heart to hear her, and as the joyless attempt gave way to tears she was ready. 'That's it, you cry all your troubles away.'

And in a way, that's what Penelope did. Oh, it wasn't as simple as that; there would be many times when a great wave of loneliness would swamp her; there would be times when her body would ache for Tom's touch. If he'd been taken from her in death she could have accepted it. What bruised her soul was the knowledge that their marriage had been built on pretence. It must have started off in love but how many of her memories dared she examine closely? How many were based on truth and how many on pretence? Where was the dividing line? No, unhappiness can't be shed like a snake shedding its skin. But all the same, even if she didn't cry all her troubles away, at least as she blew her nose and wiped her tears, then washed her face at the kitchen sink, she felt she'd taken another step or two along that road Muriel talked about.

'Where's Pa?' For with the closing of the munitions factory he had happily drifted back into a life of leisure. Peggy worked in the local auctioneer's office, Cath on the switchboard at the telephone exchange (surprising the snippets of information she was able to share with her sister). Mavis had married an American soldier and sailed

246

away to the New World. So the room she and Emma had shared was now taken by two young men from the bank. Add to that Miss Helspeth, manageress of Moody's Fashions, Timothy Hunter who'd just come out of the Navy and was teaching at a boys' private school, and Mrs Mary Greaves, a young war widow who'd found work in the chemist's shop and that was full house at number fourteen Alexandra Square. No more summer visitors for Muriel, to these people Clifford House was home. During the war the four girls had lived as if they were family. They'd eaten in the kitchen, even helped wash the dishes sometimes. Now, though, the dining room was in use and a new pattern had evolved – or more accurately the original one had been restored. And from that pattern Oliver had picked up the thread that had always been his.

'Your pa?' Muriel laughed. 'Now where would you expect him to be on a nice sunny afternoon? Wouldn't mind betting he's listening to the band. Well,' and she winked, her eyes dancing with affection, 'that'll be what he'll tell us anyway. Never you worry about your pa. May not be what other people would say, but I reckon I know him better than they do.'

Again Penelope was lost for an answer. Hadn't she thought the same about Tom?

'I'll take Avril down to the sand presently, shall I? When the others come in from school they could come and find us. Tell them I'll buy them an ice-cream cornet from the dairy.' Then she added: 'Be better if we're all out when Pa comes home, wouldn't it? Be better if the others didn't hear everything that's said.'

'Better indeed. Your pa's pretty wild about – well, I said, he's always had his ideas about who the father was. But to give you the push so that the two of them can set up house together . . . no, Ollie's better to hear it without the children's ears taking in what he'll have to say.'

'Mother, the push was the one thing he didn't give me! He even wanted us to keep the act going. But I've other

247

plans. If they'd not been so keen to protect my feelings I would have given up Perce ages ago. I had a better chance then, I was offered an audition with Douglas Mountford. Can you imagine it, Douglas Mountford! And what did I do? I turned it down because of keeping Perce and Tommy going. Well, now I'm going to think just of myself. Myself first, last and all the way.'

'Douglas Mountford?' Clearly she'd never heard of him. 'That's nice, Penny.'

'It would have been. I was to have had an introduction to him, get in through the back door. Now I have to take what I can get. But I auditioned for "Song of the Dawn". I'm to have a solo in that.'

'Still in that tatty old suit?'

'Perce is dead and buried. From now on Penelope Drew is herself. And you know – this is just between you and me, I wouldn't repeat this to Pa because he thinks stage people are pretty rotten at best – I'm excited about it. It's a sort of rebirth. Me! Not some character I built and then hid behind, but actually me. I ought to feel crushed and hopeless, I got the push from Tom as you say. Half of me is still. But the other half is just waiting to come alive, to be let free. Oh, I don't mean free for other men – men, you can have them! – but free to be myself, do things *my* way. Succeed or fail, whatever I do, it'll be *my* way.'

Brave talk, staring life in the face and daring it to think she was defeated. There were so many hurdles still to cross. Down here in Challington, everywhere was wrapped up with their past. The pier, the fishing boats, the boat yard, even the pawn shop . . . it seemed wherever she looked some ghost or other was waiting to jump out and take her by surprise. The hardest thing she had to do was to go and tell Alf.

'I don't believe it, Pen! It must be a passing fancy, a sort of reaction after the war. War does funny things to men.'

'No, Alf, it's nothing to do with the war. I'm not looking

for loopholes. The truth is we got married before we'd had time to look around.'

There was a twitch in the side of his face that was still Alf. If the other side had been more than a disfigured mask the physical sign of emotion might have gone unnoticed. As it was, Alf was unable to hide his distress.

'It's all right, you know. I'm going to be all right.'

'The sod! All right, you say? Well, I've done with him.' With clenched fists he repeatedly beat his hands together. Alf still had a long way to go before his own war was behind him.

Emma put a hand on his shoulder. Penelope looked at her helplessly.

'I'm not going to let it get on top of me, Alf. I've got plans.'

'You had plans before, 'til he and that damned woman took them away from you.'

'Don't you remember what we always said: "Life ain't all you want, but it's all you're gonna 'ave, so 'ave it, put a — "'

It was Emma who finished it off. To a stranger it might have sounded like nothing. To Penelope there was no doubt of her 'geranium in yer 'at and be 'appy'.

The tension was eased. Alf had a long way to go before he fully accepted the new situation. But to tell him that Tom had rejected her had been another hurdle for the new Penelope Drew to climb, and now she was over it.

She had three weeks before rehearsals started. She'd come down to Challington meaning to spend them there. But ghosts make poor companions – and the flesh and blood variety weren't that much easier. Oliver could do no wrong in Muriel's eyes; the Pa of days gone by was safely on a lofty pedestal in Penelope's heart. Yet that same love she'd always have for him made it all the more difficult to be with him now. Often she found him looking at her with an expression that made her uncomfortable. Not dislike, not affection, it might almost have been taken for fear. Most of the time he ignored her entirely.

In the summer evenings the children liked to be out; on the shore there was always plenty to do. Because of serving an evening meal to the lodgers, Muriel had never had time to spare for chasing them off to bed and she believed fresh air did them more good than lying in a hot attic. But on this particular July evening it was raining steadily. Oliver had been out playing darts but there hadn't been many of the regulars in the Standard so he came home early, to find Penelope and the three children round the kitchen table playing the Places Game.

'I sailed out of Southampton and crossed the Atlantic to America, docking at – two words – NY.'

'New Zealand,' suggested Bruce hopefully, his geography poor and his spelling no better.

'New York,' Amanda corrected. 'My go. I took a train down through France to a sea beginning with M.'

'Pa!' Penelope looked up as he came in. 'Fancy your not teaching them the game! All the geography I ever learnt you taught me with the game.' Such a strange look he gave her. 'Pa . . . come and play too.'

'Having a good time, kids?' He rumpled Bruce's hair. Yet he behaved as if Penelope weren't there at all.

'Please, Dad. Penny said you're the champion.'

'I'll play another time. You get Penny to teach you – and get your atlases out and learn some places. I don't play with ignoramuses, you know.' The game went on. Ollie folded his newspaper and took a pencil from his pocket. The crossword puzzle had recently made its appearance and quickly been adopted as part of his daily routine.

It was much later, even Merrick had gone up to bed and Muriel was seeing they were all settled, taking a second peep at sleeping Avril. Each night she was still with them was precious. Any day they would hear that Sylvia was coming to fetch her.

250

'Give me a clue, Pa. Let's see if I can do one.'

Her voice caught him unaware, gazing into nothingness. If she'd thought him to be puzzling over the crossword she was vastly mistaken. He threw the paper to one side.

'Never much good to you, was I? Poor little bastard! Stuck there in that rotten hole.'

'Pa, don't talk like that.' She knelt down in front of him. 'You gave me more than most children have – you made me feel I was important to you. We were partners. It's love children need, isn't that what Muriel always says? I never went short of that.'

He tilted her chin, looking deep into her eyes.

'Love – hate – fear too.' His mouth was wobbling again.

'Fear? Of what? Not having the rent for Mrs Sharp?' Anything to keep emotion out of it. Penelope wanted them to laugh together, to remember the happy times and be happy remembering.

'Fear of you – fear of letting myself love you.' His hands on her face were soft as a woman's – and why not? He never did anything to soil them.

'Oh, well, you hid it very well. I think you imagine it. You and I were pals, Pa.'

He smiled, like a naughty boy. 'We were, weren't we?' Then, as quickly again, what she thought of as 'the wobbly look' was back. 'Forgive your poor old pa? Not been much use to you, Tuppence. Things haven't been kind to you – a father not worth calling one, a husband who doesn't want you. I know what you must be feeling.'

'It's all gonna be all right, Pa.'

'Going to be – you're as bad as the children! Going to be all right, is it? I knew, before the baby was born, I knew it was that sod Tom Beasley's. I hoped you'd never find out.'

'You guessed? But how?'

'He used to write to her when she was here.'

'I know. That was no secret.'

'Ah!' He leant forward towards her as she still knelt

there, his face only inches from hers. 'No secret that he wrote. But I read the letters. She kept them in the drawer with her underwear.'

'You looked in her drawer?' The picture of him hunting through Sylvia's things shocked her.

'I did it for you.' But there was something in his expression that repelled her. He'd done it for himself too. He'd fed some unsatisfied lust of his own by reading their letters. 'Shall I tell you – '

'No. I don't want to hear about it. Let it be finished.'

He shrugged. 'As you like. But it won't be. Nothing is ever finished. When your mother went off I pretended too, just like you are. Let it be finished.'

'And so it is.' She knelt up very straight, forcing him to meet her eyes. 'If you saw my mother now you probably wouldn't recognize her, and if you did you probably wouldn't like what you saw. You're being maudlin. Well, I'm not going to be. I honestly don't want them to be unhappy together. If they were it would be such a waste – a waste for me, I mean. But I'll tell you one thing, Pa. I'm going to climb to the top of the tree. They'll never be able to reach me, but they'll see me up there. They will! That's where I'm gonna be.'

'Going to – '

They heard Muriel coming down the stairs. He picked up his newspaper and Penelope stood up. The moment was over.

She stayed just over a week at Challington, but they never came as close to each other again as they did that evening.

Like so many small people, Penelope had an outsize determination and she needed every ounce of it as she went back to London to sort through what had been her home. She gave notice that she was vacating it, found herself digs – this time not in Finchley. She'd promised herself a new beginning, with no shadows of yesterday. She took a room in a boarding house not far from Marble Arch and moved in in time to start rehearsals halfway through August.

The age of musical comedies, influenced by the American stage, had arrived in London. Penelope had one solo number, but no part in the story. One song, and if Laurence McLeod could have heard it he would have felt a twinge of satisfaction. It had been her own choice that she should sing a blues song for her audition, something so removed from Perce that it was like making her debut all over again.

'Two minutes, Miss Drew!' She heard the familiar call as the knock came on her door. A West End first night. Not a variety show with different artistes each week but a show that might run for months, even years! Out there in the front would be critics from the national newspapers. Tonight mattered as no other performance had. One last look in the mirror. Even her costume was daring enough to get her noticed! It fitted like another skin, covering her body, arms, legs in shimmering silver. Her short hair was cut in a fringe – fashionable now, although it had raised eyebrows eight years ago when Perce had first been shorn – with a silver band around her forehead. Her cue came, the first throbbing notes from the orchestra. Her heart was banging wildly, but then it always had before she walked out on to the stage. Now, as then, it wasn't nerves, it was excitement. Audiences had loved Perce. Penelope Drew as a person they'd not known; even her name hadn't been as important as Perce's. So tonight she had to forge a new bond. With Perce they'd laughed. Now she reached out to deeper emotions. Laurence had said her voice 'melted', and so it did. Low, soft, husky, full of heartbreak; and then her body took up the theme. As supple as a snake . . . but no snake had the balance, the poise. As the final notes faded the theatre was full of the thunder of applause.

Her first First Night party. She was being swept along on a tide of congratulation, floating on a sea of champagne. Maybe she had been only one small part of the show, but it had made a big impact. She knew it even before she read the morning papers.

The night was nearly over by the time she got to bed. It had all been so exciting . . . she felt full of bubbles, champagne bubbles . . . for one foolish moment she imagined coming home at the end of the evening and talking to Sylvia . . . how they used to sit into the early hours . . . she wished . . . but even before the wish was formed she was asleep.

CHAPTER TEN

Nearly a fortnight on and the excitement still held. The
theatre was booked to capacity. Penelope had been lucky;
her first solo without Perce to hide behind might so easily
have been in a show doomed to failure. 'Song of the Dawn'
was modern, bright. It belonged to an age that had come
through four joyless years (four years at half cock, as Tom
might put it), to hurtle at full pelt into an almost hysterical
gaiety. Too soon yet for the 'flappers' to have taken the
floor, but they weren't far behind.

Until now a woman on the stage had fitted into one of
two categories, both of them caricatures, exaggerations of
the truth. In the first she'd been depicted as a model of
drawing room decorum, singing songs of devotion, songs
so respectable even her Victorian grandparents would have
found her acceptable; or dancing as Christine and Terry
had, presenting a tabloid delightful to watch yet devoid of
sexuality. Into the second category had come the 'naughty'
ones, the women who kicked their legs and enticed the
men in the audience with a display of frills – or as Mr
Bailey had put it to Penelope 'showed next week's washing'. Sex had been their theme, blatant, often crude, certainly a sex with no fusion of love and passion.

But things were changing. During those four years of
war women had made a new place for themselves in
society. The changes might not be official yet, they still
hadn't been given the right to have a say in shaping the
future; the battle for equality was to prove a long one, but
when a chick once cracks its shell it's on the way out. And
the shell that had held the women of the previous century
in check was well and truly cracked.

'Song of the Dawn' was setting the scene for them and

for the wild enjoyment of the 1920s. And Penelope's part in it was something quite new, an expression of passion that had everything to do with sexuality, and nothing to do with frilly underwear and suggestive nuances.

Tonight she'd taken two curtain calls. Buoyed up by the excitement she came through the wings and made for her dressing room.

'I just put a cablegram on your table, Miss Drew,' the call boy told her.

Years of war had taught her to dread cablegrams. Even now her heart missed a beat at the words. She'd lived in fear of that buff envelope for so long. Now, in her moment of success, it was a cruel reminder. Reason came to the fore. If there was bad news, it must be from Challington. Pa . . . ?

She ran down the rough wooden panelled corridor to her tiny dressing room. The envelope was propped against the mirror.

"Can't be anything awful. Surely they would have made a telephone call." But, even so, she ripped the envelope open, half frightened to read the message.

'Congratulations. Glad at last you have come to your senses. Penelope Drew is on the way up. Good luck. Laurence McLeod.'

He'd sent it from New York! He must have read about her in the newspaper in America!

Sitting before her make-up table, wide-eyed, she and the girl in the mirror stared at each other, brown eyes meeting brown.

'Penelope Drew, did you hear that? You're on your way up.'

She'd not thought of Laurence for a long time. Now, re-reading his message, she pictured him. With her elbows on the table, her chin in the palms of her hands, she let her thoughts ramble. Almost she could hear the sound of his music. What was so different about his playing? Other people sat before the keyboard and 'commanded'; Laurence drew the music from it. She chuckled softly, laughing at herself that she could be so fanciful.

'Miss Drew.' This time it was the dresser who put her head round the door. 'You've a visitor. I'll come back and see to your things presently. It's your mother.'

But what could she be doing here? She'd never been anywhere further than Brighton. Mother in London! Penelope turned from the mirror to greet Muriel, so out of place in the setting of the cramped dressing room. But the woman who came in was a stranger. Small, thin, her face painted, her hair darker than Penelope's but cut in the same way. Not in a full-length evening dress for the theatre, nor yet in everyday clothes, she was wearing a low-waisted taffeta dress reaching to her mid-calf. Her arms were covered but if her legs were any indication they would be as thin as sticks. Around her forehead she wore a sparkling band from which sprouted a white ostrich feather. Draped about her shoulders was a musquash cape.

Often Penelope had wondered about her real mother, the dancer whose memory still haunted Pa. For eight years she'd been on the stage and always at the back of her mind had been the unacknowledged craving to see her. And here she was. There was no doubting that she was who she claimed to be.

'My little girl! Penelope. If you knew how often I've wondered about you. Did you even know of my existence? Is this a shock to you?'

Penelope was glad of the stream of words, she needed time to collect her wits. It was the words 'My little Penelope' that made her recoil. Whoever she was, she certainly wasn't this stranger's little Penelope!

'I don't even know what to call you,' she heard herself say, no hint of welcome in her voice.

'Call me Mother.' The woman reached out her hands, but Penelope clasped her own firmly behind her back.

'I can't do that. I'll call you Anna. Will that do?'

'Ah, so he's talked to you about me? You know my name.'

'Someone told me. Don't remember if it was Pa. Might have been Mrs Sharp.'

'Pa!' Her laugh was light and sweet. 'Fancy that! Oliver as Pa. What's happened to him? Does he remember me?'

'He's very well, thank you. He's married, has three other children besides me. He's very happy. I don't know what he remembers.'

'You're frightened of me, aren't you? Don't be. You and me could be such friends. Look at us. It's frightening, isn't it? I used to look just like you do.' Again that tinkling laugh. 'And I ask whether he remembers me! One look at you and he'd hardly be able to forget.'

'Why have you come to see me? After all these years, what's the point of it?'

'I could hardly have come before – where would I have found you? I saw the name on the notice outside the theatre: Penelope Drew. Could it be you? I didn't know what he'd have done about you. Drew . . . you've always been Drew, have you?'

''course I have. It's Pa's name.'

Anna didn't answer; she was fingering the jars of grease-paint, looking in the mirror. Her thoughts seemed to have strayed somewhere where Penelope couldn't follow.

'You think you owe everything to Oliver Drew, don't you? But you don't, you know. You owe it all to me. I watched you tonight. It was like looking down the wrong end of a telescope into the far, far distance at some creature that was me. You don't want me – ' her huge brown eyes were full of tears. 'Silly tears' perhaps? Could they too be something Penelope had inherited? ' – but you *are* me. I was born too soon. Penelope, if you knew how I envy you! At the start of your career and the time right for you.'

'Why did you leave Pa?'

Anna sat on the stool in front of the mirror, holding her head first one way, then another. She picked up a lipstick

258

and went over the outline of her mouth. She gave every indication of concentrating solely on her own face, but Penelope knew she was weighing up the question.

'We only get one life, only one bite at the cherry. I didn't love him enough to give up everything I wanted for him. In fact, I'm not sure I ever loved him at all. I believed he was gentle and kind – and perhaps he was. After all this time I really don't know. Gentleness and weakness are only a hair's breadth apart. But pretty soon I just wanted to be free. I knew he wasn't my man so I left him. Was that wicked?'

'I don't know. There was me. Didn't I come into it? Couldn't I give you enough in common to make him your man?'

'Ah, you.' Anna shrugged. 'I ought never to have had children. Children, did I say? I only had one. You came just when I felt I might be getting somewhere.' Through the mirror they looked at each other. 'It was because of you I didn't. Babies weren't for me. Of course, Oliver was head over heels in love with me.' She smiled, not at Penelope but at her own reflection. 'His father was a real tartar. After I'd gone, did his family take him back?' Penelope could sense that she asked it not out of interest but in mockery of the browbeaten young man Ollie had been.

'I don't know anything about it, and I don't want to! If Pa thought I ought to hear, then he would have told me.'

'Dear me, but he's got a champion in you, I see. So, if you don't know, then they clearly didn't. Brought up soft, he was, as the youngest son. You've heard of Drew's Smelling Salts? That's his family. When I first met him he was working for his father, helping with the book-keeping or something, nothing that took too much skill. Poor Oliver, he and work never saw eye to eye.' Again she laughed. 'I was on tour in the Midlands. He thought heaven had dropped into his lap.'

'What's the point of all this? I don't think you've any right to tell me, if he hasn't.'

'Followed me to Challington where I was booked for the summer. No, all right, I won't tell you any more.'

'Just one thing, not that it's important. Are you older than Pa?'

'Do I look it?' She peered at her own reflection, then answered her own question. 'Yes, I probably do. Actually, I'm not. Just look at us, you and me, Penelope. Time Past and Time Future. Frightening, isn't it? Frightening for you to see what's ahead of you – and for me to know that it's all finished.' Then she giggled, a mischievous laugh. 'Must drive him wild having you around to remind him of his fall from grace. What's his wife like?'

'She's the dearest, kindest – '

'What you mean is, she's no beauty!' Again Anna laughed. 'Still in Challington, is he?'

For a moment Penelope felt trapped. What was this woman's game? Her mother . . . her real mother . . . the woman whose genes she must have inherited.

'We moved,' she half lied. Well, so they had, away from Victoria Place. Like mother, like daughter, she told herself. If Anna could be cunning, so could she. 'Now tell me about yourself. Have you married? Where are you living? In London?'

'No to all three. I arrived in London yesterday and happened to pick up a newspaper which was a couple of days old and see the review of 'Song of the Dawn'. Naturally I wanted to see what this girl called Penelope Drew was like. If I'd had any doubts of your being my little girl, one look at you and they were gone.'

Penelope felt drawn to her yet at the same time repelled.

'I do seem to have got all my looks from you. Always been a shrimp. Not a bit like Pa.'

'Oliver?' Her thin face gave nothing away, only the eyes laughed. 'No, you're certainly nothing like him.'

'Are you still on the stage?'

'I haven't danced for a long time. I'm only in England

for a few days, I had an appointment to keep. I live in Switzerland.'

"I couldn't get there by boat – beginning with S," came the echo of the Places Game.

'Actually live there?' For the first time there was a smile in her voice. She didn't need to fear Anna; it seemed she wasn't here to rock Pa and Mother's boat.

'People do, you know. I haven't come to touch you for a few pounds now that you've got your foot on the golden ladder. Money is the one thing I'm not short of. I wasn't cut out to be a poor man's wife – or mistress either. I said I wasn't married which is true now. I'm a widow. Maxwell died two or three years ago. We were already living in Switzerland. No, I've not come to scrounge, just to see you.'

Again she put out her hand and this time Penelope took it.

'I don't think I'll tell Pa you've been.'

Anna shrugged. 'Why bother?' Clearly she didn't care one way or the other.

'Look, I'll clean my face and change quickly then we'll go out to supper. Bright lights or a little place in Soho – which would you prefer?'

'Neither tonight.' Anna took out a lacy wisp of hanky and dabbed at her nose. 'Perhaps tomorrow. Silly . . . it's the excitement . . . tired tonight.'

'Tomorrow then. I'll book us a table, somewhere quiet where we can talk.'

Anna nodded, no longer pretending it was her nose that needed dabbing. 'Silly, stupid tears,' she sniffed.

It was Penelope's turn to laugh. 'If I needed proof that I'm your daughter, that's it! Silly tears at all the wrong moments. The bane of my life.'

And because they had been emotion's safety valve and nothing to do with sadness, Anna could laugh too.

In that moment they came as near as they ever would to each other. It must have been the tears that gave her mother's face that haggard look. Both shrimps, the same build as each other, Penelope had thought. But as Anna stood up to go she could see how wrong she'd been. The older woman was so thin she looked brittle, her hands like claws, her luminous eyes with dark smudges under them.

Penelope was surprised by just how excited she was as she booked their table for supper the next evening. Perhaps it was wrong to leave Pa out of things, but kinder than telling him she was sure. Without his feelings to consider, she found she could look forward to exploring this new relationship. She remembered all the bitter things he'd said about Anna, probably all true, but they made no difference. Between Penelope and the woman who'd come so unexpectedly into her life there was unspoken sympathy. She didn't need to be told how those eyes would shine in mocking laughter when life dealt a hard blow, any more than she'd had to have the 'silly tears' explained.

Free of responsibility for anyone's feelings but their own, knowing that in two days Anna would be gone, for this evening at least they could take down all the barriers, meet not as mother and daughter but as two women, Time Past and Time Future.

That night when the curtain fell, Penelope hurried to her dressing room to take off her make-up and to dress, quickly but taking special care.

Anna was late. What could have kept her? She'd give her another ten minutes . . . another ten . . . just five more. Everyone had gone; even the wardrobe people were calling their goodnights to each other. She'd wait outside . . . perhaps there had been a hold-up somewhere on the way? She didn't even know where Anna was staying. Give her five more minutes . . .

Carriages, taxicabs, omnibuses, so many people all hurrying on their way, all going somewhere; or more likely at this time of night going home from somewhere. But no Anna. Sadly Penelope watched the world rushing on its way, only now realizing just how buoyed up she'd been at the prospect of their outing.

Would she never learn? You mustn't look forward, mustn't let yourself feel certain . . . Something else must have cropped up, something more exciting. Wasn't that what had happened that other time, when Anna had walked out on Pa, preferring the baritone lead from the Prince of Wales Theatre? And then what? Who would she have dropped him for? A more exciting prospect must have presented itself.

As she made her way back to Marble Arch, Penelope whipped up an active dislike of last night's visitor. She wrapped it round herself like an armour, not daring to think of the brief moments when their personalities had seemed like mirror images of each other.

Later, drifting into sleep, it wasn't so easy to hold her thoughts in check. There must have been a reason, something must have prevented Anna coming. Tomorrow when she got to the theatre she'd find a message . . . Comforted, she slept.

But no message came. The days went by. Anna's time in England was over.

Vernon D. Frankham mixed business with pleasure. In the twenty years he'd been involved in the changing scene of Broadway theatre he'd developed a flair for recognizing what was sufficiently ahead of its time to attract attention; and therein lay his pleasure. Experience had taught him to discern where investment could combine daring with safety, a subtle blend on which he based his successful business.

Just as Laurence had, so he'd read those reviews of 'Song of the Dawn'. A cablegram on its way to Penelope, and Laurence had given it no more thought. Vernon D. Frankham's approach was quite different. The production had been in the West End for about nine months when he arrived unannounced from New York, booking a seat in the front row of the stalls. Before he made any decision he intended to see the show as every other member of the audience saw it. He never put a cent of his money into anything on any opinion but his own. It wasn't just his faith in his own judgement that carried him on to a higher plane than any other impresario so much as his confidence that no one but a fool would turn down a chance to sign a contract with Vernon D. Frankham.

Unknown to the cast, discussions were soon taking place between the American, the composer, the lyric writer, the producer. And out of the melting pot came the announcement that 'Song of the Dawn' was to be produced on Broadway. It would run in London until the end of October with the original full cast while replacements were rehearsing ready to step into the shoes of those who were being taken to America. Vernon D. Frankham creamed off just those he wanted here in London; there was plenty of native talent waiting for him back in New York.

'Penelope Drew.' Leaning over the desk she signed her name carefully on the contract, then stood up straight to admire it. Yesterday she had stood in Court listening to her petition for divorce; she'd felt soiled and humiliated, not by Tom, not even by Sylvia, but by what she'd been certain was going on in the Judge's mind. Contempt for Tom who had been unfaithful, contempt for Sylvia who had encouraged him, contempt for Penelope herself that she'd not been able to hold her husband. She'd come to the theatre last night knowing herself a failure. Perce's old suit and muffler would have suited her mood. Instead, she found herself a symbol of sensuality; she, who couldn't even satisfy one man who had been genuinely fond of her.

'Penelope Drew.' What better to heal her wounded spirit than the sight of those two words written round and clear? Vernon D. Frankham had offered contracts to only five of the English cast members. New York! A New Life (even if only a temporary one) in the New World! Yesterday she'd been granted a decree nisi, today had opened a fresh door – and tomorrow she would go through that door and find . . . what? Whatever it was, Penelope was ready to meet it.

The short Channel crossing to entertain the troops had been nothing compared with the rigours of an autumn Atlantic. And even the Channel had got the better of her! Surprisingly for one who seemed as comfortable on her hands as her feet, who could hurl herself through the air in a somersault and not bat an eyelid, who gave the impression that her slight body could bend and twist any way she chose, let Penelope feel the merest roll of a ship and it took all her strength of character to walk the deck. As for food . . . the sight or smell of it and she was defeated. And that on a calm sea. It was November. By the time they were two days out of Southampton, the Atlantic was set to prove itself the master. Some of the stalwarts still strode the deck, wrapped up against wind and spray. Not Penelope. When she was at her lowest ebb, caring neither for past nor future, she vowed that once she reached land, even if she were to be dropped on some far flung desert island, that's where she would stay. Anything rather than go through this again.

Then, as they came within sight of America, the mood of the ocean changed. After what they'd gone through this might even pass for calm. Youth is remarkably resilient. Penelope's spirits revived even though her body felt weak and bruised. Gingerly she knelt up and looked out of her porthole; even such a simple action suggested to her there might be a future after all! Today they would dock. Somewhere on the horizon was hope. So she washed, struggled into her clothes, made an effort with her face, brushed her short hair and groped her way to the deck.

And so it was she saw her first glimpse of the New World. The sun was going down, the long beams of hazy light glimmering on the water. And out of this sea of golden mist, the sun already sinking behind the tallest of its buildings, rose New York. Penelope gripped the rail with shaking hands.

'Are you feeling all right, Penelope?' It was no less than the great Vernon D. Frankham himself standing by her side.

'Yes. Oh, yes.' He'd noticed those eyes before, but never more than today in her pinched, white face. 'So beautiful . . . I remember coming back from France, when we saw the White Cliffs of Dover . . . just like this. No words, are there?'

'Could it have anything to do with the fact you're at journey's end?' His laughter was kindly enough; it gave no indication of what was going through his mind. 'Looks like a half-starved waif. Sexy, that's what I thought! I remember the impact she made. But, dear God, the destitute immigrants come in looking more promising.'

The journey over, Penelope's natural good health took over. Rehearsals started, an easy ride for the five who'd come from England, and she found herself with time to explore.

She wrote home to Challington: 'Bits of it remind me of home, especially Greenwich Village. Not a village like we think of one, but it might almost be part of an English town. The roads are largely cobbled, and there are trees. Most of the people who live there are artists, it has a flavour all its own. There's a girl in the cast, Lana McBridie (that's what she calls herself, actually her name is Laura Biggs but she chose the other one because it sounded better) who wants us to share rooms in the Village. At present my digs are quite near the theatre.

'I walked up Wall Street today – "The money centre of the New World starting with W.S.", wasn't that what we used to say in the game, Pa? Can you believe it, I actually walked along it, stood on the steps of the Treasury Building! That would have looked at home in England too. But there's so much here that's quite different. I suppose because Manhattan is a small island the buildings have to be tall; it's the only direction to build in. Bit like the Tower of Babel. It's exciting here, noisy and pushy, people all seem in a hurry, yet everyone is friendly. Tell you what you'd miss, Pa – you'd miss the Royal Standard, and all the others too. There aren't any pubs, of course, you wouldn't get your darts matches here; they don't allow alcohol into the country. I don't know how they manage it, but some people still seem to get hold of liquor. I've seen it at parties but don't ask questions!

'People live well here. I suppose they never had the shortages we did while the war was on. But there is dreadful poverty as well. Men who've come home from the war and got no work.

'We open in just over a month. The costumes are going to be absolutely spectacular. And instead of only having one number – guess what? – I've been given a second in the last act. I'm glad, 'cos it's a happy sort of song and my dance is more the sort of thing Perce would have done! Not that I don't love "the blues" as we call the sad sort, but I want to show I can do both. Have you heard anything of Tom and Sylvia? I thought perhaps you might have seen his mother. If you do, be sure to ask her to tell them about me. I'm not sure whether I'm supposed to get in touch with them myself, not until the divorce is finally made absolute.'

She stopped writing, letting her mind ramble where it wanted. Why was it so important that they knew how she was getting on? Was it pride that prompted her to send her message? Or was it that they'd been close for so long she still needed them? But did they need her? She pulled her thoughts back to her letter.

'And what about Alf and Emma? Isn't it lovely that they've got a baby coming? I wrote as soon as I heard. Do you see him, Mother? Emma told me that he was working at home, that he'd put a notice in the paper that he mended toys, pots and pans. Does that mean he's still hiding away? Or has he just not been able to find a job?'

That triggered off a spate of day-dreams. Men she'd seen begging, dragging thinly clad children around with them in this dreadful cold of a New York winter. Alf – was he trying to earn a few shillings from home by choice or necessity? In London she'd seen plenty of poverty: men selling matches or bootlaces, playing mouth organs or fiddles. Sitting in her boarding house bedroom, an oil heater keeping it warm (and smelly!), she looked out at the sullen sky, the flurry of snow that blew against the window. She thought of the riches of the costumes being prepared for 'Song of the Dawn'. What sort of a dawn was it for the people with nothing? She'd been pleased with herself to be able to send the message home to be passed to Tom and Sylvia – but was there really any cause to be proud? Being part of this artificial, glittering world . . . This morning she'd seen a little girl standing holding a tin with a few cents in it while her father played a concertina. The memory of the little girl haunted her. Perhaps what struck a chord in Penelope was her over-large boots and long light brown hair.

She finished off her letter then took it to post. The snow hadn't come to much, no more than a coating of wet slush. Penelope had learnt to find her way around in the immediate vicinity, and knew if she turned left at the next corner she'd be heading towards the Hudson and the park. Head down as she rounded a corner into vicious wind – and that's where she crashed straight into someone coming from the other direction.

'Penelope Drew! So he brought you over with the show!'

'I've been hoping I'd see you. I thought I couldn't work on Broadway without bumping into you.'

'And you surely did bump.' He laughed. 'Here, let's get out of this wind. My apartment's just down the street. You're not in a rush, are you?'

Even if she had been she certainly wasn't now. How

268

good it was to see Laurence again. It was over three years since they'd been caught in the Zeppelin attack. He looked no older. In fact, out of uniform he seemed younger than she'd remembered. It must have been the greying hair that had made him seem senior to the rest of them – that and the fact that he'd been the only person she'd met who'd already climbed to the top of his own particular tree.

The lift carried them up, then he unlocked a door and ushered her into a spacious living room. It was blissfully warm inside; the thick carpet silenced their footsteps. But most of all it was the piano she noticed, a baby grand, and on the music rack a hand-written score. She smiled, not so much at him but with pleasure in the musician's comfortable surroundings.

'So, you saw the light! Is Tom with you?'

She shook her head.

'No. Just me. Penelope Drew being herself.'

He raised his eyebrows, but didn't ask. Which was probably why she told him.

'It must have all been my fault. Tom and me, we were always pals. But that's not enough, is it?'

He watched her as she talked, his expression giving away none of his thoughts. "I could wring the young bastard's neck!"

Penelope stood straight, felt she was standing tall. She defied pity.

'He suggested I stayed in the act, kept Perce going. But I couldn't do that. Not after us being a proper partnership – or at any rate, that's what I thought then. So I made my mind up to stand on my own feet.'

'And I, for one, am glad. I told you just what I thought long ago. And it seems I was right. I look forward to seeing "Song of the Dawn" when it opens.'

'Did you know I was in New York?' she couldn't help asking. If he had, then surely he must have been able to see her before this if he'd wanted?

'Not until yesterday. I've been down in Georgia for a

269

month or so. I didn't get back to town until then.' She supposed he and his family must have been holidaying to escape winter here on the eastern coast, until he went on: 'Sonny contracted infantile paralysis about eighteen months ago.'

Against that tragedy, her own affairs seemed trivial. She understood why his voice was expressionless: he was afraid to let it be any other way. Her sympathy was heart-felt, her brown eyes full of visible concern.

'And now? Is he in Georgia?'

Laurence nodded. 'He was always so fit, full of energy. It happened quite suddenly.' He sat on the piano stool, not facing the keyboard but looking at her. 'Seeing you here, Penelope, brings those wartime days back. Whatever we lived through then, we were both so sure that with peace everything would slot into place, the wheels keep running along the old familiar grooves.'

'Tell me about him, Laurence.' She'd always held him on a pedestal, marvelled that anyone of his stature could bother about her at all. Now, suddenly, he seemed the weaker. Hardly realizing she did it, she held her hand towards him and felt it taken in his.

'It seems a lifetime ago. Eighteen months. Before that he had everything to look forward to. And now? you ask. They say he won't be crippled. He's certainly bright enough.' He smiled as he said it, clearly picturing the boy he was so proud of. Her vision misted with 'silly tears'.

'You can see that he's getting better?'

'You know what it is, infantile paralysis, what it does? It destroys the tissues of the nerves of the brain and spine. He's had the best care money can buy, but money can't buy health. For some months he seemed to get no better, he was in hospital here in New York. Now he can be looked after at home and lifted to sit in a wheelchair.'

'You McLeods can't be kept in wheelchairs!' she smiled. 'They say he won't be crippled, Laurence, just hang on to that. When you love someone it's hard to be unable to help, isn't it?' Then, wanting to cheer him up: 'You've left his mother with him in the sunshine, I suppose?' For she clearly wasn't here.

'Helen's staying in California at the moment. No, I've left him being cared for better than he could be here. He needs the sunshine, and they say the water at Warm Springs does more to help than anything. So that's where he must stay. I get there whenever I can.'

He let go of her hand and turned back to the piano. He was upset by the conversation, she knew that; he turned to the keyboard just as he had an uncountable number of times over these tragic eighteen months, she knew that too.

'What's the music, Laurence?' She pointed to the manuscript on the rack, playing along with him, expecting to be able to put them back on the old familiar footing.

'That, and a lot more, is the beginning of a new musical. I've been working on it while I was in Georgia. There are hours each day when Sonny is being exercised and so forth, times I can't be with him. So I work. Listen, what do you think of this?'

Perhaps it wasn't as familiar as she'd expected, for after playing and singing a couple of numbers he turned to look at her. At her? Into her, it seemed.

'What's wrong?' she asked, feeling at a loss. He must have some reason for studying her with that thoughtful expression. What was wrong with her? What was he expecting? Her newfound feelings of maturity melted. She was the same inexperienced girl who'd first met him in France.

'It's what's been bothering me. When I've written before I've always had a clear idea of who would play the lead, or at least the same type. This time I knew at the back of my mind, and yet . . . Penelope Drew, here, take the sheet and sing this through.'

An hour or more went by, one song following another. Laurence outlined the story as they went along.

271

'That's about as far as I've gone,' he said finally. 'So, Penelope Drew, I take it you agree? We'll work on this together. How long are you signed up with Vernon for?'

'He's agreed to pay me until one month after opening night, my contract to be re-negotiated then. In case I was no good or the show wasn't, I suppose.' Even now she told herself Laurence was offering her a support part; more than that she dare not hope for.

'When you come to re-negotiate, we'll talk again. Penny, I'm backing a hunch. The first day I saw Perce I knew I'd found something special. And this last month while I've been working I've been puzzling over who could play the lead. Now it's so obvious. We'll build this into something that'll make all Broadway take notice. What do you say?'

It's hard to say anything when your heart is banging into your throat and 'silly tears' threaten to disgrace you if you blink. Just at that second she was saved from answering by a humiliation even worse: her stomach gave a long, loud and unmistakably empty rumble.

It couldn't be ignored. She felt the colour flood her face and neck.

'There's a timely reminder,' he teased, somehow making it possible for her to laugh too. 'How about we eat here? We can work again later. What do you say?'

'I say thank you. Must be the excitement making me so hungry.'

He went through a communicating door into another room and she saw him unhook the earpiece of the telephone on the wall and turn the handle. It was clear he often ordered meals that way, he didn't have to look up the number he wanted. She didn't like to let him think she was listening, although while she thumbed through the sheaf of manuscript it was hard not to strain her ears.

She was hungry enough to eat almost anything, but the meal that was delivered was an education in itself to anyone whose palate had for so long suffered the vagaries of stage boarding houses — where food shortages were cited as the excuse for the poor fare offered. The meal came from a Hungarian restaurant: rouladen, red cabbage and apples, followed by a concoction of hazelnuts and cream. What a moment to remember the little girl she'd seen this morning with her almost empty begging tin!

With Lana McBridie, Penelope moved into a small apartment off Amsterdam Avenue. Whether or not they would ever have struck up a friendship had they both been English, or both American, is doubtful. But each brought her own national characteristics to the relationship and Penelope felt that, living with an American, she saw her new country more clearly. It was Lana who introduced her to Harlem, to the music of the coloured people; it was Lana who took her to Chinatown, new scents, new flavours and above all here, too, new music. What a far cry it all was from a Challington unchanging in the slow, even pace of its days. Challington, the same for today's children as it had been for her. 'Last one to the pier . . . ' Talking about it to Lana she never realized just how much of the feeling of England she brought with her into their home.

There was one thing she told no one, not even Lana, and that was Laurence's offer that she should play the lead in a new musical. She spent a good deal of time with him, trying out songs, listening to ideas, letting 'Girl of my Dreams' take shape in her imagination. Just as Perce had kept Tommy's place warm for him because it would be tempting fate not to, so that inborn superstition in her made her hug this secret to herself. There was no need to hide the fact that she knew him; she'd told Lana about meeting him again and often mentioned seeing him. But nothing more. Her hopes for a star role were between herself and the all-hearing infinity of the sky above.

The first seeds of doubt had been sown in Vernon D. Frankham's mind as he'd stood by Penelope's side on deck. Back in London, he had delighted in her natural sensuality.

273

But the London production had been less spectacular, the shading more subtle. Was Penelope Drew what was wanted in New York? The scales tipped even further against her when Elayne Emery was auditioned for a place in the chorus. Now there was a girl with a figure to make every man in the audience stand up and take notice! Certainly the great Vernon D. did. Penelope's sexuality stemmed from her spirit, there was nothing of the vamp, nothing that obviously titillated; Elayne used every nuance in the business.

'Penelope!' He called her down into the auditorium where he sat watching, as always a cigarette stuck in the corner of his mouth. 'Come and sit down here a minute. We need to have a word.' There was something else he didn't feel comfortable about. This skinny child made him feel guilty. But if Elayne did to the rest of the audience what she did to him, then he was on to a winner.

'Vernon D. Frankham isn't a man to make mistakes but this time, Penelope Drew, you've got him beat. I've run through your numbers with someone else. I'm sorry but she's got something that you lack. So there it is, kid, that's show business.'

'You mean I'm out?' The way she sat so straight, only her eyes hinting at what his words had done to her, put him at a disadvantage. If she'd argued, he could have handled it.

'Now, now, not so fast. Have I ever broken a contract? I've guaranteed your money until a month after we go into production – but I brought you out here, I want to treat you right. No good offering you a place in the chorus line.' He laughed, not needing to spell out to her just why. The chorus line all measured the same five foot six inches, and even in these days of 'straight up and down' fashions, a chorus girl needed a bosom. 'I'll give you your passage back home. How's that, can't treat you fairer, can I?' He was pleased with himself. He'd expected a scene, tears perhaps, pleas for another chance.

'Just tell me one thing, Mr Frankham. Who is replacing me? What's she like?'

She looked no more than a child, holding her back straight and minding her manners. Difficult to look her in the eye though – undersized kid like that, who did she think she was, sitting there like a duchess!

'It'll soon be common knowledge, no point in not telling you. Elayne Emery – the blonde in the front chorus row.'

That afternoon she told Laurence.

'So you're free?'

'If I'm not what Frankham's audience wants, then I'm not going to be right for "Girl of my Dreams" either. Having me play the lead could ruin the whole thing. Audiences want – need – glamour. The show has to come before everything – that's what Sylvia always told me.'

He tipped her chin up so that she looked at him.

'You're the girl I want. If I'd been writing for some blonde bombshell, do you think I would have offered you the part in the first place? You're right for it – and it's right for you.' His finger gently pressed her lips shut. 'No more! It's settled. Tonight I'll take you out to the best dinner you've ever eaten. Tonight we'll celebrate. With Vernon D. Frankham out of the way there's nothing to hinder us now. We can start making production plans. We're a team, and we'll prove we're a good one.'

She and Tom had been a team too.

In the excitement of the opening of 'Song of the Dawn', Lana didn't concern herself over Penelope's apparent lack of work. It was a professional hazard, something they were all used to. Auditions started for the casting of 'Girl of my Dreams'.

'Is it true, Penny?' Lana hardly got inside the door before she shouted. 'They're saying at the theatre that your Laurence McLeod has picked you for the lead. Someone even said you didn't have to have an audition, it was cut and dried.'

275

'You make it sound horrid.'

'Might be horrid with old Vernon D., but I wouldn't say no to worming my way into Laurence McLeod's good books.'

'Don't be silly. He's not a bit that sort of a person – anyway, neither am I!'

Lana kicked off her shoes and reached for a cigarette.

'Sorry. Expect I was kidding. Anyway, congratulations! Bet our Vernon D. is scratching his head and wondering. Fancy him firing you, and you landing right in McLeod's lap!' Lana flicked her lighter and inhaled the first puff of cigarette smoke. 'Not that sort, you say . . . Laurence McLeod, I mean. Is that why his wife is always chasing rainbows?'

'I don't know his wife.' But she couldn't resist adding: 'What sort of rainbows?'

'Don't know what it is she's after but they say she goes to a medium somewhere out near Harlem River. I don't know how much truth there is in the gossip that gets about. Give a woman a well-known husband and folk'll dig into the dirt to make a story.'

'Calling up the dead, you mean? Do you believe it, Lana?'

'Heavens, no. Think it's the most awful rubbish. But I was in a show with Miriam Kinsley – you remember, before the war she and Jack, her husband, were dancing partners? You probably never heard of them back in England. He went to the war and was killed. She used to go to this same medium, paid him a fortune to call up Jack.'

'Did she find him? Did he speak to her?'

'Not to her! To the medium, so she said. Sometimes Miriam would come back looking as though she'd been given a million dollars; those were the days some little snippet had been passed on to her. Other times the medium hadn't made contact and she'd not be fit to be near. But one thing I am sure of, she handed over her money whether

276

Jack was in a chatty mood or not. Do you think there can be anything in it?'

'Gives you a cold shiver down your spine to think about it.' Penelope sat on the divan, folding herself up in her favourite position, legs crossed, feet tucked almost under her. 'But I've never had anyone I really loved die. If I did, I don't believe a stranger could get nearer to them than I could myself. If Tom had been killed, I believe I would still have felt I could talk to him.' Lana gave her what Mrs Sharp would have called 'an old fashioned look'. It seemed a funny way to talk about a man you'd just divorced. 'But Laurence came safely through the war. I wonder who his wife tries to talk to. Do you know her? What's she like?'

'I've been in the chorus a couple of times in McLeod musicals, and I've seen her. What's she like? you say. Tall, elegant, good-looking too. I've never spoken to her – but there were all sorts of whispers, you know what gossip is, it grows with each telling. I do know it's fact about the medium. Any person who has to resort to that sort of thing must be dreadfully unhappy, mustn't they? You wouldn't think she would be, married to a handsome brute like your Laurence. I know they've got problems with the son, but he's not dead, so it's not him she's calling up. Anyway, it was before that, during the war, when I first heard about it.

'Come on, Pen. Never mind Helen McLeod – tell me about you! How come you're to play the lead if you didn't audition and you didn't do anything Mama wouldn't approve of?'

'Probably because I've been there to practise the numbers and try them over with him. He says it's a role for my sort of person. It's not for someone beautiful – glamorous, good figure, all that.'

'Sounds a back-handed compliment to me!'

Penelope had always read the newspapers, followed what was happening in the world. World events were one thing, gossip and scandal another. As 'Girl of my Dreams' went into rehearsal, Penelope's mind was taken up with her own affairs. It could encompass the headlines on the front page but certainly not the column on page four written by 'Our Man About Town'.

It was late evening, and just as on that previous occasion (and quite a few in between) Laurence had had a meal sent to his apartment where they had been working. Rehearsals were a daily event, but rehearsals were for everyone. Here, together, he moulded Penelope alone into what he wanted. A Laurence McLeod musical was just what it sounded — written and produced solely by him.

In the kitchen Penelope poured the boiling water on to the ground coffee she'd heaped into the jug. The pungent steam was full of promise.

'It's one of life's disappointments, isn't it, coffee?' she said as he wandered in. 'If only it could taste as good as it smells.'

'Umph. I'll get the cups. Bacon — grilled bacon — that's another.'

Neither of them had heard the outer door open.

'What a delightfully domestic scene!'

In that instant the easy atmosphere was changed. Penelope turned towards the stranger who stood in the doorway of the tiny kitchen. She didn't look at Laurence, she didn't have to; simply from the way he put the cups and saucers on the table she could feel his irritation.

'Penny, this is my wife, Helen. Helen, Penel—'

'Oh, but you don't need to tell me who Penelope is. The whole of New York probably knows. "Little English beauty." It's all here, that's what they call you.' Her red mouth forced itself into a poor imitation of a smile. '"No need for an audition" . . . "for weeks the world of theatre has watched and speculated" . . . "no time lost, Miss Drew arrived with members of the London cast of 'Song of the Dawn' only weeks ago" . . . "do we detect romance?" . . .

There, read it for yourselves.' She threw the paper folded open at page four on to the kitchen table.

'Mrs McLeod, this is nonsense! He hasn't any right to print such lies. Tell her, Laurence. We met during the war and became friends, nothing more than that. Don't believe these beastly stories!'

'Dear me, the little English rose is more worried than I am, that's quite clear.'

'Helen, that's enough. You know as well as I do that what Penelope says is true. Just say how do you do nicely and let's get another cup out for your coffee.'

For weeks she'd been away. Now she'd come home to be confronted by malicious insinuations in the newspaper and this apparent confirmation of the truth of them in her home. Penelope told herself she ought to feel sympathy for the lovely creature – but she didn't. Even Laurence sounded like a stranger, humouring his disagreeable wife. She wanted just to get away. It had been such a happy evening; now it was spoilt, soiled.

'Don't get her another. I'll go. Let her have this one.'

But he put the third cup on the tray and carried it through to the sitting room.

'When did you arrive home, Helen?'

'Home, you call it? I don't know, some time earlier. I had people to see. Home . . . '

'Drink your coffee.'

'If anyone calls, Laurence – ' Her eyes were wild, full of fear.

'It's all right. No one will call. Drink your coffee. You'd better go, Penny. I'll telephone for a cab for you.'

'It's not far, I can walk.'

'I'd rather see you safely into a cab.'

A long five minutes later the bell rang. The cab must have arrived.

'Laurence!' Helen grabbed his arm.

'It's Penny's cab, that's all. I'll take her down and see

her into it. Lock the door after me, if you like. I have my key.'

'Goodbye, Mrs McLeod.' Penelope held out her hand pretending all these strange undercurrents had passed her by. For a second she almost believed they were a product of her imagination as, with a regal inclination of her head, Helen McLeod bid her goodbye. 'And please don't give a thought to all that silly gossip. If newspapermen haven't got a story they have to make something up.'

Helen took her outstretched hand normally enough, but instead of dropping it again she stood holding it, leaning close to Penelope.

'Newspaper? Oh, that. Yes, of course.' She let go of the hand but not before Penelope had caught the smell of spirits on her breath. 'Laurence,' Helen pulled at his sleeve, 'you will lock the door?'

'Penelope,' he said to her as the lift sped them down to the ground floor, 'she was upset. One day I'll explain.'

'She had every right to be annoyed, reading that rubbish.'

'It wasn't that. It's on your account I'm angry about that, not hers.'

'Laurence, I've known people to drink before, I know not to take what they say to heart.' It was no use pretending she hadn't noticed.

'Drink — and in this country! But that's only half of it. Penny, I hate to ask this, but if anyone mentions her, you haven't met her. She's away.'

It had started out as such a lovely evening. Like coffee and grilled bacon, it hadn't lived up to its promise.

Lana had collected the mail before going to the theatre. On the table was a large envelope with a Challington postmark. Penelope tore it open eagerly. Inside was yet another, this time of heavy parchment, sent to the London theatre, from there to her agent, from there on to Challington. It was too soon yet for her divorce to become absolute.

Normally Penelope haggled envelopes open, but the look of importance of this one demanded more respect. She took a knife out of the drawer and slit the end.

CHAPTER ELEVEN

She drew out a single sheet of paper – if anything as thick and heavy could be called a 'sheet'. From a firm of solicitors in London. Chadwyck, Collingbourne and Shand: Solicitors, and Commissioners for Oaths.

Sitting on the divan she instinctively adopted her thinking position, scanning the words as she did. Two short paragraphs, stark sentences, no words of regret. Dead! All these weeks, months in fact. ' . . . recent death of Mrs Anna Neubinsky.' But this was ages ago. The letter was dated November.

Anna, her mother; Anna, who'd not come back when she'd promised, had left her waiting. Was this why? Perhaps she'd fallen ill, perhaps there had been an accident that very evening. With the piece of paper half read Penelope's thoughts strayed back to the brief contact she and Anna had had. Now that they would never meet again she was conscious of a feeling of loss and disappointment.

"It wouldn't have done for us to get close . . . for Pa's sake I couldn't have . . . yet we were close. Whether I meant us to be or not, I could feel that we were. I knew it . . . so did she . . . " Then, pulling her thoughts back to the letter, she re-read the first paragraph and went straight on to the second.

' . . . beneficiary under her estate . . . communicate with me as soon as convenient . . . meeting may be arranged . . . '

She'd imagined she was being informed simply because Anna had been her mother. Getting to her feet again she let the letter slip to the ground and walked to the window. She, who as a child had so longed for curtains to shut out the world, never closed them in the evenings here. She and

Lana lived on the third floor; no one could look in on them from the street and she liked the sight and noise of the city clattering about its business. Now it was no more than a background to her confused thoughts. Had Anna known she was ill? She'd been so thin. Was that why they'd gone to live in Switzerland? But her husband couldn't have been English with a name like Neubinsky. She knew so little . . . now it was too late. Penelope rested her forehead against the cold window pane. The streets were brightly lit, the sky no more than black emptiness. With an uncharacteristic sigh, she turned back to the lighted room.

She must write to the solicitors, explain why she'd only just heard. Determined to write a letter as properly expressed as theirs, she took her writing paper, pen, a bottle of ink and set to work.

The next morning at the theatre where rehearsals were under way, Penelope showed Chadwyck, Collingbourne and Shand's letter to Laurence.

'I'm going to buy some good thick paper to write it on, but do you think that's the right sort of thing to say to Mr Collingbourne?' She passed him last night's final attempt.

Could that be a leading lady speaking!

First he read the letter from the solicitors, making no comment as he started on her reply.

'It's a good clear letter, Penny,' he said as he passed it back to her, rewarded by her glow of pride at his praise. 'But — and don't take my word for it, I may be wrong — I don't think this sort of thing can be handled by post as simply as this. This afternoon I'll take you to see an attorney. It may well be that this will have to be dealt with legally.

'Penelope, I thought when you told me all about yourself . . . remember that night in London, the night of the raid?'

'The night I drank too much wine,' she put in.

'Yes, that's the night.' He laughed. They seemed to be

283

drawn closer by the shared memory of a world so different from this. 'You never mentioned having a mother. I imagined your father to have been a widower.'

'They weren't married. I'm illegitimate. Perhaps I ought not to tell you that.'

'Penelope, what difference can it make if your parents are Mother Twankey and the King of England – ' what a delightful giggle she had, it bubbled up from the depths ' – it's you who matters.'

'I'm so glad I've told you, and shown you the letter. If you say I should see an attorney then, of course, I will. So I won't bother to buy a box of posh writing paper – not 'til he says.' Pushing the letters back into her purse she remembered the other events of last night. How frightened his wife had been of being left on her own. She supposed that by now she'd sobered up and he didn't have to worry. 'What about Helen? Won't she expect you home? If you tell me where to go, I'll go by myself to see him.'

For a moment he hesitated, then answered: 'Helen was tired from her journey yesterday evening. No need to worry about her, she won't be on her own.'

Even then she thought he was going to say something else, but his attention was distracted by a shout from the director. Someone was having a bad rehearsal! Laurence turned back to the action on the stage, giving it his full attention. Sitting next to him, Penelope sank back in her seat, not looking at him yet seeing so clearly every line of his face, every nuance of expression. She'd never felt like this about anyone, not Tom, not Pa, not Alf. With Laurence she knew she was safe, protected . . . almost she added 'loved' but that was nonsense. No, she mustn't even think of love. He looked on her still as hardly more than a child despite her being halfway into her twenties. He wanted to help her up the ladder she'd made up her mind to climb, believed she had a talent. That was enough for her. What else could she expect? She turned her head just a fraction so that she could look at him. He didn't notice. When Laurence was working he noticed nothing else.

Again she asked herself: what else could she expect? Her heart began to knock against her ribs. She tried to swallow, but her mouth was dry. What did she really want? To be loved, the answer screamed at her, to be loved and to love. It wasn't really because of Laurence that she felt like this. It was all to do with having been married, then suddenly having no one to reach out to in bed and touch, no one to hold her, make love to her . . . that's all it was. Something about hormones. In this dawn of a new era she'd read an article about them in a magazine.

She risked another look at him. But it couldn't be just hormones, whatever they were! It couldn't even be habit. Look at those years during the war. Tom had been away yet she'd never felt this aching, hungry feeling. This was just for Laurence. Penelope gripped her hands tightly together in her lap, as if making sure they didn't reach out to him. She'd met lots of men, even here since she'd been in New York. If it were just a physical need then there was opportunity enough. But she didn't want any of those others.

What she wanted was what she couldn't have: Laurence. Not some light affair, casual, something that set out to be no more than fun. Her body tingled with longing just for him.

"Hormones be damned! I love him."

Laurence got up and walked over to the stage. Still she sat there, watching his every move.

"He has a wife. But she's not a real wife, he wasn't even pleased to see her come home. It's a funny sort of marriage. He must want to – well, don't men have hormones? It's not just that though. Remember him that first day, sitting in his wheelchair? Did I fall in love with him then and not know it? Too busy keeping the bed warm – "

No, she wouldn't think about any of that. Even now

the shame of not being wanted, of what she'd offered Tom not being enough, hurt too much. Perhaps it always would. Her husband had cast her off while to Laurence she was just a skinny youngster he was fond of. She wouldn't let herself forget that. He was her friend who wanted to help her. She must take only that and be grateful.

That afternoon they went together to the attorney. She swore on oath that she was Penelope Drew, she signed forms, Laurence and the attorney's clerk witnessed her signature. The whole thing was very formal and unlike the letter she'd penned last night. Still, on the way home she bought the stationery she felt she needed if Mr Colling-bourne were to do as she asked of him. And that evening, sitting alone while Lana was working, she wrote to him again, asking him to tell her more about ' . . . the recent death of Mrs Anna Neubinsky.'

'Girl of my Dreams' opened at the end of April. With all the publicity, the success of the new Laurence McLeod musical was virtually a foregone conclusion – so long as the star caught the public's interest. Penelope didn't fail him. The press hailed her 'rare combination of the gamin and the chic', 'sensuality with no hint of posturing or pretence', 'magnetism that reached out and held the audience enthralled'.

How she wished the folk from home could have peeped in at her afterwards as the cast celebrated behind closed doors in Laurence's apartment. Parties in New York couldn't rely on receiving a boost from alcohol, at least not openly. Everyone knew there was bootlegging. Even if one couldn't get Scotch malt, if you had contacts and enough money, a nod in the right direction could produce home distilled rye. Wine from France seldom came nearer than the dreams of connoisseurs, but California provided a sweet substitute which Laurence mixed with fruit and spices. Tonight the punch bowl was full, although the laughing, excited cast barely needed the stimulus.

Since the night when Helen had arrived home unexpectedly and in such a strange mood, Penelope hadn't seen her. Laurence never willingly talked about her. Then, a couple of days ago, they'd been talking through the arrangements for the opening night.

'Everyone will come back to my place. It's a crush, Penny, but traditional.'

'Will your wife be in New York?' she managed to ask casually.

'Helen wouldn't miss a first night party. Yes, she'll be there.'

So this evening as she'd come on to the stage Penelope's first glance had gone to the front row of the stalls where she'd known Laurence would be. And there by his side had sat Helen, looking expensive, elegant and thoroughly composed. Then she'd forgotten. Penelope had given herself heart and soul to the show.

When, after the final curtain, shouts had gone up for Laurence McLeod, Helen had gently pushed him forward, holding her hands out in front of her as she'd added her applause to the rest. Yet hers hadn't been the same. All around her people had clapped, brining their hands together as loudly as they could. Not Helen. Arms outstretched she'd tapped her palms together, fast, almost silently, the gesture somehow intimate, attaching herself to him rather than to the audience.

Back here in this crowded apartment she moved amongst the guests, absorbing the praise that came his way as if it were her own.

'Well, Penelope Drew, it seems I backed a winner.'

So engrossed had she been in watching Helen that Penelope hadn't noticed Laurence move through the crush to her side.

'I was just thinking – I wish people at home could have

287

a peep at all this. I suppose what I really mean is that I wish Tom and Sylvia could.'

He gave her a probing look.

'Tonight belongs to you. Don't let it be spoilt by thoughts of Tom and Sylvia.'

How clear those wonderful eyes of hers were as she looked up at him. 'Oh, but it's not. It's not spite – it's just that I can't write and tell them, actually put in words what a fuss people have made of me, it'd be showing off. But I do wish they could know all the same. Do you think I can have another glass of punch? It's lovely, isn't it?'

It looked as if Lana thought so too, propped against the wall on the other side of the room with one of the male members of the cast of 'Girl of my Dreams' dancing attendance. They were two of the first to leave, off to finish the night in Harlem dancing at the Cotton Club.

There was only one similarity between tonight and that other time when Penelope had been here with Laurence and Helen. The two of them never seemed to come together. Helen lapped up the glory of being his wife, yet she never looked at him. Certainly he watched her, but who could tell what was going on in his thoughts? Certainly not Penelope.

'Can you call me a cab, Laurence? It's time I went home. It's been a day and a half already.' Suddenly she'd had enough of the laughter, the noise, the air thick with the smoke from cigarettes. There was a ring of artificiality about the congratulations: 'Darling, you were the greatest – but the greatest!' 'We knew you'd be good but, honey, you were tremendous.' She'd had a lot of fun rehearsing with these people, yet there wasn't one amongst them that she would call her friend, her real friend. Sylvia was her friend . . . She felt isolated, surrounded by strangers.

Then Laurence came back with her wrap. He draped it around her thin shoulders and just for a second she felt his hands on her.

'Gotta say goodbye t' Helen,' she mumbled. Still he kept

288

one arm around her as he steered her towards Helen who was listening to some intense young man talking about himself.

'Penelope is off now, Helen. I'm seeing her home. You won't all be gone before I get back, will you?' As he said it he looked at George Randall, the director.

'You bet we won't! Don't get a first night every day.'

Such an ordinary question and answer, yet Penelope felt they'd left things unsaid.

'Goodbye, Mrs McLeod, it's been a lovely party. Thank you.'

'So glad you could come.' Helen touched her hand.

Helen was 'glad she could come' when the party had been partly in Penelope's honour! Whatever the morning papers might have to say about the new star that had risen so high above Broadway on this April evening, clearly Helen saw no further than herself, wife of the creator of yet another success. Penelope knew that her poise was part of the role she played, her expensive gown a fitting costume.

On her shoulder she felt the pressure of Laurence's hand as he guided her out of the door.

He told the cab driver her address, adding: 'Drive us round the park first.'

'Won't they wonder where you are?'

'George will be there.'

'Is he an old friend?'

'I've known him since we landed up here about the same time, sixteen years ago. That's when you make your real friends, isn't it? When you're struggling.'

'You weren't struggling when I met you.' She heard the pout in her voice. This evening she'd been at a fever pitch of excitement, but now she was on a slide, slipping, she couldn't stop herself.

'Work, money – those aren't the only struggles.'

How did she come to be gripping his hand? Was it her doing or his?

'Would have been nicer walking.' Which was hardly an answer, but it was difficult to talk when the taxi cab smelt so of petrol.

Laurence knocked on the partition. 'Stop, will you? Wait for us here.' Then, to Penelope: 'I remember bundling you off the tube train.' He got out first, then put his hand in to help her, pushing her wrap back on to her shoulders.

They moved into the darkness of Central Park. The cab driver took out a cigarette and lit it. Wouldn't be seeing them back for a while. Looked as if the gossip columns might have got it right then. Well, nothing new in it. Plenty of girls knew the way to land themselves on a good number; on the stage, in an office, working in a hotel, didn't matter where they were. If a pretty girl knew how to play her hand, she couldn't lose. Now him, he was just a driver, nothing to tempt a girl with. His Bessie wanted him just for himself – and that's more than some of them could ever be sure of. Arms folded, cigarette between his lips, he settled down for a long wait.

'It's beautiful. Dark, quite. No one jostling us . . . only you and me.'

'I ought to have remembered to watch you. I know you don't drink. Take in the air – '

An hour ago she'd been riding so high. Now her night had see-sawed, brought her to the depths. 'Remembered' to watch her. Why should he watch her for any other reason than fatherly concern? Even saying that she didn't drink made her sound immature.

'You suppose I've had too much to drink! I'm sober, sober as a judge. I'm just – jus" . . . And she'd thought she was sober! The tears were warm on her cheeks.

'What is it?' In the near darkness they could just see each other. Gently, he raised her chin. 'Tell me. There's no one else to hear. I'm your friend. Whatever it is, you know you can tell me.'

'Can I?' she snorted. 'Dunno what's the matter. I'm a drunken sot.'

290

He pulled her into his arms. He hadn't meant to. She was lonely, heartbroken about that young swine of a husband who'd walked out on her; she was the worse for drink, the sweet-tasting punch making her maudlin. Her arms went around him, her fingers caressing the nape of his neck, her lips were parted, so close, so close . . . Then his mouth was on hers. Like a young animal she nestled close against him. Her tears were of pure joy, a joy that had to find expression. He was aroused as she was herself.

'Love me . . . love me . . . ' her mouth against his. Control had gone, she wanted it gone. 'You want to . . . you know you want to . . . '

His cheek was damp with her tears. One of them must hang on to sanity. It had to be him. Tomorrow she'd be sober – and with a headache. Firmly but gently he took her arms from about him.

'Yes, I want to.' Hands on her shoulders he stood back from her. 'I doubt if there was a man in that theatre who didn't want to.'

'Theatre! Damn the theatre!' she croaked.

With one arm around her shoulder he started to walk. Fresh air and exercise would help her regain her composure. She had to, they both had to.

'You don't mean that, Penny. You've always been in tune with your audiences.'

But she hadn't been. It came to her quite suddenly. Tonight her audience had been no more than a pale sea of faces; they'd made no call on her, she'd felt nothing for them. She'd given to 'Girl of my Dreams' everything that was in her, but not for them. She'd done it for Laurence, because it was his work, because she wanted him to be proud of her, to make him fall in love with her.

'Bugger the audience,' she snorted, delighting in sinking to the depths. Even in the dark the ground was swaying, her stomach lurching. ' . . . gonna be sick . . . ' She pulled away from him and ran into the darkness.

He let her go, following her at a distance. Let her preserve what dignity she could when she looked back on the evening.

'Penny!' After waiting a minute he called softly, pretending he didn't know just where she was. 'Penny! I'm over here. Where are you?'

Out of the gloom, dimly he saw her coming.

'. . . sorry. Behaved badly . . . disgusting . . . so ashamed.'

'Wine doesn't agree with a lot of people. Are you better?'

'Yes. Just ashamed . . . not only about being sick . . . about all the other . . . throwing myself at you . . . not sure what I said . . . '

'Neither am I, Penelope. Perhaps we both had first night fever. Can't we just be glad we shared it together?'

Somehow, his saying that removed him even further from her. It was as if he was promising that as far as he was concerned it had meant nothing, it was already forgotten. Having parted company with the wine she felt more in control of herself. She'd made a fool of herself, shown how much she cared about him. Let him believe it was only the wine talking! Clearly he preferred it that way.

They didn't talk as they went back to the waiting cab. And after that they made only one stop on the way home. The morning papers were just being delivered to the distributor. Leaving Penelope in the cab Laurence rushed off to buy copies – for him, for her, and spares for her to send home.

'I'll send them to Tom and Sylvia.' She was pleased with the composed tone of that.

'Now that the show's opened I'm going away, Penelope. Going down to stay with Sonny for a few weeks.'

'When? Not yet?' Her composure was easily shattered. 'But you'll want to see more than one night, won't you? Make sure the seats are going . . . ?'

'The seats will be booked sure enough. It isn't me who'll

bring the crowds, it's you. No, I shall go tomorrow. Today, I suppose I ought to say.'

She nodded, not able to think of anything bright and inconsequential to say.

'Just you? Or will Helen go with you?' The painful question popped out of its own volition.

'I hope she will. I doubt if she'll want to stay in New York on her own, and Sonny likes to have both of us there.'

Again she nodded. Of course that's what Sonny would want. His father and his mother. The three of them a happy family.

'Things will get better, Penny.' For a second he took her hand in his. 'You're young, you've got everything before you. Set your sights on the future.'

She didn't pull her hand away but without actually moving seemed to sink into the corner of the seat. He was going away with Helen. Penelope was nothing to do with his real life, just a girl who fitted the part he'd written – and ended up falling in love with him; he was sorry for her; he was trying to let her down lightly. Tom had done that too. Didn't want to hurt poor Pen . . . All of them frightened of hurting poor Pen.

'Please, you mustn't worry on my account. I hope you'll have a good holiday. We'll keep the show going for you. And, Laurence – my mind's a bit muzzy – don't take any notice of anything I said.' Taking her hand from his she made a pretence of adjusting her cape. 'It was overexcitement and the wine. I'm sorry.'

'No, Penny, it's me who should say that. I'm sorry. I took advantage of you in a weak moment – '

The cab lurched to a standstill and the driver climbed out to open her door.

She got out, then turned for what she was determined would be a cheery goodbye. 'Have a good holiday.'

'Here, don't forget your morning papers.' He passed her a large pile of newspapers.

'Thank you. I'll go through them and cut out the clippings. Half for me and half for Tom.'

"Tom's a bloody fool," Laurence told himself silently. And if that silent voice added anything else he wouldn't let himself listen. Tomorrow he would head south for Georgia. After tonight there would be a change in Penelope's life. She would no longer have the anonymity of a small-time artiste. For Penelope Drew, there would be interviews, invitations, admirers. Perhaps the divorce would never be made absolute. Let young Tom just read these reviews and he'd surely come to his senses.

It was as if a fire smouldered in her, only waiting for the flames to be fanned into life. Faithful Penelope who'd waited for Tom with Perce, and who waited for him still.

Laurence was right in part. Penelope was interviewed by the newspapers, by women's magazines; there was no shortage of parties and no shortage of escorts. The theatre played to full houses, and no one guessed at the emptiness she felt as night after night the applause echoed around her.

What a long way it was from a little girl with a concertina making a queue of cold people waiting for the gods smile and stamp their feet. And what a long way from Tommy and Perce, the fun they'd had together in those days before the war. At the summer concert parties they'd played to people set on enjoying their week's holiday; in the winter they'd brought cheer to plenty who found escape in the Music Halls. Then Perce All Alone, waiting for Tommy just as the members of the audience had been waiting for someone. Penelope had never entertained for the acclaim it brought her; her happiness had come from a contact she'd felt to be almost tangible between her and the people out there in the auditorium.

Perhaps the fault was hers – certainly the loss was. And what removed her even further from those who watched was that no one even recognized that the magic wasn't there. A decade of entertaining had taught her more than she realized. 'Smile, even if your heart is breaking.' That's what Sylvia had always said. Not for the first time Penelope wondered whether she could ever be a real 'stage person'. Not that she considered giving it up. To sing and dance, to learn lines and be someone else while she was in front of the footlights, these things came easily; anyway she was well paid and there was nothing else she knew how to do. All that – and magic too! What did she expect!

A letter from Muriel made it even harder to feel herself a part of the gloss and glitter of her new surroundings.

'We're the lucky ones. We've enough room to make ourselves an income. I've got some bookings for the summer too so we'll really be a full house for the holiday weeks. What a funny mixed up world it all is! Not so long ago everyone was in the same boat, their menfolk off to war, all looking forward to better times. But what better times? All very well for us. Like I say, we've the room to take people in and that's what we came here for, so you might say we've picked up the thread and are back where we started. Not like that for so many. Breaks my heart, Penny love, to see some of them. What chance have some of the poor chaps got? Never been so many beggars about. A few bob a week pension – and for that they've lost a limb, or some of them their sight.

'It's the children that worry me, poor little souls. What do they know about war? None of it their fault, but it's the war that's done it. Fathers come home too damaged to look after things, or not come home at all more likely. Mothers who either take cleaning jobs (there are still plenty of people very comfortable, thank you!) and have to leave the little ones at home on their own, or else who take in washing. Just one or two and I wouldn't feel so helpless. I'd give an eye to them at play here while their mothers had to leave them. But there are so many. The orphanage down Cumley Street is full right up!

'The work of the devil, that's what war is, and I don't care who hears me say it. Must be the same thing in Germany, in France – and as for Russia, they've even been fighting each other! Heaven knows how many lives have been torn apart. Why do we do it, Penny love? I lie awake at night and think of those poor little children. Probably gone to bed hungry, not enough covers over them . . . But what's the matter with me, burdening you with all my miseries. I don't like to talk to Ollie about it, he sees it for himself. He'd never see a child wrongly used, you know that, same as I do. Just I get so upset, and even putting it down on paper makes me not quite so tangled up.

'Emma tells me that Alf tried to get his old job back. Took him a long time to get his courage together, poor lad. Anyway it was no use. They said times are hard. Of course another young lad had taken his place when he went off into the army, and it seems this other one was lucky, he came through in one piece and went straight back. Any road, Emma says he's still taking in what bit of work he can get at home. She goes down to Watling Street to the Model Laundry in the mornings, that helps things. But she's only got two months to go before the baby comes, she can't work down there much longer. And between you and me, I think it does Alf more harm than good, feeling he's at home while she goes off to work. Oh, Penny love, reading back I'm ashamed of myself. You will think I'm a proper wet blanket today!

'We're waiting to hear how this show of yours is shaping. Fancy, going out with just one solo and instead ending up as a leading lady. Your pa isn't one for stage people, I don't have to tell you that, but he's a real swank when he talks about "my eldest, just opening in the lead in a new show on Broadway". I've heard about it when I've been shopping. Everyone at the Standard is proud as punch. And I made jolly sure that Mrs Beasley got to hear, never you fear! As soon as the newspapers come out with their reports, you see you send them to us. They're bound to be good. Back here in Challington there's lots of people waiting, looking forward to a bit of brightness in their lives from hearing how well you do . . . '

Muriel only wrote about once in three months, and when she did she almost needed to make a parcel of her letter.

By the time it arrived the reviews had gone on their way. But to Penelope that was the least important part of the long rambling missive that seemed to bring the people she knew and cared about right into the heart of New York. Muriel said she felt helpless. How much more so was Penelope, so far away. She did the only thing she could think of: she went shopping. From stores that set her in mind of Aladdin's cave she chose presents: a skirt and blouse for Muriel; a silk bow tie, matching handkerchief and pair of spats for her father; ties and checked socks for Merrick and Bruce and a dress for Mandy. She wished she could send to Alf and Emma; the shops were full of tins of food. But he might think she'd heard about him not getting his job, he might think it was charity. So she bought for the baby, sending a bundle of clothes fit for a prince. And so they should be, too, if they were for Alf's child.

Her mind still wasn't easy and, as if to remind her of what Muriel had written, on the way home from mailing her parcel she saw the little girl with the long brown hair standing by her father and shaking her begging tin. A dollar added to their meagre cents would be enough to bring them hope. Penelope imagined the evening they'd have; perhaps they'd be making plans . . .

Another letter arrived from England. From Messrs Chadwyck, Collingbourne and Shand, or more accurately from Mr Collingbourne. Sitting cross-legged on her bed Penelope read it, fitting together piece by piece what she could of her mother's life and receiving the first hint of what that meeting with her had really meant. When the solicitor's first letter had come, she'd been able to show it to Laurence. If only he were here now! This time she showed no one, told no one.

It was June. New York sizzled. 'Girl of my Dreams' had been running for seven weeks and in that time Penelope had heard nothing of Laurence. She'd been to parties, she'd had what is commonly called 'a good time', but it was all as superficial as the performances she gave every night. The audiences were fooled; her acquaintances were fooled, even Lana. None of them knew that always he was there in her mind. Each day she looked for him, longed to see him, yet dreaded it for fear of the transitory pleasure his casual greeting would hold.

It was Helen she met first, coming face to face with her on Riverside.

'Mrs McLeod, hello. I didn't know you were home.'

For a second Helen seemed undecided whether to recognize her, although Penelope was perfectly sure she did.

'Laurence's little girl from the theatre! He isn't back.'

Somehow that killed the conversation. Laurence's little girl from the theatre wished she'd not spoken.

'The theatre's well booked. I expect he knows how things are going, but in case he doesn't . . .'

'I told you, he's not here. And, um – um – Miss Drew – '

'That's it, Penelope.'

'Miss Drew, I'm only here myself for a day or so, seeing friends.'

'Is Sonny getting on well?'

Not for the first time, Helen put her in mind of a trapped animal. What a strange woman she was! Today so full of fear and hatred. Why?

'Are you questioning me? Is that it? When did you last see your son, is that what you're asking? Where have I been? What am I doing? Well – is that what – '

'Mrs McLeod, I'm dreadfully sorry. I didn't mean to pry.'

'Then don't! Now you've made me late. You're hindering me.' And without another glance she was gone, head forward, hurrying as if all the devils in hell were at her heels.

Penelope would have liked to tell Lana. But because Helen was Laurence's wife, she didn't. She didn't want his affairs a matter for public gossip. And she wasn't proud of herself that her spirits could be so raised by Helen's being in New York while he was still away. What about that cosy threesome she'd supposed they were sharing in Georgia?

It was late summer when he returned. Summer in New York had been hotter than Penelope had ever known, but summer in a city never produces the look of tanned health that was his. She didn't know he was back. Then, coming into her dressing room halfway through the performance, she found an enormous bouquet in front of her mirror. The card read: 'Still she's worth the biggest bouquet in town. Is she free for supper, I wonder?' No name, no initials. No need for either. She knew that when the curtain finally came down Laurence would be there.

He drove her out of the city, over Madison Bridge, neither of them saying more than a few formal words of greeting. Then silence. She revelled in his nearness while the night wrapped itself around them. She wanted no petty talk.

'We're going to a little place I know. It's simple, quiet. You're not wanting the bright lights, are you?'

She shook her head. 'You know I'm not.'

'Tired of the high life already, Penelope Drew?'

She considered the question. 'Yes, I suppose so. One party is always much the same as the one before and the one after. Even the same people, most of the time.'

He took his eyes off the road long enough to give her a thoughtful look.

'Anyway,' she changed the subject, 'tell me about Georgia. How is Sonny?'

'They're pleased with him. His legs are in braces, but he actually walked a few paces the day before I left. With sticks, but he walked. You've no idea, Penny – seeing him standing again . . .'

'For him too. He must have been so glad you were there to see it.' It wasn't just her words, it was the way she said them. Penelope understood. He'd known she would.

'And you? What news from England? How were your reviews received?'

'Everyone's quite cock-a-hoop. Pa's boasting about me down at the Royal Standard!'

'And Tom?'

'They wrote to me, both of them. I knew they'd be glad for me. I mean, I'm not pretending I wasn't pleased to be able to show off about playing a lead part – wouldn't be any use pretending that to you, 'cos you know I was – but it was lovely to have their letters. It makes things right, gives us a way forward, still friends.'

'Penelope, what if they'd brought him back to you?'

'Good reviews? Why should they? Anyway, I do understand how it was for them. It's right that they're together, I know that. And it could never be right for me to be with Tom now. We're different people. I suppose we've grown up.'

He'd parked the car in front of an out-of-town road-house but he didn't attempt to get out. Instead he turned, looking at her by the soft light of the outside lanterns.

'Different people, you say. Is there someone else? For you, I mean. Do you love some other man – after all those years of being faithful to Tommy, you're telling me you're different?'

She was studying the dashboard with concentration, anything rather than look at him. 'Yes. And I can understand about Tom and Sylvia.' Then, forcing herself to look at him she smiled, her eyes large and luminous. 'And I've heard again from those solicitors. Anna's affairs will take some time to sort out; I told them I'll come and see them when I get back to England. If she wanted me to have a ring or something I'd hate to have it get lost on the way.

300

There's no hurry – I never wear things like that anyway. I'm disgustingly hungry. Shall we go in?'

That was the first of many suppers. No more parties, no more empty flattery from people she didn't give a fig for. Only if Laurence was out of town did he not collect her after the performance and either take her out or, often, back to his apartment where the Hungarian restaurant round the corner supplied the meal. The ever vigilant press missed nothing; what they didn't see they guessed and had no scruples about printing.

It was an evening during what Penelope was learning to call 'the fall'. Joseph Komaronski, the Hungarian restaurateur, had delivered their meal and they were taking their time over it, the atmosphere easy and natural. Too easy and too natural; it lulled them into a false sense of security.

It was Penelope who rocked the boat, almost capsized it. Some devil in her mocked at the cosy domestic scene, reminding her she was living in a fool's paradise.

'When's Helen coming home? You remember she wasn't too pleased when she found me here last time.'

'I never know when she's coming home. Penny, you must know she and I have no ordinary marriage. Haven't had for years.'

'But there's Sonny.'

'Yes, there's Sonny. Because of him, and because we never quarrelled, we stayed together while going our own ways. Helen has never cared for New York. We have an apartment in Washington where she has a host of friends. Her friends aren't mine, mine aren't hers. It's been an amicable sort of arrangement, and it's lasted because of Sonny.'

'But she comes to New York.' She wondered how much he knew about Helen's visits to the medium.

'Yes. Poor Helen.'

She wanted to ask him what he meant. But she mustn't. She wished she hadn't started the conversation. The easy atmosphere was changed, charged with undercurrents.

'I'll make the coffee, shall I?'

'No, don't go. It's time I told you about Helen.'

'No. Please, you don't have to. It's not right for me to come here and talk about her. It's her home.'

Ignoring her outburst he took out his cigarette case and offered it to her, then took a cigarette himself, knocking its end against the table before putting it in his mouth. Then his lighter, holding it first to hers then to his own. She wondered if he'd changed his mind and wasn't going to tell her after all. She ought to be pleased.

'I suppose we were happy enough together in the beginning. There was the excitement of coming to New York, then Sonny was born. We were quite hard up – I played the piano in a night spot. Perhaps it was me, I don't know. I had a career. Even in those early days I knew where I was going, it was the driving force in my life. Not much fun for a wife. She got into a circle of friends I didn't know and wasn't interested in. I'm not blaming Helen, she had to have something. And I only had room in my life for two things – one was my career, the other was Sonny.

'We were getting better off, I was selling songs, we could afford someone to help with Sonny. We settled down to run along in parallel grooves, comfortable grooves but our only real point of contact was our son. I was aware that some of the company she kept wouldn't bear too much investigation – a country where there's Prohibition leads men into all sorts of temptation, and especially when each state has its own laws on the subject. Liquor in one state, not in its neighbour. I'm not saying Helen was doing anything illegal, but I was damned sure she was mixed up with people who were. Like I said, we kept our own counsel, went our own ways.

'Then in 1914 war broke out in Europe. My English roots wouldn't let me stay here, safely out of the fighting. Here I was surrounded by isolationists. I wasn't prepared to wait for them to see sense. So off goes Uncle Sam's big brave son to fight for Mother England. It was while I was

302

away it happened. In fact, I'd just heard at the time I met you in France. George filled me in on the facts. All I read in the papers in England was that someone called Sam Bernhard, a known handler of spirits and, worse, opium, had been taken by the police and had shot himself.

'The full story was that knowing the police were out to get him and he was for the high jump, this Sam Bernhard had gone to ground. It seems enough was known of him that they were pretty sure if they kept a watch on Helen, in time she'd weaken and go to him. And that's what she did. He had a cabin out in the Green Mountain area. They tailed her and got led right into his lair. The cabin was surrounded, Helen inside with him, knowing that it was because of her he'd be taken. He waved his gun, threatened that if the police came in he'd shoot his hostage – Helen. But in fact when they broke the door down he blew his brains out. Right there in front of her.'

Penelope's eyes were full of pity. 'And she really loved this man, Sam Bernhard?'

'I'm sure she did. Whether it would have lasted, I don't know. But by then the damage was done.' He crushed out his cigarette. 'Let's get that coffee, shall we?'

She jumped up willingly. If he didn't want to dwell on the past, who could blame him? But following her out to the tiny kitchen he went back to the tale.

'Most of the time she's quite calm, completely in control. Whether she has any men friends I've no idea, but I dare say the old pattern is still there. Every now and again though, poor Helen, it haunts her. It's then that she gets hold of drink by whatever means, and dope too. And of course it's a vicious circle. She's depressed and frightened so she smokes doped cigarettes to give her a lift, she drinks – but none of it drives the devils away. You saw her when she came home that time, imagining the police were after her. Then there's some damned medium she goes to, God knows what sort of stories he feeds her with. She tries to get messages from Sam. Sometimes when she's been under

303

the weather she's blurted it all out to me. The strange thing is, Penny, when she's frightened, when the devils are at her, it's me she comes to. As if I were a kindly brother or uncle.' He shrugged. 'Guess it cuts both ways. That's about how I feel for her. I'll take the tray in.'

'I knew about the medium.'

'I guess everyone does.'

'It's a wretched story, isn't it? No happiness for anyone.'

He didn't answer but wandered to the piano, letting his fingers touch the keyboard in chords and arpeggios, hardly aware of what he did yet getting some sort of comfort from it.

'Penelope, I ought to send you away, not have you with me every evening. You should be out enjoying yourself with some young man who can offer you the sort of future you deserve.'

'Please don't talk like that. You know I'd hate it.'

'Would you?' He turned, looking at her and into her.

She couldn't control the tears that blurred her vision; her arms and legs seemed to have turned to jelly.

'You know I would!' She heard the croak in her voice and the sound destroyed the remnants of her self-control. 'Damned silly tears . . .'

'Come here.' He held his hand towards her.

'Don't want anyone else, just you . . .' Beyond caring she held his hand to her wet cheek.

Then she was in his arms. How different from that other time in Central Park. Now he held her gently, kissing the top of her silky, straight hair, over and over again he murmured her name.

'I love you, Penelope. I believe I must have loved you since you somersaulted into my life in that ridiculous old suit with a muffler around your pretty neck.'

She chuckled, rubbing her tear-damped face against his shoulder.

'Shall I pour us some more coffee? All this loving is

304

making me thirsty, isn't it you?' Her pent-up emotion had evaporated. She'd never felt so happy, nor yet so content.

It was later that he said: 'I ought to take you home.'

She shook her head. 'Please, no.'

'Penny, you know what you're saying?'

Oh yes, she knew what she was saying, what she was almost begging. For answer she wrapped her arms around his neck, her mouth opening hungrily under his kiss.

'There's nothing of you.' But he said it lovingly as he swept her up into his arms and carried her to the bedroom. Just for a moment she thought of Tom, of Sylvia, of her own inadequacies. She wished she had a thirty-eight inch bust and rounded hips. But only for a moment. And a little later, when Laurence looked at her as she lay naked on his bed, his expression quietened all her self-doubts.

'Penny, my little Penny, you're as beautiful as I knew you would be.' His touch was tender. She drew his head down, welcoming his lips. And he? Hadn't she known exactly how his body would be? Hadn't she dreamt of this, night after night as she'd lain in her lonely bed? No, she had no self-doubts, she felt like a goddess. Afterwards, still lying close in his arms, she was sure of the rightness of what had happened. She'd loved him before; she loved him even more now.

The shrill bell of the telephone shattered the silence. If he answered it the moment was lost; if he didn't answer it the sound of its ringing was there between them. He climbed off the bed and pushed his arms into the sleeves of his dressing gown.

'Laurence McLeod speaking . . . yes . . . where? . . . Oh God! . . . yes . . . yes, of course I will . . . You'll allow her to do that? . . . ' Most of the talking was being done at the other end of the line. 'Yes . . . Is the doctor with her? . . . Yes, of course . . . How much did you say? . . . I see. Yes. I'll get there as quickly as I can.'

Then, hanging the ear-piece back on its hook, he told Penelope: 'I have to go. It's Helen. She's been taken in by the State Police. They'll let her home on bail.' What was it he'd said earlier? Helen looked on him as she might a big brother or a kindly uncle. There was no doubting his concern. 'We'll have to get dressed quickly, she oughtn't to be left there alone with too much time to think about what she's done. I'll drop you off and then drive straight out to get her.' He ran his fingers through his iron-grey wavy hair, looking at her with a boyish and apologetic half-grin.

But she couldn't smile. She felt like a child who'd been dismissed out of earshot when the grown-ups wanted to talk. She felt like a plaything put to one side when games time was over. Yet it hadn't been like that, she was sure it hadn't; certainly not for her nor yet for him either. Now the telephone call had pushed everything else from his mind, bringing him firmly down to earth again. Scooping up her clothes she went to the bathroom to dress. She'd never been any use at hiding her feelings and this time she wasn't letting him see her face.

He drove her home, neither of them speaking. As he drew up outside the block of apartments where she and Lana lived she turned to open her door. Like a hurt animal she wanted to run away and hide.

'Penny.' He reached across and covered her hand with his. 'If we hadn't had that call –'

'Doesn't matter. Forget it all.'

'I must go to her. She tried to kill herself. They took her in because of drink, drugs, God knows what. Then, in the cell, she used a penknife to try to cut her wrists. What must she be going through to have come to that?'

'"course you must go to her.' She was ashamed that she could feel so little charity towards another human being. Yes, he must run to his wife, just as he always did when she made a mess of living; just as he always would.

' . . . together to stay with Sonny.' She reined in her runaway thoughts in time to hear the end of what he was telling her. 'Penny, tonight – I ought not to have let it happen – there aren't the words – '

She took her hand and held the palm to his mouth. She might have been made of stone. She didn't move, hardly breathed. Then she pulled herself away, out of the car and through the revolving doors of the apartment block without a backward glance. She didn't dare look at him. She heard the engine start, then the sound of it was lost in the roar of the city as Laurence drove away from her.

It was the next night that Penelope made her decision. It came to her as clearly as if she'd heard the words spoken, just as she took the fourth curtain call. There were two reasons why people applauded: one was because they'd enjoyed what they'd seen, felt in tune with the artistes; the other because loud applause was their way of saying, "This is where the smart set come, it must be the best else why would *we* be here?" And just as if the clamour of their applause were speaking to her smugly, Penelope knew what she must do. "I'm going home. It was fun while it lasted, but it's over." She hadn't the courage to examine the rest of her motives: that she couldn't stay here, so near Laurence and yet never closer to him than on the fringes of his life. She'd remember all their good times, the many, many evenings, the companionship, and above all their one brief hour.

'But you can't do this,' George Randall objected, 'not now, especially not now with Laurence away.'

'George, I'm going. Millie Musgrave understudies me well, you know she does. As for Laurence being away, heaven knows how long that'll be for! Anyway, he's the one person who would understand. He wouldn't try and hold me here.'

George gave her one of Muriel's 'old fashioned looks'. There wasn't much he missed. But he said no more. No doubt he went home to ponder on whether he ought to write to Laurence, cable him, or do nothing. Next morning

Penelope bought a passage on the earliest sailing to South-ampton.

She'd been sea-sick coming out, travelling tourist. For the journey home she booked first class, telling herself that better accommodation would make a good traveller of her. The first night out, she was invited to have dinner at the Captain's table. And that was her last meal-time appearance. It seemed nothing would make a sailor of her. With legs that felt like jelly she walked down the gang-plank at Southampton. Her trunks were to be sent by rail to Challington. With no more than she could carry in one case she caught a train to London, intending to spend a night there; tomorrow she'd tell her agent she was home, then call and see Mr Collingbourne, before following her luggage.

Up until this point she'd pushed to the back of her mind that she would have to tell her father that she'd met Anna. In the first instance she'd thought it better to say nothing. Why, after all, need he ever know? Supposing she was to have that diamond ring Anna had been wearing, need she say anything? She didn't wear jewellery; Pa wouldn't know what she had in her trinket box. Yet, it didn't seem honest. Anna had been important to him, perhaps she always would be. And perhaps now that she was dead, he'd want to know that she hadn't forgotten. Penelope couldn't put off her decision any longer for tomorrow she'd collect whatever it was from Mr Collingbourne and then be free to go home to Pa. All so simple, or so she imagined.

Her decision was made. Pa felt bitter about Anna because she'd treated him badly. So, she'd tell him that Anna had been to see her, she'd tell him the nice things she'd said about him: that he was kind, gentle, that she'd known that with him the baby would be cared for. She'd tell him that the solicitor had informed her of Anna's death. As for the ring (if a ring it proved to be) she'd see what his reactions were before she showed him it. As Penelope planned her campaign she ate her dinner, which

308

she'd had sent up to her room. The first proper meal for weeks. As with all travel sickness, once it was over it left one feeling well and hungry. She ate everything they sent up, leaving the plates as clean as Chummy used to.

She put Anna and Pa both out of her mind. A long, hot bath, then bed. Once there she let her mind wander where it would. It was just two weeks ago that she'd balanced on that high peak of happiness. He loved her, she was sure of that. But Helen had a prior claim. Duty and conscience too dictated that for hadn't he said himself so much of it must have been his own fault? He'd not given her the sort of attention she'd wanted; he'd failed her, been too wrapped up in his own affairs, his own career. Then there was Sonny, the one thing that bound them, the person who loved them both and needed them both. Sleep was miles away and willingly Penelope let herself remember. No one can build a future on memories, she wasn't fool enough to think she could, but for tonight they bridged the great divide she'd put between them.

It was late morning by the time she went up the steps and into the tall Georgian house whose brass plate bore the names Chadwyck, Collingbourne and Shand.

CHAPTER TWELVE

A cab from the West End got her to Charing Cross just as the 3.55 to Challington was due to leave. This time she didn't travel first class. The carriage had no corridor and, as the guard already had his whistle in his mouth ready to give the signal for the train to pull out, she got into the first compartment that had a space. On one side sat a woman with three children, plus a young baby, on the other an outsize man, and two women, one of them already getting her knitting out and the other with her hands folded, eyes downcast. Home! Where folk 'kept themselves to themselves', and nowhere more so than in a railway carriage.

Penelope would have liked to have been by the window so that she could watch the fading daylight as they travelled. But, without raising her downcast eyes or unclasping her hands, Mrs Touch-Me-Not folded herself into the corner seat, leaving Penelope just enough space to sit between her and the long wooden knitting needles. Opposite, the mother got out a paper package of sandwiches and before Charing Cross was five minutes behind them four jaws were busy champing on them.

None of them paid any attention to the pretty, dark-eyed girl who'd so nearly missed the train. Their silence, their disinterest, wrapped itself around her. Home! Another world from the glitter and gloss, the bright lights, the affected endearments, the clamour of empty applause. Just as everyone else did, she gazed at nothing. But surely their minds couldn't all be in this turmoil? Penelope must think! She must plan!

It was after six when, with a long gush of steam, the train shuddered to a standstill in Challington's familiar station. Once on the platform, she let everyone hurry past her. She'd imagined the excitement of her unexpected arrival at Alexandra Square, but now, quite suddenly, she wanted to put the moment off. She'd walk. Time didn't matter. She'd go along West Street, down Kings Road past the corner of Victoria Place, she'd see the lights of the Grand, walk along the gas-lit Promenade. Picking up her suitcase she came out into Station Square.

A man was selling bootlaces by the station entrance, a man probably no older than she was herself. Ought she to recognize him? Had he been at Merchant Hill Board School, or perhaps at St James'? Around his neck he wore a notice telling the world that he'd been 'Blinded at Ypres'. She put a shilling in his tin. Along the road were four children playing hopscotch; three of them had no socks and the fourth no shirt under his too large jacket. It was only October but the evening was cold, mist rolling in from the sea. The children weren't begging, they looked happy enough, kept warm by their game. In West Street the large Victorian houses gave the same appearance of comfort and prosperity she remembered from the past: brass door knockers shining, steps scrubbed and whitened. Occupants of the West Street houses had always prided themselves on keeping 'staff' – more accurately some poor drudge who worked in the basement kitchen and slept in the attic.

Outside the Barley Mow in Kings Road was another war veteran. 'Out of work' told only half his story; no mention of the wooden stump that served as a leg. He was standing propped against the wall of the building, just away from the beam of light from the porch. She might not even have noticed him but for two things. One was the little boy by his side who hopefully shook his tin as anyone went in or out through the door; the second was the tune he played on his ukelele. The Sausage Song! This time she dug in her purse for more than a shilling.

311

'Cor! Thankyer, Miss.' The lad looked as if she'd given him the Crown Jewels.

How could she have forgotten? It took the innocent hope in a child's eyes to bring it all back. Herself and Pa, the hope that a good day brought, the pretence that things were better than they were. As if it were yesterday she remembered the feel and smell of the basement that had been their home. In all the months she'd been away – in all the years, too – she'd never felt so near to what they'd shared as she did tonight coming home. She'd seen plenty of poverty in New York and in London too. But nothing touched her like this did. Muriel had told her; she ought to have expected it. Had she been so busy lapping up the flattery, tasting the high life, that she'd not understood? Silly tears stung her eyes, tears welling up at the sight of that small boy's hope. Hope for what? Curtains at the dark empty windows, warm food on a plate? It was the little girl she'd once been who knew just what that 'Cor! Thankyer, Miss' had meant. She wanted to get home, to Pa and Mother and the others. Her people. An omnibus was coming, she could hear its noisy motor. Running to the stop at the end of Victoria Place, she was just in time.

The lodgers had had their meal, the family were just about to sit down around the large wooden table in the kitchen.

'Got enough for an extra?' She'd known the garden gate would be unlocked, no one ever worried about locking doors in Challington.

'Penny love! Where have you come from?'

'Up the garden path.' A silly question and a sillier answer. Enfolded in Muriel's bear-like embrace she looked over her shoulder at Pa. He seemed older, he'd put on weight. But from a bush in the front garden he'd found a rose for his buttonhole. The debonair charm was still there.

'Is something wrong?' He took his turn for her kiss. 'You haven't got the sack?'

'No, Pa. You can hold your head up still. It was my own decision. I've come home.'

'But why? You must have been earning splendid money, you got good reviews – '

'More to life than money, Ollie. If she wasn't happy, then home's the place to be.'

'I was happy.' "I never knew I could be so happy! What have I done! How can I make a future with no hope of being with him!"

'Then why? Oh, it's nice to see you. Looking very smart and successful too. Is the show coming off, is that it?'

'It's not my sort of world, Pa.'

'Never did think much of stage people, never pretended to.' But she knew he was disappointed. He'd enjoyed the glory her success had brought him.

'I've not done with the stage, Pa. I loved the part I played, I hate to think of anyone else doing it. But it wasn't like the Halls. The audiences were all so smart, all dressed up. They never seemed to be one with you – I don't know how else to explain. It's a sort of social accolade to get tickets for an important first night; and, at any time, coming to the theatre is a social necessity. If you don't see all the worthwhile shows then you aren't in the swim. You should see the smart clothes, the jewellery! Not a bit like the folk who queued up for the gods, out for a good sing to forget their worries.'

As usual Muriel had her own brand of wisdom. 'I dare say it's all much of a muchness. If money's short then sixpence for the gods makes as big an outing as whatever these smart folk of yours have to pay to sit in the stalls. And everyone wears the best they've got.' There was never any jealousy in her. 'Don't stand there looking tongue-tied, you three, haven't you got a kiss for your big sister?'

'Big?' It was Merrick who said it, his smile so like his mother's. At sixteen he was as tall as his father, and had the makings of a man just as handsome, although his nature owed more to Muriel. Even Mandy, Oliver's daughter through and through, could top Penelope by two inches. Only Bruce showed signs of inheriting his mother's chunky build, although there the resemblance ended, for in every other respect he was like neither of his parents.

'How's the boatyard, Merrick?'

'Tophole. You wait 'til I tell them you're home! Old Man Bailey likes to think he took a hand in launching you and – ' He bit back his words.

' – and Tom?' she finished his sentence. 'Yes, he did. If he hadn't let us practise there in the evenings, I doubt if Tommy and Perce would have seen the light of day. And you, Mandy? Making beautiful hats for Madame Bearne?'

Pretty Mandy nodded. Her tongue was still tied.

'I'll take your case up to your room.' Bruce picked it up. 'Is this all the luggage you've got?' Which meant, "Haven't you brought any presents?"

'My trunks are coming by rail. I docked in Southampton yesterday, they'll get here in a day or two.' She grinned at him. 'You'll have to wait for your presents 'til then.'

'You got us something? Cor, jolly good!' The sandy-haired lad gave her a broad wink, then disappeared up the stairs to the attic, two steps at a time.

'He's a monkey, that one,' Muriel tut-tutted. 'Don't take any notice of him, Penny.'

There was so much Penelope knew she must tell them. She'd planned to wait until the young ones had gone to bed, but of course she'd been away so much and so long that she'd overlooked the fact that Merrick and Mandy would be up as late as anyone else.

'Do you want to come with us, Penny? Mandy and me – and a couple of mates – we're going to the cinematograph. There's a Mary Pickford, Doug Fairbanks.'

'No thanks, Merrick. Where's the Picture House?'

'Not far, just round the back of the Grand.'

'Pass me my purse. I'll treat you. Is that enough for the four of you?' She took out a ten-shilling note.

'What, half a crown each? Poshest seats in the house

are only one and six! Look at that, Mandy! Up with the nobs tonight. Thanks, Pen.'

'Throwing your money about, aren't you, for a girl out of work?'

'Ollie, don't take the pleasure off.'

'Let's go, Mandy. Get your hat on.' Merrick had sensed the change in atmosphere just as surely as Penelope had.

'Have you got to play your darts this evening, Ollie, or can you stay in with us and hear all about New York?'

For answer he pulled out his empty pockets.

'Unless my famous daughter's largesse extends to a pint for her poor old father, it seems you've got to put up with me.'

'Stay in, Pa, please. I want to talk to you.'

Muriel as always understood what was left unsaid.

'Now, how would it be if young Bruce was allowed to see the picture show? You've enough money there for the five of you. Take him along, give him a treat.'

'Cor, super. Can I, Dad?'

'If your mother says so and your sister pays for you, I don't come into it.'

'"course you do. But it's all right for me to go, isn't it?'

And in a couple of minutes the back door shut on the young Drews.

'What dears they are,' Penelope said.

'Young Mandy could have done without Bruce's company,' Muriel laughed. 'Another lad from the boatyard, and a friend of hers from the milliners, a nice little four-some. Then I have to inflict young brother on them.'

'And a good thing too.' Oliver looked as though his supper hadn't agreed with him. 'Fifteen years old and wanting to be off after the boys.'

'I was fifteen years old when I left home, Pa. At fifteen you feel so grown up, think you know the lot.'

'And look where it got you with ruddy Tom Beasley, young sod!'

'Hush, Ollie.'

315

'I expect we were too young, too ready to believe we were in love. Tom and Sylvia were made for each other. They didn't mean to hurt me. I love them both dearly.'

'Can't understand the morals of you people.'

Penelope laughed.

'Tell me about Challington. It's funny, isn't it? I saw poverty enough in New York and London, but it seems dreadful to see it here. Men who went to fight and came home to nothing.'

'Breaks my heart . . . well, I've written you about it. Women struggling to bring up families on their own, trying to make ends meet on nothing but that bit of pension money. It's the children I worry for, poor little mites, and another winter coming. I know it's no worse here than anywhere else but, like you say, it brings it home to you, seeing it here in Challington. You don't expect it somehow.'

'Then I don't know why not!' Oliver was indeed in a bad mood. 'Penny ought to know what it feels like.'

Penelope shook her head. 'You and me, Pa, we were a team. We were never without hope.'

'Can't live on ruddy hope.'

'Oh, but you can. While you're young you can. Hope, plans, dreams . . . '

Oliver took out his handkerchief and made a pretence of wiping his nose, but not before she'd seen his mouth wobble.

'Here, Ollie love,' Muriel took some coins out of a pot on the mantelpiece and put them in his pocket. 'You go and get yourself a pint while Penny and I clear away the supper. Don't be all evening, though, it's you she wants to talk to.'

'It's both of you I want to talk to. But after we've washed up.'

Had she told them her news now while they sat together at the table, the whole future might have worked out differently. A pint with his friends invariably put Oliver in a happier frame of mind, and working in the kitchen with Muriel had always been a time for confidences.

'Have you seen Alf and Emma lately, Mother? I shall go in tomorrow and meet little Gwendoline. Who's she like?'

'Too tiny to say yet. Bluest of blue eyes, dear little soul she is. I just wish someone would give poor Alf a bit of work. He's handy as can be with his hands. This is just between you and me – don't let on to him I saw him – but the other night I popped out to post a letter. Don't know what made me take the long walk home, a nice clear, dry night it was and I suppose I'd been indoors all day. Anyway, as I turned into Crown Street, just by the end of the cutting from Elgar Street, I saw Alf. Never let him think I recognized him. Out there with a tray of matches trying to sell. Little Alf! No doubt of it. His hat was pulled right down and he was wearing a coat with the collar up, even though the night was mild enough. Who did he think would buy his lucifers there in the dark? Poor boy.

'Oh, I dunno, Penny, sometimes I feel sick with fright for what the world's coming to. It's happened once, the cream of the youth all gone, that's what folk say. But they wouldn't say it so calmly if it was their own sons, their own husbands. Like I say, it's happened once and people took it. Sometimes I look at Merrick and that young rascal Bruce and I feel sick with fright for them. When I was a girl war was for trained soldiers, men who went off into the Army because they wanted to. No more though.'

'But surely we've learnt. Mistakes are the way to learn, Mother. We've seen. We know.'

'Yes, we've learnt all right, learnt never to trust the politicians and the promises they make. I remember when we used to see the wounded soldiers in town, all dressed in their blue uniforms from the hospital at Prospect House. Boys pushed in wheel chairs, boys with limbs lost . . . we never doubted that things would improve for them. Only if a man loses a limb you can't make it up to him, no matter how much you may want to. But we expected they'd get the dignity of sufficient to live on properly, raise their families in this land fit for heroes as they were promised. Where's the justice, Penny?' Muriel's kindly face was troubled as she turned, hands plunged in the hot water. 'Here they all are, sent off home with a few bob a week, no hope, no work. Is that the way to thank them for what they did for us all? Boys like poor young Alf never hurt a soul. They were better off in that hospital. At least there they still had hope.'

'Is Prospect House still a hospital?' She wasn't really interested in what had happened to the old mansion standing in its gardens at the far end of Prospect Street. She asked the question because she'd never heard quite such an outburst from Muriel; even her letters hadn't shown how upset she was by the misery all around. Talk of the hospital seemed safe.

'No. Why, I thought it was closed before you went to America. There it stands empty. Up for sale, I believe, but what it's good for I can't think. Some folk say it would make a smart hotel, but it's too far from the beach for a seaside holiday yet not in the country neither. Who'd want to spend a holiday at the back end of town?' One after another she stood the plates and dishes to drain. 'Come on, dreamer,' she laughed, her outburst had done her good, 'wake up! Standing there with the cloth in your hand and your thoughts a thousand miles away.'

But they hadn't been.

'Now it's your turn to talk, I've done my share. Oh, but it's good to have you home, another woman I can speak my mind to, I don't like to worry Ollie with my grumbles. Life hasn't always been kind to him, he deserves a bit of comfort, bless his heart. Take this big dish next, will you, and give it a wipe.' Typical of Muriel to jump from one thing to the next. 'And what really made you come home

318

so suddenly? Unless you want to keep it to yourself? When a woman runs away there's usually a man in the picture.'

'I suppose what you've said is true too, but I haven't run away, not like you mean. He's married and his wife needs him. Oh, not because she loves him, but she depends on him. She has a sort of split personality. Half the time – in fact, most of the time – she's the same as anyone else though she and Laurence live separate lives. But there's this other side . . . oh, it's a long story. He'd never leave her as long as she needs him. And they've a son. I think Helen, his wife, is truly fond of Sonny. Of course she is, she's his mother! And Laurence – oh, Mother, he was so proud of Sonny, he told me about him in France. Then, after the war, he contracted infantile paralysis. He's just taken his first few steps after all this time. His legs are in braces. He's only fourteen.'

'Poor lamb.' And Muriel meant it.

'That's why I came home. Laurence and I could have been so happy, it's so right for us to be together. But I can't make it harder for him than it already is.'

'This is the man who writes the songs, the one who wrote "Girl of my Dreams"? And what did he have to say about your coming back to England?'

'He didn't know. I didn't even write to him. He'll understand, he won't need me to tell him.'

'Here's your pa back. That's good timing, Ollie love, we've just put the last of it away. Now we'll draw our chairs to the fire and be comfortable.'

'There are things I have to talk to you about.' Penelope couldn't put it off any longer. 'Pa, when I start you may not like what I'm saying. But let me tell you the whole story, listen to it all. Promise.'

Ollie frowned. He smelt trouble.

'It was when I was in London, playing in "Song of the Dawn". One night a stranger came to my dressing room, a woman. Pa, it was Anna.'

'Anna . . . ' His mouth dropped open. 'Your mother?'

'I called her Anna.' Penelope's eyes said far more than words as she looked at Muriel. 'This is Mother.'

'What did she want? Thought you were earning good money, I suppose, wanted to touch you for something.'

'She was expensively dressed and didn't want money. She told me that. Money is the one thing I've got plenty of, she said. No, I honestly believe she just wanted to see me. She was only in London a few days. She'd lived in Switzerland for some years, apparently.'

'Why didn't you tell me then? Can't think why you should be so sly, so deceitful! Didn't I have a right to know?'

'There would have been no point. She only came once. She was in London on business, she told me, but I didn't know then what business.'

'Well, if it wasn't important enough – or I wasn't important enough – to talk about then, why do you dig it up now after all this time. Has she come back? Have you heard from her again?'

His voice was harsh, but there was no disguising his eagerness. In all these years, had he never given up hope? Muriel heard it too, Penelope knew she did by the way she was examining the lines on the palm of her hand, not letting herself look at him.

'Anna was a widow. She'd been married to a man called Neubinsky.'

'That wasn't the chap she went off with – '

'Oh, I imagine she shed him. She was very honest, she told me she could never have been a poor man's wife. This Neubinsky, whatever nationality he was, was certainly not poor. She didn't tell me anything about him on that night – '

'So, when did you see her again? In America? Is that it, she's been with you in New York?'

'Pa, Anna is dead. I never saw her again after that one night.'

'Just tell me – did she say anything about me?'

'She said that when she went she'd known I'd be cared for, that you'd always be kind.'

His mouth wobbled, he sniffed, his eyes were bloodshot.

'Kind, she remembered me as kind. Anna dead. So much life – now she's dead.'

'She'd been ill for years.' Penelope was surprised to find herself speaking in such matter-of-fact tones. Her father's grief didn't touch her nearly as much as the hurt it might be doing to Muriel who loved him so dearly.

'It was her idea for you not to tell me, I suppose?'

'No. I asked her if she'd rather I didn't and she said she didn't mind one way or the other. She'd done a lot of living since I was born, Pa.' It was brutal but it might put a bit of mettle into him. 'I'd been in New York a few months when I had a letter from a firm of solicitors in London asking me to contact them. Anna Neubinsky had died. It seemed she'd left me something in her Will. I thought if she'd wanted me to have a ring or something there was no hurry, so I wrote and said I'd call when I came home. That's what I did this morning. Her husband had been a financier, they had a house in Switzerland, investments in South Africa. The thing is – ' she looked from one to the other ' – the morning after she came to see me she went to her solicitors and signed a fresh Will. Except for a legacy to a clinic in Switzerland, she has left everything to me.'

'Good God!' There was nothing wobbly about Oliver's face now. 'You hear that?' to Muriel. 'Young Penny a ruddy heiress. No more having to prance about on the stage for you, my girl, you'll be able to live in style.'

'That's what I want to talk about.'

'What are you going to do, Penny love? Fancy! A house in Switzerland.'

'I told Mr Collingbourne – that's the solicitor – I wanted it sold, and all the investments too. I wasn't sure what I wanted to do, at least I wasn't sure how to set about doing it. But now I know. And I want you to help me, both of you.'

'Help you! With all the money you've got, how can we help?' Oliver laughed. 'Unless it's help with the spending of it you want. Fancy her leaving it to a child she never cared a rap about.' He leant down and took up the poker, concentrating on jabbing at the coals in the range as he spoke. 'Who looked after you? Even when you were no more than a baby? Not her! The rows we used to have – old Ethel Sharp must have heard them – all on your account. Father and Mother too, that's what I had to be. And what have I ever been able to do for you? Nothing. It'll be her has all the praise, all the glory, now you're a wealthy woman.' He'd done the fire no good at all. He hardly noticed as Muriel took the poker from him. 'A poor man wouldn't have done for Anna. That's why she left me. I was the man she loved, never doubt that. But she had a weakness for money. Neubinsky could afford her, obviously. Now she's gone – and his money comes back to us. Got the laugh on him after all, eh?'

'Not to us, Ollie. To Penny. And quite right that it should. I expect you and she were alike, weren't you, Penny? I've heard say you look like she used to.'

'She was ill. So thin she looked brittle. But, yes, we were alike. Time Past and Time Future she called us when we stood in front of my make-up mirror.'

'Oh, don't say that, not Time Future, not if she was ill like that.'

'Mother, you said earlier that Prospect House is up for sale. My mind was full of half-formed ideas, pictures of children who need caring for, need good dinners and warm clothes. But I couldn't see what I had to do. Then you mentioned Prospect House and it all fell into place. What better way to use Anna's money? There's so much room in that great place. Why pay rent here if you could live there? Every home needs a mother and a father.'

Oliver frowned. 'You haven't even got your hands on

322

the money yet. Not so fast in wanting to get rid of it. The place may need too much doing to it.'

'I doubt it. It was used as a hospital, it can't be that bad.'

'Young Alf would give a hand, and gladly.'

Muriel and Penelope exchanged a glance. Not for the first time they read each other's thoughts.

'Time I made the cocoa for my upstairs lot.' Muriel stood up. Just for a second a shadow fell. If all these schemes came off she'd have to tell the lodgers to go. The Carling sisters had been with her for more than five years. Still, they were all grown people and with work to go to.

After she'd plodded up the stairs bearing her tray of steaming cocoa Oliver spoke again of Anna. Leaning back in the wooden armchair, his legs crossed, he looked remarkably pleased with the turn of events. Between his thumb and finger he idly felt the crease in the leg of his trousers, while his gaze rested with satisfaction on his highly polished shoe.

'It's gone full circle, Tuppence. It was Anna who pulled me down in the world. I've told you before, I'd been used to better things. It's only right that she should set the score straight.'

A giggle threatened to erupt from Penelope. Anna might have left her her fortune just to hear this! She put her hand lightly on his. Still the same Pa!

The picturegoers came home, each talking against the other as they tried to re-kindle the magic of the screen. Mandy went straight to bed, wide awake, starry eyed and with dreams of Douglas Fairbanks waiting for her. The boys put first things first. More cocoa had to be made, thick slices of bread held on a fork to the bars of the kitchen range to make toast. No wonder they grew so tall, they never stopped eating! Relaxing in his chair, his thumbs hooked into the armholes of his waistcoat, Oliver surveyed the scene with satisfaction. Head of the household . . . provider . . . it was to him these fine young

lads looked . . . it would be to him those other fatherless
children would look . . . governor . . . mentor . . . A smile
played at the corners of his mouth.

'Come on, now, Bruce love, time you were in bed.'

'Just finished, Mum. I'm off now. 'Night, 'night Dad.'
A light kiss on each forehead.

'Goodnight son,' from the head of the house.

'D'ye reckon the trunks'll come tomorrow, Pen?'

'Do you – not d'ye – you must be more careful.' Again
the head of the house.

'Sorry, Dad. Do you, Pen?'

'I wouldn't wonder.'

Satisfied, Bruce went off. Then – with dreams of
Mandy's friend from the millinery workshop waiting for
him – Merrick too.

'Suddenly gone quiet!' Muriel laughed.

So the three of them put another shovel of coal on the
fire and went back to what had always been one of Penelope's favourite pastimes: making plans.

That was in October. It was April by the time Anna's
affairs had been settled and Penelope actually had the
money to complete the purchase of Prospect House. And
by then so much else had happened.

A fortnight in Challington was enough for the wheels to
be set in motion. On Penelope's first visit to Prospect
House, Oliver and Muriel went with her. On the second,
Alf and Emma.

'It's almost frightening, it's so right for what we need.'
That old superstitious dread of Penelope's nudged at her.

And so it was, even to the lodge where Alf and his
family would live. He was to be in charge of the gardens
and do the odd repairs in the house.

'We don't know how many will actually live here. We
shall have to see what the need is. Mother thinks she'll
have a houseful of children to care for, but I believe they'll

324

mostly be left here while their mothers do a job of work, then taken home again at the end of the day.'

'Och a'ou hool?' Emma asked.

'School? Well, if they go to school they can still come here at teatime, have a good meal, play together in the garden in the summer, or indoors in the warm in the winter, until their mothers are home from work.'

'I think Mrs Drew's idea is nearer the mark,' Alf said. 'Have you read the lists on that memorial they've erected in Bradley Park, seen just how many from this one town didn't come home at all? Plenty of women were left with children, women who've tried to make a fresh start, don't want reminders always underfoot – of if they do, probably their new men don't. There's nothing like a war for producing illegitimate kids. You'll find your beds are full, Pen.'

'Well, we shall see. The only thing I'm sure of is that any children Mother and Pa look after will know what it is to have a good home.'

'Yes, she's splendid.'

'They both are,' her dark eyes defied him to think otherwise, 'and I should know! It was Pa who made a home for me, all by himself.'

Alf remembered.

Two days later Penelope left for London, for Charlie Cribbans, her agent, and for work. He thought she was crazy, that from Broadway to the variety theatres she insisted on playing was to slide down that all too slippery slope. Instead he suggested an acceptable compromise. From Boxing Day until March, each weekday evening and twice on Saturdays, Penelope was to don the guise of Peter Pan. The idea appealed to her. In Peter Pan, the boy who never grew up, she saw a combination of Perce and Penelope; she looked forward to playing to children, to the honesty of their enjoyment.

A fool to herself, that's what Charlie Cribbans thought. And he was determined that before very long a suitable bait would be dangled before Peter Pan to persuade him to put his wings away.

With every ounce of energy she possessed, Penelope threw herself into rehearsals. There had never been such a Peter as hers. She brought to the part all the acrobatic agility of Perce, and added to it the supple grace Broadway had loved. Christmas approached, the set was ready, Peter had flown across the stage hoisted by wires. She was thrilled, excited; she had to be, she wouldn't let herself think of the 'might have beens'. Easy enough for young Perce to tell his audience to put a geranium in their 'ats and be 'appy – he hadn't known the battle one had to fight to do it. Time and again she reminded herself of that little rhyme.

Charlie Cribbans had his ear to the ground, waiting for something that would tempt her, while unbeknown to him she was making up her own mind.

It was Christmas Eve. Dress rehearsal was over, all was ready for the Boxing Day matinée. Penelope pushed her way through Berwick Street Market, listening to the traders shouting their wares: fruit that had felt the kiss of sunshine of faraway lands, sprouts all the sweeter for the kiss of the December frost in England. She imagined the fun it would be next year, buying the Christmas fare for that large family Mother was so sure she'd have to care for. Solicitors moved slowly. They seemed no nearer acquiring Prospect House than they had been in October. No, that wasn't true. A letter had told her how Muriel and Oliver had been allowed to have the key to measure the windows; a bale of material had been delivered to number fourteen Alexandra Square and Muriel was spending hours turning the handle of her sewing machine. Always in the front of her mind, Penelope kept the picture of what they planned to do, what it would mean to the people she loved in Challington; at least that's where she tried to keep it, but sometimes her mind rushed away out of control taking her to forbidden fields.

Two and a half months she'd been home and she'd

heard not a word from Laurence. "But of course I haven't, I didn't expect to. Anyway he doesn't know my address . . . " she made silent excuses as she watched the bustle of market activity all around her. "But he could find out if he wanted to. That attorney we went to, he has the address of my solicitor – or Lana, she knows where I used to write to in Challington. If he wanted to, he could get in touch with me. Not even a card for Christmas. That's because he respects the decision I made. Anyway I haven't sent a card to him, either. It's right – it's wise – "

'Mind yer back, Miss. Gorblimey, are y'deaf? Mind yer back, I gotta hundredweight o' spuds 'ere. Wotcha think I am? bleedin' Goliath?'

So lost in thoughts was she, she might not have made way for the far-from-Goliath humper even then if someone hadn't tugged her arm.

'Pen! Ma wrote weeks ago that she'd heard you were home!' Tom, with four-year-old Avril riding high on his shoulders, enjoying the colourful scene she looked down on. 'She said she heard you were looking for work. The high life not what you expected?'

'I'm in panto.'

'Bit of a comedown, eh?'

'It's fun. And what about you and Sylvie?'

'I'm in the production team these days, making out quite well. What do you think of this one, eh? Isn't she the tops.'

'She's just like you, Tom Beasley, if that's what you mean.'

'Yep, that's what I mean. The tops.' He gave her a broad wink.

She could feel a giggle bubbling up. Tom Beasley, her one time husband! And here they were, talking together just the same as they used to in the days they'd raced from school to climb on the rocks before going home for tea – or, in her case, usually no tea.

'You're not at Challington for Christmas?' he asked. 'I

suppose you can't be if you're opening in panto, you'd not get back. Where are you? Some frusty old boarding house? Come to us, Pen. Sylvia'll be tickled pink, you know she will. You haven't got something promised that you can't get out of, have you?'

'No.' She pictured her small flat, tomorrow a day she hadn't cared to think about. Only now did she realize how much she'd been dreading it. 'But, Tom, I wrote and told you I was home. Ages ago. As soon as I got to London I sent you my address. Couldn't think why I didn't hear.'

'Probably because we didn't get your letter. We've been moving – it's worth the drive to get out of town. We've gone upmarket! Harrow-on-the-Hill. Got a nice house, Pen, and a nursemaid, a garden with a lawn to mow, all the trimmings.' Tom was bouncing with pride in their domestic bliss. 'Tell you what, go and get your nightdress and toothbrush and come home with us today. There won't be transport on Christmas Day, and anyway it'll be a lark. We'll listen out for Santa Claus, all of us together.'

'You sure, Tom? I won't be spoiling any plans?'

'What, for Sylvia, you mean? Don't be a dope. There's nothing Sylvie likes better than an unexpected visitor.' He gave her a curious look. 'What's so funny?'

'Nothing really. It's just, I was picturing Pa's face. He says he can't understand . . . ' She wished she hadn't started to explain.

'Oh, I see what you mean.' Tom laughed too, taking the situation in his stride. 'You and me, you mean? Lot of water under London Bridge since those days. How's old Alf? Did you see him when you were home? And Emma. Rotten shame about her. Pretty girl. He seems to make out what she tries to say. Me, I couldn't understand a word. Hope the kid's going to be all right.'

'Gwendoline's lovely. And I can understand Emma perfectly, we all can.'

'Honestly? We couldn't, it was embarrassing. I felt sorry

for poor old Alf. A wife we could admire would have been a feather in his cap. And the poor lad could do with one.'

'Look, Tom, I must do some shopping before I come,' with a barely perceptible nod towards Avril, 'and get my toothbrush. Where's your motor car?'

'Tell me where you live and I'll pick you up. Door to door service.'

An hour later she was sitting by his side, Avril on her knee, as they headed for Harrow-on-the-Hill.

Sylvia's pleasure was genuine. Just like Tom, she appeared to have forgotten that he and Penelope had ever been married. There had been a time when Penelope wouldn't have believed she would ever look on Tom with affection, simply as the boy she'd grown up with, but Laurence had taught her that her heart had come out of her marriage with no worse damage than a bad bruising. So everything was set for them to have a good Christmas.

Yet almost from the first, Penelope was disappointed at a new affectation in her 'chosen sister's' manner. 'Darling, we read your reviews, such raves you had' ... 'You're always so gloriously slim, straight as a boy. If you knew how I envy you' ... 'You wear such simple clothes, I'd look a real frump if I dressed like you do. No one could guess you'd been the belle of New York' ... 'Oh, we read about it all, didn't we, Tom? Penny darling, how could you bear to pull yourself away from it all and come back to smokey old London?'

Tom was just the same as he'd always been, full of fun and good humoured. Unconsciously selfish, perhaps, but never greedy. It was Sylvia who had changed. Penelope felt a sense of loss.

'I never liked Christmas.' Her friend busied herself mixing cocktails. Penelope thought perhaps she was remembering that Christmas at Hampstead, the letter from Ken's Commanding Officer, until she went on: 'Miserable digs, landladies who produced wretched plum pudding and cooking sherry.'

'A day off with knobs on, that's what you used to call it, remember, Tom?'

'Sing-songs round the parlour piano, everyone pretending to be having a wonderful time. Yes, I remember. Be different this year, though. Avril's going to go wild when she undoes all the things we've got for her. What's up, Pen? You shivered. Come nearer the fire.'

'I'm not a bit cold.' But she sat on the humpty near the fire just the same. 'Just a ghost walking over my grave. Something about Christmas . . . time past, time present, time future, it all gets mixed up in your mind. Ghosts of yesterday, hopes, wishes.'

'Oh, sweetie, you're getting maudlin. That won't do. What possible ghosts could be haunting you after the successful year you've had?' Where was the understanding Sylvia of time past?

'I'm not a bit maudlin. But that's it, isn't it? It's because it's the end of the year you sort of take stock.'

'Here, Tom, fill her glass,' Sylvia laughed. 'If she's like this on Christmas Eve, I don't think we'll invite her to our New Year do.'

'Things are all right, aren't they, Pen?' Tom looked concerned as he refilled her glass. 'Chucking up a Laurence McLeod show won't put the kibosh on your getting anything else? Perhaps we can help. I'm doing well, I told you, and Sylvia is lead dancer. We'll put in a word – '

'Tom, things are fine. I gave up because I found something out.' The cocktails were strong and Penelope had never been a drinker. 'I found out I hate posh audiences, people all decked out as if they've got the Crown Jewels on, going to the theatre just to be seen. That's not for me. It was different during the war, people liked Perce.'

'You should have stayed with me. We could have kept the act going. I told you at the time.'

'No, that's not it. I'd done with Perce. The pantomime's

something I shall love doing. Children are honest. After that, I don't know. Huge theatres, dark auditoriums – that's not for me. But it's the only thing I can do, and I have a living to earn.'

'If you want to retire, then you'd better look for a rich husband while you've got the chance. It's what you call "posh" audiences that have led many a showgirl to a life of leisure.' Sylvia laughed lightly. 'We heard all sorts of gossip, you know,' she prompted, 'you know what the grape vine is for passing the word. We heard that you and your famous Laurence McLeod were having an affair. I always did think you were a bit sweet on him, and out there, away from all the old gang, I thought a middle-aged man might have been just what you fancied.'

'Who did you hear that from? What grape vine?'

'Don't look so maiden auntish, you're a free agent. I heard it from Dick Bridges. Shouldn't think for a moment you ever met him. You don't actually have to know a person for a story to be passed. He was playing in New York. Came back during the summer, soon after "Girl of My Dreams" opened. That's how we knew what a rave it was, apart from the notices you sent. He said it was common knowledge the great McLeod's marriage was on the rocks and there was talk about him and his little protégé. Of course, we didn't really believe it, we know what people are. Anyway, he and his wife seem to have found love's re-awakening from the latest one reads. Do you hear any news from out there?'

'I have letters from the girl I used to live with. But she doesn't know much about Laurence.' She wanted to be told yet she dreaded what she'd hear.

'Well, this isn't idle gossip. I read it for myself. Fancy you not noticing, it was in our daily paper. Did you know he has a crippled son? Well, the paper had some story about Mrs McLeod having been before the Court. She'd been picked up by the police the worse for wear – illegal alcohol and drugs too. I can't think how she got off so lightly. The write-up didn't give much space to it, I had to read between the lines, but it implied the police had met her before, had their sights on her. The Court imposed a hefty fine, I forget how much, but no prison sentence, not so much as had her wrist slapped. I wish I still had the newspaper to show you. Her attorney pleaded that there were mitigating circumstances – the son being a cripple, I suppose. I bet back there the press made a meal of it and dug up all the dirt.

'Apparently your famous Laurence spoke in her defence in Court and undertook to be responsible for her good behaviour, see she keeps on the straight and narrow. It said the McLeod family – that's him, her and the crippled boy – were off on holiday to a secret destination, taking a nurse along. To keep the lad out of their hair, I imagine.'

'He's getting better, don't call him a cripple.'

Sylvia shrugged her shoulders. 'Sorry, sweetie, don't sound so aggressive. I'm only repeating what the paper said.'

'If a newspaper can dig into the dirt, it will. Why can't they just leave people alone!'

'Cheer up, it's Christmas. Top her up, Tom, it's nearly midnight.'

'Sure you want any more, Pen?'

She wished she hadn't come. She wished she'd kept her memories of them as they had been . . . of them, of Laurence, of time past . . . what about time future? Empty dreams. She daren't blink, almost daren't breathe. Where was he now, where was the secret destination? Didn't matter where it was – right next door or on the other side of the world. If he'd died he would still have been near her, nothing could have come between them. But he was alive, the Laurence who belonged to Helen and Sonny. He'd loved her – she was sure he'd loved her at the time – but that time was over just as surely as her brief triumph in 'Girl of My Dreams'.

'Pen – more?' Tom still waited for her answer.

'Why not, it's Christmas! Hark, it's striking.' Glasses were clinked, kisses exchanged all round, another log thrown on the fire. By nature they were all night hawks – and tomorrow was a day off with knobs on.

There was nothing new in starting the year with good resolutions, most people did, usually to forget them long before January was out. Penelope made only one, and had two good reasons why she must keep it as the months of 1922 went by. She resolved to make her mark on this side of the Atlantic as clearly as she had on the other. Success must be her goal.

'But you had success over there and you chucked it in, Pen,' Alf said as they walked together along the seafront, heads down against the January gale. It was Sunday, she was there until the following afternoon. 'I thought from what you'd said you were fed up with being a celebrity. Now here you are, hankering after it all over again.'

'That was different. I knew I had to get away, Alf. But now I have special reasons for wanting to be sure I make good.'

'Are you going to tell me?'

She laughed. 'I shouldn't have thought I had to. For one thing I need to earn as much as I can so that things can stay on an even keel at Prospect House. I don't want us to keep it going on capital or we'll soon be in the cart.'

'And the other reasons?'

'Pride, I suppose. So that I get reviews good enough to be read in New York.'

The left side of his face was towards her, the side with expression. But, if he obviously didn't understand why it mattered so much to her, at least he had the tact not to probe.

By the time Anna's house in Switzerland had been sold, her investments redeemed and Penelope was able to sign the contract for Prospect House, winter was almost over. It was April when Oliver and his family moved in, and

Emma became mistress of the lodge; in fact, quite by chance, it was Avril's fifth birthday. Penelope never missed an omen, whether good or bad, and to open a home for children on Avril's birthday must surely be a good one. Hadn't she been equally sure of Muriel's unfailing understanding when she'd written and shared Sylvia's secret with her five and a half years ago?

Bradford, Manchester, Brighton, Windsor, London, Scarborough, Torquay, Leeds, Edinburgh, Plymouth, up and down the country she travelled, Sundays usually spent on a train, the weeks in provincial hotels. It was a lonely life – she hadn't even Young Perce for company! Acquaintances everywhere but no friends – 'proper deep-down kindred spirit friends' would come the echo of those two little girls in the attic bedroom.

Penlope was in her dressing room one night, wriggling into her skintight all-in-one costume, when the call boy knocked loudly on her door.

'Telephone call for you, Miss Drew.'

'Shan't be a tick. Who is it, did they say?'

'It's a man. Long distance. Said it was important.'

CHAPTER THIRTEEN

In as long as it took her to run to the stage door keeper's cupboard of an office, fumbling to finish fastening hooks and eyes down the front of her costume as she went, every possible permutation of disaster flashed before her mind's eye. Pa? Who else could it be? No one knew she was in Reading this week except the family. Alf perhaps? Only something really terrible would send either of them to make a call on the unfamiliar telephone. An accident? A fire? Oh, she saw it all. No wonder her voice was barely more than a frightened whisper.

'Hello? What's happened?'

'Charlie here,' a voice yelled in her ear. 'Can you hear me?'

Charlie Cribbans. Why hadn't she thought of him? Of course he knew where she was!

'Are you still there?' he shouted. 'Are you hearing me?' Surely they must be hearing him right up his street. He never could trust the wires to carry his voice without a bit of extra help.

'Yes, clearly. Is something wrong, Charlie?'

'Now just you listen – and have the good sense not to rush in with a "no" 'til you've had time to sleep on it. Just had a visitation from Douglas Mountford on your behalf, young lady. Did you hear what I said – Douglas Mountford!'

'What did he want with me?'

'He's been communicating with Laurence McLeod.' Whatever she'd expected it hadn't been to hear *that* name. Her grip on the earpiece tightened. 'Trying to negotiate bringing "Girl of My Dreams" to London.'

'Yes?'

'Well, what would you say to that? Did you hear? "Girl of My Dreams" in London,' he yelled.

'Why should Douglas Mountford worry whether I mind, Charlie, it's nothing to do with – '

'Use your brains, young lady. Would I call you to ask you that! It's this Laurence McLeod. He says the show only comes to London if you play your original role. Kathy Malone is the third since you packed up, seems you made your mark on it. You still there? Mountford wants you and he doesn't go begging for leading ladies. Don't you be a fool and play games with him.'

'You say Laurence has asked for me.'

'Only you or he won't play ball. It was written for you, he says. Coming off at the end of August on Broadway. McLeod says none of the others have fitted the part.' Then, as if he were in the room with her instead of forty-odd miles away, she heard his familiar guffaw. 'Anything made for you ain't going to be much use to anyone else, now is it? What do you say? No, don't say anything, not now. Sleep on it.'

'Charlie – ' But he didn't stop talking long enough to hear.

' . . . not an offer that comes every day. Turn Mountford down and he'll not ask – '

'Charlie!' Again she tried. He was deaf to interruptions.

' . . . plain crazy, that's what it is, this obsession – '

'When do I start rehearsals?' she yelled almost as loudly as he did himself.

'Eh? What d'you say? Rehearsals? You mean you've come to your senses?'

'Yes, Charlie, I'll do it. After that it'll be variety again – but I'll do this.'

Of course she'd do it. Laurence had asked for her, said it must be her! Written it for her! No one else!

Tonight the citizens of Reading were given a performance that was touched with magic; but then tonight Penelope's whole world was touched with magic.

*

336

Rehearsals were to start at the beginning of October. In September she went to Challington for her first proper visit to Prospect House. She'd been twice during the summer, once when she'd travelled south to play in Brighton, then again on her way to Portsmouth, but each time she'd arrived late on Sunday and left again Monday morning. Now, with a warm spell obligingly hanging on for her benefit, she had a fortnight free.

There was no slipping in through the yard gate and surprising them here. Walking up the drive, the first person she saw was Alf busy trimming the long hedge that went round the perimeter of the two acre garden. An endless task. Alf, who only a few months ago wouldn't have ventured out of the house without a hat, its wide brim pulled down to shield his face; now here he was bareheaded, no collar or tie; his shirt open at the neck, sleeves rolled up. And busy helping sweep the clippings were two little boys who clearly accepted his appearance as readily as anyone else's.

'You haven't got all that to do?' she shouted as she crossed the grass to join them.

'Pen! Em's been watching out for you for ages. Now she's just gone to get the fish for Mrs Drew, the boats'll be unloading. Do you know these lads? This is Arnie and this is Ted. They're giving me a hand.'

'You can do with it, too, I should think. You're not considering cutting all this lot?'

'Bit by bit. We do an hour or so a day. By the time we've got round we'll be ready to start again.' He held her gaze. 'Pen, it's great work. Any work is good, you know, the feeling of doing something useful – but all this, growing the veggies, keeping the garden together – sometimes I just stand and listen. Nothing, only the kids playing, the birds . . . I say, hark at me, I'll be bursting into song next!'

'You reckon you've got a geranium for yer 'at, is that it, Alf?'

The left side of his face grinned.

337

'And me. Reckon I have too, Alf. "Girl of My Dreams" is coming to London. We go into rehearsals in a fortnight.'

'Shouldn't have thought you'd need to rehearse, you've done it before.'

She smiled, a quiet smile, hugging her secret to herself. How could Alf know that for her rehearsals meant evenings at the piano with Laurence, mornings sitting in the theatre by his side, suppers sent in to his rooms . . . being with him, sharing with him, loving him . . . in her heart surely she must always have known that one day he'd come back to her.

Bruce appeared from the vegetable plot, greeted her with his cheery 'Hello, Sis', then shouted to the house at large that Penny was home. It wouldn't be true to say Laurence, rehearsals, everything she was sure was waiting for her, was forgotten. Not pushed out of her mind, but safely stored at the back of it, her certainty of the months ahead putting her in the mood to enjoy what would be the longest visit she'd had with the family.

In the days when Prospect House had been the home of George Bradley (he who surveyed the park with disdain from his marble plinth), its largest room had been a drawing room. In those days it had held the grand piano, no less than three small settees, numerous chairs, an embroidery frame, a fireside table, whatnot, china cabinet, all the impedimenta of gracious Victorian living. Now, to the children who were left here daily, it was simply 'the room', the place where they played when the weather was too wet for the garden. Not that in Prospect House there were restrictions on where they could go. Just as Penelope had known they would, the majority of the children gravitated towards Muriel.

Children need to feel their way. Penelope was a stranger, so today they kept their distance from her.

'So far there are just the three of them living here,' Muriel told her, 'Arnie and Ted – you saw them outside with Alf. Twins, they are.'

'Are they orphans?'

'Might as well be, poor mites. Their mother's consumptive, been taken into a hospital in Hampshire. Didn't have any marriage lines. How the poor girl was managing I can't think, not fit to drag herself about. The lads are picking up nicely – and I drop her a line every week or two, just to let her know they're all right.'

'Three of them, you said. Who's the other?'

'Margaret Bligh. Wasn't the war that robbed her of a home. Her grandfather did his best for her 'til she came here. Lost her mother when she was quite a babe, her dad made some sort of a home for her. Got tired of his responsibilities, though, went off with some floosy and poor Margaret got sent to her grandfather. He's a fisherman, brings his catch in to the market here. That's how I came to meet Margaret. Sitting on a pile of fish boxes, waiting for him to come into harbour, she was. I got talking to her, made friends with her, you know. Old man Bligh was glad enough for her to come here. To start with I wondered if she'd settle. She's nearly twelve, an in-between age. But she and Bruce palled up. She's one of us now. A girl and an old man together wasn't right, just at that growing up age. Good for her to have Mandy to talk to. So that's our little bunch. Plenty more beds. But we've got to grow slowly. This house isn't going to turn into a Home with a capital "H".'

While she talked Muriel had been busy beating up the ingredients for a cake. Penelope remembered those packages she used to send from the kitchens of the Grand. Anna might have been a blatant fortune seeker but Challington had cause to be grateful for the use that was being made of her money. Of all the things Penelope had done with her life, nothing had given her the satisfaction that this did. Yet her own part was so small. No amount of money alone could give these children the sense of security that Muriel could.

'Mostly the little ones get left here so their mothers can

339

go out and do a bit of work, earn a bit of independence. I never ask for a penny, not unless they really want to pay.'

'But do we need them to? Doesn't that defeat what we're trying to do?'

'That it doesn't! There are those who wouldn't let me keep an eye for them if they felt it was charity. Not only mothers, sometimes it's fathers, you know. A man doesn't like to be made to feel he can't provide for his young. Women gone off, dead or simply flitted. Not easy for a man, bringing up children on his own. I can give an eye to the mending when I see holes – you know – the sort of thing a man wouldn't know how to set about. And Emma helps no end. It's good for her, and she's good for the children. We all have to rub along together in this world; sooner they get to know everyone has their troubles the better.'

'How do you decide what to charge them, Mother? How do you know what they can afford?'

'Can't afford anything, or they wouldn't be having to come to us. But independence is sweet. If a person's down on their luck the best way to help them hold their head up is to give them their independence. Twopence ha'penny a day – it pays for their dinner, I tell them. P'raps it does, p'raps it doesn't. Cooking for a lot, all in one go, you can fill them up on good wholesome, hot food for not much more. Alf's done well with his veggies – and by next year he'll be bringing even more from the garden. Twopence ha'penny – that's the cost of a pie from the shop – and a day's food here does them a power more good than that.'

Penelope leant forward and rubbed her face against Muriel's plump shoulder. She couldn't stop herself. Silly tears did more than blur her vision, they robbed her of her voice.

'Now it's your turn.' Muriel scraped the last of the cake mixture into the tin and put it in the oven, pushing in the damper to keep the fire from blazing too fast. 'Glad to hear you're taking a proper two-week rest, dashing up and down the country like you do. Where are you off to next? I've been hogging all the talk. How's that theatre of yours?'

'That theatre' as she called it was a world quite unknown to her. Only because she cared about Penelope did she try and muster any interest.

'I shan't be dashing up and down the country when I go back. I shall be in London.'

And when Muriel heard about "Girl of My Dreams" her reaction was the same as Alf's had been. What possible need could Penelope have for rehearsals?

'Except for me the cast will be new. We need to rehearse together.'

'That man – the man who wrote it – '

'Laurence McLeod.'

'Ah, that's the one. You be careful, Penny love. So easy to scorch your fingers when the warmth of the fire pulls you too near. You don't give your heart lightly, that I know. What if it all starts over again? You say he's got a wife – and that poor lad with the infantile paralysis. It'll be you who'll be the one to get hurt.'

'It won't start again, Mother.' Penelope took the cloth to wipe the cooking bowl Muriel had washed. 'It never stopped.'

'Oh, Penny love. If only you could find yourself a nice young fella, someone free to love you too. No good ever came out of taking what's not yours to take. It may seem fine at the time, but life has a way of seeing everyone gets their just desserts in the end.' It was the nearest she'd ever come to criticizing.

'There are all sorts of ways of loving, Mother. It was you who taught me that. At the time I didn't understand. But I've learnt a lot since then.' She hung the cloth on the bracket by the range. Then she went on, changing the subject – or perhaps not changing it: 'I had a letter from Tom. He'd heard about "Girl of My Dreams". He and Sylvia had been fussing because I'd gone back to variety.

They're heart and soul in musicals, think variety is infra dig.' She chuckled. 'To me it's the heart of entertainment.'

'But you want to do this "Girl of My Dreams" piece?'

''course I do. That's different. Look, here comes Pa. My word, he's like the Pied Piper.'

At the far end of the garden was a small rough area of shrubs, brambles and grass that was lucky if it saw the scythe once a year. A favourite play place for the children, and it was from here they ran now to meet Oliver as he walked up the drive.

'Never known him so happy – so at peace with himself.' Muriel came to the window. 'When I first knew him, he was – oh, I don't know, sort of torn. He'd failed you, or thought he had, and had a rotten sort of life himself too.'

'Because of me, you mean?'

'Not like that, I don't. He was a young man – '

'Pa?'

'Yes, love, your pa. When I first met Ollie he was a good few years younger than that Laurence McLeod of yours is. Had you ever thought of it that way? No, 'course you hadn't, and what child ever could? Poor Ollie, he was worth so much more than life had given him.'

'Because of me.'

'Because of Anna. Oh, I'm not daft. I always knew how he felt about her. But this place has sort of healed the wounds. It's as if she's said to him that she was sorry for the unkind way she used him. Look at him, regular Lord of the Manor is Ollie.'

'The children take to him.'

''course they do. I've known him hours at a time in "the room" with them. Plays the games he used to with you. That's what he tells me. Funny, really, he never did with our three.'

'Do you all have your jobs, like we used to? Does Pa have to shop for all this lot?'

'It's not a man's place to do the marketing. He has his own part to play. Most of these poor little souls haven't

342

got a man to look up to. Leastways they wouldn't have, but for Ollie. But jobs, you say? Yes, we got it all worked out. And the children have their own responsibilities, those that are old enough. It's good for them, makes them feel we're all part of the same team. Couldn't manage otherwise. Emma's a real little work horse too.'

'Can they understand her?'

'The children? Why, of course they can. Funny, hearing you say that. I never give it a thought, talk to her as easy as I do to you. It's 'cos people are nervous, frightened they won't hear aright. They're the ones don't understand her. Now, with children there's no problem. Like I say, it's good for her and good for them too.' Then, as they heard the front door open, 'Ollie! Here in the kitchen – Penny's home.'

There was a timelessness about those two weeks. One day merged into the next; hours spent at the lodge with Emma or in the garden helping Alf (even doing a few yards of the hedge); shopping in the market; visiting Mrs Sharp; taking Arnie and Ted to climb on the rocks; setting them off on a race to the pierhead and, this time, making sure she was the sissy who got there last.

There was a timelessness too about the house. Nothing haphazard in the way Muriel ran things, but to every one of those struggling parents who made use of it, it was a lifeline always within reach. Not just between the hours of nine and five, but for them to come when they liked and leave the children as long as they needed to. No doubt there were one or two who abused Muriel's kindness, and as she was no fool she must have realized it. To her way of thinking, though, parents who would do that might otherwise leave their children waiting outside the public house or at home alone, and she'd rather they were here.

It was on Penelope's last evening that a thunderstorm broke, the rain pouring off the guttering and dancing on the front steps. Anyone who hadn't already gone would certainly stay until it lifted.

'Penny,' Bruce put his head round the kitchen door, 'Dad says have you got your squeezebox with you?'

'Yes, it's upstairs. Why?'

'He says why don't we have a sing-song? Thing is, you see, one or two of the girls don't like the thunder. We didn't let them see we noticed, but Dad said let's have a good loud sing and you could play the squeezebox. Are you coming?'

Muriel's expression seemed to say: 'There! What did I tell you?' After all this time he could accept her mother's music. Prospect House had laid his old ghosts. Two at a time Penelope leapt up the stairs to fetch her concertina. And when, her work done, Muriel took her mending and went to join them in 'the room', thunder would have stood no chance against the lusty voices raised in song. Around the large table were Alf, Merrick and three lads, all of them doing fretwork as they sang. Mandy, Donald (Merrick's workmate from the boatyard), Bruce and Margaret sang as they played rummy. In his wheelbacked armchair sat Oliver, not joining in but by his presence conferring his approval on the scene. Penny was in her favourite position, cross-legged on the floor, leading them from one chorus to the next while in front of her, sitting just as she was, were the rest of the young audience.

'Here, what about this one?' she shouted. 'Doesn't matter if you don't know the words, just la-la to it, clap your hands or stamp your feet.'

They were all having such a good time the storm was forgotten. No one even noticed that the rain had stopped until the front door bell pealed and parent number one arrived. The exodus began. Penelope took her concertina upstairs to re-pack it ready for tomorrow, listening with one ear to the sound of childish voices outside. She watched from her window – she had a room on the first floor now, not in the attic. The little girl must have been about five or six, holding her mother's hand, chattering non-stop, sure in the way children are that every smallest detail of her day had been important and would be interesting. The mother was young, probably not as old as Penelope was herself, yet youth was gone. She was painfully thin, her shoulders hunched. Her clothes were shabby, those shoes must surely let water in. Where was her husband? Perhaps she'd never married, perhaps this was one of the wartime illegitimates Alf talked about, or perhaps he'd been killed or maimed. It was for people like her that Prospect House existed.

Daylight was fading fast but now that the storm was gone, there was a hint of gold in the western sky.

"It's just the beginning. Like Mother says, it'll grow gradually. All those children will know that it's here." Silently she shared her thoughts with the golden horizon. "It's not just the food, or even the warmth in winter. It's what she said about them all being a team together. And it's Pa, too, what it's done for him. I do hope Anna knows I'm grateful to her. I wonder if she would have wanted me to have her money if she'd known what I would do. Is she glad? Hope so. It sort of sets the record straight – heals the wounds, wasn't that what Mother said? Just look at the streak of gold. Don't get skies like this in London. Tomorrow I'll be there. Perhaps he's come already. Or is he somewhere out there under that golden sun, perhaps on the sea, on his way. Coming to me, 'cos that's what he's doing, he knows he is. He asked for me to be there for him, as if I – "

'Are you packing, Penny? Can I help?' Mandy interrupted and Penelope's silent confidences to the western sky were over.

The next day she left Challington and the one after that, the 1st October, rehearsals started. Douglas Mountford was a hard taskmaster; most of the cast were put thoroughly through the hoop. Not her, though. It must be that her performance was based on Laurence's direction,

345

he didn't want it changed after the producer had been so insistent that she should play the role. As the days passed by, the theatre seemed full of his presence. His music all around her; every song she sang, she'd sung standing by his piano. With every throb of the rhythm of the blues her heart called out to him to hurry. Not here for rehearsals . . . he'd be sure to come in time for opening. Her leading man was David Fellows, a young Welshman. In New York the male lead had been a back-up for her. David was a dancer in his own right, and a tenor of rare quality. Never until now had Penelope enjoyed dancing with another person, but with David it was a joy.

Stage sets, costumes, everything was building towards opening night. By nature Penelope was an optimist. Her first disappointment that Laurence hadn't come in time for rehearsals gave way to anticipation. He'd be here for the first night. Never once did she doubt it. If he wasn't going to be here, why should he have been so insistent that she had to play the lead?

'Have you heard when Laurence is arriving?' she tried to keep her voice level as she spoke casually to Douglas.

'Laurence McLeod? Coming here? I'd not heard anything about it.'

'But it's his play. I thought – '

'So were "Spring Time" and "Beyond the Sunset" – I put them both on here. This time he certainly had a say in you playing your original role, but that was just sound business sense. Not an easy part to cast. He was right.' Then, turning away from her, he shouted the magic words: 'All right. We'll call it a day.'

'What's up?' Penelope hadn't heard David coming. 'You look as though you'd dropped half a crown and picked up a tanner. Is something wrong?'

''course not. Just a touch of pre-opening jitters.'

'You! You're the one person who has no need. The rest of us are on new ground – and me? I'm a new boy altogether when it comes to playing a lead.'

346

Even his speaking voice held the lilt of music.

'We'll make it a real success, David. You see, we'll be hailed as another Fred and Adele.' There was a smile in her voice, no sign of the effort it cost her to put it there. Nothing to suggest the tumult inside her; disappointment that Laurence wasn't coming, anger at him and at herself too. Had he just used her? Was that all it had been? But whose fault was that? Hers! She'd known he had a wife, he had duties, responsibilities. Helen was the mother of his son, wasn't it possible he cared for her more than he even realized? What if he did? That was his business. As far as she was concerned, it was finished. Weren't all men the same? Look at Pa with his bevy of pretty ladies, Tom who broke his vows. Ah, but that's where Laurence was different. He still clung to the vows he'd made – all he'd wanted outside marriage was a casual hour of love, and a woman fool enough to fall for it. Round and round went her tortured thoughts. Her smile gave nothing away and if her eyes were bright with anger, David was keen enough to misread their message.

'The Astaires? No, not that, Penelope. They're brother and sister.' His meaning was clear. This time yesterday she would have laughed the remark away. But there was no turning the clock back to yesterday. She recognized David's tentative advance and went more than halfway to meet him.

Always she'd loved to dance with him, but that had been because she loved to dance. From that day, nothing was quite the same. On opening night the courtship ritual of the dance must have been apparent to everyone in the packed theatre. Nothing new in it, it was nature's way. But it added to the performance of two talented dancers, bringing a touch of perfection, of magic. Wordlessly David wooed her, at least in the beginning. No message from Laurence, no cablegram, not even a bouquet of flowers with a card that told her she was worth the best in town. So, like an ostrich burying its head, she wouldn't admit to

347

the hurt. Instead, she let herself be carried on the tide of a success shared with David. What was it Muriel had said about her finding a 'nice young fella' she could fall in love with?

The show was in its fourth month. It was Easter, Good Friday, and the air heavy with the sounds and scents of spring. A hamper of food, a rug and some cushions, and Penelope and David drove out of London, heading for Richmond and the Thames. It was the first weekend of the year for hiring boats, and too early for many to venture on to the water. What better way to prove one's manliness than to wield the long pole and glide silently up the river, while a pretty girl relaxed on the cushions with nothing to do but admire? Many a young man had come unstuck, but David was on sure ground. He'd taken boats out plenty of times before and was confident he'd score high points today.

For once Penelope disappointed him. 'I wish we'd brought paddles, I could have had a go too. I hate just sitting. Let's tie up over by those trees, shall we?'

So much for his prowess with the pole.

But once moored and sitting close by her side, the punt gently rocking and the water lapping against the bank, his spirits were restored. It wasn't often he got her to himself like this. When his hand reached for hers she didn't pull away.

'This is nice, Penny. Just you and me, the day drifting by.'

'Umph.' She took off her hat and wriggled down until she was lying almost flat, her face turned towards the sun. 'Feel the warmth, David.' Her eyes were closed. They flew wide open though when she felt the touch of his lips on her forehead.

'Sunshine or rain, Penny, I want to be with you.'

For a second he thought she recoiled from him. But he must have imagined it. Her hand reached out to touch his dark hair.

348

'Let's just enjoy the day, David.'

'You know I'm in love with you. Penny, you must know it already. I never want to dance with any girl but you.'

She wasn't ready. She tried to make a joke of it. 'Well, the way bookings are going, it looks as though we shall be there for – '

'Marry me, Penny. We're right for each other. You feel it the same as I do.'

'We dance well together, but marriage is about more than that, David.'

She hadn't bargained for the way he took her in his arms. The punt rocked. His hands moved over her body, his mouth covered hers. Then, holding her close, one leg anchoring her to the cushions, he whispered: 'I know what marriage is about, I know I want you, just you. And you?'

She knew what he said was true. He wanted her. Lying on her back she looked up at the high springtime sky. From that clear infinity surely she must find her answer. David wanted her, he loved her. How desperately she needed to be wanted and to be loved. What a fool she was! After all this time, the only answer that came back to her was the knowledge that somewhere far, far away, under that same sky, was Laurence. But he was gone. It was all over. She was twenty-eight years old. Did she expect to live the rest of her life on memories of a few brief months?

'Me? I don't know if I love you, David. No, that's not true. I do love you. But – marriage?'

'It's because you've been married before, isn't it? Penny, I'll make you happy, I'll make you forget.'

She closed her eyes, shutting out the sky.

'Then I'll marry you, David.'

They were to be married in June at a registry office in London. But first David must come to Challington. He was part of Penelope's world at the theatre; it was important she saw him against the background of that other side of her life. They drove down on a Sunday morning in May and she felt she was seeing the town she'd always thought of as home with new eyes. Always before she'd arrived at the railway station. Today they came in from the Brighton Road, through the back of town. There was no need to go along the Promenade to get to Prospect House. But she'd never before come home without a sight of the sea, not known whether the tide was in or whether there were children clambering on the rocks. All that would come later. It just emphasized to her that this visit was like no other; this time she was introducing into the family the man she'd promised to join her life with.

There were ten of them around the table. Working on her usual principle that good food loosened tongues, Muriel timed the meal to be ready when they arrived. Arnie and Ted were almost too shy to eat: Margaret too excited, with a handsome London actor as their guest. Just wait 'til she got to school tomorrow! She missed most of the conversation, dreaming about how she'd be the envy of her classmates. Oliver was his most charming, Lord of the Manor indeed.

'Look at that.' Afterwards Muriel drew Penelope to the window. It was during the afternoon and outside in the garden David was talking to Alf and Emma. Clearly the conversation was moving along well, with no embarrassment on either side. 'Yes, Penny love, you've found yourself a nice young fella. I could see at dinner time that Ollie approved too. And you're happy? Didn't I tell you that – just keep travelling along the road and suddenly you come on a signpost and know that's the way you have to go.'

Penelope smiled. It was the best she could do.

They spent the whole of Monday there.

'I know you said your mother cared for children – but, what a raggle-taggle mob! In that beautiful house! Wonder what the original owner would make of it.'

'He ought to be jolly glad. It was a hospital during the war, then it was empty for ages before we took it.'

350

'You mean it doesn't belong to the Town Council? I thought your parents were employed there.'

Penelope shook her head, but she didn't elaborate.

'Come on, David, let's go to the beach. We've been here nearly twenty-four hours and haven't even seen the sea. I'll show you where Tom and Alf and I used to play. Us and Chummy . . .'

He fell in with her plan – up to a point. The tide was low. To Penny no visit to the beach was complete without climbing over those familiar rocks. And that's where David drew the line.

'Come back. One slip and you could gash your leg – or even break an ankle. You shouldn't take risks. I certainly can't afford to.'

'Don't be silly. If you slip you won't get hurt if you just let yourself go. A wetting won't harm.'

But nothing budged David. And somehow there was no fun at all in leaping from one familiar foothold to the next by herself while he stood by watching her every step. But the visit to the beach was the one dark spot in their stay. On Tuesday morning they set off back to London, with Oliver and Muriel standing on the steps to wave them off, Alf and Emma by the lodge, and various of the raggle-taggle bunch of small 'waifs', as David jokingly named them, shouting their goodbyes as the car set off down the drive.

'They must pay an enormous rent for that place.' They were well into their journey when David referred again to the house that had so impressed him.

'It's not rented.'

'You mean they bought it?' But they hadn't struck him as people to have that sort of money.

'Mother is his second wife.' Near enough to the truth. 'My real mother was a dancer, they split up. She went back to the stage. Later she married some financier. She died a couple of years back.'

351

'You mean it was hers and she left it to her first husband? What an odd thing to do.'

'No, Prospect House wasn't hers. I bought it. With money she left to me.'

Penelope knew nothing about driving motor cars, she had no idea what David did with his feet; stabbed at the wrong pedal, no doubt, it nearly threw her off her seat. Then he drew to a stop at the side of the road. A road sign told them they were one and a half miles from Weybridge. She never heard of Weybridge again without remembering.

'You're telling me Prospect House is yours.'

'I said I bought it. David, I didn't want Anna's money, not for myself. She'd walked out on Pa and me so long ago I don't remember it even; she told me she could never have been happy without money. Well, she got rich all right, her husband was wealthy – but it didn't save her health, poor thing. I only met her once when she was already a widow. For me to have what had been her husband's after she died – I just couldn't. It was like accepting her conscience money for the way she left me when I was tiny – and Pa, too. You can see how I felt? Of course you can.'

'Sounds rather high and mighty to me. But you didn't refuse your inheritance, you took it.'

'Of course I did! Heavens, look around you, see the poverty. Of course I took it, but not for myself. When I was little Pa and I were hard up. Have you ever seen your father without enough money to bring home the food you needed? I have. Although to me it was just part of everyday life, I'm not pretending I ever felt deprived. I didn't. With Pa around, I never was.'

How pretty she was, sitting up straight on her seat, her big dark eyes serious as she tried to make him understand. And up to a point he did understand. She and her father had come through hard times together, and there's nothing cements two people together firmer than troubles.

'They don't need that glorious old house, though, Penny. Not for that raggle-taggle lot. It's a sin. Children can't possibly appreciate it. That room they play in – it has an Adam fireplace, do you realize that? I see why you want to do something for the kids, honestly I do. But we could find them somewhere not so grand, just as suitable, smaller. Between us we could manage it. Then Alf could stay on at Prospect House, caretake for us. It's your house, after all, Penny. Listen, sweetheart, we're only at the beginning of our dancing partnership, but even now we both know we've got something very special. Fred and Adele, you said. As husband and wife we've a lifetime together ahead of us. Think of it – weekend parties at Prospect House. It would be so right for us. Penny darling, you and me, we're going places!'

'David darling,' she answered in the same tone, 'until you switch that engine on we're not going places, we're sitting here and getting late. We have a show ahead of us. Remember?'

It was the nearest to an answer he would get today. But he was confident he'd sown the seed of an idea. That night after the performance he suggested seeing her the following morning. Her reply gave him reason to hope. The seed must have started to germinate.

'No. I want the day free. I need to see my solicitor. I haven't an appointment so I don't know when he'll be able to fit me in. What I want may take a lot of organizing, I've no idea how long I'll be with him.'

And the next evening at the theatre he didn't probe. In her own good time she'd tell him. Then as the days went by and still she made no mention of what she'd been arranging with Mr Collingbourne, he suspected she was planning a surprise. Perhaps the weekend after the wedding she'd suggest they drive to Challington, they'd find the family gone, the house empty, waiting for them to turn it into the sort of home he wanted for them. "David and Penelope have such houseparties!" "Have you never been to one of their weekends at their place on the coast? Oh, but you must get yourself an invitation. Prospect House parties are like no others!" "What a pair they are, and what a host and hostess!" The stairway to stardom was steep; Prospect House would lift them into the social sphere of those who'd already reached the top.

They were to be married on 3rd June. Only Oliver came up from Challington, arriving the day before the wedding. It had been Anna who had fostered in him his mistrust of 'stage people', but it was Anna's money that paid for his two-night stay and that garnished the trip. From the window of his hotel bedroom he could look on to the Strand. Refreshed from his journey, he brushed his hair, rubbed a duster over his highly polished shoes and was ready to grace the bar with his presence while he waited for Penelope and David to join him as his guests for lunch.

Oliver was enjoying himself. The Pied Piper had been left at home. Here in London he stepped into a new role, Lord of the Manor from his south coast seat, father of a famous daughter. One last look in the mirror, his reflection giving him back a wicked wink. "This is the life, Oliver my lad." As if to reassure himself he tapped his jacket, making sure his wallet was there, then adjusted the silk handkerchief (the one Penelope had sent him from New York) in his top pocket.

Lunch went according to plan, his pleasure enhanced by the fact that he could feel the interest being taken in him by a pretty little lady sitting alone at a nearby table. It was natural that, feeling her eyes upon him, he should present himself in as good a light as possible. Penelope saw through his every move, but she was older now and wiser. Nothing would ever change Pa. He was harmless, and she and Mother loved him just the way he was.

But if lunch went according to plan, he was less pleased with the evening when he went to see 'Girl of My Dreams'. Muriel would have said he was 'proud as punch' watching Penelope, and so he was. Yet what was there about this young fellow she was marrying that made him uneasy? He'd thoroughly approved of him when they'd come to Challington; had found him good enough company at lunch time today. So why, suddenly, watching him on the stage, did he feel uneasy?

Among the few people in the registry office the next day were Tom and Sylvia. Oliver was affronted by that. Penny treated the fellow as if she'd never been his wife – and fancy Sylvia, the woman who'd broken up their marriage, being asked to sign the register!

'I know you'll be happy,' she said, hugging Penelope, 'you're tailor made for each other.' It seemed she was right; David, standing by Tom's side, was inches the shorter, slightly built, graceful, a dancer from head to toe. Then it was Tom's turn to kiss the bride. Oliver looked on with undisguised disapproval. The whole thing was beyond him. And whoever heard of a couple being married in the morning and back on the stage in the evening!

But, his farewells said, he put it out of his mind, hailed a taxi cab and settled down to plan his remaining time in London. He had invited that pretty little lady from the next table to accompany him to the theatre. If he'd felt a pang of disappointment at her choice of entertainment he was far too gallant to let it show and, on the way to collect Penelope for her wedding, he'd stopped to book seats for 'Oliver Cromwell' at His Majesty's.

It had been a quiet wedding but the day wasn't over when the curtain came down that night. Two leading players, a whirlwind romance, what better ingredients for a story in tomorrow's newspapers? The party was Sylvia's idea, so was alerting the press to where it was being held. Publicity could do nothing but good for Penny and David, she told herself, and if some of it came her way that was no bad thing either.

'They want us to dance for them, Penny.' David had been talking to a reporter and now he came to lean over her shoulder at the table. 'The press are getting their cameras ready.'

Walking out on to the floor, hand in hand with David, a voice from the crowd opened the floodgates of memory. Involuntarily Penelope turned her head, hearing the American accent. It wasn't him, she'd known it wasn't. Yet the sound made her heart miss a beat. Today was her wedding day; this was her husband, David, always kind and caring; and theirs would be the greatest dancing partnership ever. Willingly she let herself be carried on the tide of rhythm and movement, its effect almost hypnotic. Together they couldn't put a step wrong. The applause was part of the magic of the night. These people knew it was their wedding day. Once again Penelope felt the pull between herself and her audience. It was as if all the world shared her happiness. Or so she imagined. She didn't take into account the champagne she'd drunk.

Later, the floor once again crowded with dancers, she moved with the throng, held tightly in David's arms.

'Let's go home,' she whispered.

'One more dance . . . '

One more dance, one more drink . . .

Inspired by having so many of the cast of 'Girl of My Dreams' there, the band struck up with a medley of Laurence McLeod music. 'Hold Fast to Tomorrow' someone crooned, so sure of the pleasure they must be giving the bride. Her tomorrows had nothing to do with Laurence, he and Helen had been reconciled for ages . . . he hadn't even come to see the show, he never would come. Anyway, if he did, what was it to her? David was the man she wanted. They were tailor made for each other, like Sylvia had said.

'Are you all right, Pen?' Back at the table it was Tom who asked.

''course I am. It's my wedding day. 'course I'm all right.'

'It isn't, you know,' he laughed, 'yesterday was your wedding day. It's pretty well three o'clock.'

'Wish they'd stop banging that drum.' She felt as though it were in her head. 'Wanna go home.'

'And so you shall,' David approached as she spoke. 'One dance and we'll go.'

The McLeod medley was over. They danced a tango. She felt slightly dizzy, her feet didn't seem to touch the ground but, an optimist by nature, her spirits rose. And then true to his word he took her home.

They had rented a two-bedroomed flat and David had claimed the smaller one as a dressing room. He was a man of the theatre, understanding all about timing and entrances. So Penny found herself alone as she got ready for bed. Uninvited came the memory of her wedding night with Tom. 'Turn your back – I want you to see me in one piece.' No fumbling with their backs to each other for David and her. In a minute he'd come in; she imagined him in silk pyjamas, silk dressing gown. He'd never been an ardent lover, he was gentle, sensitive. Again she remembered that other wedding night, Tom's desire outweighing his finesse.

She did wish that drum would stop beating in her head. Taking off her clothes seemed a major operation tonight. She must put everything away out of sight. Instinct told her David wouldn't want to see her stockings or her underwear draped on the chair. Like a stage setting she made sure the bedroom was ready. And still that drum beat. What a long time he was taking. She decided to pull back the covers and lie on the bed. The next half hour was an important point in her life, she told herself soberly – at least she thought it was soberly. Her hands moved over her body, just as in a minute his would. Another memory whispered to her, one her mind had fought to be deaf to: 'My lovely Penelope, you're just as I knew you would be.' So silly . . . her heart was banging . . . her head thumping. She turned and buried her face against her pillow, as if that way she'd escape.

Seconds turned to minutes. Her breathing grew deeper. The bride slept.

When she half woke and put out her hand, David was there, lying as near the edge of the bed as he could without actually falling out. She moved closer, not sure whether he was asleep; it seemed he was. The warmth of the bed lulled her back into the unconsciousness she'd never quite left.

Next time she opened her eyes it was daylight, his side of the bed already empty. She could hear him moving about in the kitchenette, singing softly to himself.

'David, I'm awake.'

'Ah, good morning.' He put his head round the bedroom door. 'I got up quietly, you were so tired last night I tried not to disturb you.' He smiled at her, almost she thought he laughed at her. 'None the worse for the party? Can Madam face breakfast? You'll find I've got a pretty way with a frying pan and some rashers.'

'David . . .' Her waking mind was seething with questions, each trying to push to the fore. Had she failed him? But what man would let his bride sleep? Had he had too much party too? No, she was sure he hadn't. Tom wouldn't have let her sleep, even knowing the children had been keen not to miss out on what was going on. But David wasn't like Tom. He was sensitive, he'd never take what she didn't offer. Dear David, looking at her now with smiling eyes. Sitting up, she held out her arms to him.

"There's nothing to hurry for." And what could have been plainer? 'Good morning, darling David, our first good morning.'

He took her hands, bending forward to kiss her forehead lightly.

'The start of our first day. Come on, lazy bones, after breakfast we'll take a walk. We must buy the morning papers. There were photographers outside the registry office.' Then, as he went back to start cooking the breakfast he was so keen on: 'Don't be long. I'll take you somewhere smart for lunch if you like. We have to make the most of today, you know. I suppose until we turn up at the theatre this evening, it could be termed our honeymoon.'

Yes, she thought, it could be.

On that same morning, as they set out to buy the papers, Oliver ordered a taxicab to take him to Charing Cross, the finale to his brief spell of riotous living. At journey's end it was an omnibus that took him from Challington Station to the nearest stop to Prospect House.

Seeing him walking up the drive, his young friends rushed to meet him. By the front doorway Muriel waited. Whatever was he doing? He put his case on the ground and, children all around him, dug into a paper carrier. Each child was given a chocolate mouse, a present from London. The Pied Piper was home!

'Dancer Weds Girl of His Dreams' ... 'Partners in Step for Life' ... the London evening papers carried the report of the wedding. With the added interest of their romance, Penelope and David were playing to a full house each night for there's nothing the public likes better than a peep into someone's private life. They were physically well matched and both of them attractive, yet it was something more than that which held their audiences. Penelope had always danced with the whole of her body, become lost in the spirit of the dance. To find one performer with that natural talent is rare; for partners to be blessed with the same gift must be almost unique. As David had said, together they were 'going places'.

The audiences loved them. Penelope could feel their goodwill, she rode it in a fragile bubble of happiness. She believed the feeling was born of being with David, but in truth it stemmed from the fact that the invisible link between her and her audience had been re-forged. So as the weeks of June went by, her confidence in the step she'd taken grew. If 'life ain't all you want', you have to take what it sends and mould it. So "er 'at' wore an invisible geranium, her face wore a smile. She and David were fast climbing the ladder together.

Then two things happened that almost made her lose her footing. The first was when they'd been married about six weeks, a period during which he'd purposely dropped no more hints about the use they could make of Prospect House. She was arranging something, he was sure of that; on two occasions she went by herself to see Mr Collingbourne. He smiled inwardly at the way she was handling it, indulging her in the game she played. When it was all finalized and the 'waifs' installed somewhere less grand, then she'd be ready to include him in the plans.

Anticipation buoyed up his spirits just as a few months ago it had hers as she'd waited for Laurence, so sure he would come. Realization had brought her down to earth suddenly. David's descent was more gradual as confidence gave way to doubt. At last he could stand it no longer.

'Why don't we take a drive down to Challington on Sunday?' He put out his first feeler.

'I'd like that. I'll write and tell Mother to expect us, shall I?'

Her answer disappointed him. For him to visit there now must surely take the gilt off her surprise.

'Look, Penny, we're grown-up people. Don't play cat and mouse, let me in on the secret. I know you and that solicitor chap are up to something.'

'Cat and mouse? But of course I'm not. If you're interested, it's no secret. I didn't think you would be, though. The way you always talk about them as my "waifs", I didn't think you cared. 'course I'll tell you, David. I'd much rather we could share the plans.'

Hope reared its head. 'Go on, then. It's your house, Penny, of course I'm interested. I have a right to be interested.'

'Mr Collingbourne is drawing up all the legal documents

for me. You say the house is mine — but that's not strictly true.'

'I'm not that sort of a man. Of course what's yours is mine but, Penny, I'm not the sort of chap to expect to take over. You should know me better.'

She laughed. 'Nothing to take. Well, that's not quite true. I'll tell you. You remember how I felt about Anna, the money she'd inherited from her wealthy husband? I never had any doubts about what it should be used for.'

'You wanted to help the waifs. Very noble too. Yes, I could understand that, after what she'd done to you and your father.'

'I bought Prospect House and for the time being everything was going on smoothly. It was really you who made me see I couldn't just let it drift though. Remember you talked about the house, *my* house as it was then. It worried me when you said that. Just supposing I'd died — '

'Don't be silly. Why should you die?'

'Just listen. Prospect House is there for a purpose. Pa and Mother make it work. But nobody goes on just the same for ever. So that's why I went to see Mr Collingbourne, talked about making it permanent.'

'What the hell have you done?'

'Prospect House is going to belong to the Penelope Drew Trust. There was quite a lot of money besides what went on buying the house; invested it will bring in enough to keep things running there.'

He turned away, looking out of the window, his back to her.

'This tame solicitor of yours, didn't he make you understand that as a married woman you can't deal with affairs like this without your husband's consent?'

'But, David, we weren't even married. When I signed the first papers I had no husband. That's why I did it straight away.' Standing behind him, she slipped her arms around his waist.

361

'So that I'd not be able to stop you, because you knew – '

'Stop me! But why should you? What possible difference can it make? Until the Trust was formed I had to be responsible for all the finances. That's why I wanted it settled and out of the way. Now business matters for Prospect House can be settled by any two of the three of us – Pa, Mother or me. It's so much easier. Didn't you say yourself, we're going places, you and me. It's lovely to know Prospect House is taken care of.'

He didn't answer, didn't turn round.

'David?' What was wrong? Why was he so quiet? 'You don't think it's wrong, surely? You knew how I felt about inheriting all that money. You said you understood.'

'I'm beginning to understand a lot better. That no-good father of yours . . . if ever there was a play actor it's him! Lord Muck up here in London and – '

'Shut up! I'm not going to listen to you talking about Pa like that.' Every nerve in her body was electrified. She seemed to burn with an emotion that fought for an outlet. How dared he! What did he know about Pa! No one but she had seen the frightened, trapped look when there hadn't been any money, when they'd shared the last slice of bread, when the rent had been owing, when they'd cut a cardboard insole to repair a boot! How dare he!

'He can sign for money, you say. And what will he do with it? I should have thought that would be plain to you. You saw how he revelled in living like a lord here in London!' He swung round on her. 'Oh, for God's sake, women! You're like all the rest of them, hiding behind bloody tears!' He closed his eyes, looking pale and drained.

'David, don't let's quarrel,' she pleaded, clinging to him. 'Why should Anna's money make us quarrel? Please understand, please. Pa loved her while I hardly knew her. If her money makes his life easier, is that so bad? If you knew him better you wouldn't say such beastly things.'

'Wipe your face.'

She rubbed the palms of her hands across her cheeks. 'I don't understand why you're angry. The house was always for the children, why does it matter that Pa and Mother can sign things without having to send to me? I thought that was for the best, that it would free us to start off together, a team . . .'

'Yes, of course we are. Blow your nose and pull yourself together. We're a great team. But if you go on the stage this evening looking as if things aren't right, then the gossip will soon start. Blow your nose and for God's sake grow up, Penny. Snivelling like some kid.'

'Not snivelling.'

He turned away, and looked out of the window, not because he cared what was outside.

'If either of us has been treated badly, it's not you.'

''s not fair. I never meant to hurt you.' But she was a fighter. Snivelling, he called it. Tears had always been her downfall. 'You never told me you were marrying me for my money. How was I supposed to guess?'

The point scored was hers this time.

'You know that's not why I asked you to marry me. You just said it yourself: we're a team. I'm sorry if I shouted, Penny. It's just – I was disappointed. All this time you'd said nothing about the house, and I'd been imagining you were doing as I'd suggested, planning it as a surprise, something for us, you and me.'

Face mopped, she wound her arms around him. She'd hurt him. All those disagreeable things he'd said about Pa had been because he'd been hurt. She forgave him readily. They'd never quarrelled before. The pendulum of her emotions swung back. Now she needed the reassurance of his loving; only that way could the slate be wiped, the wounds healed. The whole afternoon was before them. Silently she led him with eyes, hands, mouth. Surely he must feel it too, surely he knew that this way they would find each other.

'Forget it all, David.' She pressed close against him. 'Just think of us, you and me.' His response was slow. It was all her fault, she thought tenderly, she ought to have talked to him about what she was doing. Her mouth was half open, close to his. 'We've got all afternoon.' Now, what could be clearer than that?

Going to bed in the middle of a sunny afternoon could have been the most natural thing. But, somehow, today it wasn't. There was something self-conscious in the way they undressed, and when, a shaft of sunshine caressing her naked body, he eased her closer towards him, she wished she hadn't brought him here. For it had all been her doing, no doubt about that. Even now, he was trying to make amends, trying to please her. He turned her on to her back, his face expressionless, and with little evidence of passion, entered her. What a moment to remember Tom! He had found all he wanted in Sylvia, but even so had brought an animal urgency to his almost nightly lovemaking with Penny. David was doing his best; for her sake he wanted it to work for both of them. It worked for neither. He gave up the struggle.

'I'm sorry, it's no use. Let's get dressed.'

As he rolled off her she pulled the counterpane over her, shamed by her nakedness.

'It's my fault,' he said, climbing off the bed. 'I oughtn't to have let you drag me in here. Can't just turn on like a tap, Penny. Sorry.' He took his pile of clothes and disappeared into the adjoining bathroom. She lay there, covered with the counterpane. A few minutes later he called that he was going out for a walk. Still she didn't move. What was wrong with her? Tom . . . she'd not satisfied him. David . . . At the memory of the last half hour she felt humiliated. A warm tear escaped from the corner of her eye and trickled down the side of her nose.

'My little Penny, you're beautiful, you're just as I knew you would be . . . '

Her warm hands felt the outline of her thin body, her tiny breasts, her flat stomach . . . How many times had her mind turned back to that hour with Laurence, how many times had she lived it again? Over these last months she'd fought to push him out of her mind. 'Love' to her meant David, of course it did, she was his wife. This time she wouldn't let her marriage fail. The quarrel had left David needing space, freedom; it had left her aching for love. 'My little Penny . . .' echoed that voice she couldn't forget. This afternoon she didn't fight it, she remembered every second, lived it again. It was to Laurence she cried out, and it was for Laurence she wept when cold reality caught up with her.

When David came home from his walk she was dressed, her face washed and made up, her lipstick a little too bright and her smile too. Neither of them referred to their afternoon, both went out of the way to make the evening smooth. And the routine they'd been building fell back into place.

It was a few weeks later, the shadow of that day almost forgotten, when they stumbled on the second thing that threatened to tip them from the ladder they climbed. They were at a party. Delighted to find Tom and Sylvia there, Penelope was talking to them when David came over.

'Penny, meet an old friend of mine. We almost grew up together – Des Pritchard. Des, this is my wife.'

Grew up together? There was none of the musical lilt of David's Welsh accent about Des Pritchard's voice. Grew up together? But Des looked much the elder. A tall man, broad-shouldered, his hair starting to recede. Flushed with pleasure at the unexpected encounter, David looked a boy by comparison.

CHAPTER FOURTEEN

The wind was from the west, a warm wind that gusted, bringing the golden leaves from the trees in St James' Park, and making ripples on the lake where the mallards swam, seemingly unconcerned by their rough ride.

Penelope shivered despite the mild October afternoon. Today she and Sylvia had met for lunch. Their old friendship had stood the test, it had reshaped itself to their altered circumstances. That unexpected reunion the Christmas before last had been the most difficult meeting. Then they'd both had to adjust to Tom's change of partner. Certainly Sylvia's manner was affected these days, but Penelope knew that under the consciously glamorous exterior she tried to present was the warm-hearted girl she'd always been. Now she thought of their conversation over the meal table: Sylvia's innuendoes, her own disbelief. Yes, of course, disbelief. So, what was she frightened of? David had been with Des often enough during the summer. And why not? They were old friends, pleased their paths had crossed again. Even if what Sylvia had hinted about Des were true, that needn't prevent him and David being friends.

She got up from her seat and went to the water's edge. She ought to have brought some bread for the ducks, she told herself, determined to keep her mind firmly in check. It was perambulators' parade along here, the nannies with their charges out enjoying the autumn sunshine. Toddlers broke up pieces of bread and hurled them in the general direction of the ducks; nursemaids parked their prams by the seats, a third of their attention on their charges and two-thirds on each other and the prospect of an afternoon's chatter.

'Surely, it's Laurence's little girl from the theatre!'

Amongst the procession of prams Penelope hadn't noticed the wheelchair. Helen McLeod's voice startled her.

'Mrs McLeod!' Penelope turned in surprise then, anything rather than let them guess at the way her pulse was racing, she gabbled: 'After all this time, fancy you recognizing me! And this must be Sonny.' There was no doubt the young man in the chair was Laurence's son. He had the same smile, the same blue eyes and crisp wavy hair. Laurence's had been pepper and salt grey as long as Penelope had known him. At one time had it been dark like this? 'I didn't know you were in London.'

'And why should you?' Helen smiled with little warmth. 'We only arrived last night.' Gone was the aggressive frightened manner Penelope remembered. Smart, elegant, poised, this woman had no ghosts plaguing her. It was two years since the evening Laurence had rushed to her rescue; clearly, Penelope thought, years in which she had re-built her shattered world.

'Are you staying long?' As if that was what she wanted to know! Where was Laurence, was he with them?

'As long as it takes.'

'Dad was told about a specialist in Harley Street, someone who might be able to help me.' It was Sonny who told her what she wanted to know. 'Are you Penelope Drew, the lead from his show in town? That's where he is now, down at the theatre.'

Laurence at the theatre! And all the while she'd been idling away her afternoon, gazing unseeing at the ducks, shivering in the warm, west wind.

'I expect he'll come to a performance while you're in London.'

'You bet!' Again it was Sonny. 'We're coming this evening, if he can get seats somewhere I can manage.'

'We read about your wedding,' Helen told her. 'According to the report you and your husband are quite a team.

What was it they headed the announcement: "Two Lovers Love to Dance".'

'David's a wonderful dancer – well, you'll see for yourselves. I'm sure they'll find a way of getting you seats. Perhaps I'll see you afterwards?' Such empty chatter. She knew it. Helen knew it. But today it was Laurence's wife who was on top of the situation.

'I must go.' Penelope felt gauche and awkward. Helen's gaze seemed to mock, watching her pull herself to her full five foot one, clutching at a dignity that was just out of reach. 'David's at home waiting for me. He'll be so pleased when he hears Laurence is in town.' Helen smiled, her thin pencilled eyebrows raised as if she didn't quite understand. 'We'll see you this evening.'

Turning, Penelope left them, cutting across the grass. How hard it was to keep her head high, walk at an unhurried pace. Everything in her wanted to run. Only when she got to the other side of the park did she allow herself to peep back over her shoulder. No, they weren't in sight. She slumped on to a seat. Laurence, here in London. Today she'd see him. But it wasn't important; it mustn't be important. Two years had gone by, he and Helen had made a life together again; she and David were making a life . . . yes, of course they were. It was just that the first bloom had worn off . . . that happened with everyone . . . life wasn't all romance. If Sylvia hadn't sown that seed of suspicion, would she have even thought about it? No. She would have filled the role he wanted of her, put that geranium in her hat . . .

She closed her eyes, feeling the kiss of the warm sun. No longer was her heart banging its tattoo. She'd go home, tell David who she'd met, tell him that tonight's performance must be special, Laurence McLeod would be there.

Word had spread, the whole cast had heard that the American writer was to be in the audience. Everyone was resolved to give their performance that extra sparkle.

David must have believed that accounted for the inner glow that seemed to radiate through Penelope's performance. It infected him. Long hours of rehearsal had gone into perfecting their routines; it was the way both of them liked to work. The acrobatics were hers, there was still much of Young Perce in her dancing. The duets, the long tap dance routines, these had to be faultless. It had been David's willingness to give a hundred per cent of himself that had first attracted her to him. And neither of them had ever danced better than they did tonight.

Three seats in the centre of the front row of the stalls had been freed for the McLeods, an arrangement brought about by the original ticket holders being given a box. So it was that as she came on to the stage Penelope saw him. Their eyes met across the footlights. She forgot Helen and all she'd imagined about the life she and Laurence had rebuilt; she forgot David, their good moments and their bad. Laurence sat back in his seat, arms folded, perfectly still. In those seconds as they looked at each other, it was as if everything that had gone between melted into insignificance. "What has been, is now and will be for ever more . . . " The words sprang into Penelope's mind with a wild surge of joy.

In the interval a note was sent backstage to them, written and signed by Helen. Would they join a small party in the McLeods' hotel suite after the show? At the hotel were one or two others from the cast, Douglas Mountford and his wife, the conductor, various other of Laurence's theatrical acquaintances. A small party, Helen had said. There must have been quite forty people. The room was heavy with cigarette smoke, the drink flowed freely, the buzz of chatter defeated any chance of proper conversation. The only exchange Laurence and Penelope had was general, shouted above the clamour, fit for any ears and shared by many. But it didn't matter, it made no difference to what they both felt.

'Helen tells me she and Sonny met you in the park this afternoon.' Laurence's smile included David.

'Not David, only me. It's one of my favourite afternoon haunts, feeding the ducks in St James'. Sonny said you're in London to take him to someone in Harley Street.'

'Yes. We're seeing Sir Cedric Guthrie tomorrow morning.'

Just that. No more. But both of them knew that tomorrow afternoon she'd walk by the lakeside and so would he.

'It went well tonight, Penny.' Later, back at home, David hung up his evening suit. Knowing the McLeods were to be there he'd gone to the theatre in tails, silk hat, white tie. He'd felt the night was to be important. And he'd not been disappointed. 'I could feel he was interested in us. This evening could have been very useful. I had the feeling he might have been looking at us with a view to something. Wonder what he's working on.' He hummed to himself as he got ready for bed. 'I was thinking, coming home, at the end of that tango in the second act, it would be more effective if I were to spin you, like this – ' he took her hand and steered her into double spin ' – now, lean right back, go on, bend, then bring your right leg up, right up, that's it, head back to the floor, your right foot towards the ceiling. I'll bend over you – but I must keep my back straight. Look, turn your head and see in the long mirror. It's a good line.'

'I'm not sure.'

'Why, can't you hold it long enough?'

''course I can. I'm not sure what it would look like in that costume. The long skirt would spoil the line. Spin me, like you said, but then what if I tilt backwards, keep my back straight, my right leg making a continuous line with my body, but not so exaggerated? The skirt would hang right then. You lean over me, your body parallel with mine, your left knee bent, your right leg back just a bit further. Yes, that's it. See! Picture it in costume.' A stranger

370

watching them might think them an odd young couple, but this was the plane where they came closest.

'We'll have to try it out first, you may be right,' David agreed, already looking forward to a chance to rehearse it. 'Hop into bed and I'll turn the light out.'

'Wait a minute. Is this yours, I don't remember it?' She picked up a fountain pen from the floor by the side of the bed.

David frowned. 'No, not mine, let's see . . . oh, yes, I know, it belongs to Des. He lent it to me.'

'What's wrong with – '

'Come on, don't fuss, Penny. Nothing criminal in forgetting to hand it back when I'd used it. I'll give it to him next time I see him. Get into bed, the night's half gone.'

She did as he said. Lying side by side in the dark, they were both wide awake. David took her hand companionably in his, linking his fingers through hers.

''night Penny. Been quite an evening, hasn't it? Rotten luck for their son, isn't it, poor lad?'

He felt the answering pressure of her fingers. Then he released her hand, turned his back and settled down to sleep. But not Penelope. She had far too much to think about.

She'd rather wait there all the afternoon than have him arrive before her, think she wasn't coming and go away again. So as soon as she'd had lunch, she hurried to St James' Park. And thinking on the same lines, so did Laurence.

What a child she still looked, standing by the water, throwing pieces of bread to the ducks. Her clothes were smart and fashionable, her button shoes even added an extra couple of inches to her height; so what was it? As he came towards her she turned -- and in that second he knew the answer. It was the honesty, the lack of pretence.

'I came early purposely,' was her way of saying hello.

'Me too.'

371

'The mallards are so greedy. That poor little moorhen isn't getting a look in.'

'Subterfuge, that's what we need. Give me some. I'll tempt them away.'

It was easier to concentrate on the birds. There must be nothing dramatic, no show of emotion. Just pick up the threads, feel the rightness of being together.

'All gone. That's the last bit.' She shook the crumbs from the bag.

'Let's walk.' She fell in by his side. 'Two years of living since you ran off from New York. How come, Penelope Drew, that while the rest of us get battered by the storms you still look as though you'd seen the fairies at the bottom of your garden?'

'I'm not sure that I take that as a compliment. Anyone who stays so untouched must be very selfish and uncaring.'

'Not necessarily. And certainly not in your case. But you never lose your faith in tomorrow.'

'How do you know? You haven't talked to me for two years, you just said so.'

Their pace had slowed. Now he stopped walking and held her back with a hand on her arm. 'I knew it the moment you stepped on to the stage last night. You and your David – you've found what it is you're looking for?' He shrugged. 'Why do I even ask? Just seeing the way you dance together – you're perfect, in complete accord.'

She didn't answer.

'Penny . . . ?' He wasn't sure what he was asking.

'What d'you want me to say?' Her voice was gruff. 'Anyway, you shouldn't be talking about us, me and David. I don't ask you about you and Helen. Don't need to. I can see she's better. I heard about the court case – that you promised to look after her and all that.'

'I took her straight down to Georgia. She was at rock bottom.' He spoke quietly, with no hint of emotion. 'So, here we are, two years on. Helen has a clean record. Sonny's to thank for that, not me. He needed her, she

372

must have seen how hurt he was by what had happened. She genuinely cares for Sonny, always has.'

'You don't have to tell me about it – 'tisn't right that you tell me.' How aggressive she sounded.

'Isn't it?' It was a question, he expected an answer.

'You don't have to explain, Laurence. Don't expect I was the first woman you'd had an affair with. It's been over for ages. Come on,' she pulled her arm free, 'let's walk.'

'Over for ages, you say. No, Penelope, it hasn't been over. It won't be over. Not for me and not for you either. And don't talk to me about affairs with other women. What we had – what we have – will always have – isn't like that.'

'You shouldn't – ' Her jaw ached, she held it so stiff. She mustn't blink, mustn't cry. Such mixed emotions were almost too much to bear. 'I'm married. I've messed up one marriage, not going to mess up another.' She was winning the battle. Her voice sounded hard, the way she meant it to. 'And what about you? When it came to it, you had to leave me and rush off after Helen.'

'Yes. And what would you have felt if I hadn't? She is Sonny's mother. He needs her as much as he needs me. And you, you wouldn't have married your David without caring for him. But none of that alters the truth of what I said. I'll never be free of you. Please God, I'll never be free of you.'

'Stop it,' she gasped, beyond hope of stopping herself now. 'No, don't stop it! Say it, just once.'

'You'll never be free of me, nor I of you. You know that's true. Did two years make any difference? No. And neither will twenty. What's between us is no ordinary thing, my Penelope Drew.'

'I know. It's not just that I love you – I don't know how to say it. It's like I'm not really whole without you. What Tom would call "living at half cock". That's the way it's got to be, though.' She wiped the backs of her hands across

373

her cheeks. 'If we snatched at what we thought would make us happy, we'd end up with nothing.'

They started to walk. After a minute they started to talk too. He told her about Sonny's visit to the specialist, she told him about the Trust she had had set up with Anna's money, about Prospect House and the children. It was only later that she realized the one thing they hadn't talked about was the theatre.

The afternoon had melted, they hardly realized how far they'd walked. From St James', through Green Park, across the busy thoroughfare of Piccadilly, heading towards Hyde Park. Near Marble Arch they went their separate ways, their parting as low key as their greeting had been. Laurence would be in London as long as there was hope that the eminent Sir Cedric Guthrie might be able to help Sonny; inevitably their paths would cross. They said nothing about meeting again, but even so Penelope walked home on air. 'You'll never be free of me, nor I of you . . . ' This afternoon that was enough for her. She believed it always would be.

David was out. She was glad, she needed time on her own. She truly loved David; he was so gentle and kind. Kneeling on the chair in the bay of the living-room window she looked out at the bustle in the street below. Every one of those people had their own hopes, their own dreams, their own ambitions too. And hers were wrapped up with David's, of course they were. Fancy, a whole afternoon with Laurence and not once had they talked about the theatre. Her ambitions tied up with David's? But were they? Deep in her heart hadn't she always known that vast impersonal audiences weren't for her? Her satisfaction came now from singing Laurence's songs, dancing to his music; and from working with David. What would happen when 'Girl of My Dreams' came off?

A noise somewhere in the flat. What was that? 'Is that you, David?' she was about to call. Something stopped her. Instead she knelt very straight in the chair, hardly breathing as she listened. Voices, soft voices, David's surely . . . Stealthily she climbed off the chair, even unbuttoned her shoes and took them off, then crept from the sitting room, across the tiny hallway towards the bedroom. She didn't make a sound, yet she seemed to hear the hammering of her heart. Suppose he opened the door, saw her with her ear close to it? What was so odd about him taking Des into the bedroom, she'd done the same thing with Sylvia often enough . . . a new gown to show her . . . Sylvia, it was Sylvia who'd warned her . . . she needed to swallow but her throat was dry. What were they saying in there? She couldn't hear, even with her ear pressed to the wood the whispering wasn't clear.

The flat was part of an old house, converted into three of which theirs took up the whole of the first floor. It had thick wooden doors, built in the days when each would be expected to lock, although they'd never been given any keys. Kneeling she put her eye to the keyhole. Until that moment she'd only half understood what she might see.

As silently as she'd come, so she crawled away. Sylvia had hinted – perhaps she hadn't really understood either. How could she? Tom, so normal. But what was 'normal'? Penelope crept into the bathroom, closed and bolted the door, and sat on the edge of the bath. Tom had been in love with Sylvia, yet it hadn't stopped him ending the days by pounding at Penelope with almost the same regularity that he scrubbed his teeth. That, she'd supposed, was 'normal'. And David? They'd been married less than five months . . . and when had they last made love? It was as if all his lovemaking went into his dancing; it was then that she felt nearest to him. But this! Was it her fault? Had he wanted things in her she'd not given him?

'You'll never be free of me – nor I of you . . . ' Biting hard on her thumb she remembered. One evening that had held a lifetime of loving . . . for her . . . for him.

The bedroom door was opening. Someone was coming.

She sat quite still, watching the handle of the bathroom door.

'Penny?' It was David's voice. 'Penny, are you home?'

'I'm washing my hair.' And as if to prove it she turned on the tap and filled her cupped hands with water, then splashed it on her short straight locks.

'I've only just come in,' he told her, 'I wondered if you were back.'

This time she didn't answer. She stayed where she was, not missing the sound of the front door shutting quietly behind David's visitor. She could say nothing; she could wait, watch, play it David's way. 'Subterfuge' came the echo of Laurence's voice, and she was back in St James' Park. But honesty was her natural way, she couldn't let a lie grow and magnify between them.

'Has Des gone?' She came out of the bathroom, a towel wrapped around her head.

'I took his pen back. That's why I was out when you got home.'

'I thought I heard the door shut. I guessed you were seeing him out.' She ignored the lie.

'Penny — he's just a mate. I've known him since I was fourteen.'

'I don't really understand, David. I don't think I want to understand.'

'Then don't dig. Just forget it. Let's go to the theatre early, shall we, try out that tango?'

'Why did you marry me, David? What did you want for us?'

He slumped down on the settee, if anyone as naturally graceful as David could ever slump.

'How much do you know, Penny?'

'I know I feel cheap, dirty. I peeped through the keyhole of a closed door. Doesn't make you feel very proud, doing a thing like that. But it was your fault. It was what I'd heard, that's why I had to know.'

'Heard? What do you mean? Who's saying things?'

'About Des? Quite a lot of people, I should think.'

'Sylvia Carstairs, that's who it'll be. Des warned me she's a gossip.'

'David, I don't give a damn about Des Pritchard. He wasn't the first man to be interested in a young fourteen-year-old boy. But that was years ago. Have there been other men – for you, I mean? Or is it just him, turning up again? Is it some influence that he's always had?'

'Stop digging, didn't I say! Forget whatever it was you saw. Look, Penny, I won't bring him here again. How's that? I promise you.' He reached out and took her hands. She pulled away. From Des to her! David looked stricken. 'Oh God, you don't even begin to understand.' He leant back, his eyes closed.

Dispassionately, she studied him. His pale face was quite beautiful, she thought, shocked by the realization. Until today she'd thought of David as handsome, but now she saw him differently. To be handsome implied masculinity. She noticed that his long eyelashes were wet. Repelled as she was by all she'd seen and learnt, yet his unhappiness had the power to touch her.

'David,' she said, kneeling down in front of him, 'I know I don't understand, I don't believe I even want to. But I do care. What difference does it make who told me? The thing is, people are talking. Not about you – not yet – but about him. Perhaps he's been soliciting – isn't that what they call it?'

'That's not true! Of course he hasn't. That's a vile thing to suggest.'

'This could lead you into awful trouble, David. People like Des always have enemies, you know.'

'Like Sylvia Carstairs.'

'She wouldn't bother one way or another. He's not likely to make improper suggestions to Tom, now is he?' A tactless thing to say. To cover it, she rushed on: 'It's an offence, don't you see? Anyone with a grudge against him could drop him right in the cart – and you too.'

'God save me from their narrow morality!'

'Nothing wrong with their morality, but God save you from their spite. You and me too.'

'You?' He opened his eyes now. 'Why you? You've got nothing to hide.'

'Just that I'm married to a man who prefers his boy friend.'

'It's not true. Well, not wholly true.' He leant forward, his head in his hands. 'Don't sound hard, don't be bitter. Not you, Penny. I am as I am. I can't help it. It isn't that I don't love you, we're right together, ask anyone who's watched us.'

'Dancing!' She wanted to shock. There was a rough edge to her voice as she dug to the lowest depths she knew. 'Bugger the dancing! Bugger the theatre!' Language so out of character. 'Bugger . . . that's what it is, isn't it? Buggery!'

'You sound like all the other mealy-mouthed moralists. Penny, not you. Please, not you. I love Des Pritchard. There, I feel better now I've said it. Is that a sin, to love another man? Oh God, what did you have to come home for? It would never have hurt you. Loving Des doesn't touch the way I care about you. Don't pull away from me, Penny, dear Penny. I'm sorry. I know I fail you. Time and time again I've wanted to be able to love you, to make it good for you. I'm sorry. I never meant to hurt you.' Protect Penelope, don't hurt Penelope . . . The shadow of that first failure hung dark over her. 'You'll stay with me, won't you?' He sounded frightened. 'You won't run out on me? Please, I beg you.'

'He could take my place here. Think how cosy you could be!'

Didn't he hear the sarcasm?

'And you talk of gossip, the trouble we could be heading for! Stay with me. For your sake as well as mine. The talk wouldn't stop with Des and me. You'd get your share too. That sort don't mind who they stab in the back. Two husbands, both left you, one for a woman, one for a man. Oh, you'd get plenty of their malice.'

But in his fright he'd made a wrong move. Penelope stood up and walked away to stand with her back to him, looking out of the window. Not much more than an hour ago she'd been with Laurence. "What was, is now and will be ever more." She ought to be distraught. Her husband was homosexual; he and his boyfriend slept together here in her own home, in the bedroom he shared with her. "You'll never be free of me, nor I of you . . ." But she was free of David. His sly warning about the gossip that would attach itself to her hadn't hurt her. Suddenly she knew, if she were honest, none of it had really hurt her. What she'd discovered had somehow erased the humiliation she'd felt at their unsuccessful lovemaking.

What a brittle blue the sky was, so clear, so high. "Such a lovely world and we don't give ourselves time to stand and look at it. Today I did. Today I really saw." Would she ever look to the clear sky through a canopy of golden leaves without hearing his voice: "Please God, I'll never be free of you . . . "

David was crying. The afternoon had unnerved him far more than it had her. Perhaps he had more to lose, she thought. After all that had happened she was surprised at the pity she felt for him as she came back to him and sat on the arm of the settee, her hand on his shoulder.

'About us, Penny,' he looked at her, his face contorted, 'this doesn't alter things, not for me it doesn't. I do love you, just as much as before Des came back to work in London. He'd been in Paris, I'd not seen him for more than two years. I'd not expected to see him again. There have never been any other girls in my life, none at all. You're the first I've ever cared about.' He took out his handkerchief and wiped his face. 'I even wanted you – like that – never felt that for any woman before. If Des hadn't come back things might have got better for us. But now –

Penny, I'm sorry. I am as I am. Don't leave me. Promise you won't leave me.'

'I won't leave you. But, David, I won't live with you either – I mean, I won't sleep with you.'

He nodded. She could sense his relief.

Would she have been so magnanimous if her own circumstances had been different, if Laurence had been free? That walk in the park was little more than an hour behind her. It still coloured her vision and her thinking.

David offered to be the one to move into the tiny second bedroom, but after what she'd seen through the keyhole Penelope was glad to take her things from her old room. It was all done within the hour. The time would come when she'd look back on that late afternoon, at her calm acceptance, and wonder at her behaviour. Hanging her clothes in their new home she felt nothing, no hatred, no anguish, no relief. Nothing.

'I shall be away at the weekend, at Challington,' she told David as he drove them to the theatre. 'I'll catch the early train Sunday morning.'

'I could come with you. We could drive down.' He clutched at any chance to help them forget that dreadful scene. How could she be so untouched? He was thankful for her lack of histrionics – and yet at the same time offended. If she'd wept, pleaded with him, put up a fight, then he would at least have known what was going on in her mind.

'No. There's no point, a train's quicker anyway. I'll be back in good time on Tuesday.'

His lips set in a tight line. He hadn't wanted a weekend in Challington, seeing the way that lovely house was being misused, watching that show-off of an old man of hers carrying on like Lord Bountiful to the 'waifs'. But even so, he had every right to go with her. She was treating him like a naughty child.

That was on Wednesday. The audience that night

applauded with the same enthusiasm. And why not? Penelope and David were professionals to the tips of their toes.
The old magic might not have been there but they executed
their dances with the same old precision; the timing of
their lines was as sharp; Penelope's comic acrobatics
tonight were a mirror image of last night – or tomorrow.
Only as she creamed the greasepaint from her face did she
allow herself to wilt.

'You look tired,' David said, driving home. And somehow he was glad. Perhaps she'd not been as unmoved as
she pretended.

'Thanks.'

Again he felt he was in the wrong.

'Penny, I'm sorry – not for myself. In a way I'm glad
it's out, that you know, that I don't have to hide how I – '

'I wouldn't shout it abroad if I were you, not unless you
want to be martyred for your beliefs. I'm glad I know too.
We can put an end to the sham.' Then, for the first time,
she let emotion creep in. 'That's what I can't bear to think
of. I feel dirty, smeared.'

'That's a hateful thing to say! I said I'm fond of you.
There are plenty of married men, men with families, who
feel as I do.'

'There are plenty of married men with mistresses too.
It's not what I want.'

'What's that rhyme you're so fond of? "Life ain't all
you want . . . "'

'And so I shall, David. I shall put a geranium in my 'at
and be 'appy. I shall do things *my* way.'

He drew up outside the front door.

'You go in. I'll park the car.' He was proud of his
Renault, garaging it in an unused coach-house in a nearby
mews.

When he returned she was already in her new bedroom,
the door closed.

Next morning she walked in Hyde Park. The sky was grey

381

and overcast. Today the glory of the leaves were nothing more than a dirty brown.

'Miss Drew!' It was a young voice. Even before she turned round she knew who she'd see.

Today Sonny was with his nurse. From the wheelchair he'd been helped to stand, and by the grin on his face she knew just how pleased he was to be able to greet her from this superior height.

'Sonny! Why, you're as tall as your Dad!'

He forced himself very straight.

'I can top Dad by half an inch.' And if he was proud of that half inch, she knew Laurence must be prouder.

'This is Sarah – Nurse Culley, if you want to be formal, but we never are, are we, Sarah?'

'Hello, Sarah. I'm Penelope.'

'Sure, I know who you are right enough. Heard nothing else since Sonny came to the show.'

'Nothing to the performance he's giving. He was in the chair last time I saw him.'

'When Mom and I go out, I don't bring my sticks. She worries, poor Mom. Feels safer with me sitting in one place. Now, just you watch. What a way to spend a morning,' he crowed, 'strolling in Hyde Park, London Town.'

"Last one to the pier's a sissy," came an echo down the years. She smiled as brightly as he meant her to. He mustn't guess how tight her throat felt or how hard she had to blink to fight her 'damned silly tears'. Sonny defied pity. Manfully he swung his legs, first one, then the other, right, left, right . . . He made slow progress, but from his triumphant expression he might have been heading the field in a marathon. Sarah stayed close to his side, Penelope pushed the empty chair.

'Look at that little boy with his dog,' Sarah said. Nothing that unusual in the way the child was throwing the ball, the dog retrieving it. But they stopped. Penelope realized it gave Sonny the chance to regain his breath. She saw just what an effort it was for him to walk, taking all his concentration and all his breath.

Affecting not to notice, she talked to Sarah.

'Is this your first visit to England?'

'It is. I guess I was about eight when I decided that's where I wanted to travel to. I had a little cardboard box. I stuck the lid on then made a slit in it to put money in and that's where all my cents went. My England Box, I called it.'

'So you've brought your spending money!' Penelope laughed.

'It wasn't much of an effort. Three dollars and five cents, that's what I found when I unglued the lid. Oh, I'd not looked at it for years. It'd been put away in my old toy box.'

'You never spent the money on anything else though?'

'Well, I couldn't, could I? It would have been like asking for bad luck.'

Penelope nodded. They talked the same language.

'I hope you get a chance to see more than London.'

They stopped for another breather.

'We're going to be here a few months,' Sonny told her, trying not to let them notice he was panting.

What had made Penelope think the morning a dingy grey? Why, surely, it was silver!

'And while we're here, Sarah will have a holiday. Be free of me for a while, won't you?'

'Maybe.'

'That was one good thing about being in variety, I got to see every corner of the country. Don't think I'm cut out for city life.'

She knew Sarah listened, was as interested as she had been herself to hear about the little girl who'd saved to come to England. What between some people was empty small talk, between others was the foundation on which friendship could be built.

'Are you country born?' the American girl asked.

383

'I grew up in a town on the south coast – quite a big town. But because it's by the sea you can never feel shut in, cooped up, like you do in a busy city.'

'I'll bet you were dying to get away from it, Miss Drew, see what the rest of the world was like.' Sonny smiled when he said it, but he, more than either of them, must yearn to throw off his own restrictions.

'You bet I was, Sonny. I was fifteen. Pa said I couldn't go – but I packed my bags and went!'

They both waited for more.

'It wasn't as dramatic as it sounds. I loved them dearly – but I loved to sing and dance and to play my concertina.'

'You played one of those things?' Imagining it, he saw her with new eyes. 'They're happy instruments, aren't they?'

'That's just about it, Sonny. You couldn't play a sad tune on a concertina.'

'And that's what you did when you left home?'

She told them about the seaside concert parties, about how Perce had come into being because she hadn't a costume. It was thinking of Challington that the idea came to her.

'I'm going home at the weekend, just for a couple of days. If you'd like to – if you could manage the journey on the train – you could come with me, both of you. There's masses of room in the house. Mother and Pa would love to have you. Merrick, he's my brother, he's a year or so older than you, Sonny; Bruce is younger. Amanda is in the middle, about your age.' They hardly knew her, she told herself; why should strangers want to come away with her for the weekend? That was the voice of reason. And it only served to make her realize how much she wanted to take Laurence's son to Prospect House. 'Or have your parents other plans for you? Would they let you come, do you think?'

'Mom's got all sorts of places to go to, people she means to look up. Anyway, where Sarah and I go doesn't make

384

any difference to her. Dad's pretty busy, he won't mind. I'll manage the train somehow, won't I, Sarah?'

'There's nothing we can't manage, Sonny. We'll get you on that train all right.' Sarah sounded more confident than she felt, but she worked on the principle that challenge and conquest was Sonny's best way forward.

'Dad'll take us to the station, we'll pick you up on the way.'

They walked on, leaving the path and cutting across the grass to the Serpentine. Like children going on an annual outing, Sonny and Sarah wanted to hear about Challington. Talking about it conjured up for Penelope all the familiar sights, sounds, even smells of the place she knew so well; to the other two it held the excitement of pastures new, a holiday town on the south coast of England, a shingle beach with fishing boats, white cliffs . . . She even told them the time the train left Charing Cross.

That evening before the curtain went up Penelope's dresser brought her a note. Laurence wanted to speak to her. Could he come to the dressing room she shared with David in the interval?

'There! Didn't I tell you he was interested!' David read it over her shoulder.

'Interested? This won't be about theatre. I've invited Sonny and his nurse to come home with me for the weekend. This'll be about Laurence driving us to the station.'

'What in the world would they want to go to Challington for? Their first weekend in London, you'd think they'd want to be here.' Already he'd lost interest. So it was that Penelope was on her own when Laurence came to the dressing room.

Plans were changed. On Saturday evening as soon as the curtain came down she rushed back to that room again, tore off her costume, slapped cream on her face to get off the make-up, threw on her clothes and, pulling her hat on as she went, ran along the corridor and out of the stage-door in a way more befitting Perce than the star of the show.

It was nearly two o'clock Sunday morning when they turned in at the gate of Prospect House. A letter had gone ahead of them, asking that a wheelchair be borrowed from the hospital.

'I have a door key. We'll come in as quietly as we possibly can so that we don't wake you,' Penelope had ended her letter. 'I know it's short notice, I ought to have written and asked if it was all right. There wasn't time for that though. Anyway, I knew it would be! I've talked to you about Laurence, and about Sonny too. It means so much that he can *do* things, that's why I want him to come.'

Now they were here. And as if to welcome them a light was burning in the hall and another in the kitchen. And that wasn't all. As she got out of the car the front door was flung open, a beam of light came shining down the steps, and there was Oliver.

'Pa! You waited up!' She hurled herself into his arms, burying her head against his shoulder.

''course we waited up, Tuppence.' Then, turning to Laurence, he held out his hand. 'Welcome, Mr McLeod. Is the lad asleep?'

'He and his nurse slept most of the way. This is surely good of you, to welcome us like this.'

Penelope looked up at a clear sky, bright with stars. The two men shook hands, Oliver with one arm still around her. She shut her eyes as if that way she'd capture the moment, keep it in her memory to be re-lived. When she opened them she saw Muriel was there too, and behind her in the hall was the borrowed wheelchair.

The nurse in Sarah was trained to open her eyes and be instantly alert. The child still in Sonny worked on the same principle.

'I'll bring the chair down the steps, then you can wheel him in through the back door. It's flat that way.'

'Don't worry, Mr Drew. Put your arm around my shoulder, son, Sarah will steady the other side.'

'No, no, let me,' Oliver insisted. So one arm around his father, one around his host, Sonny was eased from step to step and so indoors. 'Through to the right, this way.' Oliver led the procession slowly towards the warm kitchen. The fire hadn't been banked to burn slowly through the night, it was a red hot glow of welcome. The smell from a big saucepan of soup was enough to tempt anyone. Tomorrow Muriel would call on culinary skills she'd not used since she left the Grand and was excited at the prospect. Tonight, though, they'd be tired, cold. What they needed was a good plate of warm soup, then their beds.

"Poor lamb! Thank God for our two boys, both fine strong lads. What's the good of money and fame when it boils down to it? Not a jot of good. Why, those little dears who get lumped off here for me to give an eye to, they're better off than this poor lad. Penny, this Laurence she's so set on, a nurse, poor Sonny . . . what about David? And Mrs Laurence? Seems a rum thing to me, first weekend in England and here he is with our young Penny not his wife. Oh, do be careful, Penny love, sitting there with eyes like stars. You'll only get hurt. No good can come of it."

And perhaps for Penelope it couldn't.

For Sonny, though, it could. One thing that illness does to a child is strip him of natural friendship with his contemporaries. But not at Prospect House. After a short night they all woke up to a sunny morning and the sort of hearty breakfast the American visitors associated with England.

'Coming out with us, Sonny?' They were still at the table when Merrick suggested it. For one moment Penelope thought he must have forgotten!

'Come on!' Bruce joined in. 'We're going to the George

Bradley — you know, Pen, the concrete bit by old man Bradley's statue.'

'Watch the way you speak, Bruce my boy. Old man Bradley, indeed!'

'Sorry, Dad,' Bruce giggled, not a bit put down, 'but have you ever taken a real good look at his face?' He sat very straight, pulling his head back. Mouth downturned, he viewed the assembly as if they were slightly less than human. 'Like that! He stands up there on his column looking at us as if we'd all got the plague. Anyway, no offence meant, I'm sure, Mr Bradley, sir.' He touched his forelock. 'We play pitch and toss. Ha'pennies, farthings, anything'll do. It's fun, Sonny. Lots o' lads come.'

It was the first time, the very first time, that an invitation had been given direct to Sonny. No: 'Can he come?' 'Could he manage?'

'You know about me?' His faced was flushed. With pleasure or embarrassment?

Under the table Laurence's fists were clenched. Every instinct made him want to come to Sonny's rescue. But he mustn't.

'About taking the chair? Yes, 'course we do. We went with Dad to the hospital to get it. You'll be fine in that, and it won't make any difference to playing. Just as easy from sitting as standing. Go on, say you'll come.'

The tension was gone.

And half an hour later so were the boys. Penelope and Laurence had dug out all their coppers, right down to odd farthings; Muriel had threatened there'd be no dinner for them if they weren't home by half-past one; Sarah had had a private word with Merrick; Laurence had sent up a silent 'thank you' as he'd seen the eager smile on his son's face as the three boys had set off down the drive.

Prospect House had its own brand of welcome. No one fussed, no one spent time they couldn't afford on empty chatter. It was typical that when Laurence glanced into the kitchen halfway through the morning, without looking up Muriel said: 'That scuttle needs filling, Ollie, there's a love.' She saw her mistake a moment later. 'Oh, it's you, Mr McLeod. I thought it was Ollie's step.'

'Tell me where the coal is and I'll fill it. And by the way, I'm Laurence not Mr McLeod.'

She smiled. 'Right you are, Laurence. Truth to tell, that's how I think of you from hearing Penny. The coal – that's kind of you. If you take the scuttle out, you'll find the coalhouse through that door and down the path on the left. There's a shovel just inside the door. Fill it right up, won't you? When the wind's from the east the fire fair eats it.'

It wasn't in her nature to pry, but she was uneasy that he should be here without his wife.

'A great place like this is,' she said when he came in, weighed down to one side by the loaded scuttle, 'pity your wife didn't come – and young David too. Perhaps it was the space in the car that stopped them?'

'Helen is staying in Beaconsfield with friends. I think Penny said David was busy this weekend. It was for Sonny's sake she suggested it. It's so good to see him with other lads.'

She nodded. 'It's what he needs, boys of his own age. Not healthy for a young person to be always with adults. There's more to a person than two good legs. His mind needs friends. Lads see jokes in things that we don't – they're all reaching out, growing up. It's good for him to have a bit of fun and not feel the grown-ups are fussing over him.' She was interrupted by shrieks from the garden. 'Just hark at them. Talk about young people needing each other. That's Arnie and Ted, the twins, you know.'

'Shall I see if they're hurt?'

'No, it's not a hurt cry. They're both growing up at the same rate, that's their trouble. Neither wants to give in to the other. One sure way of making peace is for someone else to pick on one of them, then they gang up together thick as thieves.'

'Penny told me a lot about this place, about the Trust.'

'She's a good girl, using the money the way she is.'

He watched her, the deft way she filled her pastry boats, her fingers moving quickly, lightly.

'Yes, Penny *is* good – and I don't just mean about the money she inherited.' He spoke quietly. For a second her fingers were poised, the pastry forgotten. Now what was he telling her? Whatever it was, she trusted him. Again her hands set to work, and when next he spoke there was no second meaning behind his words. 'Where has she disappeared to, do you think? Not with Sarah, she's outside with the twins.'

'Penny'll be down at the lodge, with Alf and Emma.'

It was all so relaxed. He wandered outside and kicked a ball with the twins; at opening time he walked to the Royal Standard and had a pint with Oliver. From the window of the lodge Penelope saw them go. And from where it had been hidden, deep in her memory, sprang a picture: Clifford House; upstairs Sylvia was struggling to bring Avril into the world (or fighting against it, according to how you looked at it!); Pa meeting her on the stairs, a sheet of music in his hands, the smell of whisky on his breath. The things he'd said, the hate that had seemed to fill his mind. Had all that been because of Anna? Or had it been because of her? Had he been frightened that she'd turn against him just as her mother had, that the stage would always win? Fear, jealousy, how they can warp a mind. Was it because he'd found his own peace that he could welcome Laurence to his home now? Was it because that home had come from Anna, a sign perhaps that the life she'd had at Challington had never been forgotten?

'Pity David didn't come with you,' Alf said. 'We've not seen him since he's been a married man.' Such a commonplace remark, yet now she found herself wondering if there was more behind it. Then she pulled herself up short. This was Alf she was suspecting of veiled innuendoes. Alf who

390

had always been an open book to her. She hadn't wanted to talk about David, nor even think about him. She pictured what his weekend would be in London. She thought of him with resentment; never before had she had to speak less than the truth to Alf.

'I expect he'll come next time. He wasn't free this weekend and I was keen to come. I wanted to bring Sonny.'

It was twenty-five past one when the boys arrived back, turning in at the gate at a furious rate and, four hands on the handle of the chair, running up the drive. Their morning had been a huge success – and Sonny, with beginner's luck, had come home sevenpence ha'penny the richer!

'This chap's a born gambler,' Bruce laughed as they sat down to dinner, 'you should just see the way he flicks his coppers.'

'It's a great game, Dad. I'll have to teach you.' Today Sonny was one of the boys; anything they could do he could do better. 'Say, Sarah, I don't need to rest this afternoon. I've sat down all the morning. I could – '

'Don't be daft,' Merrick cut in, 'if you've been told to rest you jolly well rest. Stick to the rules and buck up and get better. We'll only be in the garden, you can come out when your time's up.'

'Seems a waste. I can rest all the time back in London.'

'That's rich from one who takes his morning stroll in Hyde Park,' Sarah teased.

Sonny knew he was beaten. But Merrick had made it easy for him to rest without losing face. And, his hour on the bed over, he was taken out to the garden where he met another of nature's gentlemen. For so long Alf had been out of work and out of step; he knew all too well the frustration of being dependent. Of all of them it was he who understood Sonny's need to be useful. And it was surprising what a lad could do with a pair of shears, even from a wheelchair. They all had their jobs, right down to Arnie and Ted who swept leaves and filled the wheelbarrow.

Then in the evening they all congregated in 'the room' and it was Sonny who asked Penelope if she'd play her concertina. A sing-song went so much better with an instrument to lead the way; they all shouted the words if they knew them and la-la'd if they didn't. Sitting on the window seat Laurence looked at the scene: Penelope cross-legged on the hearthrug, Muriel mending, Oliver doing nothing but managing to give the impression that it all revolved around him, Mandy and Margaret poring over some picture show magazine, the boys playing shove-ha' penny, Alf and Bruce against Merrick and Sonny, Sarah and the twins playing tiddly-winks – and all of them joining in the singing.

When Muriel told the twins: 'Time for upstairs, lads, kiss Uncle Ollie goodnight,' she put down her darning and stood up, a sure sign to the boys that no good would come of argument.

'And as soon as this game's won, I must get home to Emma,' Alf said. 'What about taking my place, Sarah?'

'Is it always like this?' she laughed. 'Like one long party?'

'Not so noisy as a rule,' Oliver told her. 'It's young Tuppence here who makes them rowdy.' He crossed his legs and admired the gleam of his shoe leather by the flickering firelight. An Englishman's home was his castle; he looked benignly down on his family. 'A pity you can't stay longer. When does Sonny have to see this Sir Cedric man again?'

'Fourth of November. He'll have reports on the tests by then,' Laurence answered.

'But that's not for more than a week! Does he have to dash off back to London? Or would you be bored here, son, with the lads both off to work?'

'We're here in the evenings. Go on, Sonny, say you'll stay. He can, can't he, Mr McLeod?'

Before his father could intervene, Sonny left them in no doubt of his own feelings.

'I'd like to, Mr Drew – what about Sarah?'

'Naturally.'

'Tell you what, Sonny,' Penelope stood up in one lithe movement, 'tomorrow I'll give you a lesson on the concertina, and you can see how good you can get by the time you come back to London.' She came to sit on the window seat with Laurence.

Alf went home. Muriel came back from seeing the twins to bed, heard that Sonny and Sarah were staying on and beamed her approval. Sing-song over, the evening progressed with less noise, whispers and giggles from the girls, and the steady knock of ha'penny against ha'penny. Then one by one the others went to bed, Sarah taking Sonny.

'I'm ready for Sheet Street, we were late last night.' Muriel rolled away her work. 'You get anything else anyone wants, won't you, Penny love?'

In Penelope's mind she saw the fireside, everyone gone but Laurence and her . . . only Pa was left and he was winding the clock, a sure sign he was on his way. There had been something unreal about the day, seeing Laurence here, fitting in so well before a background quite different from his own. They'd not spoken to each other alone since they arrived.

He took out his cigarette case and offered it around.

'Are you smoking, Mr Drew?'

'No, I won't have another tonight, thanks. I've just had my marching orders, I'd better go up. See you put the guard across the fire before you come, Penny.'

After he'd gone they still sat on the window seat. Penny felt her hand taken in Laurence's, his thumb gently caressing it. She leant against him.

'This is a remarkable place,' he said. 'I could feel a special atmosphere, and I know Sonny could. I've not heard him laugh like he has today since before he was ill.'

'It's a healing place. I think it's something to do with accepting people for what they really are, not their outside show. I'm just "Penny love" – or from Pa, if he's in an affectionate mood, "Tuppence". I'm not any more important because I've played on Broadway and in the West End, I'm just me. And Emma – no one here minds telling her to "say it again" if ever we don't understand. The way she speaks is no barrier; everyone knows her and loves her. So somehow that makes her whole. Then there's Alf. The war changed his face. At first life was dreadful for him. It's here that he's found himself again. There's more to Alf than his face.'

'More to a person than two good legs, that's what your mother said this morning. I'll come down next weekend and fetch them back. Will you come too, or will David not like you being away two consecutive weekends?'

For a minute she didn't answer. Then she sat up very straight, turning to look at him.

'Laurence, I don't have to worry about David. Not next weekend. Not ever.'

'You mean he knows about us – now I'm in London he – '

'No, no, it's nothing to do with us, nothing to do with me. There's someone else.'

'But what the hell's he playing at? You've been married no time, and you say he's found another woman?'

She shook her head. 'I didn't say that. I didn't say another woman.'

He looked puzzled, then he frowned. 'Are you saying – '

'No, I'm not saying anything, not even to you Laurence whom I'd trust with any secret. I just don't want to think about it. 'cept that, in a funny way, it's easier to take than another woman would be. I suppose it doesn't hurt my pride. Doesn't hurt at all. I wonder if it would have if you'd not come? Nothing seems to touch me now.'

He held her close.

'You can't live like that, Penny.'

'It's not like it was with Tom. He wanted to be free, he really loved Sylvia. I can't leave David just because he isn't what I believed. And, Laurence, another woman is easy. You can cite her, it's a nine days' wonder. I can't do that to David. It would be the end of him. And he's no different; he's as fond of me as he was in the beginning.'

'But why the hell did he marry?'

'He thought we'd be all right. I believe he thought he was over all that, and being married would help him push the memories even further back. This friend came back unexpectedly – oh, let's not talk about it! I'm sorry for him – but, Laurence, I'm free of him too. I'll never be free of you, you told me so yourself.'

'Never.' His mouth touched hers in a tender kiss.

'Laurence, we could say we need to be home by Tuesday morning. We could go tomorrow evening.'

'I'll do things my way,' she'd told David, little realizing the effect that her way would have on lives other than her own.

In Des's mews cottage he and David had sat a long time over their meal, home cooked with that touch of care Penelope's culinary efforts lacked. Then, together they cleared it away, got out the card table. This was true companionship; there was nothing in either of them the other didn't know and understand. The Renault was left at home, there was no car parked outside, nothing to hint to even the most curious of neighbours that Des Pritchard had a visitor. Soon the lights went out.

At Beaconsfield Helen was staying with friends she'd made during the war, Victor and Celia Stein, a couple who dealt in antiques. In the days before the war the New World had been one of their best outlets. They'd bought in Europe and shipped the goods to America. That's where they'd been in August 1914 and where they'd stayed until the beginning of 1919. It was a friendship that had seen

395

Helen through some of her worst days. The days when she'd been a nervous wreck seemed a long way behind her now. When they introduced her that evening to Rosamund Valoir, how could the Steins know the ghosts they would raise?

CHAPTER FIFTEEN

Victor and Celia had taken Helen to Windsor, pointing out all she should see, and another day to Oxford, city of dreaming spires. But she belonged to the New World. To her, buildings were 'old', be they Early English, Elizabethan or even Georgian. She wanted to dig no deeper.

There had been something not quite real about life for all three of them in those days when they'd been friends in America. So far from home and all that was going on in wartorn Europe, the Steins had taken on a mantle removed from their life in an English Shire. Helen and the trauma she was going through had been part of it. Perhaps it had been a mistake to invite her to Beaconsfield, not to accept that none of them was quite the person they had been.

On Saturday evening they'd given a dinner party but it had been no more successful than the outings. Their friends were people with interests much the same as their own: paintings, books, music, antiques, the arts. Helen didn't fit in; the evening only accentuated more clearly that she wasn't one of them.

Then they'd remembered Rosamund Valoir, and on Sunday morning offered their cook's nephew a shilling if he'd miss singing in the church choir and cycle to Troughton Hall with a note for her. And that was an offer no lad could refuse! Singing in the choir brought him a penny a service, morning and evening, paid at the end of the quarter; his cycle ride was long, but it was worth the equivalent of six weeks' earnings.

Rosamund had never fitted into the same mould as the Steins' other friends. They'd first met her soon after her husband, Clarence, had died leaving her the owner of

Troughton Hall, a large and run-down estate some seven miles away. Rosamund had been selling some of the family silver. Whether she needed the money or whether she simply had no interest in surplus possessions which had no function they hadn't known then and to this day still didn't. They'd bought silver, paintings, ornaments; she'd had no idea of their value and not much interest either, but they'd treated her fairly. When it came to horseflesh Rosamund knew and understood. So, poles apart in interest though they were, yet they respected each other and based on that respect the acquaintanceship continued.

Sunday was Helen's last evening. At least with Rosamund as a dinner guest it shouldn't be dull, for the only thing you could be sure of with her was that she was full of surprises.

'Helen's husband is connected with the theatre, you know, Rosamund,' Celia said brightly during the meal. 'One of his musicals is on in the West End at the moment.'

'Never did take to the theatre.' Their guest turned that avenue into a cul-de-sac. 'Do you ride?' she asked. 'You sit well. I'd say you'd have a good seat.'

'I've never been on a horse in my life. You're a keen horsewoman are you, Mrs Valoir?'

'Know where you are with a horse. Don't brook fools, you know. Got more sense than many a human. Horses make up their own minds, know things without being told. You've heard the saying "horse sense"? Even in America they must know what it is to have that.'

'I've always lived in town. To be honest, I'm ignorant about most animals.'

Rosamund nodded, sizing her up. 'Well, that follows. Ah, and while I have it in mind – Celia, I want something off you for the bazaar. We're collecting to send the orphanage children on an outing to the zoo. You must have a trinket or two you don't wear. Or what about jam, has your cook made your jams yet?' And that was typical of her. A trinket or a jar of jam, she bracketed them together as if the value were the same.

It was chance that changed the shape of the evening. An unexpected visit from a local art restorer and Helen and Rosamund found themselves forgotten.

'You don't go in for all this fine art nonsense? You don't care about horses.' The lady of Troughton Hall frowned. 'Dogs?' Then, seeing that didn't strike a chord, 'Not the stage? No, you're not the performing kind.' Helen opened her mouth to reply, trying not to let it be too apparent that she had one eye on the clock, when Rosamund took her by surprise: 'You've known sadness, great sadness.'

Helen started. This wasn't the kind of after dinner conversation she'd expected.

'Who told you that? What sadness are you talking about?'

'No one told me anything. Sometimes we recognize a reflection of our own hurts, our own suffering, in another person.'

Helen looked at her with new interest. After days of being taken about and 'educated', of hearing conversations about things she cared nothing for, this woman had touched a raw nerve.

'Reflection of your own suffering?' Cunningly she turned the question.

'Death strips one of part of one's very being. Or so I thought at one time.' She reached for the wine and re-filled both their glasses. 'You've much to learn. Ha! And how do I know?'

'How do you know any of it? You say no one's told you.' Helen drank half a glass of wine as if it were water.

'Steady on that stuff. You Yankees aren't used to the fruits of the vine.'

'Tell me what you see. Am I so transparent?'

'I'd say you've learnt to do a pretty good cover up job. Now's not the time to strip you of your protective shield.'

It was as if a lifeline had been thrown towards a drowning man, not quite reaching him. That protective shield slipped, the hand that raised her glass wasn't steady.

'How long are you staying? Will you come and see me while you're here?' Rosamund suggested.

'I'm leaving tomorrow.'

'Can you spare another twenty-four hours? Come on to Troughton Hall.' She leant closer, her fleshy white hand holding Helen's wrist. 'There's no distance too great for a spirit to traverse.'

'I know that.'

Rosamund let go of the wrist, drummed her fingers on the table, seeming undecided whether to dig deeper or drop the subject.

'Did you really mean that? For me to come on to Troughton Hall?'

'I'd like us to talk. We are attuned – spiritually attuned. It's impossible to talk here.'

'How do I get to Troughton Hall? Is there a railway station?'

'You don't want to stay overnight here, do you? I've got my motor car, come back with me.' Then, having settled it to her liking: 'Celia, I'm taking Mrs McLeod home with me. I've invited her for a day or so at the Hall. She might as well drive with me as take a taxicab in the morning.'

Celia and Victor's regret at Helen's early departure might have been completely genuine, such was their social grace. And less than an hour later Rosamund's Lanchester was headed towards Troughton and what proved to be a long night.

'Send Alice to mend the fire in the library, Watson, then you may all go to bed,' Rosamund told the butler who greeted them in the large, badly lit hall. 'Oh, and put out a tray of drinks, will you? I'll show you where you can sleep, Mrs McLeod.'

'I wish you'd say Helen.'

400

'Then I will. You'll find our quarters very different from what you modern Americans expect. But I don't think it'll bother you unduly. Not unless I'm much mistaken. By the time you come to bed you'll have more on your mind than the lack of electric light.'

'You make it sound threatening.'

'To reach across the divide can never be threatening. You'll not make contact with your enemies, how could you? Your spirits would never fuse. But wait! Time enough, the night is young.'

That was a little after midnight.

Soon time was forgotten. The library was almost in darkness, lit only by the flickering flames of the fire. It was almost in silence, too. Knowing nothing of Helen's history, and disregarding now that she came from a country where Prohibition ruled, Rosamund re-filled their glasses. Alcohol did away with inhibitions, it was important that nothing was kept under wraps.

'There's someone I go to – in New York. Sometimes he can make contact.' Helen leant forward, her eyes pleading. 'Is that what you can do?'

Rosamund took Helen's hands in hers and looked at her unblinking, her eyes luminous in the firelight.

'You need no one else. Open your mind . . . listen for the voice you want to hear . . . listen . . . listen . . . '

'No!' There was no mistaking her fear.

'What is it that frightens you? Is it a man, a man you love, a man not your husband?'

Helen nodded.

'Tell me. I can help you find the power – but you have to believe . . . you have to work . . . he'll cross the divide but only if you are ready to receive him. Talk about it, tell me, I'll work with you.'

Rosamund was no beauty, a plump woman of perhaps fifty, her flesh white and soft. Just for a second it struck Helen that the last thing she would have expected her to be was a horsewoman. The thought melted almost before it was formed. The grip of those soft hands was like steel.

' . . . talk about him . . . forget me, just say what comes into your mind, into your heart . . . his name . . . call him, call his name, let him hear . . . forget me . . . ' And with each burst of whispered, disjointed words, Rosamund's eyes pierced deeper. It would have been impossible for Helen to turn away even if she'd wanted to. She didn't want to. She had no will.

' . . . Sam . . . Sam . . . that's who he was. Sam Bernhard was his name.'

'Was he killed in the war? Is that it? Thousands of miles away from you, you don't know what happened to him?' Just as Rosamund's eyes pierced as if they'd see right into Helen's mind, so her whispered questions probed.

'I was there. I didn't know the police were following me, waiting to be led to where he was. Sam, I didn't know!'

A lover who'd not come home from the war was what Rosamund had expected, but whatever the story behind her visitor's fear, heart and soul she believed in what she was doing. The divide was never too wide to be crossed. Her dark eyes remained riveted on Helen's, every nerve in her body strained to help her in her quest.

'Tell me, don't push it away, don't hide from it. Share it, let me help you, let me work with you. You went to find Sam . . . ?'

'He'd been gone for so long.' It was an answer, yet she spoke as if she talked to herself. Rosamund was breathing deeply, 'working' with all the strength in her. 'There was a concert at school. Sonny was in it. I'd promised to go. Sam, all morning I'd been thinking about Sam! I told Bertha to collect Sonny. I said I'd had a message from a sick friend. I lied. Sonny would be looking for me, I knew he would, but I lied, I sent Bertha. Just wanted to go to Sam. It would never have happened if I'd not gone there.

He knew there'd be trouble as soon as he saw me, he knew they'd have followed.'

She seemed to have come upon an obstacle; the words dried up, her body tensed. Just as Rosamund's instinct would have helped her to quieten a frightened horse, so now it came to her aid with Helen.

'Because you loved him. He knows that's why you went to him.'

'He doesn't! He didn't understand!' Her eyes were full of fear. 'I felt the barrel of the gun. Why didn't he shoot me? Why didn't he let me pay? Wasn't Sonny's fault!'

She seemed suddenly to become aware of where she was. In that same second Rosamund, who'd been holding herself tense, every emotion in her brought to bear on lifting Helen's spirit so that it could cross that divide, slumped, her strength drained.

'Rest. Just rest a while. We'll work again.'

Of the two Helen was the first to recover. She drained the last of her wine.

'I've never talked about it. Why should I tell you, a stranger? Why should you even be interested?'

Rosamund re-filled their glasses and threw another log on the fire. The flickering flames gave just enough light to encourage the confidences that must flow if she were to be any help. The Steins had seen Helen through her worst times; Laurence had picked up the pieces over and over again. Yet here was a complete stranger who could recognize a torment that no one else had seen.

'You mentioned Bertha. Who was she? A sister? A friend?'

'Bertha was the maid. That day I'd promised to go to school, Sonny was playing Tiny Tim in *A Christmas Carol*. I gave my ticket to Bertha, told her to bring him home after it was over. They knew I lied – every newspaper in the state knew by the next morning.' Her voice had changed, become more strident.

It would be no use trying to 'work' until she was calmer.

403

Better to steer the conversation on to safer lines, try again presently.

'Didn't Celia say your husband is connected with the theatre? Is Sonny's interest to go that way too, I wonder? Tiny Tim can't have been an easy part for a child, the little crippled boy.'

'Sonny will never go on the stage.' Her tone put a full stop to that train of thought.

'You said there was someone in New York who made contact. I told you before – you need no one, all you need is to learn to open your mind, let your spirit free.'

'Does it happen to you? Can you contact – someone?'

'Here in this very room. I've been with Clarence – my husband – I've talked to him. It's not for everyone – the occult, supernatural, call it what you will. It's a gift.'

'What makes you think I have it? The medium never suggested it. Sam's talked to him, sent messages. Not always, though. Sometimes even he hasn't been able to get through.'

'How do I know you have the gift?' Rosamund shrugged her shoulders, holding out her plump, white hands. 'I felt it. If there wasn't something there that called to me, how could I have known you needed help? Tell me all about this Sam you love, what had he done that he'd gone into hiding?'

The log slipped, sending out a shower of sparks. Again the glasses were topped up. Wine helped them relax, took down the barriers. Their soft voices were the only sound. Helen didn't mention Laurence, nor did Rosamund ask about him; she supposed that husband and son played no part in the stranglehold of her torment.

Monday was a day charged with anticipation. For Penelope and Laurence, who set off from Challington late in the afternoon, their eyes wide open to what they were doing; for Helen, who'd taken her first halting steps into spiritualism and from them had found the confidence of belief in what was ahead.

Sea mist, they'd all supposed at Prospect House as they'd waved the travellers off. But before they'd driven many miles it was evident that it was no such thing. Already it was thickening from mist to fog. Laurence had meant them to get as far as Tunbridge Wells, but under these conditions that could take hours.

'Look, there's an inn. See the lights. Let's stop, Laurence.'

They'd been on the road about a couple of hours, moving ever more slowly. It was cold. Laurence had had to take his doorshield off so that he could look out. Neither of them knew where they were. But what did that matter? Somehow the fog cut them off from everything and everyone, they were in a world that held nothing but themselves. And tonight that was what they wanted. Gladly they pulled into the yard of the inn.

Those in the bar must have been locals, this was no night to tempt anyone far from home. Penelope had imagined the moment when they walked into the hotel, signed the register as man and wife. She felt that everyone must know they were no such thing. Now though when Laurence asked the landlord if there was a room they could have, she could feel the welcome.

'No night to be on the road, sir, and that's a fact. Travelling far, are you?'

'We're on our way to London. But I'd rather stop overnight and drive by daylight.'

'So I should think. I'll get the missus. She'll fix you up with a bed right enough – and something to eat. Meggie!' he shouted through a door at the back of the bar. 'Here a minute. Got a lady and gentleman want a bed out of the fog.'

And that's what they got. The room was clean, smelling of furniture polish. Linoleum on the floor with a rug in front of the dressing table. A marble-topped washstand, an iron bedstead, dingy brown wallpaper with green and gold scrolls on it, dark brown paintwork. And to crown it all, lighting either by candle or oil lamp. In short, a room with no flavour of romance.

'I'll get you a bite to eat. Just tell Arthur in the bar when you're ready. You can have it in "the snug", nice and warm you'll be in there. It's the damp of the fog – suddenly it's gone like winter, hasn't it? You'll find that bed well aired. I always keep bottles in just in case we get a visitor.'

'We'll be fine. And thank you, Mrs . . . ?'

'Masters. And you'll be . . . ?'

'McLeod.'

'Ah, Mr and Mrs McLeod. Well now, if there's anything you want don't you mind asking for it. I'll fetch you up a drop of nice hot water, you'll be glad of a wash. And the WC is straight across the passage.'

As the door shut behind her they looked at each other, both of them with an irresistible urge to giggle.

'Oh, Penny, what've I brought you to?' He pulled her into his arms, took her hat off and threw it on to the bed. He tilted her face up to his.

'I'm glad it's like this.' She chuckled, buffeting her head against his shoulder. 'Don't you see? It's real, proper. Not all dressed up to put on a show.'

'Real . . . like us, you mean?' He was serious now. 'I love you, my little Penelope. That's real enough – and proper too. There's no other way.' He pulled her to sit on the bed – and the springs let out a scream of protest. Somehow it was in keeping with everything else about their spartan quarters. Laughter bubbled up from deep inside her.

Later, in 'the snug', Meggie Masters brought them their supper of exceedingly good game pie.

'I've put a match to the fire in your room. Need a bit of comfort coming in out of a night like this. You'll find coal in the scuttle. Just make sure you put the guard in front before you settle for the night.'

Across the small table they smiled at each other. Penelope's mind was already moving on; she wondered if his was on the same track. The bed had showed signs of being too musical for anything but sleep. Knowing it, they'd laughed. It had seemed in keeping with everything else about this old inn. At that moment the thought of ending today and starting tomorrow lying close to Laurence was all she asked. She'd grown up knowing all about improvisation and in her quick mind had already made a comfortable nest before the fire. Linoleum? What difference did that make? There was a good thick eiderdown on the bed, there would be warmth and light too from the flickering fire.

In the way pictures from the past leap uninvited into the present, she was back in that bijou house in Swiss Cottage, waiting for Tom to come home. The stage was set for her seduction scene, even to the pose he'd find her in on the settee in her new silk nightie.

'What is it you folks say — "Penny for your thoughts"?' Laurence's voice brought her back to 'the snug'.

She looked at him earnestly. 'I was remembering another evening — but it doesn't matter. That's really what I found out.'

'An evening with Tom?'

'An evening without Tom. Don't let's spoil this one talking about it.'

'Penelope, you're pushing things under the carpet. I don't have to know about the good times you and Tom had — and you did, of course you did. But don't hide the hurts or they'll build into something that matters more in your mind than the happiness we could share.'

She nodded, her eyes lighting up as she smiled at him. 'Wasn't 'cos of Tom I didn't mean to tell you. It was in case you'd think me a fast woman.'

'Go as fast as you like, my Penelope, I'll be right with you.'

They took a long time over their meal; they talked to

Arthur Masters, the landlord; were persuaded into a game of bar skittles; Laurence bought a round of drinks for the locals who apparently used The Drovers as their habitual meeting place. The night stretched ahead of them and, sure of it, they enjoyed the whole of the preceding evening. It was a new experience to both of them, feeling themselves accepted as a normal married couple. In fact, if they could have eavesdropped on those same locals the next evening, they would have found that the American with his young English wife had added more colour and interest than they'd realized. But no one suspected that they were anything other than what they seemed; certainly the names Laurence McLeod and Penelope Drew would have meant nothing to them. Now Young Perce might have been different.

More coal on the fire. In her mind Penelope had likened it to the seduction scene she'd planned for Tom. But there was nothing of a seduction about this. They made love as the only true expression of the emotion that consumed them. It had been like this for them before, in New York. Tonight, though, there was more. As today gave way to tomorrow they discovered that 'real' and 'proper' love, as Penelope knew theirs was, had more to it than sexual fulfilment or even emotion. It held laughter and adventure.

By the time the guard was put in place and they wriggled gingerly into the musical bed, they'd travelled far and travelled together. The hours were printed indelibly on both their memories. If Penelope thought of her life as being punctuated by milestones, even she didn't know the writing on this one, didn't suspect where it was taking her.

By mid-day Tuesday they were back in London. Penelope let herself in to her first floor home, glad that there was no reply when she called David's name. Her future and his were irrevocably entwined, she'd promised him that; but to come straight from Laurence to him would have been too much. She was grateful that he was out.

At his hotel, Laurence found Helen there before him.

'What a miserable homecoming,' she greeted him. 'Where's Sonny and that nurse of his?'

'I took them down to the coast. We went for the weekend – to Penelope's people. Helen, Sonny is happy there, they have boys about his age. They asked him to stay on until he has to be home for Sir Cedric. I'll fetch him next weekend.'

'Was he agreeable to it? Can they look after him properly?'

'If you'd met Mrs Drew, you wouldn't ask.'

Helen's trips into the occult had done her temper no good. Today she was tight-lipped. Her every remark held a sting, if not in their words certainly in her way of voicing them.

'I suppose you and that "girl of your dreams" motored up this morning.'

'I brought her, yes. I've just dropped her off. Did you have a good time with the Steins?'

'I had a boring time with the Steins. And now I've come back to empty hotel rooms – they might as well be empty! You're never in, and when you are all you do is tinker on that bloody piano.' She'd been mixing cocktails despite its being only halfway through the day. Now she poured a pale pink concoction from the shaker into a glass. Sitting down, she swung her legs on to the sofa.

'Go steady on that stuff, Helen. Can't you ever learn?' He heard the criticism in his tone and tempered it with: 'You're not used to it, especially at this time of day.'

'Where is this place Sonny's gone to? Perhaps I'll write him a letter.'

All too often Laurence had seen Helen's bad moods, depression, supposed neglect, self pity that led to hatred of everyone – everyone except Sonny usually. Pleased that she seemed to have changed course he wrote out the address for her.

*

'Looks like we've got a caller, Ollie. Who do we know to come calling in a motor car?'

Oliver saw the woman at the steering wheel and, true to form, straightened his tie, pulled up the corner of his spotted handkerchief in his top pocket and volunteered: 'I'll go and see what she wants. Come to the wrong place, most likely.'

'Is this the Drew residence?' Used now to Sonny and Sarah, and having listened to Laurence at the weekend, Oliver recognized the visitor was American.

'Indeed it is.' Impossible to keep the ring of pride out of his voice. The Drew Residence! 'And I'm Oliver Drew.'

'You can't be Penelope's father?'

'Is something wrong? Is that why you've come?'

'No,' the stranger laughed. 'I was just surprised. I'd imagined her father would be a little fellow. May I get out? Are you going to ask me in? I'm Helen McLeod. Laurence said you'd so kindly offered to have Sonny for a few days, so I've put up at the Grand.'

'I do beg your pardon.' He opened the door of the car and helped her out, all his not inconsiderable charm coming into play. 'But you shouldn't have booked in at the Grand. We've room for an army here.'

'That's kind. But to be honest, Mr Drew, I think Sonny might enjoy being here better without me actually in the house. He knows I worry about him. I do fuss him. I'd like to watch him having fun, didn't want to be parted from him for a whole week, but I mustn't hamper him. Oh, look, are you wanted in the house? One of the staff coming to get you by the look of things.'

Helen the beautiful and devoted mother, that was the role she meant to play – and in playing it she believed it, forgetting the months she'd often let slip by between her visits to Georgia.

'That's not staff. We run this place with very little staff, just the odd job man and gardener and his wife. That's Muriel, my wife.'

'So this is Mrs Drew.' Making amends for her slip she held out her hand as if it were for her to welcome Muriel. 'Laurence spoke so highly of you. When I was worried that he'd come home and left Sonny behind, he said if I'd met Mrs Drew I'd understand.'

Already pink-cheeked from the kitchen range, Muriel felt the colour creeping to her neck. Yet she wasn't happy. This must be Laurence's wife, the woman who came between him and Penelope. (Or had done, until young David had come on the scene. What the situation was now she couldn't make out. Not all it ought to be, of that she was sure.)

'Your Sonny's out with Sarah. But come in the house. It's either the kitchen or "the room" with the children, so you'll be better in the kitchen.'

'Children? Aren't they at school?'

'Those that are big enough, yes, they're at their lessons. Just got five others this morning, little ones. After the fog we've had the last two days I thought the ground was too damp for them to be rolling about outside, so they're in "the room" with Emma.'

Helen was at a loss. Muriel led her down the passage to the kitchen, then drew Oliver's armchair towards the fire.

'I'll make you a nice hot drink. Tea? Or would you prefer coffee? Americans like their coffee, I believe.'

'Tea would be fine. Fancy Sonny not being here. All the way down I was picturing his surprise when I drove up to the door.'

'You've not driven right down from London? No, 'course you can't have. That's not Mr McLeod's motor car, not the one he was in at the weekend.'

'I rented this one from a garage – in London. I didn't tell Laurence,' she sniggered. 'Men! They like to think we can't do things for ourselves. "I'll drive down and get Sonny at the weekend," he said. Well, I've pipped him at the post. I've booked in at the Grand – Mr Drew did ask

411

me to stay here, he'll tell you, I explained it's better that I don't. The Grand seems comfortable and I can see a lot of Sonny without cramping his style with his new friends.'

'What did Laurence say to your coming all that way on your own?'

'He didn't say anything – I didn't tell him! I left a note that I'd bring Sonny back in time for Sir Cedric. And having the car I'm free to move around. You don't come all across the Atlantic to sit in a hotel all day. I want to see something of your country.'

'Fancy! Driving all that way with no one to turn to if things went wrong.'

'I doubt if Laurence would be much use to turn to. As far as I know, he's no mechanic. I'm used to being on my own, having to think for myself, travel by myself. Laurence's life has always been too full to have much room for an encumbrance like me.'

'Seemed to me he had plenty of time for Sonny.'

'Ah, Sonny.'

'Good thing that beastly fog blew itself away.' Muriel changed the subject. 'It rolled up Monday evening, I was glad Laurence and young Penny had got on their way ahead of it. By the time I locked up Monday night I could hardly see beyond the bottom of the front steps. And yesterday it hung all day. Yes, I said to Ollie, good thing they got on their way when they did.'

'Monday? I was in Buckinghamshire with a friend. I didn't get back to London until mid-day yesterday. But I think the fog was everywhere.'

'Well, I'm glad to have had word that they're back in London safe and sound. Never done much travelling by motor car – nor any other way come to that – but I'd say it must be quite scary when the fog comes down on everything. Especially on strange ground.'

For a second Helen hesitated, her brief pause added to what she said.

'Yes, they arrived safely enough. He got back soon after I did, yesterday. Tuesday.'

'Tuesday?' Now it was Muriel's time to pause, but there was nothing intentional in it. 'Oh, but you can't think – ' she floundered. 'Why, it must have been the fog. It wouldn't have been safe to drive through a night like that. I dare say he didn't mention it because he'd think you would have worried. You can't be thinking they – '

'I'm not even thinking. Frankly, Mrs Drew, I don't care where he goes or who he sleeps with. But it does seem an odd thing for a girl who's been married barely more than weeks. You don't mind if I smoke, do you? Will you have one?'

'Not at the moment, thank you, not while I'm seeing to the dinners. What you said just now, about Penny and your husband – she's not that sort of girl. You mustn't imagine things. On a night like that no one but a fool would have tried to do the whole journey. And who can blame him for not telling you? You see the conclusion you jumped straight to. Ah, now, look who's coming. There's your Sonny home. Just you walk out and surprise him.'

She did. His pleasure was her reward.

When lunch time came, Helen was invited to stay. Just that once she did, but never again. It seemed to her that Oliver was the only normal one amongst them (not counting Sonny and Sarah). Muriel, sitting at the table still wearing her large wrap-around overall; Alf, it turned her stomach to look at him; Emma, she couldn't understand a word the girl said, the only good thing was she said very little; five tiny children eating with more gusto than finesse, and Gwendoline still in a high chair with spoonfuls of food being pushed into or around her mouth. It wasn't Helen's idea of what a mealtime should be. In future she'd eat at the Grand.

That was Wednesday. During the remainder of her stay she came little closer to knowing Muriel, which was different from most other people. Oliver went out of his way

413

to be pleasant to her, but that wasn't to be wondered at; he took tea with her at the Grand, he joined the party when she drove Sonny and Sarah into the country. In her heart she'd wanted to find fault with Prospect House as a place for Sonny to be, but she couldn't. She hadn't seen him so happy for years. The following Monday when she drove them back to London, she was persuaded he should accept their invitation to return to Challington after his appointment with Sir Cedric.

'You'll be back for Sunday, in time for the next Pitch and Toss,' was Merrick's way of wishing him well.

'Bring lots of pennies for me to win off you,' was Bruce's.

But it didn't work out that way. Sir Cedric took Sonny into his private nursing home. Hopes were raised. Test followed test; one course of physiotherapy followed another. One week passed into a second, then a third.

Leaving Troughton Hall Helen drove to Beaconsfield then onward, intending to join the Great West Road near Slough. During the weeks Sonny had been in the nursing home she'd spent far more time with Rosamund than she had in London. Yesterday's rain had given way to pale winter sunshine, the trees cast long shadows. 'Burnham Beeches', 'Farnham Common', the signs told her where she was. Turning off the road she stopped. Driving took all her concentration, especially here where she had to remember to stay on the wrong side of the road. She needed solitude, silence.

The palms of her hands were clammy, her heart was beating hard. This would be the test. Here on her own, no Rosamund to work with her and for her. How much had she relied on those black, hypnotic eyes? But last night she'd seen him, she'd reached out her hands sure that she could touch him . . . then the scene had shifted, she'd been back by the fireside, Rosamund kneeling in front of her.

Had he heard her? Had he understood what she tried to tell him?

'You need no one else, you can reach him by yourself. Open your mind . . . call to him . . . trust . . . make a clear path for him to come to you.' Rosamund's words echoed.

She slumped over the steering wheel, eyes closed, head buried in her arms.

'Sam, hear me, Sam. She said if I opened my mind, if I trusted. Why won't you hear me, for God's sake? Wherever you are, listen.'

Nothing.

'I'm too tense, that's what's stopping him. Just a sip or two, it'll warm me, relax me. Got to stop these bloody shakes.' She dug into her handbag and brought out a flask. The spirit was comforting, one sip led to the next . . . her hands were steadier now. Already the light was changing, the yellow shafts fading, dusk falling, grey and still. So still. Now there'd be nothing to hold him back . . . there wasn't a sound. She felt he was close; now she was certain she'd make that path for him to come to her. Imagine him appearing right here from between those leafless trees, imagine the sound of his voice. His voice — but not on that dreadful day. Oh God, no, please don't let him speak like he had on that day! A trickle of sweat rolled down her side.

Just as she had before, she folded her arms across the steering wheel to make a pillow for her head.

This time she didn't call aloud. Silently she entreated him. "Sam, I didn't mean it to be like that. I wanted just to be with you. I didn't know they were watching me. It was my fault but, Sam, I've paid. Oh God, I've paid! Take the torment of it away from me, Sam, tell me you understand, tell me . . . " Her breathing grew deep and even. Helen was asleep.

Measured in time it was no more than five minutes before she stirred. But in distance there is no harnessing the subconscious. In those minutes she felt she knew what it was to be with him. In flesh they'd never been closer. It was more than six years since that dreadful day when he'd shot himself but nothing had dimmed the memory nor lessened her guilt. Often enough she'd dreamt of him, nightmares of fear and shame, dreams from which she'd wake sweating with terror, crying out for mercy. Now she raised her head, her eyes mirroring a new peace. It was as if her anguish had been just so many tangled threads. Pulling at one to unravel it had only tightened the knot of the others. Hardly daring to breathe she saw each of them, free and separate. Even now she knew the clarity would soon fade, but before it did she must follow each thread, she had to be sure that her conscious mind remembered and understood Sam's message.

She stared ahead of her unseeingly. No longer did she imagine Sam walking from the wood; she didn't need to. He was here, he was in her mind. He'd pointed out to her what she hadn't realized. Because she'd betrayed his hiding place she had been punished through Sonny, the only other person she loved. Yet until now she'd not seen his illness as her fault. Now it was so plain. Then another thread, bright and clear: Sir Cedric was going to make Sonny well. Perhaps he'd never be able to do all the things he might have, but no longer would she have to see him helped from a wheelchair to take no more than a few tortured steps.

Her face radiated a joy that came from a new certainty. Sam was absolving her of her sin and, as a sign, Sonny would be well. It was so clear, even now, minutes later, she knew exactly how it would be. It was as if a great weight had been lifted. Perhaps all along, without being aware of it, her heart had known the blame for what had happened to Sonny rested on her. It was nearly a week since she'd seen him. Perhaps even now Sir Cedric had let him come home. The cure would have started, Sam had promised. He had forgiven her.

It was getting quite dark. She got out of the motor car.

The winter countryside smelt heavy with rotting bracken. 'Sam!' And this time she called aloud, alone here in the wood, 'I'm going to see if Sonny's home. I'm going to see him. Stay near me, Sam.' Her faith in Sonny's cure was as strong as in Sam himself. In his hurt and anger he'd punished her through her son; now, through him, he'd promised to forgive.

The only answering sound was the evening call of a blackbird.

With all her strength she swung the starting handle then, as the motor shuddered to life, clambered back into the driver's seat. Southwards to meet the Great West Road, then eastwards to London. She drove as fast as the car could manage. In her present mood it was the only way. And as she went she sang, loudly and tunelessly.

'Girl of My Dreams' was to go on tour in the New Year. Penelope wouldn't look so far ahead. What about Laurence? How long would he be in England? She lived each day as it came during those weeks that Sonny was in Sir Cedric's care. As often as they could she and Laurence were together. A weekend in Marlow, another near Oxford. David asked no questions. She doubted if he was at home to miss her. As for Helen, Laurence said that she'd struck up a friendship with some friend of the Steins'; she was away more than she was in London.

It was the second week in December, a raw, grey Sunday afternoon, hardly the time to be wandering along a towpath beside the Thames. But that's what Penelope and Laurence were doing. They'd come to Henley-on-Thames. He'd signed the hotel register 'Mr and Mrs L. McLeod, London' and they'd been shown a room very much more comfortable than they'd had at The Drovers, with a view of the river and the traffic crossing the bridge.

'Something's wrong, Laurence, I know it is.' Almost timidly she touched his hand as they walked. 'I wish you could tell me? Is it us? Or is what you're working on not coming right?' She thought of those far off days in New York where each night he would play her anything that was new, where she'd felt herself to be a part of what he did.

'How could it be us?' His fingers held hers. 'I want to talk about it – yet, Penny, I can't bear to say it. He doesn't know yet – '

'Sonny?'

'There's nothing to be done. All the hopes . . . ' They'd stopped walking. Standing on the muddy path they turned to each other helplessly. She knew just how his jaw ached as he held it rigid, hers did too. She leant against him, her arms around his waist, her head against his shoulder. How could she help him? There was nothing she could say, nothing that would ease what he must be feeling. Yet she loved him so much that she would gladly have suffered for him. She felt insignificant, useless.

''s not fair.' Her voice was muffled, her face pressed against him. 'He's just a boy, not had a chance yet.'

'A person's more than just two good legs, I keep telling myself. He's whole still, he's not changed. Look how he laughed with your brothers. It hasn't warped him. I should be thanking God for that, Penny. I should be – but I can't.'

'It would have been easier for him if he hadn't been given hope. Sorry seems such a poor thing to say. But I am, Laurence, I'm so dreadfully sorry. For you, for him – for Helen. Ought you to have left her this weekend?'

'She's not there. She's gone off again to Troughton Hall. What the attraction is there, God knows. She only stayed home twenty-four hours – seemed to expect he might already be out of the nursing home. I've asked the staff there not to tell her, I don't want her to blurt it out to Sonny. I shall tell him myself next week. We'll take him back to the hotel. But you know what it means?'

'For you? For us?' She nodded. 'It means you'll be leaving England. You only came because of Sonny.'

'That's not true. I did come because of him but, Penny,

418

I came because I couldn't go on without seeing you. I had to see who you'd married, find out if you were happy.'

'Well, now you know.'

His hold on her was firm yet gentle. She shivered.

'You're cold. Let's walk.'

'Not really cold. Just a ghost walking over my grave.' But they walked on, Temple Island looking as desolate as their spirits on the dreary winter afternoon. 'Laurence, I've been thinking too. Each night I go on that stage, I do my best, honestly I do – '

'Your best! Your're wonderful!'

'No, don't *you* say things like that. There's nothing of me there, not really me. I put everything I've ever learnt into it.' She stopped again and turned to face him. 'You know what the trouble really is? I'm not a proper stage person. I never was and I never will be. Not like Sylvia – not even like David. It matters more than anything to him. But it doesn't to me.'

'What matters to you, my darling?'

'You know jolly well.'

Her answer brought his first smile of the afternoon. 'Yes, I know jolly well. But, please, I need to hear you say it.'

'You matter to me, that's what. Don't know what I'm going to do when you've gone. But you have to go – and soon – I can see that. Sonny needs to be bathing in those warm springs.'

'I'll come back. You won't be free of me, Penny.'

'There's lots of ways of loving, that's what Mother says. And we've got to get used to a way that knows we're together even when we aren't.'

His laugh was full of tenderness. 'That sounds like the girl who somersaulted into my life in that hospital in France – remember?'

'I'm serious, Laurence. You don't have to be able to touch someone or speak to them to be near them. I'll always be near you, I promise I will. It doesn't matter how

419

many miles of ocean are between us. It's the same sky over both of us wherever we are. That's what I used to do before, look up and think of you beyond the horizon but under the same sky. It's like a kind of God, the sky. It goes on for ever and ever, the same for us all, whether we're rich or poor, well or ill.'

'And it's just about to rain on us, rich and poor alike. Right, about turn, my Penelope, we'll go back to the hotel.' He put an arm around her shoulder. 'Your mother's right. There are lots of ways of loving.'

Her brown eyes were bright as she looked up at him. 'And I can think of just the one for a wet Sunday afternoon.'

An hour or more later, still holding her in his arms, he went back to what she'd been telling him about doing her best at the theatre.

'Are you tired of "Girl of My Dreams", is that what you were trying to tell me?'

'No. That's not what I'm tired of. I miss people. I'll never be a proper performer, the sort who gets stage nerves before the show, then sort of blossoms. You know what I mean. All the really good people say that's how it should be, how it always is with them. But it never was with me. I never got butterflies in my tummy. I like to see the people, I like to be able to make them enjoy themselves. I've never wanted to prove that I'm great or anything. I just like to see people having a good time.'

He kissed the top of her head as if that were an answer.

'Anyway, I think I want a break from all of it for a while. I've not told David yet. He'll have to get used to dancing with Sue Giles, my understudy.'

'You're the best in town, Penny. Have a break – but don't waste yourself. You know what we should do, you and me?'

'You tell me.' Her fingers moved down his spine, her eyes teased.

'Stop it, woman. I'm being serious. Sorting out this

420

career of yours. Cabaret. You'd like cabaret. It's personal, you're amongst the people. Can't you just see us? I'd write songs especially for you. What about that?'

'Umph. One day, perhaps we will. It's something for us to dream about.' Her voice croaked.

'Darling, you're crying.'

'All this fine talk about loving just the same when we're not together,' she snorted. ''s easy to talk . . . but it's like looking forward to nothingness.'

Lying by his side, she spoke for them both. He held her close. From outside they could hear the grinding gears of the motor cars as they crossed the river bridge, just occasionally the clip-clop of horses' hooves. In the Shires habit dies hard, there were still those who preferred to travel with a pony and trap.

'Come with me. Let David cite me. Would the gossip matter to you?'

'You know it wouldn't. I'd be proud. But Sonny has misery enough ahead of him, Laurence, we can't make things any harder.'

'Sonny's sensitive enough to understand. He's not blind, he knows his mother and I go our separate ways. She's been in the clear for a long time – no drugs – no drink either until we came here, and even now she seems to be in control. At one time I could feel how she was driven to it, driven by fear. But lately something seems to have changed for her. I don't pretend to know what it is – or who – I don't want to.'

'If I was the one to do wrong – but doesn't that show how stupid it is, as if it could be wrong for you and me to be together? – if David had grounds to divorce me, no one need guess about how he is.' Penelope hesitated, still not decided whether to keep her secret to herself.

'Go on,' he prompted, which proved to her just how well they understood each other.

'You know I said I wanted to give up, not work for a

421

while? Well, I do, I would in any case – but there's a special reason. There's going to be a baby.'

He raised himself on to one elbow, looking down at her. 'And you think I could leave you here . . . ?' That was all he said, but the way his hand touched her face spoke more to her than words.

'I know when it was. I think I knew it right from the time. Remember The Drovers? If it's a girl we ought to call her Flora.' She giggled. 'Spelt with a double "o". Remember?'

'You think I could forget?'

The rain beat steadily against the window. They could hear the splash of the tyres as the motor cars climbed the slope of the bridge. Close by, the church bells started to peal. All around them were sounds of Sunday, yet they weren't part of it, they were suspended in a world that held only themselves – themselves and the embryo of the child they'd created. She pulled him to her, wrapping her legs around him. Blinded by the sting of tears, she knew no words for the song of thanksgiving that echoed with every pulse beat. Deeply, tenderly, he loved her, both of them so aware of that new life. Only minutes ago she'd talked of looking forward into nothingness. But not now! Never again!

The next day they returned to London.

'We'll speak to David together,' he said as he turned into the road where Penelope lived.

'Not yet. It can't hurt us to wait. We know where we're going. Don't say anything to anyone about us until after Sonny is back on the track again. He's the most important. If David made a scene, got difficult – I don't see how he can, but suppose he did – and news got out, then Sonny might get to hear. His world's going to be shattered enough, we can't risk making it worse.'

'What a nice girl you are, Penelope Drew.'

'I'm no such thing. I'm a woman. It's just that children, young people, they're vulnerable.'

422

No wonder her words conjured up a picture of Prospect House. A healing house. He'd take Sonny there again, he even pictured holding back the consultant's verdict until then. Penny was right, they couldn't give him anything more to bear than he had to, he must hang on to what normality he could.

'In Henley it all seemed so easy, so straightforward.' She was speaking again. 'You said that Sonny is sensitive enough to understand. Perhaps he is. But it's not as simple as that, Laurence, I've seen it all before with Tom. When relationships break down, don't grow together, is there ever an easy way out? And your divorce would have to go through the Courts. Just think of the case Helen could put up if she chose to. A father who forsakes his son for another woman, and just when he needs him most.'

'Me! Forsake Sonny!'

'It's not me who's saying it. But if Helen wanted to make things difficult for you, she could hurt you by taking Sonny away from you. She'd have custody of him. It's usual for a child to stay with the mother.'

'He's not a child. He's sixteen years old.'

'In law he's still a child.' She gripped his hand tightly.

'Good God, Penny, she's been no mother. She's hardly more than a visitor in the home, you know that. When he was small she had a series of men friends. Then the Sam Bernhard affair left her in no state to be responsible for herself, let alone anyone else.'

'She may have been no proper mother, but she's the only one Sonny's ever known. He talks about her affectionately. 'Poor Mom worries about me. When she takes me out she likes to know I'm safely in the chair.''

'And so he will be. So he will be.' His eyes were full of pain as he looked at her. 'Why? Why him?'

There was no answer. Helplessly she shook her head.

CHAPTER SIXTEEN

'Well, well. You home on a Monday! Could Mr Wonderful be getting tired of his protegée, I ask myself.'

As she closed the front door, David's voice greeted her. Clearly her homecoming had spoilt his own plans. It would have been so easy to answer him in the same tone, it was what he wanted. She swallowed the retort, going straight to her room to take off her hat and coat. It was no use putting it off. If there was something difficult to do, best to get it over. A touch more colour on her lips, a comb run through her short, straight hair, then, squaring her shoulders, she went back into the sitting room.

'I came home early because I need to talk to you. David, I'm not going to carry on like we are.'

'You've got nothing on me! That was weeks ago. And who do you think would listen, when you've still been living here with me. Anyway, you promised, you swore you'd – '

'Shut up. It's not about you and your boy friend. I certainly don't want to talk about that. David, I'm coming out of the show.'

His mouth opened but he seemed lost for a reply.

'You know what I feel about these spectacular musicals,' she went on, 'I always said I'd never do another.'

'You've had a row with McLeod! That's what it is. You're walking out on the show to spite him. Don't be daft, Penny. You'll hurt yourself a damn sight more than you'll hurt him. Look, we may not be an ideal married couple, but we've got a great partnership. Like Adele and Fred, isn't that what we said?'

'I've made my mind up.'

'If you haven't had a row with him, what is it then?'

You're running off with him! Is that it? Forgetting all you promised me. Penny, don't do it.' He grabbed her hand. His eyes were full of tears. She felt she couldn't look at him, it reminded her of the 'wobbly look' she'd dreaded to see on her father's face. 'Penny, I beg you, please stay with me. I'm sorry I spoke like I did when you came in. It's just – well, I feel rotten about us. I know I've let you down. Sometimes when we dance together, you must feel it too, it's as if we're two different people, nobody matters except us. When we dance I know what it's like to love you. No other woman's ever made me feel like that. I almost believe then that things will be all right again for us. Be patient with me. Penny, I'd be nowhere . . . nothing . . . without you. It's as if the two sides of me are struggling – '

'I don't want to know! We're not man and wife, we're not going to be. I've promised you I'll never tell what I know about you. But I'm not spending my life doing what I don't want to do just so that for an hour or two each evening in front of the footlights you remember what it feels like to be normal.'

'That's a beastly cruel thing to say to me.' His voice told her how near the surface those tears were. 'Anyway, what is normal? To chase after any half good looking woman like your old man does? "He's a lad for the ladies", and they say it as if it makes him no end of a good fellow. God! That makes my flesh creep. Or is it normal to leave your wife behind and go off with your fancy bird at every opportunity like McLeod?'

'Shut up. I'm not going to listen to you.' She held tight to the back of a chair. Her mouth was dry as parchment; she wanted to swallow but couldn't. If only the floor wouldn't rock she'd escape to the bathroom.

'Are you all right? Penny, aren't you well?' It was the gentle David who asked, but immediately the frightened spirit inside him pushed to the fore again. 'Suppose that's why he brought you home. Wrong time of the month, was it?'

She wanted to get out of the room with dignity; but speed was the driving force as holding her breath she made for the bathroom, getting there just in time to be horribly sick. So much for the extra touch of lipstick that had given her courage. Afterwards, sitting on the edge of the enamel bathtub, she felt as though she were made of feathers. A cold wash, her cheeks rubbed vigorously with the towel and she must face him again.

'It was the car ride.' No use pretending, he must have heard her.

But David had had time to think. He was ready for her. 'Leave the show, you say.' This time he gripped her shoulders hard. 'Why?' His face was so near, the smell of the Eau de Cologne hair dressing he always wore nauseatingly strong. 'He's put you in the club, hasn't he? *Hasn't he?*'

'Don't you shake me!' Adding a silent plea that she wouldn't be sick again.

He let his hands drop and moved away from her, yet all the while he watched her. Taking a cigarette from his case he put it in his mouth then offered the case to her.

She shook her head. 'Don't want one.'

'Thank you, David,' he added as he might remind a child. 'Must remember our manners, Penelope. I take it you'll condescend to grace the theatre with your presence until we leave London?'

'Sue will have to go on. I wouldn't be worth the price of a seat. I don't feel well, I tell you.' And he noticed how her hands trembled as she held them to her head.

'Spare me the details of your condition. Well, I'll tell you what I'll do. I'll have a talk to Douglas Mountford. He'll understand my concern. Quite a laugh really. My wife, expecting. The gossip mongers can put that in their pipes and smoke it!'

Sometimes she was touched by his dependence on her;

other times, and this was one of them, she felt he was a stranger. He was like two people. But wasn't that just what he'd said himself?

It must have been this feeling of being made of feathers that stopped her brain functioning at its usual pace. His words filtered in to her mind from a vast distance, and even then her response wasn't immediate. Then the impact hit her. Her baby, the human life that together she and Laurence had created – and David, with that condescending smile on his pretty face, was meaning to lay claim to it! 'My wife expecting.'

She panicked. 'It's nothing to do with you! It's not your child, you know it can't be.'

He raised his eyebrows, the corners of his mouth turning up into a gentle smile.

'But Penny, I'm your husband. Not my child? You'll be saying next that our marriage wasn't consummated. Think how the newspapers will love that. The darlings of the theatre, that's what we've been called. Nothing the British public likes better than a good romance.'

'It's nothing to do with you!' If only she could stop shaking. 'I wasn't even going to tell you, not yet.'

David shook his head, patently puzzled.

'I don't understand. I may be old-fashioned, but what sort of a man is this Mr Wonderful? Penny, if he's leaving you in the lurch, you needn't be frightened. I mean that, honestly. I'll see things are right for you.'

'I don't want to talk about it. I'm just telling you, I've done with the show. But don't you go telling everyone why! I'll see Doug myself. Whatever the reason, it's my business. Not yours, not theirs.'

'You're frightened now, Penny – and I know what that feels like.' He poked his face close to hers, his smile threatening. 'Not my business, you say. Well, you'll have a hard time proving it.'

Again his hands gripped her shoulders, not shaking her but as if he held her prisoner. This time she pulled free of him. It was easier to fight him when he sneered than when he was kind.

'Don't you dare tell anyone about the baby.' Unblinkingly she held his gaze. 'Understand? If you do, then I'll break my word too. I could finish it for you, easy as wink. if I told them what you and your boy friend get up to. There are plenty of people wondering about you already. And who do you think would take your word against mine, that you could father a child?'

Her words were meant to cut. Just as his hand was meant to sting as he brought it across her head, sending her reeling against the table.

His blow knocked the feathers out of her and the metal back in. Never had five foot one held more dignity than it did as she went to her bedroom, closing the door behind her. Tears had been her downfall at every emotional crisis. but this time her eyes were dry. Leaning against the closed door she felt empty, drained. She could hear David crying like a child. Her husband . . . only six months ago she'd joined her life to his. Had she ever truly believed she loved him or had it been no more than a burning need to be wanted?

Remembering even the short time they'd shared, she felt degraded, humiliated. She slumped on the edge of the bed, forcing herself to think of it. Yet, truly, he did depend on her. Not as a husband, nor yet as a brother or even a friend. She knew it had been the truth when he'd told her he'd never cared about any other woman. So what was it he wanted of her? Admiration? Approval? Arms folded across her chest she sat, hunched, small. But she was guilty too, she'd been no more honest than he had. When she'd married Tom she'd truly believed that what they had was the whole meaning of love; he'd expected it was too. But they'd both learnt. She'd promised to share her life with David, knowing that what she felt for him was a pale shadow of the real thing.

'Life ain't all you want but it's all you're gonna 'ave.

428

And she'd snatched at the first chance and hoped that in David she'd found a geranium to wear in her hat.

For a long time she sat there. She heard him moving about, then the door closing behind him. Probably he'd gone to tell his troubles to his friend. From her hunched position she flopped to lie on the bed, pulling the eiderdown over her. Sleep is nature's healer; when she woke the nausea had gone, her body was her own again. Outside it was quite dark.

Some colour dabbed on her pale cheeks, rather too much lipstick on her mouth, then she brushed her hair, put on her hat and coat and went out. She needed air, she needed to walk; to walk but not to think. This time she didn't want the solitude of the park, there there'd be no hiding from herself. She needed to see the busy city rushing on its way, to be part of a throng that made no demands on her.

With a screech of brakes a motor car pulled up at the kerb just ahead of her and the driver leant towards the path, rapping on the window shield. Helen McLeod! Surely the last person she wanted to see, but there was no avoiding her. Already the car door was open.

'I'm going to see Sonny, I'm going to fetch him. Drive with me, please.'

'At this time of night? But you can't bring him out of the nursing home at this time of night. Why don't you wait until tomorrow, let Sarah go with you? She handles him so easily.' Any excuse to prevent Helen going to Sonny. Laurence would want to bring him out of the nursing home, he'd want to be the one to break the news.

'Get in. The door's blocking the sidewalk.'

Getting into the passenger seat, Penelope tried again.

'Why don't you wait until the morning? You and Laurence go together. That's probably what Sonny is hoping for.'

'Sonny's hoping for a lot he's not going to get. You

know, I suppose? He'll have told you. Only me left in ignorance. I heard this evening.'

'You were away, how could he tell you? Let's leave Sonny tonight. Things are always harder to take at night than in the morning. Don't tell him now. Or, better, why don't you let Laurence break it to him? It's not going to be easy.'

'How stupid you are! It has to be me who tells him. This is something between Sonny and me. Oh, I can't talk to you, you don't understand any of it.' Helen spoke wildly. As she changed gear the motor car jolted forward almost throwing them off their seats. Something was wrong. But of course it was! Helen was Sonny's mother. She couldn't be expected to accept the end of their hopes with no show of emotion. Still, the way she clawed the steering wheel, stabbed her feet on the pedals . . .

'Does Laurence know what you're doing? Why don't you drive back to the hotel and collect him to go with you.'

It must have been luck that saved them hitting a man pushing a barrowload of vegetables; the car swerved to the wrong side of the road before Helen got control of it.

'For Sonny's sake, won't you wait?'

By now they were in a residential suburb, out of the heavy traffic, the nursing home no more than a mile away. Helen stopped the car again, and with the engine still running she turned, trying a new approach.

'Please.' Her tone was wheedling, out of character with the woman Penelope had known. 'It has to be me. I don't want Laurence there, nor Sarah. She's only his nurse. I'm his mother.' She jabbed her fingers against her chest. 'Me . . . that's what it's all about. Laurence doesn't understand.'

'So why do you want me there?'

'They might not let me bring him if I'm driving on my own. Stupid doctors, pretend they're so clever. And you're as bad.' There was a catch in her voice. 'I know what

430

have to do. You're not going to stop me. Why can't you trust me? I know — I tell you, I know.'

'I'll tell you what — let's drive there and you have a talk to someone. There must be a doctor there, even at this time of the evening. Perhaps then you'll change your mind. Sonny'll think it so strange — why, it's bedtime by now in the nursing home.'

Helen smiled, nodding her head. Again it struck Penelope she was acting like a good child. 'Acting'? No, it was wicked to suspect her of not being genuine. Yet, there was something . . . something . . . ?

'You wait in the car,' Helen told her as they turned into the drive. 'They might not tell me anything in front of an outsider.' A laugh that was practically a cackle. 'Did you hear that? You — an outsider — that's what you are. I'll say you're waiting in the motor car, then they won't argue about my bringing him. Can't stop me.'

'No, they can't stop you, Helen. But, listen, why tell Sonny anything tonight? Why not just bring him home, let him think he'll be seeing Sir Cedric for treatment without having to be kept here?'

'That's right. Let him stay happy, let him believe.' She took a deep breath then let it go in a sigh that might have been taken for contentment. Penelope, too, was satisfied with the arrangement. Once Sonny was safely back at the hotel Laurence would choose his moment to talk to him. Her decision made, Helen walked up the steps of the nursing home with assurance. Outside in the dark, Penelope waited.

It must have been about twenty minutes later that they appeared, Sonny being pushed down a ramp by the side of the steps, two nurses helping him into the car. Helen, with all the grace and charm she was capable of, waited behind for a last word with the doctor.

'Mom said you'd come with her, Penelope. Dad came to see me this afternoon. He didn't say I was coming out.' Sonny obviously needed reassurance.

431

'Well, your mother couldn't wait, I expect. Once she heard they could treat you without your actually living here, she just wanted to get you home.'

He frowned. He might be swimming around the bait, but he wasn't taking it.

'But why tonight? Is she all right, Penny? You know how she is sometimes? Seemed a bit tensed up.'

'Excitement, I expect, that you're ready to leave hospital.'

It was then that Helen got back into the car, the doctor swinging the starting handle for her. Only as the engine fired and they moved away did she pick up the conversation where it had been interrupted.

'Free! That's it, Sonny.' Her voice sent a chill down Penelope's spine. Yet why? There was nothing in her words to merit it. 'Tensed up' Sonny had said. Oh, but it was surely more than that.

There was an uncomfortable silence. The quiet suburb was settling down for the night. With her foot hard on the accelerator, Helen drove on the crown of the road, all the time pulling further to the right.

'Mom, you ought to be on the left. We're in England, not back home.'

Did she even hear him? Penelope peered at her in the darkness. And suddenly she was frightened.

'Slow down. You're throwing Sonny all across the back seat.'

'Have to go where you're thrown – have to go where you're pushed. That's what they think. Poor Sonny – and what about me? Poor Helen.'

'Mom, it's all right. Please, Mom, don't get in a state about me. I can handle it, honest I can.' Did he have any idea what he was talking about?

Just as she'd been driving too fast, now she slowed right down, hugging the left hand kerb.

'This isn't the road we came on, Helen.' Penelope clutched at normality. 'Are you sure it's the right way?'

'This is the way, I tell you, this is the *only* way. Never going to be better. That's what they say about you, Sonny. It's my fault — did you know that? It's because of me you're like you are.'

'Helen, that's not true. Things'll look better in the morning.'

But Helen hadn't even heard her.

'He told me I'd be free. Sonny was my punishment. When Sonny was free, then I would be, too.'

'Laurence? Laurence said that?' But Helen didn't even hear her.

'You turn right here, Mom, London — West End. Right! Don't you hear me!'

Her foot was hard on the accelerator again as they sped towards the 'T' junction. Ahead was the wall of a cemetery, above it a stone angel on a marble plinth, made eerie in the pale yellow light of the gas lamp.

'Turn the wheel!' Sonny shouted. 'Mom! Wake up, Mom.'

Helen was in a world where they couldn't reach her. She had only one purpose: escape for her and for Sonny whose life she'd ruined. She drove straight ahead, her foot hard on the accelerator.

In that second all Penelope's half understood fears fell into place. She pushed Helen's hand from the wheel and turned it hard to the right. But it was too late. Swerving violently, the car crashed into the wall. To Helen it had seemed so simple; she'd not considered failure. But it was the passenger side of the car that took the brunt of the crash before it came to rest on the last remains of one Jeremiah Cray, b. 1800 d. 1881. Beloved by all who knew him.

It was like seeing dimly through a long, dark tunnel. Voices she didn't know. She was being lifted, carried. On the edge of consciousness she didn't question where she was being taken, who the men were; Helen, Sonny, the nightmare

433

drive, all these things were gone completely. There was pain, that alone reached across the divide that cut her off from reality. Then even that faded, the light at the end of the tunnel was gone.

When reason returned to her she was in a hospital bed. One eye open; the other, like the rest of that side of her face, bruised and swollen. With returning consciousness came the vivid memory of being hurled through the open door of the motor car, noise, someone screaming – her? Helen? And almost with the first thought came the second. Her baby! "Please, please, don't let me have lost the baby." From head to foot her body was racked with pain. Gingerly she started to move her hands believing that she must have broken every bone. No bandages . . . nothing . . . a great wave of thankfulness swamped her.

Laurence was by her side, his hand a steady pressure on her shoulder. She saw the flowers on the locker, the largest bouquet, 'the best in town'. Her hand emerged from under the bedcovers and was taken in his. The flowers were lost in a haze. Tears rolled down her face. Even an eye too swollen to open can weep.

David brought her flowers too, by chance or design arriving at the same time as a reporter from the national press. He behaved as though that other afternoon had never happened. But his visit was brief; illness made him uncomfortable. Penelope looked like a stranger. Jeremiah Cray might have been beloved by all who knew him, but Penelope had less cause to feel affection. Thrown from the car, his grave had been her landing place, the left side of her face sadly the worse for an encounter with his tombstone.

The accident had happened on Monday night. It was Wednesday afternoon when the crisply starched nurse rustled in to tell her she had a visitor. And there, standing in the doorway, a Christmas rose in his buttonhole, was Oliver.

434

'Pa!' She snorted. 'Pa, come all this way. Damned silly tears!'

'There, Tuppence, as if I wouldn't.' He kissed the good side of her face. 'Soon as we read it in the morning paper your mother agreed with me. I'd have a day or two in London, be able to keep an eye on you and see for myself things are going all right. I've taken a room along in the Strand where I was before.'

If her mouth had felt as if it were her own she would have smiled. The corner of it twitched. Oh, Pa, it seemed to say, you never miss a trick!

'You won't be prancing about that stage for a while, that's for sure, not with looks like yours.' He'd settled himself into the chair by her bed, prepared to be there some time. He smiled. 'Did you hear what I said, though? The morning paper! That's how I knew you'd been hurt. You've come on in the world, young Tuppence. As soon as you're fit enough for the train – if David can spare you – your mother says what about coming down to Challington. You do that, eh?'

'I was meaning to, Pa.'

'The paper said you were with Mrs McLeod and young Sonny. They seem to have got off lightly. Shaken though, they must be shaken. Nasty experience. Pleasant woman, I tried to keep her company when she stayed at the Grand.' He chuckled, crossing his legs and running the knife-edge crease of his trousers between his thumb and finger.

Almost shyly, she put out a hand to him. There was so much she wanted to be able to say to him. Her swollen face tried to smile.

'Used to get so cross, Pa, about you and all the pretty women you found "pleasant". I've learnt a lot since then – about what matters and what doesn't.'

'That Tom Beasley, you mean. You're not still hankering after him?'

'Tom's a dear, he'll always be my friend. But no, I wasn't thinking about Tom. Do you know what, you've got a lot to be grateful for, having to look after me when I was small. It made sure you didn't get taken up by some woman who wouldn't have done you any good. As things were you had to hurry home to me and Chummy – and that took you all the way along the road 'til you got to the right signpost. One that led you to Mother.'

'Are you trying to tell me something? I'm no good at conundrums.' Then, with a wink: 'Now, the Places Game, I'd beat you at that any day of the week. What are you saying, Tuppence?'

'Just that I know you truly did love Anna – even if I think you were a darn sight too good for her. If you hadn't had me to look after, you might so easily have gone chasing after happiness too quickly and in the wrong place. It's easy to do, Pa.'

If she wanted to confide in him, she was unlucky. Oliver wasn't going to listen. A nasty knock on the head like she'd had could do funny things to a person; he didn't want her unburdening herself to him and perhaps regretting it when she was better.

'Nice flowers. From David?'

'Those over there are. These by my bed are from Laurence.'

'Ah, no wonder he sent you a fine bouquet, you taking the rap and his two getting off lightly.' But he gave her what Mrs Sharp called an 'old fashioned look' for all that. 'I ought to have brought you some, but I just booked in at the hotel and hurried straight here.'

'Tell me about everyone, about Challington, all of it.'

'Not much to tell.'

'Go on talking, Pa. I like to know you're there.'

It was so good having him here, with no shadows between them. She closed her good eye. His voice was low and even, it required no effort on her part to listen to him. Sore and aching though she was, she felt a sense of peace.

Her concentration wandered, the background sound of his voice was all she asked. Willingly she let her mind drift back and forth through the years. She'd lived away from Challington nearly half her life, travelling the country, fending for herself. She'd experienced so much more than those who'd stayed at home. Of course she wasn't the same as the child who'd packed her bundle of possessions, the muffler with her money in it, and sneaked off to meet Tom.

Letting her father's voice drift over her, memories took her to the pier at Hastings, to the hairdressers where she'd taken her courage in her hands and had her hair shorn; once again she and Tom were sitting on the bed in her room at Mrs Fellows' boarding house in Finchley reading about Sylvia's wedding; then that other night, supper with Laurence, the feeling of the night air as they'd come out from the underground to find that in the midst of life there was death and destruction; Laurence, his hands drawing a sound from the piano that made her want to cry; "Last one to the pier's a sissy"; Young Perce; Chummy, the way he used to sneeze with excitement when she got home from school; "Knives and forks on the table, Tuppence, got something warm for our supper tonight"; a queue of people waiting for the gods.

Oliver's voice talked on ... Merrick ... that rascal Bruce ... your Mother ... Ted and Arnie ... Alf ... Of course she was changed, how could she have lived as she had and not be changed? Pa ... she opened her eye just enough to see him ... smart as paint he was these days. For all that, was he any different? Oh, he was older, his waist wasn't as trim, his hair was receding. But those things weren't important. The person he was, the core, the spirit, nothing could ever alter that.

What about her spirit? The core that would for ever be Penelope Drew?

Behind where Oliver sat was the window. From her room on the first floor her only view was of the pale winter sky. Lying here she felt she could see for ever, nothing between here and eternity. The same sky that had been

437

over the battlefields of France, over Hampstead Heath, over the noise and bustle of New York, over the hot springs of Georgia; the same sky that had looked down on the rocky shore where she'd played with Tom and Alf, and on Helen as she'd tried to escape from the imprisonment of her tormented mind.

What had happened to Helen's spirit, the core that would always be her? Somewhere she'd gone wrong. She'd wandered from the road, lost her way.

Penelope's head still hurt, but the mists had cleared. Under the bed covers she moved her hand, rested it gently on her stomach. She knew just what she had to do.

Joy in being with him, the void his going would leave, neither could make any difference. There was no other path for her to follow. A voice from deep within her, a voice made up of all her yesterdays, pointed her way forward. "No happiness can ever come from taking what's not yours to take." " . . . many different ways of loving . . . the gifts of the Wise Men were all different . . . " She knew Laurence so well. There could be no lasting happiness for him – or for her either – if he failed Sonny now.

To steer him down that path wouldn't be easy, but somehow she had to do it.

'It isn't just that I love you, that makes us sound like two separate people.' She groped to find the right words. 'The real me, the sort of – of essence of my being – sounds a bit grand but I don't know how else to say it – you're part of it. So even when you've gone, you'll still be here.'

She saw the way his lips twitched, felt the tight grip of his fingers on hers. 'With most people we find ourselves being what they expect. I think it comes with learning our manners when we're little, don't you?' As long as she kept talking she could stay strong. 'I've thought so much about it – about us, I mean. And you have too, Laurence. Go on, don't pretend. We've got to be honest, we must, even

438

if it can't be the way we want it. How would you feel if Sonny couldn't look up to you as his champion? Running off chasing rainbows. 'cos, that's all it'd be if we took what we weren't entitled to – a rainbow. We might think we were heading for the sunshine and blue skies but we know what happens to a rainbow when the sky gets bright. It just vanishes.'

He lifted her hand to his face, held it pressed tight against him. How strange it was that knowing how he was battling to hold on to his control, she didn't want to look away. Not like she had with her father, not like she had with David. Instead she pulled him towards her, cradling his head against her breast. Small and thin, she was as she was. And that was the answer to all of it, she realized, holding him close. 'We are as we are. Things might happen to us, to us and around us, but we are as we are.' And if they'd been different their spirits wouldn't have fused.

'I'll come back. You know that.'

''course I do. The time'll come. That's the only way I can be strong now, knowing one day things'll be right for us. But I can wait. We can both wait. "Now" belongs to Sonny.'

'Penny, Sonny's not going to be beaten by this. He's a terrific young man. He'll make something of his life.'

'I know. And you've got to be there to see that he does. Helen loves him right enough, but her sort of love isn't much help, doesn't put any ginger into him. I reckon it was that medium in New York got an idea into her head that it was her fault Sonny had been made ill, to punish her for what she'd done to that man you told me she was in love with. Imagine what it must have been like for her! If I thought I'd done that to you, there'd be nowhere to run from it. It would haunt me, just like it must have haunted her.'

'It wasn't her fault the police were after him.'

'What difference could it make to her that he'd been up

to whatever it was? It's all to do with her – her psyche – that's the word I couldn't think of before.'

'I don't know how I'm going to leave you . . . '

'You won't be free of me, I won't be free of you. It was you who told me that. And I'm lucky. I'll have the baby.'

From the far end of the corridor came the clang of the bell telling them it was time for visitors to go. Penelope's resolve held as she watched him walk away; when the doors opened tomorrow she knew he'd be back. But for how many days? She wouldn't let herself think of the emptiness ahead of her. It was easy to be brave when they were together, then she could hold the truth at bay. But now he'd gone it caught up with her. How many more times would she watch him walk away, knowing that tomorrow he'd be back? By the end of the week she would be fit to leave the hospital. Her face was healing fast, and except for bruising there was nothing wrong with her body. Sometimes there had been other visitors: Sylvia, Tom, Douglas Mountford. But always there'd been Laurence. Any day she'd be deemed fit to face the train journey to Challington where the past and the present would merge into one. But what of the future? As long as he was with her she could face it with courage, her mind fixed on the certainty that one day they would be together.

One day . . . but when? Alone here, her immediate problems couldn't be pushed out of sight. She was pregnant with a child she swore she'd never let her husband lay claim to. If she'd been simple Penelope Drew of Challington, even then there would have been gossip. But she was Penelope Drew, star of the West End stage. She was half the romantic partnership the newspaper columnists had taken such an interest in. Not that she cared what scandal she had to face. She hoped David would agree to divorce her. Surely he would? Or would he be frightened by the inevitable rumours that she'd turned to another man because he was as he was? Then there was Helen. Nothing they did could have the power to hurt her, but that didn't

440

make the way ahead any clearer. And Sonny? He was never the boy to be beaten. She remembered him walking in the park, the effort, the determination.

'If Sonny can have guts like that, then so can I. I'll show them!' Then, the palms of her hands on her flat stomach: 'We'll show them! That's what we'll do. If ever I've had a geranium to put in my hat it's now . . . Laurence's baby.' A smile played at the corners of her mouth as she lay there with her eyes closed. 'What's got into you, Penelope Drew? As if you're going to have your life upset by anything David could do. No one can force you to live with him, he hasn't any rights over the baby. Not even Pa – and he's going to be a hard nut to crack. Nothing they can do matters, not a jot it doesn't. Soon as Sonny is back on the track, then our turn'll come and we shall have earned our right to be together. Bit like when Mother gives nasty medicine to the children. Open wide and swallow it down then pop in a bulls-eye to take the taste away. That's how it'll be. Once Sonny is settled at Georgia – oh, how rotten for him, all his hopes . . . ' Thinking of Sonny, her own disappointment seemed easier to handle.

All that was a week ago. And now he'd gone. The sky was heavy with clouds. Alone on the shingle by the shore at Challington she gazed at the 'gingerbeer' sea, the waves breaking like froth. Gone? He was at the top of her mind; she was at the top of his too, she knew that. So how could he ever be gone?

She stooped down, picking up a handful of stones, and stood idly making 'ducks and drakes' on the water. Already her face was looking like her own again. Another week or two and she'd be ready to journey on along the road she'd made for herself. It might have plenty of twists and turns, plenty of hills to climb, unexpected pitfalls, but she knew just where it was heading.

In her pocket she had a letter from Charlie Cribbans; he was arranging for her to have what he called a 'screen test'. Moving pictures . . . shown in picture houses all over the country . . . shown in America too. She was going to make a big name for herself and she was going to do it for Laurence and for their baby too.

There were hurdles enough before the road they must follow would take them out into the sunshine – but she'd never been tripped by a hurdle yet!

EPILOGUE

In the early hours of 1st January 1929 fire gutted the Prince of Wales Theatre in Challington.

'Never seen such a blaze.' On the set at Downside Studio, Penelope read Muriel's letter. 'Being New Year there were plenty of revellers on the streets, some say that's how the fire came about, but it's only talk. True enough though that it seemed all the town turned out to see the end of the old Prince of Wales. You'll remember it from when you lived nearby – and Ollie tells me that's where you first got itchy feet to dance on the stage. So the old place must have its memories for you, Penny love, and you'll be sad to hear there's nothing of it but the blackened walls. Even the roof fell in. All around people had to turn out of their houses.

'No sign of Mandy's baby yet. She and Bill moved in here ready at the beginning of last week. He's like a cat on hot bricks. That jumpy he is about it, you'd think it was the menfolk had to go through it not the wives. Tell the truth, my back's been aching all day. I've heard women say that before, how they get all the warning signs for their daughters. Perhaps the little one will come tonight. Soon as you're an auntie I'll let you know.'

'Miss Drew, position please. Ready to roll. Take One.' And the band struck up.

Muriel's clear, round hand had taken Penelope into the heart of Challington. Now she was pulled back. A cluster of tables, in the background the counter of a bar, bottles on the shelves, tankards hanging from the rafters. There was no more glamour to the set of a film than there had been long ago when she'd practised in the boatbuilders' shed. Tom's mouth-organ for accompaniment, a few feet

443

to dance in, and the world had been hers. And so it was now, as if she inhabited a small magic patch in the midst of the chaos of the paraphernalia of movie-making. The brilliant stage footlights had never been like this. From table to table she leapt as she danced. Young Perce would have been proud of her; she'd lost nothing of her agility or gamin charm.

After five years of film-making Penelope Drew was known in every town in the country. This, though, was the most important part she'd ever played. Much of the success or failure of any show rested on the star, and none had ever mattered to her more than this one.

'Cut,' called the director.

Across the set her eyes met those of the scriptwriter, a young man of twenty-two with dark curly hair and blue eyes always ready to smile; a young man watching proceedings from a wheelchair.

'Ticket to Paradise' opened in Leicester Square the following April, PENELOPE DREW blazoned in letters even larger than the title of the film. They all went to the première: Penelope, Laurence, Sonny, Sylvia, Tom. It was more than merely another Penelope Drew film; tonight the triumph was surely Sonny's. At the party afterwards, as they raised their glasses to his future career, Penelope thought of his mother, seemingly content living with her friend Rosamund at Troughton Hall. They'd invited her to join them this evening but she'd declined. She and Rosamund seldom came to London. If she'd ever expected to find her release in a 'free' Sonny, tonight would have been her opportunity. But perhaps in these years she'd found some other salve for her wounded mind. She'd divorced Laurence with an eagerness that hinted she'd done with her past.

That was the première that was reported in the movie magazines. But to Penelope it was an evening in September which held pride of place. The Prince of Wales Theatre had been restored, its Victorian grandeur had given way to the elegance of this new cinema age, and it had been re-christened the Pavilion. What more appropriate than that the first time its doors were opened, it was for the showing of a film starring Challington's very own star. No evening dress here, but as Muriel had said long ago, everyone liked to put on their best when they went somewhere special, whether it was their Sunday hat or a tiara.

This time Sonny didn't go with them. The front row of the circle was no place for a wheelchair.

'Will you play the 'tina for us, Sonny? We could sing songs.' Eyes as huge and dark as her mother's, hair as dark and curly as his own, his little step-sister knew just how to wheedle what she wanted from him. Not that he needed much persuading. Here in 'the room' at Prospect House he'd enjoyed many a sing-song.

'Run upstairs and get the concertina then.'

Soon the large room was filled with the sound of young voices. Always there were children at Prospect House.

Sitting in the middle of the front row of the circle, Ollie swelled with pride. On his left was Tuppence. There! Look at that screen: "Starring Penelope Drew. Supported by . . . " and a list of names he hardly read. "Script by Sonny McLeod, Music by Laurence McLeod, Produced by . . . " He read no further. Someone tapped his shoulder and, turning, he saw Ethel Sharp was sitting behind him, best hat and all. It had been a struggle for her to climb the stairs, Ethel wouldn't see eighty again. But for an occasion like this she was determined not to be beaten. She meant to be in one of the best seats. They nodded in wordless agreement; rarely had they been in such accord.

Penelope felt her hand taken in Laurence's. The years had brought her plenty of acclaim, but tonight was like no other. She saw the screen through a blur of 'damned silly tears'. What had she done to deserve so much? The picture was bright in front of her, but she saw none of it. She was at the bottom of the steps to the gods, the wind bitingly cold. Her hat pulled down and her collar up, she stamped her feet in her too-large boots in time to the music of her concertina.

> Once in the window of a pork and beef shop
> Two little sausages sat . . .

She could almost hear the childish voice that had been hers, feel the thrill of that first ripple of interest spreading through the queue. She knew every word and movement of the film, and was content to let her mind wander where it would.

There was no party afterwards. Instead they all walked home together in the darkness of the late summer evening, going the long way round, along the Promenade, beyond Alexandra Square, then the whole length of Prospect Street. There was no moon but the stars were brilliant.

'Hark at the sea.' It was Alf who spoke. They stopped, standing still to listen to the waves breaking gently on the shingle, and to look at the rays from the gaslamps shining on the ever moving water, the dark outline of the pier beyond; all of it imprinted itself on their memories, background to a very special evening.

Penelope leant her head against Laurence and was answered by the pressure of his hand on her shoulder.

"It begins with C," silently she played the Places Game, "and tonight it holds everyone I love best in all the world."